THE

Heiress
MASQUERADE

THE
Heiress
MASQUERADE

RUBY® AWARD–WINNING AUTHOR
MADDISON MICHAELS

Entangled Publishing, LLC
644 Shrewsbury Commons Ave., STE 181
Shrewsbury, PA 17361
Visit our website at www.entangledpublishing.com.

Amara is an imprint of Entangled Publishing, LLC.

Edited by Alethea Spiridon
Cover design by Bree Archer
Photography by Period Images
Stock art by CHUNYIP WONG/GettyImages
Interior design by Britt Marczak

Print ISBN   978-1-64937-652-7
ebook ISBN 978-1-64937-511-7

Manufactured in the United States of America

First Edition September 2024

AMARA

ALSO BY MADDISON MICHAELS

DOLLAR PRINCESS

The Heiress Swap
The Heiress Masquerade

SAINTS & SCOUNDRELS

The Devilish Duke
The Elusive Earl
The Sinful Scot

SECRET, SCANDALS & SPIES

The Bachelor Bargain
The Bachelor Betrayal

To Darren.

My best friend. My soul mate. The love of my life.

I couldn't do this without you, and I treasure your love, just as I treasure you.

xxx

CHAPTER ONE

"Your plan won't work, Mother," Aimee Thornton-Jones declared over her shoulder, wincing as the modiste yanked the laces of her corset tightly together. "I have no intention of being the next Dollar Princess."

"I never said that was my plan," her mother Edith replied, leaning farther back against the lounge, her broken leg propped up on a footstool in front of her, the ruby red of her day dress draped gracefully across the hardened plaster, the rich color of the gown complementing the deep sable of her hair and the emerald of her eyes. Eyes that missed little but were now wide with innocence.

"You didn't have to say it." Another tug of the corset strings had Aimee twisting around to face the modiste, her patience wearing thin given she'd been standing here for nearly two hours. "That's tight enough, Madame Rounel. I can barely breathe as it is."

The modiste glared at her as she wrapped her tape measure around Aimee's waist. "Monsieur Worth requires exact measurements before he can finalize your travel wardrobe." She pulled the tape away from around Aimee's waist, before jotting down some notes.

"I'm certain you have every measurement you

need by now," Aimee replied. "And if you don't, then Monsieur Worth will have to make do."

"Make do?" The modiste sounded scandalized.

"Madame, please forgive my daughter," her mother said placatingly, dragging the modiste's attention back over to her. "She's obviously forgotten the great favor you and the House of Worth are providing us, having you come to New York for the final fitting instead of us traveling to Paris. And we are grateful for that."

"You're paying them a fortune for that, Mother," Aimee said as she motioned for her maid to come over to assist dressing her, while happily ignoring the daggers in the modiste's eyes as the lady began to pack her tools.

"A fortune that's entirely justified given the caliber of the dresses from the House of Worth," her mother replied, her glare mirroring that of the modiste's, before she returned her attention back to the French woman. "Will the measurements you've taken be enough? Her outfits must outshine all others and scream perfection."

"Don't you mean scream one million dollars?" Aimee asked as her maid began to button the back of her sapphire-blue gown. "Isn't that how one attracts a lord to trade in one's inheritance for a title?"

"Really, Aimee, must you always be so dramatic? Or perhaps crass is a better word for it," her mother said with an arch of her eyebrow.

"The truth is neither dramatic nor crass," she replied as her maid finished dressing her.

Her mother shook her head before turning to

the modiste. "Madame, will all be good?"

The modiste raised her chin and haughtily nodded. "Yes, Mrs. Thornton-Jones. I will send a telegram to Paris today and they will finish your daughter's wardrobe in the next week, then deliver everything to London as arranged."

"Wonderful." Her mother smiled. "As usual, our thanks to you and the House of Worth."

The modiste nodded to them both before turning on her heel and striding from the room.

"Honestly, Aimee, did you have to be so rude?" Her mother glanced back to Aimee as the echo of the modiste's footsteps disappeared down the hall.

"I thought I was rather restrained."

"Your idea of restraint is different from my own." Her mother shook her head.

"As is your idea about this trip compared to my own," Aimee said. "Because I have no intention of marrying a titled gentleman."

"Oh goodness. This trip is for you to have a London season and be exposed to English Society. It isn't about you marrying a titled gentleman."

"It feels like it is."

"Well, it isn't," her mother said in exasperation. "However, if you happen to fall in love and become engaged while there, I wouldn't complain."

"No, of course you wouldn't, because then you'd finally be invited to the Astor ball." Aimee walked over and sat on the chair next to her.

"That would be a bonus," her mother said frankly, with a dainty shrug of her shoulders.

"A bonus for you, not me. I can't believe you want me to marry a title, rather than marry for love as you and Father did." Not that she planned to ever fall in love, but her mother didn't need to know that.

"Oh, darling, of course, I want you to marry for love." Her mother reached over and patted Aimee's hand. "It's your happiness I desire above everything, and I have no intention of sacrificing my only child into a loveless marriage halfway across the world so I can join Mrs. Astor's inner circle."

The expression on her mother's face was fierce and Aimee knew she was telling the truth, even though her mother had been obsessed with being invited into Mrs. Astor's circle for as long as she could remember. "Then why are you still insisting I go to England when I don't want to?"

"Call it a mother's intuition." She squeezed Aimee's fingers lightly. "Because even though I can't accompany you anymore, I have a feeling your destiny is awaiting you there."

"I just told you I have no intention of marrying." Aimee shook her hand free. It was one of the only things she truly had control over. The rest of her life was regimented by her mother, a social routine consisting of ball after ball, the opera, the theater, and any other acceptable event deemed appropriate for an heiress. It was suffocating.

"Once you fall in love, you'll change your mind. You haven't met the right man yet. There are many eligible English lords all eager to marry, and one just might be perfect for you."

"I think you're confusing the term *eligible* for *destitute*. Lords are only eager to marry an heiress so they can fill up their depleted estate coffers, which I have no intention of helping them do."

When her mother had first told her of the trip, which was, coincidentally, after Aimee had rejected a fourth marriage proposal from a young man whose mother was best friends with Mrs. Astor, Aimee had known immediately what her mother's plan was—an attempt to ship her across the Atlantic for six weeks to attract the attention of some lord and become the next Dollar Princess to marry into the English aristocracy, thereby securing their social position in Society. After all, no one, not even Mrs. Astor herself, would dare not to invite the mother-in-law of a lord to her ball.

"We shall have to agree to disagree on the merits of the trip, a trip you *will* be going on despite your protestations otherwise," her mother replied, the militant expression Aimee had inherited shining upon her face. "You know I've already arranged everything with the Countess of Brexton, who has kindly agreed to take my place as your host and chaperone for the trip."

"I've never even met the countess." Perhaps a change of strategy was warranted. Giving up was not in Aimee's nature, even if she was starting to feel it was futile to convince her mother of the pointless nature of the trip. "Surely, she'd understand if we cancelled given your accident. I can't travel to England on my own, now can I?"

"I would never allow that. After all, a woman's reputation is one of her most important assets, especially for someone in your position."

"You've made other arrangements, haven't

you?" The thought was depressing.

Her mother smiled and Aimee knew then none of her arguments would sway her. Her mother had a plan and wouldn't be deterred. Aimee should have known, because when did her mother not have a plan?

"Of course I've made other arrangements, darling."

Now it was Aimee who sighed. "You're getting Evie to accompany me." It was the only other possibility, given her father was far too busy running his empire to take her mother's place on the trip.

"She's proven herself a reliable and trustworthy companion to you these past six years."

As much as Aimee loved her cousin and best friend, Evie, they were as different from each other as night was from day—and that was probably understating things. Well, at least understating their personality differences. Physically, everyone said they looked alike except for their hair. Evie's was a honey blonde compared to Aimee's sable black.

Evie was the sensible one, the responsible one. The completely proper and oh-so-very English one, given she'd grown up in London until she was sixteen. Aimee, on the other hand, was impulsive, determined, though some would say stubborn, and enthusiastic about wanting to experience all life had to offer—even if that was a rather difficult endeavor given her sex and the fact that her parents preferred she be wrapped in cotton wool, rather than let loose into the world.

Until now. The allure of Aimee potentially meeting an impoverished English gentleman, willing to trade his title for an inheritance, was proving enough of an enticement for her mother to relax her reins of control on Aimee's social life.

"Evie will be the perfect companion for you on the voyage across to England in my place." Her mother smiled serenely and Aimee felt the last vestiges of potentially getting out of the ordeal slip away like ether.

"She's only a year older than me and unmarried," Aimee couldn't help but point out. "Do you think she's a suitable companion for the voyage?"

Of course, Aimee knew Evie was suitable, but she started feeling the pull of desperation itching up her neck. The idea of being stuck in London for six weeks, with the only entertainment being attending dinner parties and ball after ball, was suffocating. At least here in New York she could finish her term at Eastman Business College, attending in secret of course. Only Evie knew she disguised herself as a young man and attended the college once per week. It was amazing what people expected to see if one disguised oneself. You could practically pretend you were anyone.

"Given her calm and sensible temperament," her mother continued, "and the fact she's been your companion for years now without incident, which is a feat given your own temperament, my dear, she's the perfect companion for your trip."

"At least she and I can be bored together."

"Actually, your father's arranged for something else for Evie." Her mother sounded surprisingly hesitant.

"Something else?"

"She's to undertake a six-week traineeship as a secretary at his London office, and while doing so, she'll stay with the head secretary, Mrs. Holbrook."

A pain ripped through her chest with the news. All Aimee had ever wanted to do since she was little was learn all she could of her father's business, to one day fulfill her dream of taking over from him. A dream he'd constantly rebuffed, believing her place was in a ballroom, not a boardroom. And now Evie was getting to do a traineeship? Even though being a secretary was the last thing Evie would want.

"Evie will hate that. She doesn't want to be a secretary. She loves history and rocks, not business and commerce." Two subjects Aimee adored.

"You must understand, Aimee, you and Evie come from different worlds," her mother said softly. "Evie knows she can't be your companion forever and that when you eventually marry, she'll need a profession to fall back on. Unlike you, my dear, she understands her situation in life."

"Oh, I understand my situation." Aimee jumped up and couldn't help but stomp her foot, even though she felt like a two-year-old for doing so. "I'm expected to behave like a porcelain doll with no thought or ambitions at all! I am to marry instead of following my dreams to have a career and run Father's companies."

"You're a woman, Aimee. As much as you might wish the world was different, it isn't. The sooner you accept that, the better."

"I will never accept that!" Aimee picked up the silk skirt of her gown and strode over to the far window to look out onto the crisp green lawns at the back of their residence, a rarity in New York only afforded to the obscenely wealthy like her parents. "This is America. It is the land of dreams… or at least it's meant to be, regardless of what you and Father have planned for me. I have no intention of living the life of a submissive society wife!"

"Oh, for goodness' sake, Aimee!" There was a hint of exasperation in her mother's voice. "Neither your father nor I are under any illusion you could be submissive to anyone."

"Which is why I'd be a terrible wife," Aimee insisted, turning back around to face her. "I should be doing the traineeship, not Evie. You know I want to learn about Father's businesses above anything, then eventually take over from him."

"Society and women's rights may have come a long way since the start of the century, but they haven't gone that far."

"Not yet, they haven't. But they will. Providing we don't accept those boundaries, and instead push them beyond what anyone thinks is possible."

"I hope you're right. But I fear Society will never be progressive enough to accept a woman at the helm of a multimillion-dollar company. We can't even vote, Aimee. What hope then does a woman have of running a company?"

Ever since she was eight and visited her father at his offices, she'd been fascinated with his companies, constantly begging him to teach her all about them and how to run them, knowing in her heart she was destined to take over from him when he retired, even though she was a girl.

After all, she was his only child and should be his successor despite her gender, because if she didn't take over from him, who would? Her father, however, didn't share her ideas for her future, and continued to refuse her requests, instead believing she'd eventually marry and her husband would be the one to take over from him.

Not if she had anything to do with it.

"You've always been a dreamer who thinks anything is possible," her mother continued, sounding equally proud and sad of that fact. "Just like your father."

"Yes, but at least Father made his dreams a reality, whereas my dreams are being stifled. You know I'd be far better suited to the secretary traineeship than Evie would."

"Darling, you're the sole heiress to all of this." Her mother waved her hand around the room filled with marble, gold, and priceless artifacts. "You can't learn how to be a secretary. It wouldn't be the done thing for someone in your position in Society."

The unfairness of her world was bitter. "Why should we let Society dictate to us? We are wealthier than nearly all of them. Why should I have to bend to their dictates instead of following my dreams?"

"You know it doesn't work that way." Her mother held up her hand to forestall Aimee from interrupting. "Evie will need a profession to fall back on. She can't stay your companion forever, and you know she faces challenges surrounding ever finding a suitable marriage given her birth status."

"Just because she was born out of wedlock doesn't make her destined to remain a spinster," Aimee was quick to reply. "Evie would make someone a far better wife and mother than I ever would."

Her cousin was kind and nurturing, and, yes, she was illegitimate, but that didn't make her a leper, even if most of New York Society only accepted her within their realms because Evie was, despite her birth status, still Thomas Thornton-Jones's niece. And no one dared upset Thomas Thornton-Jones.

"I still hope you will make a wonderful wife," her mother replied. "Any man would be lucky to have Evie as a wife, but, unfortunately, Society is an unforgiving beast and no matter how unfair it may be, the sins of the parents follow the child. Which is why this trip will be an excellent opportunity for both of you."

"An opportunity for both of us to be miserable!" Aimee flopped down onto the chaise longue and blew out a pent-up breath. What a waste of six weeks it would be, being forced into situations neither of them would enjoy. If only Aimee's father had arranged for her to do the internship instead of Evie, then the trip would have been enjoyable.

The very thought gave seed to an idea…

An idea as outrageous as it was brilliant, as fraught with danger as it was with possibilities. But it was an idea that would solve all their problems in one fell swoop. They could secretly switch places with each other in London, with none the wiser… couldn't they?

Suddenly, frustration was replaced with exhilaration. No one in London they'd be interacting with had met either of them before, so no one would know who they were, apart from what they were told. Evie was the same size and stature as Aimee, so they could easily wear the other's clothes, and Aimee was confident she could mimic Evie's English accent, given accents came easily to her, having learned to speak five other languages fluently.

If they did switch places, then Aimee could undertake Evie's traineeship at her father's London offices, learning all she could of his business. The idea filled her with even more excitement than the thrill she felt while secretly attending college to complete her business diploma. She'd finally get to learn all she could of her father's company from the inside, instead of having to sneak into his study each night and read through his latest correspondence to stay abreast of his deals and negotiations.

That's *if* she could get Evie to agree to the ruse…which might prove difficult, given Evie's proclivity for always doing the right thing. But Aimee had convinced her to go along with various other plans in the past, so it wouldn't be too difficult to convince her to go along with this plan, too.

She had to. There was no other option.

CHAPTER TWO

LONDON, AUGUST 1890

Harrison's knuckles slammed into the punching bag with the strength and steady rhythm born from daily repetition. Jab, jab, duck, hook, repeat. Over and over, always pushing further and harder every day, each session conditioning his body and making him stronger and sharper for whatever came his way. Which, in his position as the head of the London arm of the Thornton-Jones empire, was a necessity.

"I thought I'd find you here."

His fist stilled against the bag at the interruption, and Harrison deliberately paused a moment before glancing over his shoulder to his second in charge, Benjamin Hartley.

"Now don't bite my head off," Ben said, striding over toward him, an expression of extreme discomfort yet an equal amount of determination in his brown eyes. "I know you don't like being interrupted during your morning routine, but this couldn't wait." He pulled out a folded yellow piece of paper from the brown satchel slung over his shoulder. "You'd have throttled me if I didn't show you this immediately."

Harrison raised a brow at his friend's dramatic prediction but took the telegram from his outstretched hand and quickly read the two short sentences on the paper. Reflexively, his jaw clenched and his chest tightened at the message. "Fuck."

"Not quite the words I used, but, yes, that," Ben replied, straightening his black-rimmed spectacles before heaving a lengthy sigh. "What are we going to do? This means the deal is dead in the water, and we've wasted months of our time and resources for nothing." He threw his hands in the air, his despair and restlessness mirroring Harrison's inner turmoil. "Not to mention the company's English stocks will take a hit and the share price will plummet once news of this becomes public knowledge. It will be a disaster."

The outburst from Ben was unusual, given he was normally a pillar of reserve and composure, and so very English that it often irritated Harrison's American sensibilities. But, in this case, Ben had a right to be upset given the hours they'd spent working on this deal together. A deal that had to go through. Harrison had everything riding on it and there was no way in hell he'd let what he'd worked his lifetime for slip through his fingers because someone had changed their mind.

"It hasn't been for nothing." Harrison crunched up the paper in his fist and hurled it against the wall, before he stalked over and grabbed his towel from the hook. "And it's not the end of anything, not by any means," he said, wiping his face. He balled up the towel and lobbed it into the washing hamper as he strode to the exit, Ben following closely behind him. "If Franz Wilheimer thinks I'm going to accept this without a bloody fight, he's a fool."

"Quite so. But um…you're not *literally* going to fight him, are you?" Ben's voice was laced with concern, his footsteps clipping alongside Harrison's as they made their way down the hall and through the lobby of the Mayfair Grand Hotel, which was one of the flagship hotels in the Thornton-Jones English portfolio Harrison was in charge of growing.

"What? No pistols at dawn." They'd worked together for over five years and still Ben thought him a wild American, even though both Harrison's parents had been English.

"Very funny." There was a hint of sarcasm in Ben's voice before a sudden look of concern flashed in his eyes. "You are joking, though, aren't you? I mean, I'm aware you carry a five-shot revolver on your person—"

"It's a six-shot, actually." Harrison nodded briefly to some hotel staff he passed along the way.

"Regardless," Ben continued, "you do know dueling's been illegal here for nearly fifty years? Fighting to settle disputes isn't the done thing in England nowadays, most especially not to settle business disputes."

"It's not the done thing in America, either. Unfortunately." Striding straight past the elevators, Harrison began to climb the marble stairs up to the top floor. Besides never using elevators, he needed to work off some of his frustrations at this latest development, which six flights of stairs would help with, despite Ben's mumbled protestations behind him. "So, no, I'm not going to shoot him or fight him. At least not physically, but you can be damn sure I'll fight him with every other means and method at my disposal. He *will* see the error he's making and *will* change his mind, or else he'll suffer the consequences."

"Sounds ominous," Ben muttered as they eventually crested the top stair to the sixth floor. "But at the end of the day, it's just a deal. We can always go back to pursuing a deal with the other company you'd originally been considering."

"No. It has to be this deal, damn it!" Harrison replied, somewhat more harshly than he'd intended.

"But why this deal?"

"Because buying out Wilheimer's company will make Thornton-Jones Shipping the largest this side of the Atlantic, and the Conglomerate itself one of the largest trading companies in the world."

"True," Ben agreed. "But we'll eventually get there. It just might take us a few more years."

"Damn it, I don't have a few more years." Turning to his right, he headed to the far end of the corridor toward the suite he'd called home for nearly the past five years. "If I can pull off this deal by the end of this year, Thomas Thornton-Jones has agreed to sell me the majority shares for the English arm of the company." Meaning Harrison's goal in life, and one he'd worked his butt off for since he was a boy, would be a reality. He'd own his own multimillion-dollar company and be the financial success his grandfather told him he never would.

And no one was going to jeopardize that.

"Hence, this deal must go through," Harrison

continued. "We need to get as much leverage on Wilheimer as we can."

"I'm already ahead of you on that one," Ben said, pausing in tandem with Harrison at the door to the suite. "I've brought over all of the information I've gathered on him." He patted his satchel.

"And that's why you're my right-hand man, Benjamin." Harrison unlocked the door and strode into the lounge area, gesturing for Ben to follow. "You have a knack for anticipating things."

"Unfortunately, I didn't anticipate Wilheimer changing his mind." Ben hurried over to the dining table, while simultaneously pulling out several files from inside his bag and putting them on the table. "But, luckily, we already know most everything about him. Who he banks with, who he owes money to, what clubs he has a membership with, who he socializes with and who his mistresses are."

"Mistresses, plural?"

"Three," Ben replied with a straight face.

"The old German has more stamina than I do." Women were a complication Harrison had little time for, instead preferring to expend his energies on what was important—his business endeavors and ensuring his financial success.

It was a shame his last paramour, Lady Whitley, had started hinting at marriage when Harrison had been under the impression she was more than happy with their casual arrangement.

But it seemed most women wanted more of Harrison than he was willing to give, especially after they found out he was the unwanted heir of his uncle, the Earl of Carlisle. A fact Harrison found laughable, given his father's family had all but disowned his father when he'd gone against their wishes and did the unthinkable by marrying a maid and running off to America to start a life with her there.

Then when Harrison was eight and his parents both died from typhus, his father's family hadn't wanted a thing to do with him, refusing to send him a penny. In a way, it was poetic justice his uncle had been blessed with five daughters and no sons, making Harrison his sole heir. Something Harrison took great pleasure in. Not because he wanted to be an earl—which he didn't—but because he was sure his grandfather was turning in his grave knowing the earldom would be passed down to the son of a maid. Served the old bastard right.

But an earldom cost money, especially one as poorly managed as his uncle had made it, which was why Harrison couldn't afford for this deal to fall through. Not after he'd been promised the majority stake in the London operations of the Thornton-Jones empire if he could make it happen.

A stake that would assist with the eventual mammoth upkeep on an estate that consumed pounds like a ravenous beast and would see Harrison's dreams of being a success realized. Then, perhaps finally, this restless sense of loneliness that had plagued him since his parents' deaths would abate and he'd be content.

Which was why he had to come up with an effective strategy for how best to leverage Franz Wilheimer into selling his business. Given all men had weaknesses, all Harrison had to do was find the right one to prod. He picked up one of the files and started to flick through it. "Who does Wilheimer bank with?"

Ben reached for another file on the table and quickly thumbed through the pages, stopping on a page in the middle. A slow smile spread over his face. "The International Bank on Cannon Street, and even better, he has several loans with them totaling over one hundred thousand pounds."

Satisfaction filled him with the news. "Can he raise the capital to fulfill the loans if they're called in?"

"Highly unlikely," Ben replied. "Though, he has some solid contracts in operation, which is why we want to buy him out. Those aren't going to be fulfilled for at least another year or two. As it stands right now, if his debts are called in, he can't repay them."

"There's our leverage." Lady Luck was smiling down on him with Wilheimer banking at a bank Harrison held a huge amount of sway with, given he sat on the board of directors and owned a large stake of shares in it himself. "Contact the manager at the bank, Mr. Carter, and tell him I'll be in to see him within the hour. Then find out all you can about why Wilheimer's changed his mind. See if he's been approached by another company, or if any of our employees have been visiting or contacting anyone from Wilheimer's company."

"You think someone's been spying for him?"

"Probably." Harrison made a beeline for the bathroom, wanting to shower and change as quickly as possible. Now that he knew his plan of attack, nothing was going to stop him. "Oh, and set up a meeting with Wilheimer for Monday afternoon, and don't take no for an answer."

"Very well, but what about Mr. Thornton-Jones's niece, Miss Jenkins?" Ben asked, his words halting Harrison in his tracks.

"What about her?" He'd told Thomas he'd collect the man's niece when she arrived in England for her traineeship.

"Her ship's due to dock at midday today."

"Today?"

"Yes, it's Friday."

"Damn it." Harrison dragged a hand through his hair. The last thing he had time to do was play nursemaid to Thomas's niece when he needed to focus on this deal.

Ben shrugged. "At least it's just her you're collecting. His daughter is being picked up by the Countess of Brexton."

"A small mercy." Thomas was always lamenting how much of a handful his daughter was, as willful and stubborn as she was charming and confident, apparently. Thomas had assured him his illegitimate niece, Evie, was the more docile and patient of the two, someone who wouldn't ask too many questions nor bother Harrison overly, given fossils were her passion rather than business. Thank goodness. But still, collecting Miss Jenkins was a complication he didn't have time for. "You'll need to get her on my behalf."

"Actually, I can't," Ben replied, appearing completely unapologetic. "I promised Holly I wouldn't miss out on another one of her doctor's appointments. Which you should remember given she extracted a promise from you to make sure I attended."

The very memory of Ben's petite wife scolding him like a dragon over Ben missing her first appointment was still fresh in his mind. "The last time you missed going to her appointment, she marched into my office and nearly took my head off with her fury. For such a small woman, your wife has one bloody big temper, and one I'd prefer not to incur again."

"Yes, isn't she marvelous, especially for someone in her delicate condition," Ben said, with the usual sappy grin on his face he wore whenever he spoke of his wife, so clearly in love with the woman it was slightly nauseating. "Honestly, she would take on the Queen herself if she tried to come between me and this appointment. Which is why I must attend. Plus, neither of us wish to suffer her wrath again if I don't."

Harrison sighed. "Fine. Send Mrs. Holbrook to greet Miss Jenkins then." It made sense, given his head secretary would not only be training the girl but hosting her at her residence, too.

"Mrs. Holbrook had to have a personal day today to visit her cousin in Windsor," Ben replied.

"Am I the only one working today?" Harrison threw his hands up in the air. "Send Frederick to collect her then."

"The office boy?"

"I assume he at least is working."

"Yes, of course, but are you certain Mr. Thornton-Jones will be fine with Fred collecting

Miss Jenkins? Won't he be upset with the arrangement, given you've promised to collect her yourself?"

"Thomas is pragmatic when it comes to business and would do the same in my shoes." And Harrison should know, since he'd been mentored by Thomas since he was twelve, after he'd gotten up the courage, while shining the man's boots at the small street stand Harrison had set up on Wall Street, to ask if he could invest in Thomas's company with the meager amount of dollars he'd saved away.

Thomas had been so impressed with Harrison's reasoning why he felt the Thornton-Jones Conglomerate was the stock to invest in, that rather than just let Harrison invest, Thomas also gave him a job working as an office boy in his New York office.

Then gradually, through his diligence and determination, Thomas had seen just how serious Harrison was about succeeding, so he'd taken him under his wing and began mentoring him and teaching Harrison about all facets of the company. Eventually, Harrison had proven his worth, becoming Thomas's most trusted right-hand man, second in charge of all of Thomas's companies, only answering to Thomas himself.

It was a position Harrison took seriously, never wanting to let down the man who'd done so much for him. A man who was like a second father to him, having believed in him when no one else had given him the time of day.

"Stop worrying about it, Ben," Harrison said. "It's not like Miss Jenkins will be walking the streets alone. Fred will take her straight from the docks to Mrs. Holbrook's, where she'll be safe. Now is that all?"

"Yes," Ben mumbled. "I'll arrange everything."

"Good, and don't take no from Wilheimer about setting up a meeting for Monday."

"I won't." Ben nodded and twisted on his heel, heading for the main door.

Harrison watched the door close and latch before striding into the bathroom and stripping off to get into the shower. The quicker he could get this whole mess sorted out and get the deal back on track, the better.

Miss Jenkins's arrival was an annoyance he'd have to work around, but if she was as agreeable as Thomas said, then it wouldn't prove too difficult at all.

CHAPTER THREE

The ship's horn blared as the vessel navigated its way into the dock, while Aimee stood on the top deck, her gaze hungrily drinking in the sight of London looming large in the distance. It was a hub of activity and commerce, with people and carriages bustling about everywhere, the air thrumming with boundless opportunities.

And here she was, about to embark on the most daring plan she'd ever conceived, switching places with her cousin. Exhilaration filled her with the thought she'd learn all she could of her father's company and show him she had a brain for business. Perhaps then he might finally believe there was a place for her within his company.

It wouldn't be easy. Her father was as stubborn as she was. But standing there, with the wind whispering against her cheeks and the late morning sun shining brightly down on her as they prepared to disembark, it felt like anything was possible.

"We should reconsider this plan, Aimee," Evie mumbled nervously beside her, her porcelain complexion still tinged with a slight shade of green from having been seasick for the majority of the trip. "I don't think it'll work. How will anyone believe I'm you? Even dressed in this ridiculously expensive outfit." She nervously tugged on her bodice, the tapestry of delicate white lace and blue silk all but dancing in the sunlight.

"Nonsense," Aimee declared, turning to face her cousin, smiling in reassurance. "You look perfect. No one who saw you would think you anything less than a wealthy heiress. A million-dollar heiress." She winked and gave Evie a reassuring pat on her arm. Dressed in a glorious two-piece sapphire and white gown that clung to her cousin's lithe figure in a perfect balance of sophistication and modesty, Evie not only looked the part of an heiress, but exuded the vast wealth of the Thornton-Jones empire.

While Aimee, wearing an ensemble from Evie's wardrobe, of a simple navy skirt and matching jacket with a white blouse underneath, couldn't be mistaken for anything other than what she wanted everyone to believe her to be—a respectable companion, with little wealth to her name. No one would think they weren't who they said they were.

"I'm not an heiress, and people are going to realize that fact quickly." Evie bit into her bottom lip, her blue eyes reflecting her worry as a frown marred her normally serene countenance. "How could they not? I don't have your confidence or poise, and my American accent is dreadful."

"Your American accent is fine." Aimee reached over to her cousin and adjusted the broad-brimmed blue bonnet elegantly perched atop Evie's blonde hair. "People only see what they expect to. Dress the part and that's what people will believe. It is as simple as that. And if you make a mistake, so what? They'll put it down to you being American."

"I suppose you're right…"

"I'm always right." Aimee grinned.

Evie raised her brow, her worry now replaced with skepticism. "Always?"

"Well, maybe not always," Aimee allowed, glad Evie wasn't looking quite so ill anymore. "But I'm right about this. And you know I have the experience to back up my assertions."

"Secretly attending a male-only business college, dressed as a young man, isn't the same at all," Evie lamented. "No one would ever expect an heiress to do that."

Aimee shrugged. "People see me dressed like a man and assume I'm one. It will be the same for you, pretending to be me."

"It's completely different." Evie threw her hands up in the air and blew out a breath. "I'll be interacting with people. You sit at the back of the lecture halls and don't draw any attention to yourself."

"Which is a hard thing for me to do, especially when I often disagree with the lecturers who have no practical experience in business."

"You don't have actual experience in business, either," Evie said with a slight shrug.

"You're right, I don't, at least not *yet*. But, unlike them, I've read every business contract, document, and ledger my father has ever brought home, and I'm well aware of what goes on with his deals and negotiations."

"You know one day he'll catch you sneaking into his study and reading his papers."

"That's unlikely, given I sneak into his study in the middle of the night." Aimee raised her chin and returned her gaze to the dock as the deck hands threw ropes down from the ship to the waiting men below, who began to loop them onto the moorings. "Hopefully, one day I won't need to sneak around anywhere to know about what business he's conducting, and he'll happily discuss such matters with me." She turned back to face her cousin. "I know you think it's a silly dream of mine—"

"I don't." Evie grabbed one of Aimee's gloved hands with her own, squeezing it lightly. "When you set your mind to something, I've seen firsthand your determination to achieve it, regardless of the hurdles. I worry this plan of yours is too bold to succeed. We might be similar in stature and appearance, but that's the extent of our similarities. I'm scared I'll make a mess of it, Aimee, and I don't know if I have the courage to convincingly pretend to be you."

"Courage isn't about being fearless, Evie. It's about pressing on in the face of your fears." It was a saying her father used often, and one she took to heart. "The truth is, I'm always terrified of being caught that one morning a week when I attend college, but it's the only sliver of freedom I get. I'm more terrified of not going and living a half life, stifled by everyone else's expectations of what I can and cannot do, instead of what brings me joy."

Evie sighed, her eyes staring out across the city before she turned back to regard Aimee steadily. "Do you really think we can pull this off?"

"I know we can." She stared deeply into her cousin's eyes, trying to will the conviction she felt into her, too. "And for once you'll be able to explore London and the museums like you never could when you grew up here. Just don't go falling in love with a handsome gentleman."

"Oh goodness, that won't happen. Besides, we're only here for six weeks."

"Jenny Jerome not only fell in love with a dashing heir to an earldom, but became engaged to him, too, only three days after arriving here."

Evie shook her head. "That will never happen to me."

Aimee raised an eyebrow. "In any event, as long as we both enjoy ourselves in our respective pursuits, that in no way include men, we'll be fine, and it will be a trip to remember."

Evie nodded, and Aimee could see her worry gradually give way to acceptance, perhaps even to the tiniest bit of excitement, too.

"You're right," Evie said. "We can do this."

"I told you I'm always right."

Evie gave an exaggerated eye roll and they both laughed.

"God help anyone who tries to come up against you," Evie said. "You can convince anyone of anything, I'm sure of it."

"The only one I need to convince is my father, who is proving to be a tough mountain to move." But persevere she would, because giving up was not in her nature, no matter how immovable the obstacle. She was crossing everything she had that this trip would be the exact opportunity she needed to finally convince him of her worth. Though, she still wasn't sure how she'd convince him of that without disclosing her and Evie's switching places in the first place.

That's even if they could pull off the ruse convincingly because contrary to her assurances to Evie, part of Aimee was nervous. If anyone found out about their masquerade, most particularly her parents, they probably would send her to a convent, or worse, marry her off to someone despite their pledge to the contrary.

Thankfully, Evie's seasickness on the voyage had ensured they could prepare well. They'd both mainly stayed in their cabins and had used the time to practice the other's accent and mannerisms. Aimee had also done her best to quell Evie's nerves and school her on how to be an heiress, a rather simple and boring endeavor, consisting mainly of dressing the part and then acting as if you had not a care in the world but instead owned it. A tedious role to play, but one expected by Society.

"Excuse me, Miss Thornton-Jones?" the captain's voice spoke from behind them. "We're ready to disembark."

They both turned and Aimee had to give Evie a quick nudge to remind her the man was addressing her, and not Aimee. She found it strangely liberating that for once the attention wasn't on her as it usually was being Thomas Thornton-Jones's only child.

"Thank you, Mr. Melville," Evie said with a polite smile.

"You're welcome, Miss." Mr. Melville returned the smile, the lines around his eyes crinkling at the corners. "If you and Miss Jenkins will follow the porters, they'll take you to the carriages your father's arranged for you both."

"I still hate we're not staying together," Evie whispered over her shoulder to Aimee as they both began to follow the porters.

"At least the Countess of Brexton is collecting you, while I'll have to put up with my father's *perfect* protégé, the horribly annoying Mr. Stone," Aimee whispered back, feeling the frown start to form on her face with the thought of the man.

"How can you dislike him so much when you've never even met him? Especially given how glowingly your father talks about him."

"That's exactly why I loathe the man," Aimee replied. She'd been subjected to her father's enthusiastic accounts of the young man and his achievements for nearly as long as she could remember, and it was tiring. "My father is normally an excellent judge of character but he's blind when it comes to his protégé. No one can be so perfect or so good at his job as father infers Mr. Stone is."

"Hasn't he been mentored by your father for nearly twenty years? One would think Uncle Thomas would know him well by now," Evie said. "Especially as he talks about him almost like he would a son."

"Yes, I know Father considers him the son he never had and has essentially groomed him to take over his business, but I won't stand for it. I intend to prove to my father that I am more than capable of doing the job. He just has to give me a chance." It hurt Aimee to see the joy in her father's face whenever he spoke of Harrison Stone, and as much as she didn't like admitting it, she was jealous of him and the relationship he had with her father. A relationship that should have been hers, but for the fact she was born a girl. "And I'm not going to let Harrison Stone take what should be mine."

"I'm surprised you've never met the man."

"You know Father likes to keep his business world separate from his family life." Aimee shrugged. "Besides, Harrison Stone is nearly ten years older than me, so by the time I came out into Society five years ago, he'd already moved over here to start up this leg of Father's business. Honestly, the way my father adores him and talks about how wonderful he is, makes me think the man has to be the biggest sycophant. But enough about the infernal Harrison Stone. I intend to start this trip on the right note, not a sour one."

Aimee linked her arm through the crook of Evie's as they made their way down the wide gangway to the dock, following the porters to the first-class passenger disembarkation point, where a handsome and rather regal-looking gentleman wearing an impeccably cut navy blue suit stood waiting for them in front of a carriage.

If that was Mr. Stone, he didn't look like the cutthroat businessman her father always praised. This gentleman was dressed in extremely fashionable attire and seemed far too happy for someone used to the ruthless world of business.

"It's not too late to change our minds," Evie frantically whispered.

"Yes, it is," Aimee replied, giving Evie a small nudge toward the gentleman. "And remember your

American accent."

Evie took a hasty step forward and glanced briefly back to Aimee, an unusual expression of annoyance on her face before she turned to face the man.

"Miss Thornton-Jones?" the man asked, to which Evie nodded. "I'm the Earl of Brexton. It's a pleasure to meet you." He stepped forward and picked up Evie's gloved hand, placing a chaste kiss on her knuckles. "My mother sends her abject apologies for not being here to greet you," he continued, smiling at Evie in a manner Aimee knew meant the man liked what he saw. "She's had an emergency with a water leak in her ballroom, so she sent me in her stead to escort you back to her residence."

"That's quite all right, my lord," Evie replied with such grace and a rather good American accent that Aimee knew they'd be fine in switching places. Better than fine, given Aimee would have forgotten to call the man *my lord*. "Thank you for agreeing to escort me."

"It's my pleasure."

Aimee cleared her throat and stepped forward. "And I am Miss Jenkins."

"Oh, do forgive me," the earl said, his eyes swinging over to Aimee. "You must be Miss Thornton-Jones's companion."

Aimee held her hand out to him. "I am."

"Ai-Evie is my cousin," Evie said, nearly stumbling over her name, clearly as thrown by calling Aimee 'Evie' as Aimee was calling herself by Evie's name.

"How wonderful," the earl enthused, reaching over and taking Aimee's proffered hand in his own, his smile again flashing brilliantly as he kissed her gloved knuckles. "And you're from England, too, not America?"

"I grew up here, before moving to the States to live with the Thornton-Joneses," Aimee replied. She didn't think she'd ever get used to referring to her family like that.

"Very good," the man said with another smile.

He seemed altogether far too good-natured and jovial for Aimee's liking.

And though he seemed genuine, could it be a ruse? Could he be an impoverished earl on the hunt for a Dollar Princess and using this as an opportunity to do so? Could her mother have even known that and arranged for her to stay with the countess? Well, if that was the case, the joke was on her mother as it would be Evie staying there interacting with the earl, not Aimee. And, thankfully, her pragmatic cousin was too smart to be taken in by a handsome face. Wasn't she?

Surely, she was…even if this was a personable, charming, and very handsome earl.

Evie didn't have the same experience rebuffing gentlemen as Aimee did, being far more entranced by her history books than by any man.

"Are you aware that Aimee's father loves to hunt?" Aimee asked the earl, returning his smile with a far more glacial one of her own, concern for Evie starting to press upon her.

"Not really, but most of us men do like the sport," the earl said, looking a bit perplexed at the turn of conversation.

"Yes, well, my f—uncle Thomas has one of the largest rifle collections in America, and is an excellent shot. He also doesn't take kindly to anyone trying to take advantage of his daughter. Most especially would-be-suitors, whom he's more than willing to shoot if they even try to think about hurting her."

"Cousin, there's no need to be so dramatic, my *father* isn't that bad," Evie said with a forced laugh before she leaned in closer to Aimee. "What are you doing?"

"My dear Aimee," Aimee replied, loud enough for the earl to hear. "You know your father is ridiculously protective of you, which is only fair to warn the earl of." She turned back to stare at the earl, who appeared uncertain. "Uncle Thomas is ruthless about it. Trust me, you wouldn't wish to incur his wrath, or he's likely to shoot you," Aimee said in utter seriousness, reflecting briefly on how odd it was to refer to her father as her uncle. "Or I will, given I'm a better shot than he is." As much as her father liked to argue the point.

"An Englishwoman who shoots? How, um, interesting." The earl blinked again, several times, clearly unused to such a conversation.

"I've picked up a lot of American mannerisms," she said by way of explanation. "I even carry a derringer in my pocket." She patted the right front of her skirt, feeling the comforting metal pistol inside.

"That's, uh, prudent of you…" The earl's voice trailed off, seemingly ill at ease with the direction of the conversation.

For a moment, Aimee felt sorry for him, especially if he wasn't hunting an inheritance, though she still wasn't certain of that. "Yes, if someone tries to take advantage of my cousin, I'm well prepared to deter them. *Permanently*."

"So I see. Perhaps I shall go and see how the servants are faring loading Miss Thornton-Jones's trunks into the carriage, and where your carriage is, Miss Jenkins." He quickly excused himself and strode over to the second carriage where all the luggage was being loaded, bar a small trunk that contained the clothes Aimee would be wearing.

"He seems sweet," Evie said. "Was there really a need to try to scare him?"

"Of course there was," Aimee replied, watching as a carriage with her father's company crest pulled in behind the carriage the earl was heading to. "He was far too friendly and smiley."

"Smiley? My, what a sin."

"I'm serious, Evie." Aimee rounded on her and lowered her voice to a whisper. "Now that you're pretending to be me, they all think you're an heiress, which could place you at risk of men seeking such a fortune to replenish their coffers with and being willing to compromise you to do so."

"As lovely as it is, you wanting to protect me, you don't need to." Evie smiled. "I've been protecting myself for the majority of my life, well before you and your parents came along."

"Protecting yourself in London is different from protecting yourself against scoundrels in a ballroom," Aimee replied. "Don't underestimate how ruthless supposed gentlemen can be. Men,

especially those accustomed to wealth, can be un-
scrupulous when it comes to ensuring that lifestyle
continues. They're a different sort of creature to
deal with than a thief on the streets. They use
charm and seduction as their weapons, and those
are two implements you have no experience defending yourself against."

"I've accompanied you to hundreds of balls
over the last six years since moving to America."
There was a mutinous expression on Evie's face,
one that reminded Aimee of herself. "And I've in-
teracted with plenty of men during those
occasions."

"Interacting with waiters by taking a glass of
lemonade from their trays and thanking them isn't
the same thing at all."

"I've had other interactions, too," Evie mumbled, crossing her hands over her chest.

"Butlers and footmen don't count, either,"
Aimee replied. "Look, you're more like a sister to
me than a long-lost cousin."

Evie smiled and reached over, giving her a
quick hug. "I feel the same."

Aimee returned the hug before pulling back
and staring at her. "Good, then you know I'll always protect my sister. Especially as I'm the one
who's put you in this situation in the first place."

Aimee was starting to feel the first hints of guilt
about doing so, but not enough to change the plan.
It was too late for that anyway given they'd met the
earl, and she was still convinced it was going to be
a marvelous adventure for them both. But there
was always a possibility of things going wrong,

however small that was, and the last thing she wanted was for Evie to get hurt.

"Your trunks are all loaded, Miss Thornton-Jones," the earl said, returning back to them. "And I believe your escort is here, Miss Jenkins."

He nodded over his shoulder and Aimee watched as a boy, who couldn't have been more than fourteen, rushed up to them with a grin on his face.

"Miss Jenkins?" the boy asked, removing his cap and bowing.

"You're not Mr. Stone."

"Ah, no, Mr. Stone had to chase up something very important," the boy replied in earnest.

"He did, did he?" The man was already making a woeful impression but given the sort of man she believed him to be, it only made sense he wouldn't bother turning up to greet her cousin in person, or her as the case was.

The boy cringed. "Aye. A big deal's gone wrong, and he has to fix it."

"The Wilheimer deal?" Her throat tightened at the thought. Her father needed this deal to go ahead to expand his global reach into Europe; it would be the deal of a century if it could be pulled off.

"Aye, that's the one," the boy said, surprise flickering in his eyes. "But Mr. Stone sends his apologies."

Aimee raised an eyebrow. "*He* actually said to say sorry?"

"Well, no," the boy confirmed, looking slightly abashed. "It was his second in charge, Mr. Hartley who told me to say that, and he also organized for me to get you and then take you to Mrs. Holbrook's to settle in for the rest of the day."

That wouldn't do, not if the Wilheimer deal was in jeopardy, and though she knew she wouldn't be able to do anything, if she could find out what was going on, she might be able to help, or at least let her father know what was happening.

"What's your name, boy?"

"Frederick Lambton, miss." The boy bowed again. "And at your service, I am."

"Well, Frederick Lambton, rather than Mrs. Holbrook's, you can take me straight to my fa— uncle's office."

"Oh no, miss." Fred shook his head, his eyes wide in alarm. "I was told to take you straight to Mrs. Holbrook's house to settle in, not to the office."

"Can I call you Fred?"

The boy nodded his head once again. "Yes, miss."

"Well, then, Fred, as I see it, you have two options." She took a step closer to him, her eyes level with his. "You can either drop me off safely to the office, or I will walk to the office on my own. But make no mistake, I'll be going to the office directly from here."

CHAPTER FOUR

Stepping out of the carriage and onto the cobble-stones of Fenchurch Street, Aimee glanced up at the tall brownstone building standing boldly before her. The grand structure took up an entire block, with its four-story-high marble arches towering in front of enormous double entrance doors, the gold letters THORNTON-JONES CONGLOMERATE etched onto a marble sign above them.

It was a testament to what her family had built from nothing. Turning a small business, ferrying people and goods across Manhattan Island, into a global shipping and railroad company that had a hand in moving most everything across America and was now making strides in doing so in England, too.

A company she was finally going to be part of, rather than a mere spectator on the sidelines. She could feel the warring emotions of exhilaration and nerves creeping through her, given the charade she was undertaking to do so. But standing here in front of this building, she was filled with a confidence she couldn't explain. She was meant to be here.

"Miss Jenkins, please, won't you change your mind?"

It took Aimee a moment to realize Fred was addressing her, the surname Jenkins still sounding odd to her ears. She glanced over her shoulder at him as he poked his head out from the carriage, almost like he was hoping that by staying in the vehicle he might be able to change her mind.

"Please, miss?" he said again, for maybe the tenth time since they'd left the docks. "Mr. Stone will have my head for not taking you to Mrs. Holbrook's like I was told to."

"There's no need to fret," she replied, happy she'd become rather adept at donning an English accent consistently, which so far hadn't raised any questions. "I'll deal with Mr. Stone and make certain he knows this was my idea. After all, my uncle is the boss of the company, and Mr. Stone can't get too cranky with the boss's niece, now can he?"

Fred nodded but still appeared unconvinced. "I suppose not."

"It will be fine." Aimee winked at him. "But, just to be sure, why don't you go with the carriage driver and see that my trunk is delivered safely to Mrs. Holbrook's, while I go inside and introduce myself."

"Yes, miss." Fred didn't need telling twice. He smacked the side of the carriage and yelled, "Mrs. Holbrook's," to the driver. A moment later, the carriage disappeared into a swarm of other carriages heading down the street.

Taking in a deep breath, Aimee turned back to the building's entrance. It was time to make her mark and learn absolutely everything she could of her father's business. She lifted her skirts and strode toward the entrance, but then a high-pitched yelp echoed loudly to her left, and she swiveled around toward the sound.

A well-dressed man was rushing across the street, dragging a little brown dog behind him, yanking harshly on the dog's leash, while the animal valiantly tried to pull in the opposite direction. "You stupid mutt, stop doing that," the man growled, swatting the dog on its hind leg with his open palm.

Aimee gasped as the dog whined. "Stop that, you brute!" she called out to the man, but he didn't bother to acknowledge her as he continued down the alley, tugging the dog around the corner.

Without another thought, Aimee rushed after them, certain once out of sight the man might be even more cruel. One thing she wouldn't tolerate was an animal being mistreated.

She ran around the corner into the laneway and saw the man up ahead. He'd stopped in the middle of the road, his round frame straining while he wrestled to hold onto the lead as the dog tried to get away, with little success.

"You bloody idiot of a dog," the man screamed, his breathing labored and his cheeks reddening. "You'll come with me or I'll tie some bricks around you and throw you in the Thames."

"Don't you dare touch that animal again!" Aimee yelled, running toward the man.

The man turned to face her, while she careened to a stop in between him and the dog. He blinked in surprise before he glanced down at her attire and his beady brown eyes filled with an expression of dismissal, followed by anger. "This is none of your concern, *girl*," he said, taking a step toward her, his fists clenching by his sides. "Now be gone before I shake some sense into you, too."

Aimee felt her rage boil over. She'd never been so dismissed before, and all because she was wearing Evie's simple outfit. "I'd like to see you try, you bloated old turnip!"

"*What* did you just call me?" the man screeched, puffing out his belly, the buttons of his paisley waistcoat straining at the seams.

"You must be hard of hearing, too, for I called you a *bloated*, *old* turnip," Aimee replied, the description rather apt given the man's rotund body and pasty complexion.

The man's jaw clenched and his nostrils flared, while his whole face reddened, almost like he was about to erupt. "You won't be so insulting when you realize who I am."

"I already know who you are," Aimee replied. "You're a cruel, horrid man, and I won't let you hurt that dog again."

"Won't let me?" the man exclaimed, his eyes narrowing upon her. "How dare you! You have no rights here. My brother is a policeman and I'll have him arrest you."

"First, he can arrest you for animal cruelty."

"You're far too bold for a woman who clearly works in a menial position," he spat out, his eyes narrowing further, until he was squinting at her.

"And you're lucky I don't shoot you for mistreating an animal," Aimee replied, holding his eyes steady and raising her chin. "I warn you now, if you so much as try to hurt that dog again, or threaten me, you'll regret it."

She glanced down at the small dachshund who

was cowering on the footpath, her big brown eyes fearful. Just looking at the poor creature had Aimee's fists curling tightly into a ball.

"You're the one going to regret speaking to me like that, you strumpet," he hissed, his meaty hands reaching for her, but Aimee ducked out of his reach, then turned around and kicked him in the back of his knee. He toppled forward to the ground and lost his grip on the leash. The little dog used the opportunity to launch into a run in the opposite direction, her short legs a blur as she dashed out of sight and around the corner, her lead trailing behind her.

"That dog cost me money, you little bitch," the man roared, twisting around, his hand lashing out and grabbing at her ankle before she could side-step away from him. "You're going to pay for that!"

"Let go of me, you fool!" She used her other leg and kicked him in the chest. He grunted with the impact, but his hand didn't release her ankle. Instead, his other hand grabbed at her skirt and yanked her toward him, the momentum pulling her down on top of him.

Before Aimee knew what he was about, he used his bulk to twist her under him, his weight partially pinning her in place. It felt like a brick was on her chest, and for the first time she felt a sliver of fear crawl up her spine, but then an avalanche of fury began to consume her. How dare he!

The man heaved himself up on his arms, the exertion of doing so making his already flushed face even redder and giving her just the space she needed to slip her hand into her pocket.

"You should have minded your own business." He exhaled harshly through his gritted, yellowing teeth. "You'll pay for your insolence, you stupid girl, and then I'll have you arrested for assault."

"Let's make it a good assault then, shall we?" She pushed her derringer through the material of her skirt and pressed it against the junction between the man's legs. She cocked the hammer of the pistol and he froze. "What's the penalty for shooting you in the nether regions?"

Fear leached into his eyes but then, without warning, the man was flung off her and tossed into the street like a pile of rubbish. Aimee glanced up, and standing above her, with the sun behind his head, was a golden-haired angel, wearing a frown on his face.

"Are you hurt?" his deep voice rumbled, the timbre of it echoing through to her very core, making her feel annoyingly uncertain, when only a moment ago, with the Turnip on top of her, she'd felt confident.

"I'm fine," she snapped at him as she put her pistol back in her pocket before struggling to her feet, her annoyance increasing as the skirts of her dress got lightly tangled in her legs. "I didn't need your assistance. I had the situation well in hand."

"It didn't look that way." He raised an eyebrow and reached his hand out to help her, but Aimee knocked it away.

"Well, it was that way." She steadied herself in front of him and glared at him with as much haughtiness as she could muster. She knew she was being ungrateful, but she was so sick of men taking charge and thinking she was helpless and couldn't do anything. It was infuriating. "Trust a man to rush in thinking he has to save the day."

The angel blinked. "Listen, lady, I was just trying to help you."

She heard the twang in his accent and realized he was American, too. "I didn't need your help." She straightened up to her full five-feet-six-inches, which felt woefully short against his extremely tall stature. The man had to be at least six-foot-three and built like a brick, with his ridiculously large, muscular arms and chest. "Now, if you'll excuse me, I have a turnip to finish castrating."

She turned and stalked over to where the turnip was trying to heave himself up from the pavement without much luck, given his short and bulky frame. She pulled out her pistol and aimed it directly between his legs as he came to his feet. "Give me one reason I shouldn't shoot you."

The man froze, a look of panic flashing in his beady brown eyes. "I say, there's no need for that. I didn't hurt you. I was trying to teach you a lesson…"

"Well, now it's my turn to teach you a lesson." Aimee cocked the hammer. "A lesson that will ensure you never underestimate a woman again."

"Are you mad? You can't shoot me!" the man yelled, desperation rife in his voice, before his eyes swiveled wildly across to Aimee's left. "Aren't you going to help?"

"No," the angel said, his footsteps surprisingly silent for such a strong man as he came to stand to Aimee's left. "She's made it clear she doesn't need my help."

"I meant me, not her. Please, help a gentleman out?"

"You're no gentleman," Aimee scoffed.

"She's right." The angel gave a half smile, but there was little humor in his green eyes. "A true gentleman never lays a hand against a female. Ever. No matter the provocation. What you are is a pathetic excuse of a man."

Then before Aimee could even blink, the angel's hand darted out and grabbed her derringer from her hand, deftly disarming her as he uncocked the hammer.

"How dare you!" she yelled, a sense of fury mixed with helplessness washing through her. Without her weapon, she felt naked. "Give me back my pistol."

"As much as he deserves to be shot, I don't have the time to deal with the ramifications of you doing so." He glanced back to the turnip. "Get out of here," he told the man. "And if I see you around this area again, make no mistake, I'll be the one to shoot you."

"My brother, who's a policeman, will hear about this!" the turnip squeaked before turning and fleeing down the alley like the devil was on his tail.

As the man's footsteps receded down the street, the angel turned to face her, staring at her as if he were cataloging her soul. A shiver ran down her spine at the scrutiny, but she didn't feel scared; instead she felt more furious than she'd ever been.

"You have some nerve," she growled at him, before quickly reaching out and snatching her gun back from his hand. The weight of the pistol instantly restored her confidence. But she took a step out of the angel's reach to be certain.

"I told you I don't have time to be embroiled in a police matter."

"I wasn't going to shoot him, only scare him." She exhaled and shook her head. "You shouldn't have bothered coming to my assistance in the first place, especially when I didn't ask for your help or need it."

"Clearly, you're used to your fellow Englishmen and their propensity of doing nothing. But I'm American, sweetheart—"

"Don't you dare call me sweetheart!"

"And when I see a woman struggling with a man on top of her," he continued, "I'm going to help, despite the fact she's clearly an ungrateful wench who doesn't like help from anyone."

Aimee gasped. The man was infuriating. "I don't need help from an arrogant baboon of a man who should have minded his own business!"

"Better to be an arrogant baboon than a reckless, overconfident harridan of a woman." He crossed his arms over his chest and frowned. "What *stupidity* possessed you to confront a stranger on your own and down an alley in the first place? Do you like getting yourself into silly situations where you can pull out your gun, or are you completely without any sense? My money's on the latter."

Her mouth fell open. "Excuse me?" The man had no right to berate her.

"It's a simple question," he replied. "Though perhaps you'd prefer I call it foolhardiness instead of stupidity? Or what about reckless, idiotic, or dim-witted, to better describe your behavior? I mean, what were you thinking? Clearly, you work in an office around this area, so you should know better than to chase a stranger down a side street."

"I was saving a dog from that man!" The angel had turned into a demon. "I couldn't leave the poor thing to suffer."

"You should have gone and gotten help, not tried to tackle a man on your own. It seems your safety means little to you."

"And you don't think a woman can protect herself."

The angel raised an eyebrow. "Yes, I saw how well you were protecting yourself with that fool on top of you."

"I had my derringer pointed at his crown jewels." Aimee raised her chin in the air and narrowed her eyes at the man. She'd never instantly disliked someone so fiercely before. "So I was protecting myself quite well, and if you hadn't come along and played the role of completely unwanted hero, I would have had him off me in mere seconds."

"With that little thing?" he scoffed, staring down at her derringer with a raised brow. "Do you even know how to use it?"

"I'm an expert shot, actually." Aimee cocked the hammer. "Would you like me to demonstrate?"

His eyes narrowed, but he didn't seem concerned in the slightest, merely annoyed. "Your threat would be far more effective if you were holding a real gun instead of a toy."

"Not only do you underestimate me because

I'm a woman, you also underestimate the capabilities of my pistol, too." She shook her head. "You men are all the same. Although in fairness to other men, you're the most infuriating one I've come across."

"Anyone as ungrateful and belligerent as you, *princess*, would surely consider every man you came across as arrogant and annoying."

Aimee took in a sharp breath, straightening her spine to glare at him with all her might. The man was odious, even if he did look like a darned Adonis. "No, just you."

"Given one of your hobbies is obviously trying to pick fights with men," he continued, "you might want to carry a gun that deters a man. Something like this perhaps?" He flicked back his jacket, revealing the shining silver butt of a six-shot revolver nestled in a holster strapped around his hip. It was a beautiful piece, and one she and her father both had in their collections.

"A double action Frontier Model, Smith and Weston," she said, wondering if he was trying to intimidate her with the piece. "It's a beautiful weapon but hardly concealable in a skirt pocket like it is under your jacket. And though you might not be intimidated by my derringer, the two bullets in its barrel will still penetrate through flesh, no matter whether they're twenty-two or thirty-eight calibers."

"An Englishwoman who knows her guns and ammunition," he murmured, interest sparking in his eyes. "Rather impressive and somewhat curious…"

"I'm not surprised you'd think that, given you believe women can't take care of themselves and hence would have no knowledge of weapons," she replied. "Again, you've completely misjudged the situation."

His eyes narrowed. "I can't save you. I can't compliment you. Damn it, lady, you might be bloody stunning to look at, but you are the most ungrateful woman I've had the displeasure of encountering, with the sour personality of a bloody prickly pear to match."

"The same can be said of you!" She squared up to him, feeling oddly flustered he thought her stunning, but equally upset he thought her ungrateful and sour. "And, yes, I might sound ungrateful, but I bet you've never been constantly underestimated and always told what you can and cannot do for your entire life!"

"You might be surprised," he murmured, staring at her with those impenetrable jade eyes of his.

"Oh please," Aimee scoffed. "You're a man. You have no idea what it's like to be a woman and pigeonholed into a certain role all because of your sex and station in life."

She took in a deep breath, surprised that she'd bothered to try to explain anything to him. But for some reason the knowledge that he thought her ungrateful and sour rankled. Not that she should care what this man thought of her, but, surprisingly, she did.

"One should never make assumptions," he replied, the first hints of impatience drawing across his brow. "In any event, I don't have time for this nonsense. I've saved you from your own stupidity, and yes, a thank you for doing so would've been nice—"

"For the last time, I didn't need saving." The arrogance of the man was astounding. "You've got to be the most obnoxious, vexing jackass of a man I've ever met!" Aimee took in a deep breath, trying to recollect some semblance of calm. "Now, if you'll excuse me, *I'm* the one who doesn't have time for this as I need to get to work. Good day, sir."

She turned on her heel and strode down the alley, determined not to even glance back at him, not even for a moment.

"You're welcome, lady!" his deep voice hollered from behind her, sending a jolt of annoyance coursing through her. She paused for a moment and took in a deep breath. *Let it go, Aimee. Just let it go.* She resumed walking and kept her head held high, not giving him the satisfaction of a response.

She had a job to get to, and no one, not even a fallen angel who looked like sin incarnate, was going to distract her from that.

CHAPTER FIVE

Harrison could only stare as the woman stalked down the laneway, her stride filled with a confidence and energy he'd not encountered in an Englishwoman before. He didn't know what to make of her, and for a man who prided himself on knowing what motivated a person within the first few minutes of meeting them, not knowing what drove this woman was annoying the hell out of him.

What woman didn't thank someone for rescuing them? Even going so far as to berate him for doing so, constantly asserting she didn't need rescuing in the first place? She was either so confident in her abilities that she truly hadn't needed help, or she was one step removed from reality and had deluded herself into thinking she could handle the situation. He got the sense it could be either or perhaps both with her.

He hadn't even asked her name. Not that he wanted or even needed to know it, given he had no time or interest in pursuing such a snappish female, who clearly had a chip on her shoulder against men and would be trouble with a capital *T*. He'd only had to look at that glint of determination and sass in those ridiculously blue eyes of hers to know that.

But the problem was he suddenly found himself craving trouble. Her snow-white porcelain skin and rich sable-black hair had been breathtaking, and he'd felt an instant tug of lust in his belly, which had quickly turned into annoyance and exasperation when she'd opened that mouth of hers and started scolding him without justification.

How could a woman so beautiful be so disagreeable? Honestly, there'd been a point there he'd felt like kissing her just to shut her up. Well, that and the fact her lips had been ridiculously full and luscious.

Fuck. The fact he'd been so attracted to the most infuriating, troublesome, frustrating slip of a female he'd ever come across, when he should be focused on the Wilheimer deal, was not a good sign. It was probably just as well he'd never see her again. The last thing he needed was a distraction of any sort. This deal was the most important deal of his life and he couldn't let anything, especially not that disagreeable, bothersome harpy, get in the way of it. Even if he was undeniably attracted to her.

Blowing out a breath he hadn't even realized he'd been holding, he turned to the back entrance of the building behind him and let himself inside. It was time to get back to work and return his attention onto what mattered. Making an empire for himself, and not letting anything or anyone get in the way. A step he was now closer to achieving, given he'd successfully gotten Mr. Carter to call in Wilheimer's loans. Which begged the question: why had Wilheimer pulled the pin on the deal in the first place?

It didn't make sense, and for Harrison, who'd raised himself out of poverty through logic and reasoning, a decision that didn't make sense was a puzzle that needed solving. But first he had to work out the best tactics for the meeting on Monday.

Once again, he bypassed the elevators and instead climbed up the stairs to the fourth floor, then headed to his office in the upper east corner of the building. An office that was more like a home to him than his hotel suite given he spent the majority of his waking and sometimes sleeping hours there.

Striding through the outer doors into the first room of his sanctum, where Mrs. Holbrook usually sat along with two other undersecretaries, he noticed Mrs. Holbrook's second in charge, Miss Mitchell, sitting at her desk, a telephone receiver up against her left ear, while her right hand furiously scribbled notes about whatever was being discussed on the other end. The second junior secretary, Miss Cantor, was juggling a pile of folders in her arms, an annoyed expression on her slightly pinched face.

She froze midway to her desk as she caught sight of Harrison. "Mr. Stone," she exclaimed, her voice purring as a sickly sweet smile spread over her rouged lips, and she stumbled slightly toward him.

Harrison stifled a sigh. He'd noticed of late Miss Cantor often trying to attract his attention in the office. It was as unwanted as it was inappropriate and tedious.

"Oh dear," Miss Cantor cried, making a show of stumbling some more.

"Here, let me assist." He strode over and took the files from her outstretched hands, then walked them over to her desk, the woman following on his heels, the scent of her rose perfume cloyingly sweet.

"Oh, thank you, Mr. Stone," she gushed, battering her eyelashes at him as he dumped the files onto the mahogany surface of the desk.

He merely nodded before heading over to Miss Mitchell, who had just replaced the telephone onto its metal box, her eyes anxiously following his trajectory over toward her.

"Messages?"

She nodded and quickly grabbed a bundle of papers before handing them to him, her eyes blinking rapidly as she did so behind the thick lenses of her spectacles. The woman had always been quiet and timid, and perpetually nervous around him, but she was nearly as efficient as Mrs. Holbrook when it came to dictating and organizing his paperwork, which was all that mattered to Harrison.

He took the messages. "Do you know if Mr. Hartley's back yet?"

Miss Mitchell opened her mouth and then closed it, before finally opening it again. "I'm not certain. Would you like me to check?" She pushed the black rims of her glasses up her nose, a nervous gesture, given it was usually Mrs. Holbrook he spoke to directly rather than her.

"Yes, and get Mr. Stanton, too." Harrison would need Robert's head for numbers to strategize for the Monday meeting with Wilheimer.

"Mr. Stanton told me he'd gone to get a late lunch next door," Miss Cantor chimed in, her voice slightly breathless in a manner he suspected was attempting to be sultry but instead only sounded winded. "I can get him for you if you'd like, Mr. Stone? I could fetch both of them for you given I'm much quicker and more agile than Miss Mitchell."

Miss Cantor glanced sideways at Miss Mitchell, her gaze filled with disdain as she looked upon the other woman, whose outfit of a serviceable brown skirt and jacket was at clear odds with Miss Cantor's stylish green dress.

"Miss Mitchell is more than capable of fetching Mr. Hartley for me," he said, knowing the woman was referring to Miss Mitchell's rounder figure and not being kind about it. "While you, Miss Cantor, seeing as you're so agile, can go and find Stanton, and neither one of you come back without them."

Both ladies hastily nodded and made a quick retreat out the door.

Honestly, he had little time for women and their games. Especially women who preyed on the insecurities of others while trying to flirt with him when knowing full well he didn't fraternize with his employees outside of work, ever. It was one of his golden rules he never broke, as much as some of his female employees tried to throw themselves in his path.

Walking over to the door to his office, Harrison quickly flicked through the messages Miss Mitchell had given him. Thankfully, none required his urgent attention, though there was one from Thomas mentioning his niece's arrival.

Harrison sat down at his desk and quickly scanned over the note. It was brief and to the point, much like the man himself, and it clearly requested

Harrison keep his niece safe while she was in London. A simple enough task, given she'd now be ensconced at Mrs. Holbrook's residence, settling in.

"And in through here is Mr. Stone's offices," Ben's voice echoed down through the antechamber of Harrison's office. "Though I'm not sure where his secretaries are…"

"Off looking for you and Robert," Harrison said, raising his voice enough so Ben could hear him in the other room.

"Oh good, you're back." Ben's enthusiastic voice grew louder the closer he got to Harrison's office. "I have someone to introduce to you."

Harrison leaned back in his chair and glanced over to the door, resigned to the interruption.

"And here he is, the leader of our London operations, Mr. Harrison Stone," Ben said, walking into his office and waving his arm in Harrison's direction as a woman followed behind him. "Harrison, let me introduce you to Miss Yvette Jenkins."

Harrison bolted upright, every cell of his body going rigid. It was the maddening woman from the alley. "Bloody hell, *you're* Thomas's niece?"

How could this woman standing there, staring defiantly at him, be Thomas's niece? Thomas's supposedly *agreeable* niece, who didn't seem to be in the least bit agreeable at all?

CHAPTER SIX

The angel turned demon from the alley was Harrison Stone? Her nemesis...the man her father considered a son, and thought could do no wrong, praising him at every turn, until she'd become sick of hearing his name?

"You're Harrison Stone?" she asked, her stomach suddenly feeling like she'd consumed a lead weight. Surely, it was a joke. Fate couldn't be so cruel as to make this man her new temporary boss.

"I am." He gave a brief nod of his head, looking as annoyed by the twist of fate as she felt.

"Have you two met before?" Mr. Hartley asked, confusion rife in his gaze as he glanced between them.

"Ten minutes ago in the alley," Mr. Stone replied. "When I saved her from being assaulted."

"Assaulted?" Mr. Hartley gasped. "Good Lord, that's terrible! Are you quite all right, Miss Jenkins?"

"I'm fine," she replied, her fury softening as she turned to glance at Mr. Hartley, who'd been just lovely since she'd entered the building and met him in the lobby as he'd been returning from an appointment. "Mr. Stone is exaggerating, for I had the situation well in hand before he interfered."

"Interfered?" the man himself scoffed. "The bloody hell I did."

"You don't need to blaspheme. *Mr. Stone*," she said, turning her attention back to him, his name rolling off her lips like an expletive. She'd never known anyone to infuriate her so instantly as he did. "I was more than capable of getting myself out of that situation, but you're seemingly the type of man who believes a woman can't handle her own problems and must rush in and rescue her."

"Yes, how rude of me, coming to your rescue and pulling that idiot off you," he replied.

Aimee's eyes narrowed. "What was rude was when you called me stupid."

"You called her stupid?" Ben exclaimed, looking horrified at the suggestion.

"I asked her what *stupidity* possessed her to confront a man alone in an alley," Mr. Stone ground out through clenched teeth. "I never called her stupid, merely her actions."

"I was saving a dog," she explained to Mr. Hartley, who seemed far more sympathetic. In retrospect, perhaps it hadn't been the wisest move to run after a man showing his propensity for cruelty, at least not without arming herself with her derringer when initially confronting the fiend.

"You were brave to interject," Mr. Hartley replied, his eyes earnest as he nodded his head. "Not many people would put themselves at risk to save a person, let alone an animal."

"That's because most people have a sense of self-preservation, unlike Miss Jenkins," Mr. Stone growled, dragging a hand through his hair. "And what are you even doing here in the first place? Fred was told to take you to Mrs. Holbrook's to settle in. You're not meant to start work until Monday."

"It's not Fred's fault," Aimee was quick to point out. "I insisted he bring me here."

"You don't say," Mr. Stone replied.

"Is he always this sarcastic?" she asked Mr. Hartley, to which the man apologetically nodded. "But to answer your question," she said, returning her attention to Mr. Stone, "there was no need to settle in as I only have one trunk. I decided to get a head start on my traineeship, given there's no time like the present to see a dream fulfilled."

"A dream?" His eyes narrowed. "Your uncle said you weren't enthusiastic about learning the skills of being a secretary."

Darn. What else had her father told him about Evie? Hopefully, not too much. "I've since realized this is an opportunity I'd be a fool not to embrace." That sounded plausible, didn't it? "Why would I go to Mrs. Holbrook's when she's not even there and there's so much to start learning here?"

She stared unflinchingly over at him, as he stood ramrod straight, towering behind his desk, almost like he was ready to do battle. Surely, the man would appreciate her desire to get to work, because despite her misgivings about him, her father always said the man respected hard workers.

"Part of the learning process, Miss Jenkins, means doing what you're told," he replied, his tone clipped while he matched her stare with his own. "Which is something you're going to have to remember going forward given I'm to be your new boss for the next six weeks."

Suddenly, six weeks seemed like a lifetime. "How *lucky* for me."

His eye narrowed. "The next time you think to do something that hasn't been arranged for you, don't." There was a finality to his voice that once again suggested the man was used to being obeyed explicitly, but Aimee had never been one to go along with being told what to do.

Tamping down on the anger threatening to spill over, she plastered the most serene smile on her face that she could. It was a smile she often wore at balls and the like when she was digging her nails into her gloved palms, wanting to flee from the stifling confines of it all but unable to. "I feel it prudent to point out I don't answer to you. Boss or not."

"You answer to me while you're here in London," he said, his voice brooking no arguments. "Your uncle has charged me with keeping you safe, which I will. Though given what I've already observed, that's going to be a damned hard task, if not impossible, if you regularly disobey commands." He folded his arms across his chest and glared at her with the most ferocious scowl she'd seen on him yet. A scowl she was sure usually had most people capitulating, but instead only strengthened her resolve.

"I'm not a dog to be commanded about, and I'm most certainly not your responsibility, despite what my…uncle might have asked of you," she replied, quickly catching her near slip-up. "You may be my temporary boss, Mr. Stone, but if you think for one moment that your reach extends outside of these walls, you're sorely mistaken."

"I'm rarely mistaken about anything or anyone,

Miss Jenkins." He shrugged.

"Neither am I." She smiled tightly, the man's entire attitude of trying to control her infuriating beyond belief. "And you're exactly as I imagined you'd be." Well, except for the physical aspect of him—she certainly hadn't imagined him being so attractive, darn the man.

Harrison Stone was meant to be a sniveling little yes-man who was out to steal her father's company from her, not this Adonis who was as confident as he was commanding, wearing a perfectly tailored navy suit that only enhanced his athleticism and authority. A man she always believed she'd be repulsed by, not attracted to. Not that she was attracted to him, but she had eyes and couldn't deny he was handsome, almost ridiculously so. Not that that made any difference to her. This man was her enemy, full stop.

"You were imagining me, Miss Jenkins?" The man's lips twisted into a half smile as he walked around his desk and perched on the edge of it, now only a few feet away from her. "How flattering."

"Oh, my imaginings weren't flattering at all." How dare the man tease her, especially when she didn't want to imagine anything about him, even if some unbidden images of him had already flashed into her mind since meeting him. "They were, however, accurate about you being an arrogant ass."

Mr. Hartley inhaled sharply behind her, while Mr. Stone himself didn't seem bothered in the slightest.

"Resorting to name-calling, Miss Jenkins, when we've only just met?" He tittered, and Aimee felt her blood boil even more. "It's either brave or foolhardy of you, given most would be worried their new job would be in jeopardy doing so."

"Is that a threat, Mr. Stone?" She raised her chin and stared unflinchingly into his stormy jade eyes. No man apart from her father had dared to threaten or reprimand her before, and she was furious that Harrison Stone thought he could, though part of her was also reluctantly intrigued.

"I don't do threats, Miss Jenkins," his deep voice rumbled as he spoke. He stood and took a few steps toward her, making her tilt her neck up to maintain eye contact. "I state facts. Something you'd do well to remember."

Aimee felt her breath hitch slightly being so close to him again. "Your facts sound a lot like threats, and I will not be intimidated by you, no matter what your position is in the company." It probably wasn't the smartest move to antagonize him, which didn't even seem to be working, but everything about him rubbed her the wrong way.

"Who says I'm trying to intimidate you?"

"Aren't you?" She raised her chin, refusing to even blink as she stared him down, or up as was the case, given he was a great deal taller than her.

The sound of Mr. Hartley clearing his throat broke through the tense atmosphere like a knife. "It seems you've both gotten off on the wrong foot." He walked around to stand between them, almost like a referee.

"It's not just the wrong foot, Mr. Hartley," she said, glaring at Mr. Stone. "It's both feet."

"You weren't even on your feet when I rescued

you, Miss Jenkins," Mr. Stone had the audacity to say.

Mr. Hartley began to chuckle but hastily covered it with a cough, while the devil himself winked at her. The absolute temerity of both men! She swung her gaze between them, and Mr. Hartley had the grace to appear apologetic, while Mr. Stone's expression was the opposite.

"I might just go and answer the phone seeing as it seems your secretaries aren't back yet, Harrison," Mr. Hartley blurted out, before rushing to the outer office, leaving them alone.

Aimee took in a deep breath and plastered another smile on her face before turning her full attention back to Mr. Stone. Which she realized was a mistake as soon as her eyes clashed with his and she was subjected to the intensity in their depths. "Do you always welcome your new employees by mocking them?"

"None have ever dared talk back to me like you have, Miss Jenkins," he replied, an expression of curiosity crossing his gaze. "I don't know whether to be impressed or have you shipped back home immediately."

"I'm not some parcel to be shipped anywhere." The hide of the man suggesting he had the power to send her home. Didn't he know who she was? Actually, he didn't. As far as he was concerned, she was his boss's illegitimate niece. Darn it. But still, even Evie had leverage. "I feel it prudent to remind you that my…uncle is *your* boss. It would be wise for you to remember that fact when you interact with me."

Instantly, the amusement vanished from his eyes. "Now who is threatening whom, Miss Jenkins?" He took a step closer toward her, their bodies now only a foot from each other.

Aimee raised her chin higher, refusing to back down even an inch. "It's not a threat, Mr. Stone, but a fact, seeing as you're so fond of those." This close to him she could smell the soap and sandalwood on his skin and had to clench her fingers into fists as an unaccountable longing swept over her. Oh my goodness, what was wrong with her? She loathed this man.

"Well, here is another fact for you, Miss Jenkins," he said, leaning down until his head was but an inch away from her ear, and Aimee had to will herself not to budge as his voice sent a current of electricity through her body. "Your uncle trusts me to run the London company as I see fit. He respects my decisions, and, make no mistake, he will not interfere in them, not even for his niece."

She couldn't quite stifle a small involuntary gasp from the soft whisper of his breath against the skin below her earlobe. Damn the man. She hated not only how her body was reacting to him but that he was right, too. Her father did trust him, nearly above anyone except her mother, and he certainly wouldn't meddle in the decisions Harrison made, not for his niece, not even for his daughter.

"If you defy me again, especially when it relates to your safety," his deep voice rumbled, "I'll ship you back to New York as fast as I can hurl you aboard a steamer, Thomas's niece or not. Am I being clear?"

"Crystal, Mr. Stone," she replied. "And do let me be as equally clear. I'm not going anywhere. I intend to stay here and learn all I can about this business, and if you lay one hand on me in an effort to *haul me aboard a steamer* as you so eloquently put it, you'll see firsthand what a good shot I am with my pistol."

Mr. Stone regarded her steadily for a moment before he took a step back. "You're not at all intimidated by me, are you?"

"Did you want me to be?"

"No. Though it would have been handy given how headstrong you are," he replied with a shrug, then his eyes narrowed with suspicion. "You're not how your uncle described you. Not even in the slightest."

"I'm not?" Her father had described Evie to him? Fear clawed up her throat. She hadn't previously been worried about being caught in her masquerade but that was before she'd met Harrison Stone. If anyone was going to unmask her, it would be him. And if that happened, he really would ship her home.

"No, you're not."

Aimee forced herself to smile at him through her tightly pressed lips. Surely, he couldn't suspect she'd switched places with Evie. No one was that good at detecting deception. Not even her father's wonder boy. "Perhaps you misheard how my—uncle," she managed to just catch herself again before saying *father*, "described me."

"I didn't mishear anything," he replied. "You're not bloody agreeable, or docile, or shy in the slightest. You're the complete opposite of all of those things."

"Oh…" Relief washed over her, and she took in a deep breath. That sort of description, she could work with. "Uncle Thomas does have a bit of a soft spot for me." And he did for Evie, who was exactly as he'd described.

"A blind spot is more like it if he thinks you're any of those things," Harrison muttered.

Aimee narrowed her eyes upon him. "He might have exaggerated my temperament somewhat… though he's known for bringing out the best in people. An admirable quality you seem to lack."

"My dear Miss Jenkins, you have no idea of what I can bring out in people. In ladies most especially of all."

Aimee gulped at the gleam of heat smoldering in his gaze, and her imagination started to run riot as her eyes were drawn to his full lips. What would they feel like pressed against her own lips? Would they be as soft and full against hers as they appeared? Would the slight stubble along his jawline tickle or tantalize her cheeks?

Stop it! She wouldn't allow herself to succumb to him simply because he was handsome. His eyes, though, were almost compelling her to break her own rules, but then he blinked and was staring at her with a detachment bordering on coldness that she began to question if she'd seen any heat in his gaze at all.

"The only thing you bring out in me is annoyance," she eventually responded. "Absolute annoyance, and nothing more." *Liar*, the voice in her head whispered. *Shut up, Voice,* she silently whispered back. "Though I'm prepared to overlook that in my effort to work with you."

"My dear Miss Jenkins, you will be working *for* me, not with me." He pulled out a coin from his pocket and began flicking it backward and forward across his knuckles, using the same hand without help from the other hand.

The action was mesmerizing, and Aimee had to drag her eyes away from the silver coin and back up to his face.

"Things will be easier between us if we *both* remember that," he continued, as Mr. Hartley came back into the room, his eyes glancing curiously between her and Mr. Stone.

"That was Wilheimer's secretary," Mr. Hartley said without preamble as he walked over to them, and Aimee took a hasty step away from Mr. Stone, realizing that it probably didn't present well to be standing so close to him. "The meeting is set for Monday."

Mr. Stone nodded and then his eyes returned to Aimee. "Good. Now I have to get back to work. Ben, please escort Miss Jenkins back to Mrs. Holbrook's. And, no," he forestalled her, holding up his hand. "You can't stay here longer. I'll relent and let you start your traineeship tomorrow instead of Monday, but that's the best you'll get from me."

"But I'm here now."

"Mrs. Holbrook isn't," he countered. "And she's the one who'll be training and supervising you."

He inclined his head before walking back to his

desk and taking a seat, busying himself with some paperwork in front of him. That was it? He'd summarily dismissed her, without another thought or even a courtesy goodbye?

She'd never been dismissed before. Normally, she was the one who left or sent others on their way. Was this what it felt like to be Evie? That because of her station in life, people could simply brush aside a person so casually. It was rude, was what it was. But, really, what else did she expect from Harrison Stone?

"Come along, Miss Jenkins." Mr. Hartley held out his hand toward the door for her to precede him. "I daresay Mrs. Holbrook might be back home after her visit with her cousin, and will be able to assist you with settling in."

Aimee began to follow him from the room.

"Oh, and Miss Jenkins?"

Mr. Stone's deep rumble stopped her in her tracks and she glanced over her shoulder at him, only to find him staring at her with an intensity she felt down to her bones.

"No detours this time, or I will ship you back to New York."

CHAPTER SEVEN

Aimee spent the better part of the ten-minute carriage ride over to Mrs. Holbrook's fuming over Mr. Stone's promise. If the man thought he could boss her around outside of her work hours, he had another thing coming and would soon learn he had no control over her actions, even if he was her boss.

Albeit her temporary boss, thankfully, and just because he thought she was Thomas's niece didn't give him the right to tell her what she could or couldn't do, even if it was in a misguided attempt to protect her.

Aimee didn't need any man to protect her, and most especially not Mr. Stone.

Mr. Hartley had seemed to sense her annoyance and had said little on the trip over to Mrs. Holbrook's, instead glancing out the window and making a few brief comments here and there, pointing out various landmarks within the neighborhood that he said she might find interesting.

What she'd find more interesting, and would help her stop thinking about Harrison and how infuriating he was, was finding out what was happening behind the scenes with the Wilheimer deal. From what she'd read of her father's notes about it, amalgamating Wilheimer's company into their own would increase their trade routes across Europe and England, making the Thornton-Jones shipping arm of the company one of the largest distribution companies in the world, which meant there was a lot riding on the deal.

"Mr. Hartley?" she asked, glancing to the man.

"Oh, please, you must call me Ben. Mr. Hartley is far too formal, given we shall be working together and everyone else calls me Ben, too," he replied with a friendly smile.

"Then you must call me Ai—Evie."

"Ai—Evie?" he asked, confused.

"Um, sometimes my cousin and I swap names for a bit of fun, you see, so it's become somewhat of a habit of mine," she replied, quietly sighing in relief when he nodded, seeming to accept her explanation. "So then, Ben, what's going on with the Wilheimer deal?"

"How do you know about that?" Ben tugged nervously on his tie.

"You mentioned it in Mr. Stone's office before we left."

"Oh, yes, I suppose I did."

"And Fred mentioned there was trouble with it."

Ben blinked several times, seemingly at a loss of what to say in response. "I'm not sure if Harrison would appreciate me discussing the matter...perhaps you can ask him about it tomorrow?"

"If I must." She'd do just that, though she didn't hold out hope he would answer her. The man seemed ridiculously stubborn about certain things, and she imagined the Wilheimer deal would be at the top of his list on what not to discuss with her, as much as she could probably help him with it.

After all, she not only spoke fluent German, but

her grandmother was German and had taught her a great deal about the Germanic people and their culture. And they preferred doing business with their own countrymen. "So how long have you been his right-hand man?"

"Nearly five years now." He rubbed his chin.

"Since Mr. Stone was sent over by my uncle to start up the London arm of the company?"

"Yes." Ben nodded. "He was interviewing me for a position along with three other men, and when I disagreed with them all about the future direction of the company, Harrison appreciated my honesty."

"He didn't seem to appreciate it when I disagreed with him today."

Ben smiled. "Oh, I don't know about that. Harrison appreciates honesty above everything. He can't stand liars. Speaking up for what you believe in and telling him the truth will always serve you well with him."

"That's, um, good to hear." Aimee's throat suddenly felt constricted. She wasn't really lying to him or any of them by pretending to be Evie...well, perhaps it was lying, but it was unavoidable and a small bit of deception given she wouldn't be allowed to do what she was if she told everyone her true identity. She hadn't lied about anything else.

"Here we are," Ben announced as the carriage came to a stop in front of a two-story brownstone.

Taking in a deep breath, Aimee followed him out of the carriage and up the entrance stairs. The whole townhouse would fit in the foyer of her parents' mansion on Fifth Avenue. Though it was small, the building was well maintained and quaint, with white curtains and flowers in vases adorning the inside window sills on the lower level of the residence.

She turned back to Ben. "How does such a small residence accommodate Mrs. Holbrook and all her staff?"

Ben glanced at her with bafflement in his eyes. "She has a housekeeper and a maid."

"Two staff?" How did anyone make do with such a small number? Surely, a two-level residence, even one as small as Mrs. Holbrook's, would be staffed by a minimum of eight servants. How did only two people do the work of so many? Her parents employed over fifty servants at their residence on Fifth Avenue alone, not to mention their Hampton estate and their villas in France and Italy. "But who does the cooking, or answers the door? Does Mrs. Holbrook even have a lady's maid?"

"I don't attend any balls to have need of a lady's maid," an imperious female voice enunciated from the direction of the door. The woman's voice was crisp and she spoke with the most perfect and precise Queen's English Aimee had heard on her trip thus far.

Aimee turned to the doorway and saw an older lady, probably in her sixties, staring at her with hazel eyes that seemed to miss nothing. The lady had not a single speck of hair out of place, with the black and gray strands pulled tightly back into an efficient bun at the nape of her neck. Her back was ramrod straight, much like a military general's, and her black jacket and skirt were perfectly fitted in a style of efficient modesty. There was a manner about her that reminded Aimee of her old headmistress at the finishing school in Switzerland her parents had sent her to for the summer when she was fifteen.

"Ah, Mrs. Holbrook, how fortunate you're home and able to greet Miss Jenkins!" Ben clapped his hands together.

"Quite so," Mrs. Holbrook replied, with absolutely no expression crossing over her matronly features.

Aimee couldn't tell if the lady was happy or upset with her arrival, her expression the epitome of a polite Englishwoman who was not prone to display anything so crass as feelings upon her face. "It's nice to meet you, Mrs. Holbrook."

The woman raised a brow. "Is it? You've only just met me, Miss Jenkins, and I've yet to lay the ground rules for the house, so perhaps you should reserve judgment until I do."

Lovely. It was going to be her finishing school all over again...a headmistress who was as strict as she was demanding. That, combined with having to deal with Mr. Stone, too, suddenly made Aimee think twice about what she'd taken on. Evie thought she'd been doing Aimee the favor, but after today, Aimee suspected it was the other way around.

Mrs. Holbrook stared at her for another moment before her gaze traveled over to Ben. "Frederick tells me there was a setback with the Wilheimer deal. Does Mr. Stone need me to go to the office to assist him with anything?"

The older lady said Stone's name with such deference that it was clear she thought a great deal of him. Just like her father did, too. From what Aimee had observed he seemed competent enough, but hardly worthy of such devotion, especially given his arrogance.

"No. He has everything in hand," Ben replied to the lady. "He asked me to arrange a meeting with Wilheimer for Monday, but I'm sure he'll appraise you of all the details tomorrow morning. Oh, and he also said Miss Jenkins could start tomorrow, too."

Mrs. Holbrook nodded. "Very well. You can go back to work then, Mr. Hartley, and I shall take care of Miss Jenkins."

"Thank you, Mrs. Holbrook," Ben said, tipping his hat to both women. "I look forward to seeing you both again tomorrow. It's been a pleasure, Evie."

"Thank you, Ben," Aimee replied, watching as he stepped down onto the footpath and walked over to the carriage.

"You're welcome," he said, vaulting into the carriage. "Have a wonderful time staying with Mrs. Holbrook and the other ladies." He waved before the door closed and the carriage drove away.

"Other ladies?" Aimee asked Mrs. Holbrook, who was currently assessing her much like someone would examine an unusual specimen under a microscope.

"Yes," Mrs. Holbrook replied with a raise of her haughty brown eyebrow. "I mentor a great deal of other young ladies training to be secretaries for the

company, and those who are not from London re-
side here with me. Currently, there are three other
young women staying here," she said, preempting
Aimee's question. "You'll be the fourth and shall
be sharing a room with Miss Mitchell."

"Sharing a room?" She hadn't considered that
possibility, having never had to share a room before with anyone, but it made sense given the size
of the house, or lack thereof.

"Yes, this is not the Mayfair Grand Hotel," Mrs.
Holbrook said, appearing thoroughly unimpressed
with Aimee. "I don't have suites for everyone, now
do I? Is sharing a room going to be a problem?"

"No, not at all." After all, how hard could it be
to share some space? Especially when she planned
to be at the office far more than she planned to be
here.

"Good. Now, don't just stand there, Miss
Jenkins, come inside and I'll show you to your
room." Mrs. Holbrook stepped inside and indicated
for Aimee to follow her.

Aimee followed her over the threshold and
then up the stairs to the first floor, where Mrs.
Holbrook turned right and walked down the narrow corridor toward the back of the house. She
stopped outside of a room on her left and opened
the white door.

"This is the room you'll be sharing with Miss
Mitchell."

Aimee glanced past her into the room and had
to blink several times. The room was a small rect-
angle, with two single beds and two narrow bedside
tables between them, along with a small desk and a

tallboy that wasn't tall on the wall opposite the beds. One of the beds was pushed tightly against the wall on the right, and the other was against the wall on the left and had her trunk at its foot. It was amazing the trunk even fit into the room, given there was a narrow gap of about three feet between the beds, and about the same space between the trunks and the furniture.

There was little room for one person to move around, let alone two. Indeed, the entire room was about half the size of the closet she'd had in her cabin on the journey across. Intellectually, Aimee had always known how fortunate she was growing up with wealth and living in luxury, but until right then, she hadn't truly appreciated just how lucky she'd been.

Was this the sort of room Evie had grown up in? No wonder her cousin regularly seemed over-whelmed living with them, and Aimee could now understand the incredulousness on her cousin's face when she'd first been shown to her bedroom just down the hall from Aimee. Evie had been lost for words, literally, and then when she'd said the room was bigger than her entire apartment back in London, Aimee had thought she was exaggerating. Obviously not it would seem, if this room was any indication.

"You can unpack your clothing into the chest of drawers. I believe the bottom two are free for you to use," Mrs. Holbrook said. "Then we can store your trunk in the attic until it's time for you to leave again. Now, dinner will be served at precisely eight tonight, though I will expect you down in the sitting room around seven, so I can introduce you to the other ladies when they get back from work."

"That's a late finish."

"During the week we *all* work until around six thirty, sometimes later if there is a need. Saturdays is a half day where we finish around two. You get a lunch break of one hour each day, but aside from that you're expected to work until all of the work is done. Are those hours going to be a problem for you, Miss Jenkins?"

"No, not at all. But don't most businessmen finish work around four or five every afternoon?" Though her father usually stayed until six or seven, but most of his employees were well gone by then, and she'd assumed secretaries would be the same. Obviously not.

"Yes, *businessmen* do, Miss Jenkins, *not* secretaries." The woman pursed her lips together and stared at Aimee. "But, surely, given you've been working as a companion you should be used to long, demanding hours. Though perhaps I am not considering your time spent living on Fifth Avenue and being a companion to a family member, rather than an employer. I imagine anyone's expectations would change after residing in a mansion, and finding out their uncle is one of the richest men in the world."

"I get the impression, Mrs. Holbrook, that perhaps we started off on the wrong foot," Aimee replied.

"Not at all, Miss Jenkins."

There was little expression on the woman's face for Aimee to even tell if she was being truthful or sarcastic. It was frustrating to say the least.

"Now, I shall leave you to start unpacking."

"Wait!" Aimee lightly grabbed the woman's upper arm as she turned to leave. "There's no bathroom attached to the room?" That couldn't be right.

The woman pressed her lips together, and Aimee got the sense that she was trying not to laugh, given the hint of amusement in the older woman's eyes. "Like I said, this is not a hotel, Miss Jenkins. The bathroom we *all* use is down the hall on your right, across from the stairs. There's also a small powder room on the ground floor."

It took Aimee a few seconds to process what Mrs. Holbrook was saying. "We share the *one* bathroom? All of us?"

"Yes, we do, Miss Jenkins," Mrs. Holbrook confirmed. "In fact, we're rather fortunate to even have a bathroom, as a lot of the terrace houses along this street are yet to install plumbing to their residences."

"Oh..."

"Yes, when I was your age, it was a large white porcelain bowl in my bedroom that I had to use for my daily ablutions. Aren't the inventions of our industrial revolution simply marvelous?"

Aimee opened her mouth to reply but didn't really know what to say. A bathroom to share amongst several ladies? Good Lord. She couldn't fathom it. "What about a bath? Do you have hot water plumbing installed for that?"

Mrs. Holbrook nodded. "Yes, of course we do."

"Oh, thank goodness."

"We pour one bath a week, on a Sunday," Mrs. Holbrook seemed to take great delight in telling her. "I, of course, have the first bath, followed in order by who has been here the longest. Generally, though, most don't have a bath as the water is usually cold by the time it gets to their turn. Instead, they use a washcloth twice a day."

Aimee cleared her throat. "You all share the same bathwater?" Oh good Lord. She was used to having a bath every night, and she never had to share it, let alone use the same water as anyone else. The very idea of doing so made her feel ill. When Evie had said Aimee wouldn't do well without the luxuries she was used to, Aimee had thought she'd meant she wouldn't do well without her normal dresses and jewelry, along with shopping and gourmet meals. She hadn't realized Evie had meant the basic essentials like having a private and clean bath.

What on earth would she do? She couldn't not have a bath, but then the idea of sharing dirty bathwater made her feel filthy.

"You really have gotten accustomed to living in luxury, haven't you?" Mrs. Holbrook remarked with interest, obviously seeing the expression of horror on Aimee's face that she didn't have the strength to hide. "But don't worry, I'm sure you'll quickly settle back into living in less opulent accommodations, as I believe you were once previously used to. Like I said, this isn't—"

"A hotel," Aimee finished for her. "Yes, Mrs. Holbrook, I've gathered that." Though it did give her an idea. Perhaps she could rent a room at her father's hotel, the Mayfair Grand? She had the inheritance her grandmother had left her, which was separate from her million-dollar inheritance from her parents, which meant she could take what she wanted from that account without anyone knowing.

She wouldn't sleep at the hotel of course, as much as she might wish to, because doing so would undoubtedly be noticed. But she could surely manage to sneak away there a few times a week to have a bath in the room, given it was only a short walk from the office and she'd have an hour for lunch each day.

Hmm, it was a definite possibility, and one she'd have to look into. Because as much as she wanted to experience life from a different perspective, sharing other people's dirty bathwater wasn't a line she was willing to cross.

"Good. Then I shall leave you to your unpacking. And remember, do not be late for dinner." Mrs. Holbrook inclined her head at Aimee before she backed out of the room, shutting the door firmly in Aimee's face.

What had she gotten herself into?

CHAPTER EIGHT

The sounds of the waltz drifting up to the balcony from the orchestra playing down in the ballroom below were enough to give Harrison a headache. Why he'd come to Lord Anderson's ball when he should be back in his office trying to finish off the damn paperwork he'd been trying to get done all bloody afternoon, he really didn't know.

Though it might have had something to do with how every time he tried to do his paperwork, all he ended up doing was thinking about that darn woman and how even when she was chastising him, constant thoughts of kissing her had intruded.

How could he want to kiss such a harpy?

Thankfully, he'd kept things professional, and kept his hands to himself. Now, all he had to do was stop thinking about the blasted lady…something far easier said than done.

How could his thoughts be so consumed by a woman he'd only just met? A woman that was off-limits but that tempted him like no other? How could a woman he found so utterly annoying and bossy entice him without even trying, to the point of distracting him from his work? And his work was his everything.

Ben often joked Harrison was married to his job, but it was true. Work had been his absolute salvation during a time when he'd been completely alone and lost as a young boy. It had given him a sense of purpose and drive, providing him with more happiness and contentment than another person ever had, so he'd dedicated his life to succeeding at it. And he wasn't going to let anyone, not even a woman as damned attractive as Yvette Jenkins was, distract him from his ultimate goal in life.

"A penny for your thoughts?" a soft and sultry voice whispered from behind him.

Harrison felt like sighing, but he straightened from where he'd been leaning against one of the balcony pillars and turned around to face the woman.

"Lady Whitley," he said with an incline of his head, watching the blonde beauty flinch slightly at the use of her title coming from his lips. He didn't want to hurt her, but the sooner the young widow realized he was serious about not continuing their relationship, the better.

She wanted to marry again and have children while she was young enough to, and Harrison couldn't blame her for that, but it wasn't part of his plans. At least not yet anyhow, and not with her, even though she'd make him a perfect countess, given she never argued nor spoke out of turn. Unlike Miss Jenkins, which was all she seemed to do. Why he was thinking of Miss Jenkins again was a bloody mystery. He had to get the woman out of his head.

"My dear Harrison, just because we're no longer intimate with each other doesn't mean you have to be so formal. You can still call me Jane. We have, after all, shared some lovely times together, haven't we?"

"We have, Jane," he relented, seeing the hurt in her hazel eyes. "However, you know I'm not in a position to offer you what you want or deserve, and it's not fair to you to pretend otherwise."

"I understand that and I appreciate you being so honest," she said with a sad smile. "Though I do miss your company. Perhaps we can stay friends? I've been helpful in introducing you to my circle of acquaintances for your business, which I know means everything to you, and I do so enjoy spending time with you."

The elegant widow had been a perfect companion to take to the opera and balls; she was beautiful, poised, and knew everyone, which was helpful, but their conversations had always been so polite and calm. Then when she'd started to hint at marriage, Harrison had known it was time to end things with the lady before she became too attached. "Friends only? Nothing more?"

She smiled. "I know your work is your true love, and I have no intention of resuming where we left off. I promise it will be friends and nothing more. What do you say?"

It couldn't hurt, and she did know everyone and everything. "Friends it is then."

"Excellent." Her smile spread right across her face and she clapped her hands together. "Now, as a friend, I'm in need of dance; will you assist me?"

Harrison reluctantly smiled. Jane was always charming and personable, and most men found her difficult to resist. "Very well."

"Wonderful." She grinned and threaded her arm

through his as they commenced walking along the landing toward the stairs leading down to the ballroom below. "Now, as my friend, I also find myself in need of your expert business advice. My accountant says I have about twenty thousand pounds I should be investing, rather than have languishing in the bank. Can I take you for a quick lunch on Monday and pick your brain about some shares I'm considering purchasing?"

"Men rarely say no to you, do they?"

"You're the first to, Harrison Stone," she replied. "And I hope you'll be the last, so please don't say no to me again, because I really do need to pick your business brain, and I promise you that's all it is."

"Very well," Harrison grumbled with a small smile. He did have a soft spot for her. She was a resilient lady who'd had to endure a great deal of gossip five years ago, after being widowed only a month after marrying a man who'd been sixty years older than she was, and who unfortunately decided to meet his maker in the middle of trying to get his new countess pregnant. The details of which should have been private but had been bandied about by all of Society not even twenty-four hours after the man's demise. "Though it will have to be a quick and early lunch as I have a meeting Monday afternoon."

"I'll make certain it is," she said, squeezing his forearm lightly with her gloved hand as he led her to the bottom of the stairs and began walking along the hallway to the ballroom.

"I need to talk to you!" a loud voice boomed

from the dark corridor ahead.

Harrison watched as his uncle stepped out from the shadows of the hallway, almost like he'd been waiting there for him. Which he probably had.

"It will have to wait," Harrison said. "I've promised Lady Whitley a dance."

"It can't bloody wait!" His uncle grabbed Harrison by the lapels of his jacket and shook them, an almost wild desperation in his actions, especially considering he was a foot shorter than Harrison and weighed a good thirty pounds less.

"Remove your hands from me, *Uncle Reginald*." Harrison spat out the last word like it was a curse, knowing the man hated any reminder of them being related. "Unless you want me to break them while I remove them for you?"

His uncle seemed to realize the perilous position he'd put himself in, abruptly letting go of the material and taking a hasty step out of arm's reach from Harrison.

"This is urgent. You know I wouldn't have accosted you otherwise," his uncle replied, looking far more desperate than Harrison had ever seen him before. "We must talk now, in private." The man's eyes darted over to Jane.

"I think that's my cue to leave," Jane said, extracting her hand from the crook of Harrison's elbow.

"No, stay," Harrison said. His uncle might think he could order anyone about, being the Earl of Carlisle, but Harrison was having none of it.

"It's fine," Jane said. "The earl already seems greatly agitated and I would hate to add to that.

Good evening, gentlemen. I shall see you for lunch on Monday if I don't see you later tonight." She smiled at him before deftly walking around the earl and down the hallway, the sound of her footsteps gradually receding as she left them alone.

"You've got two minutes." Harrison pulled out his pocket watch and made note of the time on the dial. His uncle had had little time for him over the years, so Harrison was happy to return the favor in full. "So talk fast."

"You must marry an heiress!"

Of all things Harrison had expected the man to say, that hadn't even been on the list. "What the devil have you done now?"

His uncle tugged his collar and licked his lips. "Nothing a quick marriage to an heiress won't fix. In fact, another Dollar Princess has arrived in London today and she's worth one million pounds. You must court her and convince her to marry you, which should be easy given your boss is her father."

The last discussion they'd had relating to Harrison's future and marriage was nearly five years ago, just shortly after he arrived in London, when his uncle had summoned him to his residence and demanded Harrison marry one of the man's daughters, who were also Harrison's first cousins. Apparently, his uncle had rationalized in his head that that would be the only suitable arrangement to make amends for the erroneous situation of the man having no son, and Harrison being his un-wanted heir.

In his uncle's opinion, given Harrison's mother had been a base-born housemaid and should never have married into the family in the first place, the least Harrison could do to right that supposed wrong was ensure his cousins were provided for and that the earldom stayed within his uncle's line of the family as it was meant to have done.

Harrison had declined, infuriating his uncle to the point where his uncle had cut him directly, never acknowledging him at any social functions. Which hadn't bothered Harrison in the slightest as he didn't give a damn about the man or Society. But then about two years ago his uncle had approached him, begging for a loan, saying that the cost of giving his five daughters season after season without having married them off to anyone was bankrupting the estate.

Harrison had laughed, truly enjoying the irony that the lofty Earl of Carlisle was begging him, the mere son of a maid, to save the great Carlisle Estate, with the fortune Harrison had made in trade. It had been quite ironic and Harrison had sent his uncle packing, more than content for the entire estate to burn to the ground for all he cared, given they'd banished his parents and then refused to have anything to do with Harrison, even after his parents' deaths when they were informed he was all alone with not a penny to his name. They'd chosen to let an eight-year-old boy fend for himself in New York City, rather than debase themselves by accepting him.

However, Harrison had changed his mind about saving the estate after his cousin, Amelia, the Earl's eldest daughter, visited him the next day at his office, without the earl's knowledge. He'd been about to have her thrown out when she'd calmly started reciting from memory dozens and dozens of names of all their servants and what position they filled in the earl's household and how long they'd worked for the family. By simply reciting their names, she'd let him know of all the innocent employees he'd be destroying the livelihoods of if he did nothing to help his uncle as he'd originally intended.

So he'd found himself reluctantly agreeing to loan his uncle the money to ensure the estate wouldn't go bankrupt, as much as it had annoyed the hell out of him doing so. But his cousin had been on the money—Harrison wouldn't let hundreds of servants lose their positions and home, simply because of an egotistical earl who didn't have a head for money or business. His respect for his cousin grew that day, and he didn't mind having the occasional chat with her at the various Society events. She was bookish and had no interest in marrying, so they shared that in common and got on well together.

Unlike Harrison and the man currently standing before him, wringing his hands together, agitation rife in his gaze. "Tell me what you've done." Harrison annunciated each word slowly. "And I won't ask again."

His uncle began nodding, almost like he was a puppet. "Yes, well, um, you see I was trying to make some money, to um, repay the loan from you, of course, and well, um, this phenomenal investment opportunity presented itself to me, and it promised returns of up to fifty percent. It was an opportunity of a lifetime."

"No legitimate investment can offer a return that good."

"I realize that now…" His uncle's voice trailed off. "But, at the time, well, it seemed so promising, and a gentleman I trusted was investing and doing me a favor to let me invest in the scheme, too…so I did."

"How much did you lose?" Harrison said, his top teeth grinding against his bottom.

His uncle gulped heavily. "Everything. Well, everything that isn't entailed…but yes, everything else, or at least I will lose everything if I can't repay the bank by the end of the month. They at least gave me until then to try to rectify the situation."

"How many pounds?"

The man bit his bottom lip. "About two hundred thousand…give or take a little."

"Fuck." He'd known his uncle was a fool, but after nearly losing everything before with his blatant spending, Harrison had assumed the man had learned his lesson, especially having had to come and grovel to Harrison to bail him out.

But clearly no lesson had been learned in the slightest, and now Harrison would have to deal with this even bigger mess his uncle had created. Yes, *fuck* was really the only way to describe the whole damn mess of a situation.

CHAPTER NINE

The reverberation of loud banging gradually penetrated through Aimee's sleep-riddled brain. Along with a female, very English voice echoing in her head.

"Wake up, Evie," the voice kept repeating.

"Go away, Evie," Aimee mumbled into her pillow, wanting to go back to the dream of a golden-haired angel with jade-green eyes, murmuring sweet nothings in her ear as his lips trailed kisses everywhere on her feverish skin.

"Evie! Mrs. Holbrook will get cranky with you if you're late for your first day, not to mention it won't impress Mr. Stone."

Hearing the man's name was akin to having a bucket of ice water thrown on her head. She bolted upright in bed and blinked as the early morning sunlight began to creep in through the now-open curtains. She didn't recognize anything as she gazed around the tiny room and felt completely disoriented. "Where am I?"

"Mrs. Holbrook's, remember?" It was her new roommate, Molly Mitchell, who answered. "Soon to be your ex-house if you don't get up and get ready in the next fifteen minutes."

"What time is it?" she groaned and collapsed down onto the bed. "The sun barely looks up."

"It's a quarter past-six." Molly shook her shoulder. "And you need to get up because we leave at six thirty on the dot."

The gravity of the situation penetrated her sleep-addled brain and she was awake in an instant. "Oh no. How will I get ready in fifteen minutes?" She felt the first vestiges of panic claw up her throat, but she tamped down on the feeling.

Swinging her legs to the side, Aimee jumped out of bed and hurried over to the tallboy. "How do you all wake up so early without a maid to wake you or help you dress?" She quickly rummaged through some of the outfits inside and settled on a jade-green skirt and matching jacket, the color of which instantly brought images of Harrison Stone to mind. She couldn't escape the man from haunting her dreams and now it seemed he was haunting her waking hours, too. Darn man.

"You just get used to it, I suppose." Molly shrugged as she placed her black boots on and began to lace them up. "And Mrs. Holbrook bangs on the door, just like she was doing a moment ago in case one of us has slept in."

Aimee shrugged out of her nightgown and hastily began to dress. Now she knew why Evie favored such simple outfits; they didn't require the help of a lady's maid, and, oddly, shrugging on her jacket over her blouse and doing up the buttons at the front without needing assistance felt strangely liberating.

"You know, you have quite an American twang this morning," Molly said, doing up her last lace.

"I do?" Aimee cleared her throat, focusing on remembering to use her English accent. "I suppose that's because I've spent the last six years surrounded by American twangs."

"I suppose so." Molly stood up and tidied some loose hair strands using the small looking glass on the desk. "What's it like living with the Thornton-Joneses in their Fifth Avenue mansion? It must be so different from what you were used to growing up."

"Overwhelming, initially," Aimee replied, remembering how Evie had described it.

"I imagine it would be. To go from struggling to living a life of luxury, and all because your uncle found out you were his lost niece. What an incredible story."

Aimee didn't reply and pulled on some stockings, then started to lace up her boots.

"If only we were all so lucky." Molly smiled. "Well, I'm ready. I'll leave you to finish up and meet you downstairs. Don't be late, though, as Mrs. Holbrook won't be impressed."

"She doesn't strike me as the sort of lady easily impressed by anything."

Molly laughed. "She does expect a lot, but she gives a lot back, too, helping us girls try to better ourselves with a profession."

"How long have you been training with her as a secretary?"

"Over two years. I work as an undersecretary along with Deidre, assisting her with Mr. Stone."

"Deidre didn't seem happy to meet me." Aimee had tried to make some conversation with the woman last night at dinner, but Deidre Cantor hadn't wanted a bar of it.

"Oh, Deidre doesn't like anyone prettier than

her," Molly replied. "Or anyone smarter. So she doesn't like me, either, for the second part, not the first. In any event, she's far too distracted wanting to run off with one of the accountants she's having an affair with to pay either of us much mind."

"An affair? Wouldn't such a thing ruin her?"

Molly grinned, a glint of humor in her gaze. "You've been spending too much time with those in a loftier social class than us, haven't you?"

"What do you mean?"

"It's common practice that as long as a young couple is discreet about a love affair, making sure there's no pregnancies outside of marriage, everyone looks the other way."

Aimee felt her mouth drop open. "They copulate outside of marriage?"

"That's a fancy way of putting it, but yes."

"How interesting…" In Aimee's social sphere, simply being caught kissing a man would be cause for a hasty engagement. She was beginning to realize how very different things were in her cousin's old world to her own.

"It's just how it is," Molly replied. "Most end up getting married, though some don't, and as long as they don't get pregnant it's considered acceptable. I wish my mother had remembered that rule before having me."

"She didn't get married?"

Molly shook her head. "No, and by the time she found out she was pregnant, my father had already fallen in love with another woman. So I grew up with that stigma, much the same as you."

"Yes, I suppose so." Evie's parents hadn't

married, which still colored most people's perceptions about her. Ridiculously so.

"In any event," Molly continued, "I'm making my own way in the world, without a dollar spoon in my mouth, just like you will be, too, after completing your traineeship. Though I'll be avoiding men, unlike Deidre. I suggest you do the same."

"Yes, I most definitely will. To be honest, it's not done in the circles I frequent in America."

"Interesting," Molly said, grabbing her coat from the back hook on the door. "Anyhow, I hope Deidre runs off and marries her beau, because then I won't have to put up with her snide and catty remarks every day."

"Why wouldn't she work if she got married?"

"That part of Society is the same regardless of social class. Once a woman is married, she's expected to run the household and have children, so there'd be no time to work as a secretary."

"It doesn't seem right that a man can marry and give up nothing, while a woman has to give up nearly everything."

"It's just how it is." Molly shrugged before pulling open the bedroom door. "Now, do hurry up. You've got five minutes before we leave, and Mrs. Holbrook will leave you here if you're not on time."

Exactly what Aimee didn't want to happen on her first day. "I will, and thank you for waking me."

"We're alike, you and me. So we have to stick together." Molly smiled before leaving Aimee alone in the small room.

Five minutes later, Aimee found herself

downstairs and swiftly bundled inside the company carriage with Molly and Deidre, along with the other secretary, Claire, who worked in accounts, and Mrs. Holbrook, too.

"Now, Miss Jenkins," Mrs. Holbrook said as the carriage began its journey to the office. "You will be shadowing myself today and I expect you to listen, learn, and do what's asked of you without fuss. Is that clear?"

"Yes, Mrs. Holbrook." The woman really was like her old headmistress. Still, Aimee was determined to get back onto the right foot with the woman, which might prove challenging, given she didn't know what she'd done to annoy the lady. Perhaps she'd accidentally offended her with the comment about her servants?

Her agreement seemed to satisfy Mrs. Holbrook, who turned to her right and began speaking with Deidre, leaving Aimee to return her attention to the window, as the carriage turned down Fenchurch Street, meaning they were nearly at the office.

And it wouldn't be long before she'd see Harrison Stone again. Why that thought made her both nervous and thrilled she wasn't sure. She hated the man, even if her skin felt flushed just thinking of him. Which was what she had to stop doing; thinking about him was a distraction she didn't need.

The carriage came to a halt and a minute later she stepped out of the vehicle and looked up at the facade of the building, her gaze glancing to the upper levels. She gasped when she saw Harrison staring down at her from his office window, and even from this distance he seemed annoyed, which seemed to be the expression he usually wore, at least when looking at her.

"Is everything all right?" Mrs. Holbrook asked, missing nothing.

Aimee swung her gaze back to the woman. "It's fine," she assured her, unable to stop her eyes from flicking briefly back up to where she'd seen him, but there was now an empty window in his place. Had she imagined him there? Given her dreams had been filled with the man, it wouldn't surprise her if she had.

"I think it prudent to warn you Mr. Stone does not appreciate any of the secretaries forming any sort of romantic attachment toward him."

"Excuse me?" Mortification flooded her. Could Mrs. Holbrook tell she'd dreamt of kissing him? That she couldn't stop thinking about him? "That would be the last thing I'd ever do with someone like him." And it was true. She might be thinking about his lips, but the very idea of them being involved in something *romantic* was ludicrous given they couldn't stand each other.

Mrs. Holbrook didn't look convinced. "You wouldn't be the first young lady to start here and be bowled over by the man's good looks."

"I'm not bowled over by anything about him, except perhaps how rude he is." Aimee followed the ladies as they walked up the steps and through the entrance, before climbing the marble stairs. "How long have you been working for Mr. Stone?"

"Close to five years. I was the first person he

hired when he came to London to start the company here. Your Uncle Thomas recommended me, while also praising Mr. Stone as being an excellent boss. As always, your uncle was correct."

Aimee still had her reservations about that. "You're loyal to Mr. Stone."

"I am," Mrs. Holbrook agreed with a shrug, marching up the stairs to the top floor. "He's a man who expects a great deal of others but expects more from himself. That sort of work ethic inspires loyalty and hard work from all around him, which he recognizes and rewards. It's a trait your uncle shares."

"Yes, I suppose my f—uncle"—darn, she'd nearly slipped up again—"does that, too." If only he could recognize that his own daughter would be an asset, instead of relegating her to the ballroom. "How do you know my uncle?"

"I've worked as a temporary secretary for him many times over the years when he had business here in England. I also worked for your father when he was alive. Thankfully, though, your Uncle Thomas is far more responsible than your father ever was."

"You worked for my…father?" Uncle Peter, Evie's father, had been the black sheep of the family after he refused to marry an heiress that would have amalgamated their families' fortunes and companies. Not speaking to him after doing so was her father's biggest regret.

"Briefly," Mrs. Holbrook confirmed. "He was a charming man, who didn't have the same drive when it came to business as your Uncle Thomas, and though he'd been tasked with starting the London arm of the company, his personal life got in the way."

"He ran off with my mother, don't you mean?" Or rather, Evie's mother as the case was.

"Indeed," Mrs. Holbrook replied, looking unimpressed. "In any event, Mr. Stone has proven a far better replacement, even though it was some fifteen years after the fact. Under his leadership the London arm has far surpassed expectations. Mr. Stone truly is brilliant."

"Yes, you're not the only one who likes to praise him." Her father did so, constantly.

"Mr. Stone is fair, honest, and will listen to suggestions," Mrs. Holbrook replied. "He's also a tactical genius in negotiations and a decent boss everyone respects."

Where was this version of Harrison Stone that everyone except her had seemed to have met so far? With her the man was a brute…well, that wasn't being entirely fair to him, but he did vex her beyond belief.

A few minutes later, they entered the outer room of Mr. Stone's office, and Molly and Deidre went straight to their desks while Aimee followed Mrs. Holbrook over to her desk. As she walked across the room she glanced to the door of Harrison's office and was grateful that though the door was open, it didn't have a direct line of sight into the outer office area, and she couldn't see him at all.

"Miss Mitchell and Miss Cantor both assist me to ensure the smooth and efficient running of Mr.

Stone's office," Mrs. Holbrook said. "And that, Miss Jenkins, will be your job, too, while you're here."

"How...*wonderful.*" Aimee really tried to sound enthusiastic about it but evidently wasn't all that successful given Mrs. Holbrook's narrowed eyes.

"Once you've settled, I'll introduce you to him."

"We met yesterday."

"Let me rephrase," the lady replied. "I will *officially* introduce you to him after you are settled in. Now, this will be your desk." Mrs. Holbrook waved over toward the small desk adjacent to her own. "For today, I want you to observe, take notes, and ask any questions you need. On Monday, you'll do some actual work and implement what you've learned today. Is that understood?"

"Yes, and I'm looking forward to it." She had no trouble this time with being entirely genuine in her enthusiasm.

She was here and making her dream a reality. She'd prove to her father she had a mind for business and wouldn't let anyone stand in her way, not even a man whose lips had captivated her dreams.

CHAPTER TEN

After having been *officially* introduced to Harrison Stone, which Aimee had found extremely awkward, Mrs. Holbrook had decided to give her a tour of the building and introduce her to the other employees there.

Whether that was because the lady had sensed the tension between Aimee and Harrison, or it was what she'd already had planned, Aimee had no idea, but she was grateful for the respite nonetheless. And after the tour, Aimee had been sent down to the Accounts section to learn all she could from the Accounts manager. To most, that would be utterly boring, but to Aimee it was anything but.

In fact, if running her father's business wasn't her goal in life, she'd have wanted to be an accountant. The language and the logic of numbers was thrilling, and after having spent the past two hours in Robert Stanton's company discussing the actual financials for the company, Aimee was more fascinated than ever.

The man was a genius with numbers. So passionate and diligent in their application relating to reaping the largest benefits he could for the company that she couldn't help but be impressed.

"I hope I haven't been boring you overly, Miss Jenkins," Robert said, his brown eyes crinkling in concern. "I do tend to go on and on about numbers, and most ladies I talk to about the subject tend to get bored. Not that you look bored," he was quick to assure her. "I just know from past experience that it is not a topic that interests most."

"You're not boring me at all." She smiled at him. "I feel quite happy to admit to you that numbers are a hobby of mine. In fact, I adore them."

"You do?" A look of excitement lit up his earnest face, and, in that moment, he looked like a young boy even though he had to be in his midthirties. "How extraordinary. I've not really met a lady before who enjoys discussing numbers, let alone leafing through dusty old books filled with them." His eyes glanced down at the ledgers Aimee was flicking through, which listed in meticulous detail all of the London company's transactions for the last few months.

"What can I say?" Aimee shrugged. "I'm a rather unusual lady. Honestly, if I could trade in never having to attend another ball to read ledgers instead, I'd do so in a heartbeat."

Robert grinned from ear to ear. "A woman after my own heart."

"Excuse me, Mr. Stanton?" Robert's secretary interrupted them. "There's a phone call for you in your office."

"Thank you, Emma," he replied, then turned back to Aimee. "I'd best take that."

"Am I all right to keep looking through these?" She glanced down to the ledgers still open on the desk in front of her. She'd noticed a few odd entries in the most recent pages over the last month and wanted to study them a bit more.

"Of course." Robert nodded. "Perhaps I can

take you to lunch tomorrow to discuss them?" There was an interest in his eyes that Aimee had seen on men's faces before, but one she didn't want to encourage given she wasn't drawn to him. *Unlike someone else in the office*, a little voice in her head whispered. She really had to work on silencing that voice.

"Perhaps," Aimee allowed, smiling at him as he bowed before returning to his office.

Why couldn't she find herself interested in Robert Stanton? He was sweet and intelligent, and clearly seemed to like her for her, given he had no idea she was actually an heiress. But, instead, her thoughts were preoccupied by a certain six-foot-three, dark blond Adonis, who annoyed her more than any other man she'd met.

"Did you have to lead the poor man on?" a deep voice rumbled from behind her.

Speak of the Devil.

She swiveled around in her chair to face Harrison, her whole body bracing as a fission of energy raced down her spine as she locked eyes with his.

He straightened from where he'd been leaning on the doorframe, wandered over to her desk, and perched on the edge of it. His large frame filled the space so much that Aimee had to push back her chair to give herself some room to breathe.

"I don't know what you're talking about," she replied, narrowing her eyes at him.

"Please, you had him wrapped around your pinkie. But he's a good man who's far more comfortable with numbers than people. So don't lead him on, all right?"

"I wasn't doing anything of the sort," she replied in a harsh whisper, glancing around, only to see the others in the office barely paying them any mind. Thankfully, it seemed the men here in accounting were far more interested in their work than in gossip. "What are you doing here anyhow? Did you come down just to annoy me?"

And it was working, too. She was greatly annoyed at how attractive she found him. How was that possible when she hated him so?

"Don't flatter yourself," he answered gruffly. "Besides, you've been down here for over three hours now."

"Paying attention to how long I'm gone, are you?"

"I pay attention to everything that happens here," he answered. "And it's nearly home time, so you should go back upstairs to finish off for the day."

She glanced at the wall clock and was surprised to see it was nearly two o'clock. "Oh, so it is. Goodness, the day went quickly." She'd make use of the early Saturday finish to send a telegram to her accountant to get some funds wired to her, and then she'd rent a room at the Mayfair Grand and have a bath. It would be nice to have a Saturday free from having to attend a ball.

"And how has your first day gone, Miss Jenkins?"

Oddly, he seemed genuine in wanting to know. "It was a good first day," she answered truthfully and as her eyes locked with his, she couldn't help but notice his strong jaw and lips. Lips that annoyed her and enticed her. "Now, as you mentioned, I better go upstairs and finish up for the day given I have some errands to run this afternoon."

"You're not planning on traipsing about on your own, are you?" He frowned and crossed his arms over his chest.

That was exactly what she was going to do while she was here, having never had the freedom of not having a chaperone with her in New York. "I am. What of it?"

"I've promised your uncle I'll make certain you're safe. Allowing you to traipse about London on your own is not honoring that promise."

"You don't have any say about what I do outside the office," Aimee replied, infuriated that the man had taken on a self-imposed protector role. "I'm more than capable of looking after myself, and I'll be perfectly safe."

"You're the niece of one of the richest men in the world; someone could try to kidnap you and hold you for ransom."

"That's a bit dramatic, isn't it?"

"It's a possibility."

"A highly unlikely one." She'd never had an issue with being possibly kidnapped as herself, so the chance of that happening while masquerading as Evie was even more remote. "Besides, no one knows who I am, so I'll be safe."

He blew out a breath. "I suppose you're right, but do be careful."

"I have my derringer, so I'll be fine," she

reminded him for what felt like the tenth time. "In any event, you never answered my question about why you're down here in the first place."

"I had to come and see Robert about a meeting I have on Monday."

"Ah, the meeting with Wilheimer."

His whole body went rigid for a moment. "How do you know about that?"

"Aside from you and Ben mentioning it yesterday?" She pursed her lips. "I've been privy to conversations my uncle and aunt have had on the matter." If eavesdropping on her parents was what one considered being privy to. "I've also read some of the correspondence you've sent to my uncle about it." And by some she meant everything, though she didn't think he'd appreciate knowing that, either.

"Thomas has let you read my correspondence about it?" There was a sense of incomprehension in his expression.

She nodded. "How else would I read them?" It wasn't exactly a lie. Her father did leave his study unlocked, so it could be inferred he was giving her permission to sneak down and read them. "Plus, it's all anyone has been able to talk about most of today."

"Oh."

"Yes, *oh*."

"Do you always have to be so contrary?"

"I was agreeing with you, which is contrary to being contrary," she replied with a straight face. "Isn't it?"

"I suppose it is."

She grinned up at him. "Are we agreeing about something, Harrison Stone? We should mark this day in our calendars, for I doubt it will happen again."

"Perhaps we should, Yvette Jenkins," he agreed, again.

They stood there staring at each other for a moment, and Aimee found her body begin to ache with need, almost begging for his touch. Dragging her gaze away from his she glanced pointedly over to Robert's door. "Well, then, don't let me keep you." The quicker she could get Harrison to depart, the quicker she could recommence breathing properly.

Without warning her stomach growled, a loud yawning gurgle that startled them both and broke the tense atmosphere, making them grin.

"Have you even had lunch yet?"

Aimee shook her head. "No, I've forgotten to. Time tends to slip away from me when I immerse myself with numbers and ledgers, which are far more fascinating to me than food."

He peered at her oddly for a moment. "That happens to me, too."

"You also forgot to eat lunch today?"

"I did." He nodded. "I was caught up in reading my notes and figures for the Wilheimer deal and lost track of the time."

"Good gracious, Harrison Stone, first we agree and now we also have something in common? Whatever is happening? Perhaps we aren't destined to be enemies after all." She wasn't sure how she felt about it. For so long she'd built up this persona of him in her mind and hadn't liked him at all. In person, though, it was a whole other story.

"I've never thought of you as my enemy, Yvette Jenkins."

That's because he'd never had to compete for her father's praise like she had. Though that wasn't entirely fair. Her father often praised her, just never relating to business deals like she wished. "Your behavior suggests differently."

"You think I'm your enemy because I came to your rescue the other day? Or was it because I criticized you for going into the alley in the first place?"

"No—" But then she stopped short. She couldn't very well tell him the truth that she hated him because her father treated him like the son he'd never had. The son she could never be. "Well, perhaps. What gives you the right to berate me regardless of the circumstances? Especially when you didn't even know who I was then." Not that he knew who she really was now, either.

He gave a half shrug and pulled out a coin from his pocket. "Do you blame me for disagreeing with your questionable decision?" He began to roll the coin between his knuckles, using only the fingers of his same hand to do so. It was just as mesmerizing today as it had been yesterday.

"I would do it again in a heartbeat." And she would. "Though I'd confront the man with my pistol."

"Let's hope there's not another time." He sighed. "Perhaps if you keep your nose buried in those ledgers for the rest of your trip here, it will keep you out of trouble."

She blinked several times, freeing her eyes from staring at his fingers as they deftly manipulated the coin. Would his fingers be able to so deftly touch against her skin as they were doing to the coin? The very thought sent a heat spreading through her, warming her from her head to her toes. She really shouldn't be thinking about Harrison Stone touching her, period.

"I'd be happy with that, for I adore numbers," she finally replied. "They speak to me on the page and capture my attention in a way little else does." Perhaps apart from him…though in a purely annoyed way, she quickly tried to assure herself.

"I feel the same. As does your uncle." He was quiet for a moment. "You're very much like him, did you know that?"

"I've been told that before." Her mother always said that Aimee and her father were like two peas in a pod, both as stubborn and exuberant as they were impatient about life.

"Over the years, whenever we acquired another company," Harrison began, "I'd watch him spend the next day pouring through all their financial ledgers cover to cover, forgetting to eat, so absorbed by the numbers on the page."

"That sounds like him."

"He's a good man, your uncle," Harrison replied. "He gave me a chance when no one else would, taking me under his wing when I was a boy."

"Yes, I've heard everything about you since I was young—" When his eyes narrowed slightly at the corners, she realized her blunder. "—ger.

Younger."

"He's one of the best men I know." The statement was simple, but Aimee could see the absolute truth radiating from his eyes, which was at odds with her belief of him and his intentions regarding her father's company. "Like a second father to me, given my own father passed away when I was young."

"I couldn't imagine what that would feel like to lose your parents."

He seemed taken aback. "But aren't you an orphan, too?"

At this rate, he would discover her ruse and ship her home. "Of course I am, but what I meant was… Well, you see, my parents died when I was a baby, so I have no memory of them." Evie had told her so, and it sounded plausible, she hoped. "Whereas you grew up with your parents until you were eight, so I imagine you remember them to a certain extent, and um, that's what I meant when I said I couldn't imagine what it would feel like… Because I couldn't, given I don't remember my parents at all, so I don't remember losing them."

She was blathering like a fool in his presence, and lying to him, which she hated, but what else could she do? Perhaps try not to talk to him at all for the next six weeks? The man was so sharp that if they kept conversing, he probably would put two and two together and her opportunity of a lifetime would be ruined.

"I suppose sometimes the memories I have of them are both a blessing and a curse," he responded before falling back into silence for a moment.

Then he stood up. "In any event, I'd best go and see Robert. Now go and get some lunch before it's time to finish work."

"But aren't you worried someone might kidnap me?" She didn't bother to hide the sarcasm in her tone.

"Very funny. But, like you said, no one knows who you are, so you should be fine. Though, I can accompany you if you wan—"

"No, that's not needed." The last thing she wanted was for him to go with her. Her body already felt like it was wound up like a clock being this close to him; she could only imagine what she'd feel like if she spent another hour in his company. "I'll go myself, thank you."

She was enjoying this aspect of the masquerade, being able to go outside without a chaperone or a companion. It was exhilarating. A tiny bit of freedom she rarely had as herself but planned to take full advantage of while pretending to be Evie.

"Just don't go rushing down any alleyways trying to save more animals."

"How hilarious you are." She narrowed her eyes at him, while he winked and tipped his head to her, before striding across the large room toward Robert's office.

Reluctantly, she found her eyes following his athletic figure, unable to do much but admire the man's backside, and a darn fine backside it was. A backside any woman would admire, and the fact Aimee was doing so meant absolutely nothing.

Not a darn thing.

CHAPTER ELEVEN

"Two shillings? That's highway robbery," Aimee declared to the telegram clerk who she was sure was trying to overcharge her for wanting to send a two-sentence telegram to New York. "In America, it's half that."

"Well, we aren't in America, are we," the man behind the counter said, his voice a nasal whine. "Now, did you want to send it or not?"

"Yes, fine," Aimee grumbled, pulling out two shillings from her reticule and passing the coins across the wooden counter to the man's out-stretched fingers. Even though two shillings was nothing to her in the grand scheme of things, it felt like she was being cheated given she could get the same service in New York for half the price. And Aimee hated being ripped off.

"What did you want to say? And remember two shillings gets you up to thirty words," the clerk said, picking up his pencil and placing it against his note paper. "Anything more and it's extra."

Paying such an amount for only thirty words was ridiculous, especially when she could have used one of the specially installed telephones at the office, but then someone could overhear her request and it could get back to her father, or worse, Harrison, which wasn't what she wanted at all. "Please write, 'Transfer five hundred dollars from my personal account into my Bank of England account, stop. All is well, I simply require more spending money to shop with, stop. Regards, Aimee Thornton-Jones, stop.'"

"That's thirty-three words. It'll be an extra shilling to send that."

"It's thirty words exactly, actually."

"We count the word 'stop,' too, and you got three of those."

"That's thievery."

The man shrugged. "It's just how it is."

Aimee blew out a breath. "Fine then, get rid of the words 'all is well.' That should be exactly thirty words including the three stops."

"Aye, it is." The man peered at her. "Is five hundred gonna be enough, though, considering you're complaining about a few shillings? Why not make it an even thousand? Or two, perhaps? Goodness, I don't know, maybe even ten thousand? That might see you through to the end of the week." The man cackled, clearly thinking her to be delusional to be asking for such a sum in the first place.

"Please send the telegram as is." She'd calculated that was what she needed to rent a suite at the Mayfair Grand for the duration of her stay, and having her accountant transfer the funds from her separate account her grandmother had set up for her meant her parents would be none the wiser about her request so soon after arriving. Which, if they did know about, would warrant their scrutiny.

"It's your money to waste, ain't it, Miss Thornton-Jones."

"Oh no, that's not *me*, that's my cousin," Aimee was quick to correct. "I'm just sending the telegram on her behalf."

He shrugged. "Whatever. Now wait here, I won't be long."

She watched him walk over to the telegram machine in the far corner behind the counter, and then start to punch her words into the machine.

"Ah good, you found the office," Molly's voice said from behind her.

Aimee turned around to see both her and Deidre. "I did, thank you for the directions," she replied, noting the smile on Molly's face and the scowl on Deidre's. "What are you two doing here?"

"Mrs. Holbrook needed a message sent to her cousin, and as she still had some work to finish, I offered to do it for her." Molly glanced over to Deidre. "Deidre decided to accompany me." Molly didn't seem happy with that fact.

Deidre cared little for Molly's apathy. "In truth, when Molly said *you* were sending a telegram, I thought I'd come see what you were up to. So, what are you doing here? Do you have someone back in America pining away for you? I daresay you must, to spend such a lot of money on a telegram."

Aimee blinked at the sudden barrage of questions. "Um, no. I just have some business to attend to on behalf of my cousin."

Deidre pouted. "Oh please! I don't believe that for a second."

"Deidre, leave her alone," Molly said, her eyes sending an apology to Aimee.

"I'm trying to be friendly," Deidre replied, her gaze glancing up and down Aimee's outfit, almost like she was sizing her up. "Though, of course, if you don't want to be friends, that's fine, keep your secrets. You're not the only one here who has them."

"Oh, I've already heard about your secret flirtation with an accountant at the office," Aimee couldn't resist saying.

Deidre's face went red. "You told her?" She turned to Molly with an accusing finger.

Molly shrugged. "It wasn't a secret, was it, given you've been telling everyone about it for the last few weeks." Molly glanced back over to Aimee. "If you want to wait for us after you're done, we can all walk back to Mrs. Holbrook's together?"

"That's kind of you, but I have a few errands to run before I return to Mrs. Holbrook's." A bath being at the top of that list.

"How do you have errands?" Deidre's sharp voice questioned. "You've only just arrived."

"All done," the clerk's voice from behind the counter interrupted them. "Anything else?"

"No, thank you—um." She glanced to his name tag. "William. That's all I'll be needing." She turned back to Molly and Deidre. "Anyhow, I best be off. I'll see you both back at Mrs. Holbrook's later on," Aimee said, wasting no time to wave and leave the shop.

She hurried through the door and turned right, wanting to get lost in the crowd in case Deidre wanted to follow her, which she wouldn't put past her. She glanced back over her shoulder to check when she nearly collided with a brick wall of a man's chest.

Her whole body tensed as the man's hands

grasped her upper arms to steady her and stop her from falling backward. The man's touch, his scent… "Are you following me?" She stared up into Harrison's face, and instantly she saw the pulse at the base of his neck jump.

"No, of course not," his deep voice rumbled, and she swore she could feel the reverberation of it, being so close to him.

"What are you doing here?"

"I was across the road and saw you leaving the telegram office and thought I'd see if you needed any assistance."

"So, you were spying on me." She brushed off his hands and glared at him with the full force of her displeasure. "I knew it."

"I wasn't spying on you, Yvette."

It was the third time he'd called her by her supposed first name and it felt uncomfortable and wrong, him using Evie's name. Not that he could call her by her actual name, given he had no idea she was masquerading as her cousin… But, still, for one mad moment she wanted to hear her name roll off his lips, not her cousin's.

"We're on a first-name basis now, are we, *Harrison*?"

"We'll be seeing each other a lot over the next several weeks, so when we're alone, why not? You and Ben are already on a first-name basis."

"Call me Evie then and not Yvette." At least if he called her that she'd have a better chance of thinking it was her he was speaking to, given Evie sounded far more like Aimee than Yvette did.

"Very well, Evie. So, what are you doing sending

a telegram?" he asked, falling in step beside her as she recommenced walking down the street. "You know you can use the telephones in the office. Even to call New York. Unless, of course, you didn't want anyone to hear whatever the message it was you sent."

Damn the man for his astuteness. "What are you suggesting?"

He stared steadily at her. "Selling company secrets and information to competitors can be a lucrative endeavor. Especially for someone who's gotten used to luxuries but doesn't have money of her own."

"Are you suggesting I'm a company spy when I've only been here for two days? How industrious of me."

He frowned. "You were interested in the company ledgers a short time ago, and let me tell you, no other secretary has ever shown the slightest interest in them before."

"That's because I love numbers, and I have a talent for them. I'm certainly no spy. This company means everything to me." The hide of him to suggest she would sell out any of their secrets.

"Then why send a telegram?"

"Because the man I was sending a message to doesn't have a phone." It was one more regrettable lie, given her accountant most certainly had a phone in his office, but she wasn't willing to explain to Harrison why she didn't want to be overheard, which had nothing to do with spying and everything to do with protecting her identity.

"A man?"

"Yes, a man. What of it?" She turned down a side street, caring little if he followed or not, but feeling oddly elated when he did.

"Are you spoken for back in New York?" His voice was devoid of all emotion.

"Why would you all assume that just because I was sending a telegram?"

"*All* of us?"

"Molly and Deidre were in the telegram office, too, and that was what Deidre assumed I was doing," she said by way of explanation. "Which is not the case at all."

"It's a logical assumption to make," he replied. "So, who is this man, and does your uncle know about him?"

"That is none of your business, but if you must know, yes, my uncle knows all about him." She was glad for once to be telling him the truth as her father was the one who'd referred her to his accountant in the first place. "Now, is there anything else you wish to interrogate me about?"

He was silent for a moment. "Did you have lunch like I suggested?"

"You're not my keeper, and most certainly not my husband to be telling me what to do." She could only imagine how horrid it would be to be married to such a bossy, controlling man. Though, perhaps his kisses wouldn't be so horrid… Oh good lord! What was wrong with her to think such thoughts about Harrison Stone?

"I was only asking because I haven't, and there's an excellent pie store around the corner if you're hungry and wanted to accompany me."

"Oh." She hadn't eaten yet and she was hungry, darn it. She could always go to the Mayfair Grand after. "Perhaps I will accompany you." She just had to not think about kissing and Harrison Stone together again in the same sentence. Which should be simple, even if his lips did look absurdly kissable.

"I thought you might, given your stomach's still rumbling, and loudly, too." A grin stretched across his face.

"A gentleman wouldn't point that out."

"But I'm an American and most certainly will point that out," he countered. "Come on, this way." He took her hand and crossed the road with her by his side, and though Aimee knew she should yank her hand away, her body was refusing to listen to her head. His fingers were so strong, and firm, wrapped around her own, that a part of her instantly missed the contact when he let go as soon as they got to the other side.

She felt like shaking her head at her foolishness. "So, you consider yourself American, even though both your parents were English?" she asked, wanting to distract herself from him, but also feeling curious, far more than she should.

"You seem to know a fair bit about me."

"Like I said, my uncle speaks of you, *a lot*. Too much in fact." And that was downplaying it.

He laughed at that, a rich, deep tone, that had Aimee smiling, too.

"You know, Thomas talks a lot about you and his daughter, too."

"He does?" She'd always imagined her father to be too focused on his business deals to talk about her or Evie to anyone, except perhaps complaining about one of her latest escapades.

"All the time," he replied, leading them down a street on his right. "Though he does discuss his daughter a little more, given she causes him the headaches."

"Headaches?" Aimee nearly screeched. "I don't—" She caught herself just in time once again. "I don't think my cousin causes him that many problems. Certainly, she and um, my uncle butt heads a lot, but that's only because he doesn't listen to her or take her seriously."

"He says the same about her."

"Of course he does. He and her mother think they know what's best for her future, which is marrying some boring old English lord, rather than listen to what would actually make her happy."

He shrugged. "Not all lords are boring or old."

"Oh please, they're all stuffy, pompous creatures who think a woman should hover silently in the background, seeing to her husband's comfort and never speaking up for herself. English traits you've obviously inherited."

"And ones you've obviously discarded," he murmured, before pointing to a sign up ahead. "Here we go, London's best pies."

As they approached the store, the smell of buttery pastry wafted from the door and Aimee closed her eyes for a moment in bliss. "They do smell good." Suddenly, she was ravenous, aware she hadn't eaten a thing since the hastily grabbed apple before she rushed out the door of Mrs. Holbrook's that morning.

"The best I've tried in the years I've been here."

He opened the door for her, and she stepped inside to be confronted by row upon row of delicious pastry concoctions, along with a plethora of people all packed into the space to get a late lunch, too.

"The chicken mushroom pie is one of my favorites," he said, leaning down to murmur close to her ear. Again, a tingling sensation his nearness seemed to evoke rippled through her. "Along with the steak and pepper pie, which is also delicious."

Aimee glanced up at him, and their eyes locked, and she didn't want pie. Unexplainably, she wanted him with a burning desire she'd never felt before. She licked her dry lips and noticed his eyes following the movement while his chest expanded as he heaved in a deep breath.

Even though they were surrounded by people, it felt as if it were just the two of them, alone together, aware of each other on a level Aimee had never experienced. Heat filled her cheeks, and she knew she had to get out of there before she did the unthinkable and kissed him, right then and there, in front of everyone.

"The chicken pie will be fine," she hurriedly said. "I'll wait outside." Pushing past him, she ran over to the door and yanked it open, before stepping outside on the footpath and finally feeling like she could breathe again.

She inhaled several deep breaths, and slowly her skittering heartbeat started to steady. These feelings he was making her feel were as foreign to her as they were unwanted. Well, perhaps not exactly unwanted…

"Excuse me, miss?"

Aimee turned around to be confronted by a policeman. "Yes, officer?"

"I need to question you about a stolen dog."

Oh dear…could her day get any worse?

CHAPTER TWELVE

For a moment there, as he and Evie had stared at each other, Harrison had felt an almost overwhelming urge to kiss her, and he hadn't even cared that they were in public and surrounded by a shop full of people. It was impulsive and so completely out of character that he didn't like it one bit.

After his parents had died, his sole focus had been on proving his grandfather wrong, that he wasn't a good-for-nothing bastard and he could succeed and amass a greater fortune than his grandfather. And he was so close to finally succeeding, he couldn't let anyone get in the way of that goal. He'd just have to keep her at arm's length, like he'd kept every other woman his entire life.

What was it about Yvette Jenkins that made him want to abandon all rational behavior and give in to his base desires? There was something about her that he was so attracted to, and it wasn't just her pretty face. No matter how he tried to rationalize it or pretend it wasn't the case, the truth was he desired his boss's niece. Damn it.

"What would you like?" the serving girl asked him as he got to the head of the line.

He placed an order for two chicken pies, then handed the money over to the girl, who went and got his pies before giving them to him in paper bags. "Thank you."

Turning around, he made his way through the

crowd of people and headed over toward the front door, where he saw Evie on the footpath talking with a police officer. Wonderful…

"I don't know what you're talking about," Evie said imperiously, her voice commanding, as Harrison stepped outside and walked over to them. "Do you see a dog anywhere near me?" She gestured in a sweeping motion with her hand all around her. "I don't. So your allegation that I've stolen a dog is ridiculous."

"Is there a problem, Officer?" Harrison asked, staring into the police officer's eyes with an unflinching intensity he always used to intimidate his competitors.

The policeman didn't look pleased by the interruption. "This is a police matter, sir. I would suggest you leave before I arrest you for hindering me."

"That won't be happening," Harrison said. "She is under my protection while she's visiting England, and I've promised her uncle, Thomas Thornton-Jones, that I will ensure she's looked after. You have heard of the Thornton-Jones Conglomerate, haven't you?"

"Aye, it employs a lot of people in these parts." The policeman nodded his head, his police hat bobbing as he did so. "She's his niece then?"

"Yes, and I'm sure you realize that if she wanted a dog, she could quite easily buy one given her uncle's wealth." Harrison flicked off some lint from his jacket. "She'd have no need to steal one, would she?"

"I suppose not, but I've received a complaint from a reliable source that a woman fitting this lady's description has stolen a dachshund."

"Would that source happen to be your brother?" Harrison raised a brow.

The policeman slowly nodded. "Aye."

"I don't blame you for taking your brother's word for it. However, as an officer of the law, you're obliged to look beyond family ties and regard the evidence. At least that's what my good friend Adam Darrow always says. I'll ask him his opinion of the situation when I meet with him tonight at my club."

"You're friends with Magistrate Darrow?" The man gulped, his expression turning pale.

"Very good friends," Harrison replied. "I hope we now understand each other, and this will be the end of the matter?"

The policeman nodded slowly. "Aye, it will be." He turned to Evie and tipped his head to her. "Apologies for worrying you, Miss."

"I wasn't worried in the slightest," Evie replied, lifting her chin to stare boldly into the policeman's face.

"Do be sure to tell your brother he's mistaken and to leave well enough alone," Harrison added. "Or I'll have him arrested on assault charges for daring to touch Miss Jenkins."

The man curtly nodded, then turned on his heels, his legs carrying him swiftly down the road and out of their sight.

"Now before you berate me again for coming to your rescue—"

She launched herself into his arms and hugged him, which was the last thing he'd been expecting, and rendered him speechless for a moment. He stood there with his arms out to his sides, a pie bag in each hand, not quite knowing what to do. He'd never really been hugged before, at least not since his mother died. Even his paramours never hugged him.

"Thank you, Harrison!" she gushed, squeezing her arms tightly around him once again before she stepped back and smiled.

Harrison gulped. The press of her body against his had stirred all sorts of reactions in him. Reactions that would get him in trouble if he didn't control a certain part of his anatomy, and quickly, too. "You're welcome?"

"You don't have to sound so surprised." Her smile turned to a frown.

"You threatened to shoot me yesterday for coming to your rescue, yet today I get a hug?"

"That's because I could have handled the situation yesterday." She plucked one of the bags from his hands. "But today I couldn't very well pull out my derringer against a police officer, now could I?"

"Only if you wanted to spend the night in jail."

"Exactly, so thank you. It would have been a difficult situation if that officer had decided to take things further, so it's one less thing I must worry about. Is this pie mine?" She glanced down at the paper bag she was holding.

"They're the same." He shook his head, thinking not for the first time how bloody difficult women could be.

"Good." She pulled out the pie and tucked into it with gusto.

"You really are hungry."

"Ravenous," she managed to say between mouthfuls. "This is so good."

Harrison grinned, oddly pleased she thought so. "Come on, let's eat as we walk back to the office. Robert mentioned you were interested in studying the company ledgers."

She paused with the pie halfway to her mouth. "You want to discuss the ledgers with me?"

"Yes. You want to learn about the company, and I'd be interested to hear your opinions on where you think we could improve, coming from an outside perspective."

"You want my opinions?" There was shock in her eyes as she came to an abrupt stop on the footpath.

Harrison stopped, too. "If you want to share them."

"Absolutely." A smile unlike anything he'd seen lit up her face, and he'd never seen anyone look more beautiful or filled with so much joy as she was right then in that moment. Suddenly, all he wanted to do was scoop her up in his arms and kiss her, tasting her sweetness and zest for life. To feel the joy she was feeling, which had been missing from his life for as long as he could remember.

But he refrained. Only just, with *she's trouble and Thomas's niece* repeating over and over in his head. Mantras he desperately hoped he'd be able to keep at the forefront of his awareness while she was here in London.

Because if he didn't, he knew he wouldn't be able to resist the pull she had over him, a pull that was beyond tempting but that would lead to devastation and heartache in the long run. It would lead to Thomas never forgiving him and destroy any chance Harrison had of being sold the London side of the company, and that was a risk he couldn't take, not even for what promised to be bliss.

Yet, standing there, staring at her, Harrison was tempted to throw caution to the wind. To do something wild and daring for once in his life. Damn, she really was getting under his skin for him to be considering that.

He couldn't allow it to continue and the more time he spent alone with her the harder it would be to resist her. And he wouldn't risk his dreams he'd worked so hard for crumbling. "Actually, I forgot I have to run an errand. An important errand, so you'll have to excuse me, but I don't have time to listen to your little ideas right now."

Her smile fell and confusion shone in her eyes. "My *little* ideas?"

"Yes." He cleared his throat. "Women tend to think a lot smaller than men." He didn't, of course, believe it; in fact some excellent ideas had come from Thomas's wife, and Mrs. Holbrook, too, but if Evie thought he was a pompous ass, surely she'd refuse to spend time alone with him. Which was exactly what he needed her to do right then. "I imagine I'll be amused by your thoughts, but I have more important things to attend to at the moment."

"Thank you, Harrison Stone, for proving to me first impressions are usually always correct." She spun around on her heel and marched in the opposite direction.

Harrison sighed, knowing he hadn't handled that at all well, though he resisted the urge to run after her and apologize. He watched her cross over to the other side of the road, her hips swaying enticingly, before she disappeared. Shaking his head with a lengthy exhale that amply captured his turmoil, he started the short trek back to the office, his pie tasting like sawdust with every mouthful.

It was far better she maintained her dislike of him than start liking him anyhow, even though the thought made him feel oddly hollow inside. He'd only known her for two days and she'd already turned his world upside down; what the hell would he be like after six weeks in her presence?

A candidate for Bedlam most likely.

• • •

The following afternoon, after meeting Evie at a coffee shop and finding out Evie was also having difficulties with an annoying duke, Aimee wondered if perhaps all men were difficult.

Though she doubted Evie's duke was as frustrating as Harrison Stone. No man could compare to him in terms of his obstinacy and rudeness. Honestly, she was still seething at how he'd essentially dismissed her and her *little* ideas yesterday. She couldn't understand what had happened. One moment they'd been getting along, and then in the blink of an eye he was cold, distant, and condescending. Exactly the man she'd originally imagined him to be.

Little ideas? Oh, she'd show him. Especially

when she confronted him about the anomalies she'd detected in the accounts ledgers, having gone through them more thoroughly after checking into a suite at the Mayfair Grand and finally having her bath.

A bath she'd been in dire need of, though it wasn't as relaxing as usual, given thoughts of that blasted man kept intruding and distracting her. Thankfully, though, after she'd finished her bath, she'd pored over the ledgers, which had proven a great distraction when she realized someone had been doctoring the numbers, making it seem as if the London company was starting to run at a loss. Which only made sense if someone was trying to sabotage the company.

It would be interesting to see what Harrison had to say about that, especially since he'd accused her of being a corporate spy, which was simply ludicrous. He could be the one to have doctored the ledgers for all she knew, though that was doubtful given she was certain the man was trying to be her father's unofficial successor, and he did seem to live and breathe the company.

In any event, before she presented him with her findings, she wanted to gather all the data first. It was why she was on her way to the office to go through the rest of the ledgers in Robert's office on a Sunday, which hopefully meant she could do so uninterrupted given no one else should be there.

The office came into view and Aimee ducked around the alley behind the building, to where Molly had said the back entrance was, noting it was close to where the turnip had accosted her the first day. Instinctively she reached into her pocket and gripped her derringer. She had no intention of being caught unaware again, but the alley was silent. Using the key Molly had given her for after-hours access, she let herself in, making sure to lock the door behind her.

Ten minutes later, she was rifling through Robert's office looking for the ledgers which he'd mentioned he kept on his desk, but try as she might, she couldn't find them anywhere.

The nape of her neck prickled in awareness, and she knew even before turning around that Harrison was there. If he wasn't invading her thoughts, he was invading her space.

"And you still say you're not a corporate spy?" he murmured.

CHAPTER THIRTEEN

"Oh, for goodness' sake, I'm not a spy!" Aimee replied. "And what are you doing here anyway? It's a Sunday. No one should be here."

Harrison straightened from where he'd been leaning against the doorjamb of Robert's office, curiously watching as Evie rifled around on the man's desk. "I'm here every day. Surely, the better question is what are you doing here?"

Her brows drew together in a frown. "If I'd known you'd be here, I wouldn't have come in."

"You're not still upset about yesterday, are you?"

"Please," she scoffed. "It matters *little* to me what you say, given I have such *little* ideas."

Yes, Harrison was going to pay for that remark; he'd known it as soon as he'd said it. Though it had served its purpose in giving him much-needed breathing space. "Look, I apologize for what I said yesterday. Can we move past it?"

She gave a half shrug, but she didn't seem overly congenial to the idea. "How about we see how you go today with what you say."

"How kind of you," he replied with a reluctant grin. The fact that she wasn't intimidated by him was refreshing. "And don't think I haven't forgotten you still haven't told me what you're doing here."

"What does it look like I'm doing? Clearly, I'm here to work."

There was an indignant expression on her face

that Harrison found oddly endearing. "By rifling through Robert's desk?"

She sighed. "I suppose it appears nefarious."

"What, like you're spying for another company by coming into the office when everyone isn't here, clearly looking for something?"

"I'm not a spy." She huffed, blowing away a strand of hair that had fallen loose over her face. "I was hoping to find the other accounts ledgers Robert was showing me yesterday. I've detected several anomalies in the few that I borrowed to read, and I wanted to see if the others also contained the same discrepancies."

Harrison frowned as he walked into the room. "What anomalies?" Anomalies in accounts ledgers were never a good thing, and certainly not something he expected to see in the ledgers for the London company he ran.

She pulled out several ledgers from a satchel over her shoulder and opened one, pointing out several incidents where it appeared the figures had been doctored and changed to other numbers than what had originally been written.

"It looks like someone's changed the last month's worth of figures to make it appear as though the company's started to run at a loss," she said.

"You detected that by just looking through the ledgers?"

"I told you I was good at numbers," she replied. "Though I can't work out why someone would want to do that, at least not someone within the company. Certainly, a competitor would, and perhaps they paid someone here to do so, but why would somebody risk going to jail to forge some numbers in our company books? Especially when they're discrepancies that would be picked up at the next quarterly audit?"

"The damage might've already been done by then, particularly in light of the Wilheimer deal we're working on," Harrison said, picking up one of the ledgers and scanning through its contents for the last month. She was right. Somebody had doctored the books. The question now was who? "Have you mentioned this to anyone yet?"

She shook her head. "No. I thought I'd come in today to see if any of the other ledgers also showed evidence of tampering before I mentioned it to anyone. But I can't find any of the ledgers, even though Robert said he usually keeps them on his desk."

"They're in the company safe," Harrison replied. "They're kept there overnight, then retrieved in the morning to be left on Robert's desk for the day, for easy access."

"Then why did he let me borrow these ones?"

"Guess."

"Because of my uncle."

"I think it more likely because the man is besotted with you."

"Nonsense," she declared, her hands fisting on her hips. "He only just met me."

"I saw how he was looking at you." And he hadn't bloody liked it at all. Not that he should care. And he didn't, not really… "In any event, let's go and retrieve the other ledgers. I'll be interested to see if they also reflect any discrepancies."

"Me, too," she said, following as he headed up to his office, where the safe was.

"You really do like numbers, don't you?"

"I told you I did," came her rather indignant reply. "Men are all the same, you never listen."

"Oh, we listen, we just don't know if you ladies are telling the truth." He glanced across at her as she kept pace with him as they walked to his office, and he could have sworn for an instant she looked guilty. He wondered if she'd been lying about what the man she'd sent the telegram to meant to her? The thought was surprisingly upsetting.

"Who do you think might be behind the alterations?"

"It could be a number of people," he replied. "Robert, obviously, comes to mind, given he's in charge of the ledgers and is the only one authorized to write in them."

"But you don't think he's guilty, do you," she said perceptively as they walked through the outer room before entering Harrison's office.

"No." Perhaps he shouldn't have brought her here with him, especially as they were literally the only two people in the entire building. *Not the smartest move, Stone,* he chastised himself.

"I don't think he's responsible, either," Evie replied, walking over to the back of the room where a picture of her uncle hung on the wall, the safe nestled behind it. "He seems far too honorable and nice."

"Nice people commit crimes," he said, then frowned. "How do you know that's where the safe is?"

"I'm a cat burglar in my spare time," she replied with a completely straight face, before laughing. "How do you think? It's the only picture frame on the wall, so where else would a concealed safe be? Honestly. You men are so suspicious of everything."

"And you women love to pigeonhole us," he grumbled, walking next to her and pulling on the hinged picture frame to swing it open.

"That very statement is itself pigeonholing women," she replied with a smug smile.

Harrison turned his eyes away from her and stared straight at the safe in front of him. Perhaps if he focused on it, and not on the woman beside him, he might have a chance of getting out of the situation without compromising her or his morals.

He pulled out a set of keys from his pocket and opened the safe, retrieving the ledgers inside.

"Does anyone else have access to this safe?" Evie asked.

"No. Just me," he replied. "Which is why the books are kept on Robert's desk through the day. Though he hasn't previously loaned any of the ledgers out like he did with you. However, no one who wants to look through them is as pretty as you." He mumbled the last part under his breath.

"You think I'm pretty?"

"Yes," he admitted, frowning as she smiled. "Pretty annoying, that is."

Her smile turned into a scowl. "As are you. In any event, if Robert was the one responsible for doctoring the entries, it's doubtful he would've allowed me to borrow some to look through. Though it's lucky I did, isn't it?"

"You've saved me about a week until I check them again as I do every fortnight," he conceded.

"My...uncle does the same thing...checking them fortnightly, that is."

"Who do you think I learned the habit from?"

"Does everyone know you look over the ledgers fortnightly?" she asked.

"Robert and Ben do," he replied. "But no, that fact isn't generally known."

"So whoever did this would have assumed the anomalies wouldn't have been discovered until the quarterly audits in about one month's time."

"Yes. When the figures would've been posted for the shareholders."

"And if kept as is, would have been detrimental to the share price of the company," she replied.

He was reluctantly impressed by her quick grasp of the situation. "You know, for someone who apparently doesn't like business, you're taking to it like a duck to water."

She smiled; however, it seemed slightly forced. "I've told you I've decided to embrace this opportunity, so embrace it, I am."

"Well, you're certainly doing that." He still couldn't quite work her out, but she was a fascinating puzzle. One that he wanted to unravel and solve. Unravel to the point of her being naked and in his bed.

"Are you all right?" She was staring at him in concern. "You look a bit flushed suddenly. You're not coming down with something, are you?"

"I probably am," he barely managed to say, as images of her naked, soft curves wrapped only in the silk sheets of his bed dominated his thoughts to the point where he could think of little else. He kept trying to tell himself that this was Thomas's niece, but even that didn't seem to sway his imagination. "You better go, right now." Because he was coming down with a case of foolish idiocy.

She ignored him and instead raised her hand to his forehead. "You feel a little warm, but not fevered."

He pressed his eyes tightly together, trying to ignore the softness of her fingers against his skin. He was fighting a losing battle with himself, and he knew it. "If you don't leave right now, I'm not going to be able to help myself and I'll kiss you, right here and right now."

She gulped. "You will?"

"Yes," he said, opening his eyes and staring down into her wide ones. "Which we both know is a terrible idea."

"It is a terrible idea," she said, though she made no effort to move away from him.

There were so many problems with kissing her, but right at that moment he couldn't articulate any of them, and his body began swaying toward hers with a mind of its own.

"Though we are adults and can kiss whomever we want," she whispered, her body also moving in toward his, her lips now only inches from his.

"But you're Thomas's niece…" Harrison tried to clear his suddenly foggy head, the voice warning him that this was a bad idea getting very distant, until it was nothing but a far-off echo. "And you're an employee…"

"A *temporary* employee," she reminded him, her mouth getting precariously closer to his. "Don't you want to kiss me, Harrison Stone?"

"I thought I was your enemy?" Surely, if they could both remember how much they disliked each other, this madness would end?

"Don't they say to keep your friends close and your enemies closer?"

"They do," he said in a gruff whisper, breathing in the sweet scent of jasmine on her neck.

"Then kiss me."

"You don't know what you're asking." Harrison's voice was a choked groan, as he stared at her with desperation in his gaze.

"A simple kiss is all I'm asking for."

"There's nothing simple about kissing you," he groaned. She was Thomas's niece, and nothing would change that.

But then she boldly grabbed the lapels of his jacket and before he could protest, she pulled his lips down onto hers.

The touch of them against his was like an explosion, and he couldn't help but groan at the sweet taste of her. Heat burned through his body as she moaned when he opened his mouth against hers, kissing her with a thoroughness bordering on obsession. She tasted so good; he never wanted the kiss to end.

The thought stopped him cold and abruptly he dragged his mouth away and took a step back. "I'm sorry, that should never have happened," he said, resisting the temptation to kiss her again.

For a moment, she looked flustered as she

pressed her fingers up to her lips, an almost confused expression in her eyes. "It was just a kiss," she replied, hastily dropping her hand from her mouth, and spinning on her heels, striding to the door. "Nothing worth apologizing over."

And then before he could say another word, she left, without a backward glance, and he was the one to feel confused. What had just happened? She'd been urging him to kiss her and then was acting as if it was nothing when Harrison's whole world felt rocked.

Damn it, women were confusing. This was why he didn't get too involved in his relationships—not that this was a relationship, God, nothing of the sort. Thomas would kill him if he began a relationship with his niece.

No. Evie Jenkins was off-limits, and he'd just have to remind himself of that when he saw her next. She wasn't worth risking his dreams over. Dreams that had been his constant companion since he was a boy and had given him hope in what had been a bleak and barren existence.

Dreams he wouldn't abandon for anyone. Intuitively, part of him knew she had the power to possibly mean something to him, and the last people who meant something to him had died and left him all alone.

He wouldn't suffer through that pain again, even if his body was urging him to. No. She was a temptation that could ruin everything he'd worked for, ultimately leading to heartache and loss. Two things he refused to ever go through again.

Not ever.

CHAPTER FOURTEEN

First thing the next day, before anyone else had arrived, Harrison had arranged to meet with Ben and Robert in his office to discuss the discrepancies in the ledgers. A meeting that would distract him from his obsession over Evie, which was growing stronger each day, and couldn't be allowed to continue, no matter how much a part of him wanted it to. He still couldn't believe he'd kissed her.

And what a kiss. She'd tasted both innocent and so delectable all at once.

"What do you mean there are discrepancies?" Robert asked, jolting Harrison out of his musings as he stood up from the chair across from Harrison's desk and rushed over to glanced down at the ledgers in front of Harrison.

Harrison relayed the problem in more detail to them, after which both men appeared shocked at the news that the ledgers had been tampered with.

Robert pressed his lips together, an expression of concern and uncertainty on his face. "How is that possible? Everyone knows I alone am allowed to write in them, given their importance."

"Then why would you lend them to Miss Jenkins?" Harrison asked.

A light red blush spread over Robert's cheeks. "Given she's Mr. Thornton-Jones's niece, I didn't think it would be a problem for her to read them, as she was keen to. Why? Do you think she's the one who doctored them?"

"No, I don't," Harrison said. "Though there's something she's hiding, I'm sure of it. I just don't know what it is." But he was determined to find out.

"I'm glad to hear you don't think she's responsible," Robert replied. "It's rare one meets a woman who likes numbers, let alone is good with them, as well as being so well, um, beautiful. It's a fascinating combination indeed. Don't you think?"

"I don't think about her, period." If only that were true. "In any event, we need to find out who was behind the alterations of the figures."

An expression of embarrassment flooded Robert's face, but he didn't shy away from Harrison's gaze. "I should have discovered the anomalies and I fully accept responsibility for my failure to do so."

"But why would someone alter the ledgers?" Ben spoke up, glancing at Harrison and then down to the ledgers themselves.

"Someone is trying to sabotage the stock prices." Harrison tossed one of the ledgers over to Ben who deftly caught it and began to flick through some of the pages.

"Yes, it certainly seems so," Ben said after his perusal. "The question, then, is who?"

"It could be a large pool, unfortunately," Robert replied with a sigh. "Given all my staff in the accounts section have access to the ledgers through the day, as they need them for the various reports and projects they're working on. But still, I couldn't imagine one of them doing it; they're all such good workers."

"Even good workers will stoop to dishonesty for money," Harrison replied. "Especially given the current deal we're working on."

"You're right," Robert said. "If Wilheimer or his team had seen the ledgers in their current state, it would have jeopardized the entire deal." He straightened his posture and took in a deep breath. "Though I promise you I didn't have anything to do with changing the numbers, ultimately I must take the blame for this, and I see no other option but to tender my resignation, effective immediately."

"I appreciate your willingness to fall on your own sword," Harrison replied. "However, I won't accept your resignation."

"You won't?"

"No. You're far too smart to want to sabotage a company that you yourself have a portion of shares in." All heads of departments throughout Thomas's companies got shares as part of a recruitment bonus when they joined the company. It was an effective scheme that ensured loyalty and hard work to make the company a success.

"Whoever changed the figures presumably wanted our stock prices to plummet and the deal with Wilheimer to fall through, so we need to find out who has a motive for that, then we will find who is responsible."

And whoever it was had better run, because when Harrison found them, they'd wish they'd fled.

CHAPTER FIFTEEN

After waiting nearly the entire morning for an opportunity to speak to Harrison, Aimee finally got her chance when Mrs. Holbrook went downstairs to the shipping department, while Molly and Deidre were off running errands. She quickly ducked into Harrison's office without bothering to knock on his open door.

"I have a plan about the ledgers," she said, hurrying over to where he was sitting at his desk, scribbling on some papers.

He glanced up from his work and raised an eyebrow. "Dare I ask?"

She perched on the edge of his desk, trying not to think about the kiss they'd shared yesterday, which was hard, given it had been constantly replaying in her head since. But that was only because it was her first real kiss, not because of the kiss or the man himself. At least, she kept trying to tell herself that. "Robert mentioned going to lunch with me today, so I thought I'd use the opportunity to superciliously find out what he knows about the alterations."

"He's not going to lunch with you today. He's far too busy after the meeting I had with him and Ben this morning trying to rectify the situation."

"You had a meeting with them about it, without me?"

"I did."

"But I was the one who discovered the issues. I should have been part of it."

"I didn't see the need for you to be there." He leaned back in his chair.

"Of course you didn't." Aimee threw her hands in the air. "Trust you not to think a woman could assist. Even though it was a woman who discovered the issue in the first place!"

"It has nothing to do with whether you can assist or not, but more to do with my wanting to assess Ben and Robert, without you there to distract me."

"I distract you?" She didn't know if that was a good thing or not.

"Yes. You're constantly annoying and interrupting me, so of course you're a distraction."

"You're quite the comedian. But you don't suspect either Ben or Robert, do you?"

"Not really." He gave a half shrug and then sighed. "But you never really know the secrets someone is keeping, even someone you trust."

She felt a stab of guilt from his words, knowing if he ever found out her secret, he'd be furious, which was probably too tame a word for it.

"Wilheimer is downstairs!" Ben said, interrupting them as he rushed into the room. "His interpreter says he's demanding a meeting with you now, not this afternoon."

"He's obviously found out about his loans being called in." Harrison didn't seem concerned with the news. "Very well then, we'll have the meeting now."

A few minutes later, Harrison had organized for Miss Mitchell to show Wilheimer and his men to the boardroom, while Mrs. Holbrook fetched Mr. Stanton and Ben was getting his notes from his office, leaving Aimee alone again with Harrison.

"What should I do?" Aimee asked.

His eyes swiveled over to her and narrowed. "You can stay here and look after the office."

"You can't be serious. I've come here to learn all I can about my uncle's company, not twiddle my thumbs. Please let me attend the meeting, too. I promise I won't say a word."

He paused and stared at her in what she assumed most would think an intimidating manner, but she didn't budge an inch, and instead raised her chin.

"How can you possibly assist when you said you won't say a word?"

"I speak fluent German so I can pay attention to what's said and done, and we can discuss it after."

He was silent for a few seconds. "Fine. You can come to the meeting." He bent his head down toward hers, until his lips were mere inches away from her own. "But that's it. You will not interrupt, interfere, or do anything to make your presence known. Do you understand me?"

"I do." Aimee gulped as she felt the heat radiating from him, and a shiver of excitement ran down to her toes.

"You'd better understand," he murmured, his tone suddenly softening as he leaned in closer to her.

Aimee felt her breath hitch, his mouth inches from her own. Would he kiss her again? She licked her suddenly dry lips and was fascinated when she noticed the pulse at the base of his neck starting to thump rapidly.

Was he, too, feeling this strange pull toward her, as she felt toward him? Almost like her body had a mind of its own and was urging her to close the distance between them. But darn it, she couldn't do that. She had to prove to her father that she was more than capable of taking over the company from him, and an office flirtation would never prove to him how serious she was. Though he would never find out about it…

"I won't say a thing," she finally managed to whisper back.

Time stood still as they stared at each other, only inches away, but then Harrison blinked, cursing lightly under his breath.

"You damn well better not," he said, rather stiffly. "I will not have this deal jeopardized. And I do literally mean you're not to say a word. If you so much as—"

Aimee couldn't help herself; she closed the distance between them and pressed her lips against his, kissing him with all the pent-up frustration she was feeling. Then she pulled back from him and grinned. "What an effective way to silence someone."

The muscle in his jaw twitched. "You kissed me to silence me?"

It felt wonderful having the upper hand for once. "It worked, didn't it?" Really, she'd done so just to get the feeling out of her system, hoping that that would be an end to her thoughts of kissing Harrison. Though it hadn't worked as she'd intended, she still wanted to feel his lips against hers. Damn it! She had to keep what was important to her in focus, rather than the man's lips.

"My dear lady," he all but purred. "If you want to silence someone then you need to kiss them more effectively."

Before Aimee knew what he was about, his lips were against her own, kissing her with such passion that his kiss from yesterday all but faded in comparison. Her body came alive under the sweet onslaught, her heart skittering and her breath catching in her chest as his tongue caressed and tasted hers, tempting her as little else had.

Lust, hot and heavy, cascaded through every single part of her body, pushing aside all the reasons she knew she shouldn't be doing this. She wound her hands around his neck, pulling him more tightly against her, as their kiss deepened into something wild and dizzying. Something she didn't want to end, despite her head knowing it was a terrible idea.

A low growl rumbled deep in his throat, and his hands slid around her skirt, cupping her buttocks, then gently squeezing them as he pulled her firmly against his hard length.

She moaned at the feel of him. Never had she felt so wanton, her body begging for his touch, craving it even.

"Um, Harrison?" a voice, and an accompanying knock from the doorway, interrupted them.

They both froze, and then with a curse, he dropped his hands from her and spun around to the door.

Aimee glanced over and saw a petite and beautiful lady dressed in a light blue Worth day dress, her pale blonde hair swept effortless up into a chignon, with a beautiful blue bonnet perched daintily atop. She appeared the epitome of effortless elegance, though she couldn't fully disguise the hint of upset in her eyes as she stared at Harrison then swung her gaze over to Aimee.

Instantly, Aimee knew the woman and Harrison were involved, and her heart sank. Then, she got angry. Furious in fact. How dare he kiss her if he was already seeing this woman! The nerve of him, but could she really expect anything less?

"Jane," Harrison said, dragging a hand through his hair. "I hadn't been expecting you…"

Aimee never thought she'd see the man squirm, but clearly having his paramour catch him kissing another woman was enough to make even the great Harrison Stone flustered. Just as he deserved to be, the cad.

"So I see," the woman replied, with a smile. "And who is this?" Jane's gaze swung over to Aimee, and though her smile didn't slip, there was loathing in her eyes.

"This is Yvette Jenkins. She's Thomas's niece, and here to train as a secretary," he replied. "Miss Jenkins, this is the Countess of Whitley, a…friend of mine."

Aimee had to restrain herself from scoffing. A friend? What a load of nonsense. There was more than simply friendship between him and this woman, who was staring at Harrison like she owned him.

"It's nice to meet you, Lady Whitley," Aimee replied, lying through her teeth.

The lady inclined her head at Aimee, but instead of repeating the sentiment, she turned to Harrison, dismissing Aimee out of turn.

"Did you forget we had a luncheon date today?" Lady Whitley asked Harrison, her voice refined yet sultry, which Aimee assumed many men would be entranced by. The lady also seemed happy to pretend she hadn't found him in a compromising position. If Aimee were in her place, she would have already pulled out her derringer and threatened the man's nether regions for daring to dishonor her so. She still might, she was that upset with him.

"Damn it, I did forget," Harrison swore. "I'm sorry, Jane, but I have to attend a meeting right now for the Wilheimer deal. We'll have to reschedule lunch."

"You'll still need to eat," the lady replied, an enticing smile on her face. "And I can wait until you're done."

"It could take a while," Harrison replied, having all but forgotten Aimee was even there.

She felt like throttling the man and couldn't wait to give him a piece of her mind when they were alone.

"That's fine. Now go and sort out what you need to. I'll wait here for you, for as long as I need to." She directed her last comment straight to Aimee, and Aimee knew she wasn't just talking about waiting for him for lunch.

That was fine with Aimee. She had no plans to

ever kiss Harrison Stone again.

"Very well," Harrison replied, before glancing to Aimee. "Come along then, Miss Jenkins, we need to get to the meeting."

"Of course, *Mr. Stone*," she said with caustic sweetness, following him out his office and into the outer room. And just as she was about to launch into a scathing attack, Mrs. Holbrook came rushing through the door.

"Ah, there you both are," Mrs. Holbrook said. "Everyone's waiting in the boardroom, and I came back to collect Miss Jenkins after I realized I'd left her here. If that's all right with you, Mr. Stone, that she attends?"

"I've already told her she can," Harrison said, his eyes never once looking at Aimee. "Provided she doesn't say a thing."

"I've already said I won't," Aimee replied. And she wouldn't, not unless she had to.

CHAPTER SIXTEEN

Harrison sat at the head of the table in the board-room, with Ben on his right and Robert on his left, while Mrs. Holbrook sat next to Ben, and Evie sat on a chair over near the side table, staying silent so far, as she'd promised. And even though Harrison's entire future hinged on this meeting, he couldn't stop thinking about her or the kiss they'd just shared. Damn it.

He could have groaned in disgust at himself and his lack of willpower. As it was, even thinking of kissing her had aroused him to the point his cock was beginning to strain against the material of his trousers, which thankfully was hidden from every-one's view by the large table.

He had to get control of himself and ensure the situation of kissing Evie never happened again. Ever. He couldn't risk his future and all he'd worked so hard to achieve.

Returning his attention back to the matter at hand, he glanced over at Wilheimer and the three men who'd accompanied him. They were sitting on the opposite side of the large table, none of them seeming happy to be there. Harrison knew from past dealings that the man on Wilheimer's right was his German accountant, Josef Bernstein, and the man on his left was his brother and business partner, Eric, who had a lesser share in Wilheimer's business, though he was influential with the decisions made. The third man was the interpreter they'd bought with them given Wilheimer and his men spoke very little English.

Currently, Wilheimer's brother and accountant were yelling at each other, and occasionally turning and yelling at Harrison—all in German of course, which the interpreter was having a hard time interpreting given the pace and volume they were yelling with—while waving their hands furiously toward Harrison, both talking over the other. Wilheimer sat there staring at Harrison, his face giving away nothing.

Harrison met his stare, wondering when Wilheimer was going to take charge of his men. He raised his eyebrow at him, and Wilheimer's eyes narrowed, but he gave the briefest of nods.

"Das genügt!" Wilheimer's voice reverberated around the room as his gnarled fist banged on the table, silencing his men in an instant.

"That's enough," the interpreter translated for Harrison.

"What do you want, Wilheimer?" Harrison asked the man directly, to which the interpreter translated, and then Wilheimer began answering back in German.

Though his eyes stayed locked on Wilheimer, from his peripheral he was aware of Evie and the glint of excitement in her eyes to be included in the meeting.

Her enthusiasm was at odds with the picture Thomas had painted of her, and Harrison was beginning to wonder if he'd been purposefully misled about her temperament and desire to be here. But that didn't make sense, either. Thomas had never misled him before, so why would he now?

It was peculiar, though, because from what Harrison had observed of her, she really seemed to want to be here and learn all she could, with a passion that was obvious.

"Mr. Wilheimer says how can you ask him what he wants when you must know why he is here, given you're trying to destroy his company," the interpreter translated after Wilheimer finished responding to Harrison's comment.

Harrison returned his attention to Wilheimer, who looked as stubborn as an old goat and was glaring at him with undisguised animosity.

Not that Harrison could blame him, when only yesterday, Wilheimer had thought it was business as usual, only to find out today his whole company was about to go under if he didn't find the capital to repay his loans in full by the end of the week. An undertaking that wasn't possible, and every one of them there knew it.

Normally, the thrill of corralling his prey into a position of weakness would satisfy the part of Harrison that longed for justice and retribution against every wealthy and entitled gentleman out there. But seeing the stress and fear at the edges of old Wilheimer's face didn't make Harrison feel thrilled at all. Quite the opposite.

"I'm not trying to destroy anything, and if you hadn't backed out of our negotiations, I wouldn't have had to instigate anything," Harrison replied. "But you did, so you need to understand I will use everything at my disposal to ensure this deal goes through. If that means forcing your hand, then so be it."

The interpreter turned to Wilheimer and translated what he said. In response, Wilheimer banged his hand on the desk and started speaking in rapid German, his voice booming around the room.

"He says you're either a liar or a fool," the interpreter began to translate back to Harrison. "And maybe both if you think calling in his loans won't destroy his business and cause the company shares to crash. He demands you undo what you did and do so immediately."

"The only way out of this for you, Wilheimer, is to sell the majority of your shares and voting rights in your company to the Thornton-Jones Conglomerate. Once you do, I will ensure your company debts are paid off and that you personally receive five hundred thousand pounds. It's a fair deal, and one you must accept if you don't want to see all you've worked for disintegrate into ashes."

He waited while Wilheimer's interpreter translated what he'd said and wasn't surprised when Wilheimer stood up and pointed his finger at Harrison and began to curse vehemently; at least that's what he assumed he was doing, given the tone of his voice and the fury on his face.

From the corner of his eye, he saw Evie waving her hand in the air, trying to gain his attention.

Dammit, the last thing he needed while negotiating was to be distracted again by her. With more effort than it should have taken, he ignored her and kept his attention on Wilheimer, who finished off his rant and then sat back into his chair with a grunt.

"Mr. Wilheimer declines your offer, and I think it best not to relay the specifics he said, given there are ladies present," the interpreter translated, a note of apology in the man's voice as he glanced toward Mrs. Holbrook and back over his shoulder to Evie, who hastily stopped flapping her hands about. "They were rather ungentlemanly comments."

Evie scoffed and he got the sense she was desperate to say something, but with a quick eyebrow raise from him, she stayed silent, though from the corner of his eye he saw her press her lips together tightly. The woman was not happy.

"If you can't pay back your loan to the bank by Friday," Harrison turned back to address Wilheimer, trying his best to ignore Evie, "and we both know you can't, then the bank will foreclose on your company, and all your years of hard work will be for naught. You must accept my deal. The repercussions of not doing so would be catastrophic for you and your employees."

While the interpreter was again translating his words, Evie once again impatiently waved her hands in Harrison's direction. He sighed; at least she was keeping her word not to say anything, he supposed. He motioned for her to come to him, to which she wasted no time jumping up from her chair and rushing over.

"The interpreter's lying," she whispered in his ear, and a small shiver ran through him as her breath brushed across his skin.

He turned to her and scowled. "Explain yourself."

She leaned down and put her hand in front of her mouth before whispering in his ear once again. "He's leaving out important details you're telling Wilheimer, and he's doing the same for Wilheimer's replies to you. Not to mention he omitted the full terms of the deal you outlined. He told Wilheimer you were offering to give him fifty thousand pounds, not five hundred thousand."

"And you truly speak fluent German?"

"I do. I speak five languages other than English, all of them fluently."

He couldn't help but be impressed, and if what she said was true, he and Wilheimer were being played for fools. He glanced over to the interpreter whose attention was on Wilheimer and the two other men, as all three of them were talking in a muddle of German words. Was the interpreter purposefully trying to ruin the deal, or was he simply incompetent? It wouldn't be the first time Harrison had encountered corporate espionage in the way of sabotage.

Swiveling his head back to Evie, his eyes narrowed upon her. "Are you certain he's not translating what's being said properly?"

"One thousand percent." She nodded, her eyes wide in earnestness. "Whether it's ineptitude or deliberate, he's sabotaging the dealing and making it seem like you're trying to steal Wilheimer's business for a pittance."

Ben cleared his throat. "Is everything all right?" he asked, disguising his words behind his hand as Evie was doing.

"Miss Jenkins, who speaks fluent German, tells

me the interpreter is not interpreting properly,"
Harrison replied, his voice deliberately loud
enough for everyone to hear, including the interpreter, who gasped at the accusation.

"That's not true," the interpreter replied, his
voice cracking on the last word.

Wilheimer and his men stopped talking, clearly
aware something was going on, even if they didn't
understand what.

"It's true," Evie countered. "And you know it!"

"I don't know what you're talking about," the
man exclaimed, his eyes beginning to blink rapidly
as they pivoted between Harrison and Evie. "I'm
interpreting properly." He glared at Evie. "Perhaps
you need to learn German better."

Harrison glanced to Evie. "Tell Wilheimer and
his men what you told me."

She nodded and began speaking in rapid and
what sounded to be flawless German to the three
men, each of them turning to glare at the interpreter.

"Ist das wahr, was sie sagt?" Wilheimer asked.

"He's asking me if what I'm saying is true," Evie
informed Harrison and Ben, before turning back
and addressing Wilheimer. "Es ist wahr—" she began, speaking at such a fast pace that Harrison
could barely make out the words she was saying,
but whatever she was telling Wilheimer, clearly the
man understood it, as he began nodding and narrowing his eyes toward his interpreter.

"I told Mr. Wilheimer and his colleagues their
interpreter is either deliberately misleading them
or entirely incompetent."

Harrison felt his lips twitch at the expression of outrage on the interpreter's face from Evie's blunt assessment of the situation.

"Es ist nicht wahr!" the interpreter insisted, getting to his feet, a flicker of panic in his eyes.

"He's saying it is not true, but it is true, and you know it." She pointed at the man. "Are you merely incompetent or being purposefully untruthful?"

"You're mistaken," the man said, tugging on his collar as beads of sweat broke out on his brow and his eyes desperately sought out Wilheimer. "Du kannst ihr nicht vertrauen."

"How dare you say that!" Evie said, leaning forward and slamming her hands on the table between Harrison and Ben. The interpreter flinched, and Wilheimer and his other men were staring at her in fascination. "He just told Mr. Wilheimer he can't trust me."

She then recommenced speaking in rapid-fire German, wagging her finger at the interpreter much like a schoolmistress chastising an errant pupil, and all Harrison could do was marvel at her confidence. Every one of them was staring at her as she berated the man, far more confidently than what Harrison would have expected from someone who'd been a companion for years.

The interpreter responded by yelling something in German, to which Evie's frown grew.

"Yes, you do have to listen to me," Evie replied.

"I will not," the man said, switching to English. "You're disparaging me and it's unacc—"

"Enough!" It was Wilheimer himself who yelled the word aloud.

So, the old man did speak a little English. Harrison had suspected so, but just how much was another guess, though obviously not enough to have realized the interpreter hadn't been translating properly.

Wilheimer turned to the interpreter. "Wer hat dich dafür bezahlt, uns anzulügen?"

"He's asking him who paid him to lie to us," Evie informed them.

"A good question," Harrison said, watching as the interpreter's face blanched.

The interpreter replied in German, sounding terrified as he glanced nervously over to the door.

"He says how dare you accuse me of that," Evie said.

Then before anyone could stop him, the interpreter bolted from his chair, yanking open the door and sprinting down the hall, leaving them all staring after him.

Wilheimer turned to Evie and stared intently at her, saying something in German.

"Danke," she replied before turning and grinning at Harrison. "He says my German is excellent, and he'll find out who was paying the traitor."

Her grin lit up her entire face and made Harrison want to taste the sweetness of those full lips of hers. Goddamn it, not again... He couldn't keep thinking of wanting to kiss her. She was Thomas's niece and an employee. Harrison never mixed business with pleasure when it came to employees, no exceptions, ever. So why the hell did he want to make an exception for her? Badly, too.

"Ask Wilheimer how long the interpreter has

been interpreting for him," Harrison told Evie.

A moment later after speaking with Wilheimer, she turned back to Harrison. "Only for the last month after his usual interpreter had to suddenly return to Germany. Apparently, his business, Interpreters International, was recommended by a friend."

Interesting that it was around the same time they'd started the negotiations between their companies. Harrison didn't believe in coincidences, and it was seeming more and more likely that someone didn't want this deal to go ahead.

"Ask Wilheimer if he wants to continue this meeting with you interpreting," Harrison said.

Wilheimer's brother Eric was the one to respond after Evie had translated, his eyes assessing her with a great deal of suspicion in their depths.

"He's asking why they should trust me." She shrugged and turned back to Wilheimer and his men, and again spoke to them in German.

For a moment, Harrison wondered if he should be trusting her, too? He barely knew her, and though she was Thomas's niece, she'd only been living with the Thornton-Joneses for the past six years or so. Could he really trust her to translate for a deal worth millions?

"I told them they shouldn't trust me," she turned back to him.

"You did what?"

"They shouldn't trust me given I work for you, and you shouldn't have been relying on their interpreter for such an important deal, either," she said. "The stakes are too high to risk a miscommunication occurring from a poor translation. You both should have checked the interpreter you were using could speak fluent German and would interpret what you both said properly. It's what I would have done had I overseen the negotiations."

She turned to Wilheimer and seemed to be chastising him, too, given the expression of incredulity on the man's face, but then respect shone in his eyes as he replied in German. "He agrees with me that it was poor form on both of your parts," Evie said. "And he's happy for me to continue interpreting."

"Poor form? Remind Wilheimer he was the one who brought that interpreter with him," Harrison said.

"That will only antagonize him further."

He narrowed his eyes. "Translate it, Evie. That is, after all, the only reason why I'm allowing you a voice in this meeting."

She sighed. "Fine." Quickly, she translated what he'd said and Wilheimer's expression grew darker.

She'd been right. Damn it. Normally, he was a tactical genius in meetings, but with this meeting everything was out of kilter. The only difference was the presence of Evie, and though he never blamed others for his mistakes, he was certain having this woman in here was the cause of his sense of imbalance.

Granted, she'd also discovered the deception the interpreter had been perpetrating, and if that had been allowed to continue unchecked, then the deal really would have had no chance of survival.

In that respect, she'd been invaluable, but in every other aspect she'd been a liability.

Wilheimer stood up and said something else in German to Evie, to which she seemed surprised.

"Bist du sicher?" she replied to Wilheimer, who nodded in response.

"Evie?" Harrison said. "A translation might be nice, if you wouldn't mind."

She glared back at him. "Mr. Wilheimer says he's decided he's not prepared to discuss the matter any further today—"

"But we need to discuss—"

"Did you want me to translate or not? Because if you want me to, you need to listen to the full translation first." She glanced back to Wilheimer and quickly spoke in German to him, Harrison guessed translating what she'd just said.

Wilheimer grinned and said something else to her, to which she grinned back and replied in German, too.

Now Harrison was starting to get annoyed with being left out of their little conversation, and he certainly didn't like how the old lecher was smiling at Evie. Didn't the man have enough mistresses already? He couldn't bloody well have Evie, too. Not that she was Harrison's for him to have any say in the matter, but he owed it to Thomas to protect her. He probably should also start protecting her from himself, too, but that was another story.

"Now, as I was saying," Evie continued, "Mr. Wilheimer doesn't want to continue discussing the matter today. However, he'll consider your proposal if you agree to get the bank to delay the foreclosure for a fortnight so you can attend his house party the weekend after this, where you can both further discuss the matter."

"He wants me to attend his house party to discuss the matter?" Harrison was incredulous. "Is he joking?"

"Not at all." She shook her head. "He says if you want him to seriously consider your business proposal, then he wants to find out what sort of man he would be entrusting his company to."

"And he thinks a house party is the best way of discovering that?" Did the man really expect him to believe such nonsense? The request for the delay would only be to see if he could pull together the funds, not to measure him as a man at a damn house party.

Wilheimer said something else in German to Evie.

"He says there will be sports and hunting competitions over the weekend that reveal a great deal about a man's character," Evie relayed. "And he says if you want him to consider selling his shares to a man proposing to destroy everything he's built, then you will attend."

"I'm not going to destroy anything," Harrison said through gritted teeth. "And this is a business negotiation, not a social club. Tell him that and tell him he's not in the box seat to be dictating terms to me. He needs to agree to my proposal, or he'll lose everything."

Evie translated his words and the old man shrugged, before replying again in German.

"He says if it is God's will for him to lose

everything, so be it. However, if you're willing to compromise, he's willing to genuinely consider your offer."

"Tell him I know he's trying to delay to find the money somehow, but he won't. Mr. Carter from the bank has already let the other banks know that the Thornton-Jones Conglomerate will blacklist any bank who agrees to lend him any funds."

The man shrugged after Evie translated, then he replied.

"He says then you have nothing to worry over with the delay, do you?"

"He's really prepared to risk losing all he's worked years for, if he doesn't come to the table and negotiate?" The man had to be bluffing.

Evie translated his words, then listened as Wilheimer spoke. "He says, are you also prepared to see this deal fall through simply because you don't want to attend a house party? Especially when you also have much to lose given your uncle's recent financial issues." There was a hint of curiosity in her gaze as she translated the last part but thankfully, she refrained from commenting.

"Ask him how he knows anything about that."

Evie translated and Wilheimer shrugged again before replying.

"He says you're not the only one with contacts in banks."

For several moments Harrison and Wilheimer stared impassively at each other, both trying to get a read of the other.

"I'll get the bank to defer until the Monday after his house party," Harrison said. "And I'll attend, but he will give me an answer while I'm there, or I'll ensure all his loans are called in, and I'll not give him another chance."

After Evie interpreted his words, Wilheimer nodded to Harrison, then glanced to Evie and said something. Whatever the man said had Evie blinking rapidly, before she started shaking her head furiously and responding back in German.

Wilheimer said something again and Evie appeared more annoyed than Harrison had seen her so far, and in his very short acquaintance with the lady, he'd seen her annoyed too many times to count. "What's wrong?"

She blew out a deep breath and glanced back to Harrison. "He's insisting I interpret all your negotiations from now on."

"I can't see a problem with that." Harrison gave a half shrug; it would be the most convenient way forward. "You seem to have done an adequate job thus far."

"Adequate?" She narrowed her eyes, her annoyance at Wilheimer paling in comparison to her annoyance with Harrison.

"A very good job, then?"

"You seriously need to work on your adjectives." She blew out a breath. "In any event, Mr. Wilheimer is insisting I attend the house party, too, so I can interpret for you both."

"He's what?" Harrison's whole body went rigid, and he had to resist swearing aloud at that little revelation. A weekend house party, with this woman present? Such a scenario was a damn recipe for disaster.

"I don't like it any more than you do." She fisted her hands on her hips and glared at him. "Which is why I was trying to convince him to find someone else." She turned back to Wilheimer and rattled something in German to him.

The man shook his head but smiled as he replied.

"Unfortunately, he's insisting I attend given he's impressed by my interpreting skills."

Harrison scoffed. It wasn't her interpreting skills Wilheimer was impressed with; it was the woman herself.

"And now he bids us all farewell."

The man nodded to them, then pushed back his chair and headed straight for the door, his two other men hurrying after him, both glowering at Harrison.

After they left, everyone was silent for a moment.

"I can't go to a house party with Mr. Stone!" Evie blurted out. "It wouldn't be proper without a chaperone."

"My dear girl, in this day and age it's only someone of noble birth or an heiress who ordinarily requires a chaperone," Mrs. Holbrook replied.

"Yes, I know that…" Evie replied. "I suppose I assumed, um, that in England, you were all a bit more proper than everyone in America."

An odd choice of words for her to use, given she was English, too, but she was an unusual woman, he couldn't deny that.

"Oh, we are far more proper, my dear, even if some of us do forget that on occasion," Mrs.

Holbrook said, her face perfectly expressionless. "However, in this instance, I feel it's prudent I attend, too, don't you agree, Mr. Stone?" She turned and stared at Harrison, and he knew she suspected something had gone on between himself and Evie.

"I do, Mrs. Holbrook," he replied, having to clear his throat slightly. "Make the arrangements and ensure Wilheimer's informed of your attendance, too."

The woman nodded and stood. "Of course. Now, if that's all, Miss Jenkins and I will return to our duties." She glanced at Evie, who followed her out of the room.

Harrison let out a deep breath, finally able to relax.

Though he didn't like the idea of being in such proximity to Evie at the house party, given what had already occurred between them, at least with Mrs. Holbrook present there was no way he'd even consider kissing her again. Well, perhaps he'd consider it; he was only human after all, and Evie was an attractive woman.

But he wouldn't act on it, even if every inch of him was screaming for him to.

CHAPTER SEVENTEEN

"I know I wasn't meant to say anything," Aimee began as she hurried along after Mrs. Holbrook down the hallway to their office. "But that translator was jeopardizing the whole deal."

"Relax, Miss Jenkins, I'm not going to berate you for doing the right thing," Mrs. Holbrook replied, walking into the office, and stopping short. "Lady Whitley? I didn't know you were here."

Aimee heard the subtle censure in Mrs. Holbrook's tone and guessed that she was also not a fan of Lady Whitley's. It was one thing they shared.

"Didn't Harrison tell you he's taking me to lunch today?" the lady replied to Mrs. Holbrook, a definite hint of annoyance in her tone.

"No. Obviously he didn't," Mrs. Holbrook replied.

"He does like to keep things to himself, doesn't he," Lady Whitley tittered, her gaze landing on Aimee. "So typical of a man. In any event, has his meeting finished?"

"Obviously, because I'm not still there," Mrs. Holbrook replied.

"And how long will he be then?" Lady Whitley ground out, smiling tightly at Mrs. Holbrook, nothing friendly in the gesture.

"How would I know, Lady Whitley?" Mrs. Holbrook replied with a dainty shrug. "When, as you've just pointed out, he likes to keep things to himself."

There wasn't a hint of an expression on Mrs. Holbrook's face and Lady Whitley clearly didn't know how to respond, so she swung her eyes over to Aimee. "We didn't get properly introduced when I walked in on you and Harrison. Miss Turner, wasn't it?"

"It's Miss Jenkins, actually," Mrs. Holbrook replied on Aimee's behalf. "Now if you'll excuse us, Countess, we need to get back to work." Mrs. Holbrook inclined her head and strode off to her desk.

Aimee went to follow but Lady Whitley reached her hand out onto Aimee's and stopped her.

"It won't work," the countess said.

"What won't?" Aimee replied, even more conscious of her English accent in front of an actual countess.

"Trying to seduce him." She shrugged her shoulders, almost dismissing the matter. "He might have his fun with you, but, in the end, he'll return to me."

"You're more than welcome to him," Aimee insisted, mindful of Deidre trying to eavesdrop from her desk. "What you witnessed won't happen again."

"Yes, well, it wouldn't have meant anything to Harrison, I've known him for years to know that," she replied, her gaze scanning down Aimee's length. "And how are you English? I thought the Thornton-Joneses were American."

"My mother was English, and my father was American," Aimee explained, glad that her accent was adequately fooling the woman. "I grew up here until I was sixteen."

"And you don't go by your father's surname?" the woman asked with such an innocent tone that to the casual listener she sounded completely sincere, but Aimee could see the calculation in her eyes.

"My parents weren't married." Was this what Evie had to deal with every time she spoke to someone about her parentage?

"Oh." The woman's mouth formed a perfect little circle as she slowly nodded. "I see... Does Harrison know that?"

Aimee shrugged, wondering why the woman would care. "I'd assume so, given it's not a secret, though I haven't spoken to him about it specifically." No, they'd been too intent on arguing or kissing each time she'd been alone with him to do anything as mundane as have a proper conversation. "Nor can I see why he'd care."

The man had grown up himself as an orphan, practically on the streets from what her father had said. Despite Harrison's faults, which were many, he didn't strike her as someone who would care about someone's background.

"You're correct, he wouldn't. You are, after all, *only* a trainee secretary," the lady said dismissively, almost like she was trying to convince herself of that fact. "I'm sure you've barely even spoken."

It was hard to speak when kissing someone, that much Aimee had discovered. "Not overly."

"Yes, well, he's been far too focused on the Wilheimer deal," the countess replied. "He's tenacious when he wants something and won't let anything stand in his way. I'm much the same. Once I set my mind upon something, I'll not let anything, or *anyone*, get in my way. Probably why Harrison and I get on so well, we're so alike."

"You seem to know him well."

"*Intimately*, my dear," the woman returned with a self-satisfied smile. "Harrison has been so wonderful to fill the void of my late husband. He's such a kind, considerate man, and is so talented in so many ways. If you understand my meaning."

The woman couldn't have made it plainer she was in an intimate relationship with him, and Aimee felt equally sick and furious he'd kissed her, all the while being involved with this woman. Men like that disgusted her, and she couldn't believe how gullible she'd been. Her initial assumptions about him were correct—he was a bastard, plain and simple. "I think you two are just *perfect* for each other."

"How sweet of you to say," Lady Whitley purred, your eyes narrowing slightly at the obvious sarcasm in Aimee's voice. "And, can I say, what a lovely outfit you're wearing. It's so simple and so delightfully *plain*. So appropriate for someone in your position to dress the part, isn't it? I commend you for it."

It might be a simple dress, but it fit Aimee to perfection, the blue of the skirt offsetting the blue of her eyes, and Aimee knew then and there the woman was jealous of her, perhaps even threatened, too. Well, she didn't need to be, Aimee's level of respect for Harrison Stone had plummeted to rock bottom.

But, still, she didn't take kindly to those who thought they could use their positions to intimidate or belittle others. Which this woman was trying to do in spades. Aimee hadn't navigated the waters of New York Society for her entire life without learning the skills needed to thrive.

"Why thank you, Countess," Aimee replied. "One couldn't likewise claim your Worth gown was plain at all."

The lady arched her eyebrow. "You know your designers?"

"Indeed. The House of Worth is my aunt's favorite, and I regularly travel to Paris with her and my cousin for their fittings."

"You do?" The lady appeared disconcerted with the fact.

"Oh yes," Aimee purred in the exact tone the countess had used earlier. "And now it is I who must commend *you* on your bold choice to wear a gown from their ready-to-wear collection. Goodness, no one in New York Society would dare to wear something from the rack, even if it was a Worth design. It must be different here in London."

The woman's mouth dropped open. "You're very much mistaken. This isn't from Worth's—what did you call it? Ready-to-wear collection. This was custom designed for me by Mr. Worth himself."

Now it was Aimee who arched her own eyebrow. "Lady Whitley, if you're going to tell lies about your outfits, don't do it in front of someone who knows the brand well. Firstly, Mr. Worth doesn't design anything nowadays, given he's ninety years old. It's his sons, Gaston and Jean, who have taken over the reins. Secondly, I was in Paris two years ago and saw that very outfit on their ready-to-wear rack. So, no, it's most definitely not a custom-designed gown of theirs."

Lady Whitley's mouth opened and closed for several seconds as she tried to respond but couldn't find the words to.

"Jane, you waited?" Harrison Stone's deep voice rumbled from behind them, and Aimee felt every inch of her body go on the alert.

He entered the room, his large strides covering the short distance to them with ease, with Ben just behind him, and she had to stop herself from launching at him and punching him for being a two-timing bastard.

But it was her own head she needed to knock some sense into, given her body was still craving him despite knowing what she did. What was wrong with her?

CHAPTER EIGHTEEN

Harrison didn't know why seeing Evie talking with his ex-paramour made him so uncomfortable, but it did. Especially as Evie was glaring at him with daggers and he got the sense she'd draw her pistol on him again if he wasn't careful.

"I said I'd wait for you, and wait for you I always will." Jane smiled graciously at him as he came to a stop next to them.

"I'm sorry, I'm going to have to take a rain check for lunch." He dragged a hand through his hair. "Some unexpected complications have arisen with the Wilheimer deal."

"There's no need to apologize," Jane assured him. "Of course you must attend to business. A rain check won't be a problem."

She was always an astute lady to the goings-on around her, and not for the first time the thought she'd make him an excellent wife flittered through his head. Not only was she poised and elegant but she knew absolutely everyone in Society, and already had experience being a countess. If he were to marry anyone, she was the logical choice given she'd never distract him from his business goals, which was his true love in life. But it wouldn't be fair to marry her or anyone, given he doubted he'd ever love anyone.

Not that that was her fault; after the agony of losing his parents, he'd decided then and there as a young boy that love was too painful, and he didn't want to experience it again. And he'd managed to steer clear of it ever since, having respectful yet emotionally distant relationships, which had served him well and would continue to.

"How about dinner, though?" Jane asked. "You do need to eat sometime today."

He was acutely aware of Evie standing there, listening with a look of haughty distain on her face. "No, I'll have to pass," he responded, noting the slight tightening around the corners of Jane's eyes. "But I'll catch up with you at the Bentley soiree later in the week, perhaps."

Jane inclined her head. "Very well. I shall leave you to your work then."

She extended her hand toward him, and he kissed the back of her glove before she turned on her heel and glided from the room. Harrison glanced at Evie, who seemed particularly unimpressed, and was even, he'd go so far to say, staring at him in loathing.

He felt the urge to explain everything to her, but he wouldn't, because there was nothing to explain, given he hadn't done anything wrong. Well, perhaps apart from kissing Evie herself. That was wrong on far too many levels.

"In my office, Miss Jenkins," he growled. "Mr. Hartley and I wish to discuss what happened in the meeting in more detail with you."

Having Ben with him would ensure nothing untoward would happen again with Evie. Which, if it did, would be a recipe for disaster. A recipe he couldn't afford now, no matter how much he might be craving it.

• • •

After spending the past hour going over exactly what was said, or more specifically what the interpreter didn't say, Aimee was about ready to scream at the two men still barking out question after question.

Ben wasn't so bad but having to be in such close proximity to Harrison, especially after realizing what a jackass he was for kissing her while he was involved with another woman, was pure torture. Particularly when she never wanted to speak to him again, after she gave him a piece of her mind about the situation.

Instead, she was biting her tongue and doing her best to answer their question with a measure of professionalism, unwilling to jeopardize her traineeship over a feckless man. If only her body would subscribe to that, though, instead of being hyper-aware of his every movement. Especially now she knew exactly how it felt to be pressed against him while he kissed her senseless.

"Are you certain he changed the figure to fifty thousand instead of five hundred thousand?" Harrison asked once again.

"Yes. For the tenth time, I'm *positive*. But feel free to ask me an eleventh time, just to see if my answer changes." She pinned him with her eyes. "I dare you."

He cast her a veiled glance. "Every single detail needs to be analyzed."

"Which you've done," she replied. "Honestly,

I've told you everything, in exact detail. I really don't know what else you want me to say. The interpreter was sabotaging the deal."

"The question, though, is why?" Harrison asked, his eyes boring into her own.

"Perhaps he was being paid to by someone like Wilheimer thought?" Aimee shrugged. Her father had spoken of such things happening with other deals over the years.

"One of our competitors perhaps?" Ben added.

"Possibly," Harrison replied.

"I can speak to the agency who hired the interpreter, if you like," Ben said. "See what I can find out about him."

"No. I'll go and speak to them myself," Harrison replied. "What I want you to do is start an internal investigation."

"You think someone from here was responsible?" Ben asked, his eyes filled with doubt.

"I think if someone was prepared to pay Wilheimer's interpreter to sabotage the deal, they'd most likely hedge their bets and pay someone here to do so, too, which may have included tampering with our ledgers."

"Makes sense."

"It's what I'd do." Harrison shrugged.

"Why doesn't that surprise me?" Aimee said, again wondering how her father could think a man like Harrison Stone was worthy of his praise and affection, when he so obviously wasn't. "Dirty tactics seem to be a hallmark of your modus operandi, Mr. Stone."

"It's back to Mr. Stone, is it, *Miss Jenkins*?"

"It is," she confirmed. "Especially after having met your *friend*, Lady Whitley."

Ben cleared his throat. "Perhaps I should leave the two of you to discuss this in private?"

"No!" Aimee and Harrison said simultaneously.

"We're done here anyway," Harrison continued, standing from his chair. "I need to visit that agency before the interpreter has time to hide his tracks and go to ground."

"You do realize I'm going to have to go with you," Aimee replied, supremely annoyed at the thought of being alone with him, though at least they'd be out and about, and not left in a private office. Not that she had any intention of ever kissing him again. No, thank you. He could make do kissing Lady Whitley as far as she was concerned.

"Like hell you're coming with me," Harrison swore, his eyes boring into her own. "You are to stay here and go about whatever duties Mrs. Holbrook tells you to."

Aimee stood and placed a hand on her hip. "And what will you do if you need my interpreting services?"

"The agency *is* an interpreting service," Harrison growled, walking over to the coat stand and taking his jacket from the hook. "I'm sure they'll speak English, don't you?"

"Oh, most certainly. And I'm sure if the German interpreter is there, and he speaks in German, that whoever else is working there will *accurately* and *honestly* translate what he's saying to you in English, won't they?"

He swore again and dragged a hand through his

hair, in what she was beginning to recognize was a mannerism he often employed when frustrated. Which seemed to be a lot in her presence.

"Fine. You can come." He exhaled harshly, a furious expression spreading over his face as he stared at her. "But I'm walking there, so you better keep up."

CHAPTER NINETEEN

Aimee knew she shouldn't be feeling this thrill of excitement to be going with him, especially given her anger toward him, but the idea of assisting him investigate who was behind the attempted sabotage was exciting.

They zigzagged through various thoroughfares and alleys, with Harrison focused on getting to their destination in the quickest time possible, it seemed, barely speaking a word or glancing at her at all. It would be a boring fifteen-minute walk if that continued, and she was still furious with the man for thinking he could toy with her without consequence.

"Does your paramour often visit you at work?" she asked, unwilling to be anything but blunt about the situation.

His steps faltered for a millisecond. "Lady Whitley is not my paramour."

"Oh please, I'm not a fool. It was clear you and she are involved, though she doesn't strike me as the sort of woman who'd appreciate you kissing another woman while you're in a relationship with her. But what would I know? You're the one who knows her *intimately*."

Aimee knew it was inappropriate to be having such a conversation with her boss, but it was a perfectly acceptable conversation to be having with a man who had only recently kissed her.

He stopped in his tracks, his hand reaching over and pulling her to a stop, caring little that several people had to dart around them. "I'm not in a relationship with Lady Whitley."

Ignoring the fission of electricity shooting up her arm from the brush of his fingers against her sleeve, Aimee glowered at him. "I think she might disagree. She made it plain that she considers you hers."

"Well, she's not." He peered at her. "You sound jealous."

"I'm not," Aimee insisted, shaking her hand free from his. "I don't appreciate being kissed by a man who's already in a relationship with another lady. It's not what a proper gentleman would do."

"But I'm not a proper gentleman. My mother was a maid after all."

"Is that how you justify your reprehensible behavior?" This close to him she had a hard time ignoring her desire to lean into him and breathe in his scent fully. "How dare you kiss me while you're seeing her!"

"I'm not seeing her!" He exhaled sharply. "I broke things off nearly two months ago, so there's no reprehensible behavior on my part to justify. Except perhaps for kissing you, which I never should have done, and certainly won't be doing again."

"I'm the one who won't be kissing you again."

"You instigated our kiss today."

"That was to prove a point."

"Is that so?" His voice was a challenging whisper, his head bending down precariously close to her own, until their lips were mere inches away.

The man wouldn't be so bold as to kiss her on a crowded street, would he? Aimee gulped, uncomfortably aware that the thought excited her rather than horrified her. "I thought you said you won't be kissing me again."

"It's your body that's leaning in toward me."

Aimee belatedly realized she was doing exactly that. Darn traitorous body. She straightened back and took a deliberate step away from him. "A derringer is far more effective at close range, perhaps you should remember that."

He stared at her for a moment, with a look that could only be described as baffled amusement. "You're still threatening to shoot me? You know, not one other woman has ever done so before, yet you have on numerous occasions in our short acquaintance."

"That's probably because most ladies you've dealt with before didn't have a derringer to threaten you with. If they'd had one, I'm sure they would've used it."

"My dear lady," he murmured his eyes traveling down the length of her body, making Aimee feel naked. "The furthest thing those ladies were thinking of doing to me was shooting me. They had far more enticing activities in mind, *that* I can promise you."

She believed him, too. Any woman with a pulse could see how darn attractive he was, exuding a raw masculinity that was compelling to the point of impulsiveness. And she was having a hard time not being impulsive when it came to him. But she had to resist. If anyone ever caught her kissing him, she'd be ruined, and worse, possibly forced to marry him with her dreams of ever running anything of her father's swept away in a heartbeat.

She'd never give up her dream for any man, even if he did kiss outrageously well.

Clearing her throat, she dragged her eyes away from his, realizing that even in a crowded street she wasn't immune to the man. It was a weakness she had to put a stop to. "I'll take your word for it. Now, perhaps we should continue on before the interpreter flees the country and this whole endeavor becomes a waste of time?"

"Then stop bloody talking about kissing," he mumbled as he resumed walking down the street while Aimee followed next to him.

"You were the one to mention it," she didn't hesitate to point out. "Are you really not in a relationship with Lady Whitley?"

"No, I'm not," he said candidly. "I promise you that."

And for some reason, she did believe him.

"Are you in a relationship with the man you sent that telegram to?" he in turn asked.

"I suppose it depends on how you define relationship."

His expression grew thunderous, and Aimee couldn't help but grin.

"Oh relax, I'm only joking. I'm not in any relationship with him except for the fact that he's a business acquaintance."

"A business acquaintance?"

"Yes. Now you're the one sounding jealous."

She grinned, enjoying teasing him for once, rather than arguing with him.

"Hardly." Now it was he who rolled his eyes.

"Well, you sound jealous, Harrison." His name sounded so intimate rolling off her lips, and he must have sensed that, too, because for the next several moments neither of them said anything, the atmosphere between them surprisingly charged and uncomfortable. She didn't like it at all. And she especially didn't like that now she knew he wasn't in a relationship with Lady Whitley, thoughts of him kissing her again kept flittering into her consciousness.

Would it be so bad to kiss him again? Of course, it would be if her parents discovered she'd done so, but here in England, with a measure of freedom she'd never had, having always been chaperoned and told what she could and couldn't do, it was highly unlikely anyone would ever find out.

But, no, she couldn't kiss him again. Already he was filling up far too much of her thoughts; thoughts which should be focused on learning her father's business, not thinking about how wonderful his tongue felt caressing hers.

Oh God, even just the thought of that had her eyes glancing over to his mouth, noticing the fullness of his lips from his side profile, and remembering the heady thrill of what they felt like pressing against her own.

She had to stop thinking about his lips. It was distracting and a complete waste of time when she had far more important matters to attend to. "Who do you think is trying to sabotage the deal?" she asked, returning to her safe space of discussing business while dodging out of the way of several street hawkers as she followed him down another street. She had no idea where in London they were, but the flow of pedestrians and carriages had increased.

"It could be any number of possibilities," he eventually replied.

"Who would benefit most from this deal being aborted? It would have to be someone who didn't have stocks in either company, given both ours and Wilheimer's shares have been steadily soaring for the last month since rumors first began about us buying them out. If news leaked that the deal might fall through, stocks in both companies would plummet."

"That's a deft assessment of the situation," Harrison replied.

"If it's correct, it means whoever wants the deal to fall through must want to see the stock prices of both companies fall and would undoubtedly make a profit from them doing so." Then a thought occurred to her. "Is Sampson's Shipping and Building still Wilheimer's main competitor?"

They stopped at a crossing as several large carriages lumbered past, and Harrison glanced over to her. "They are. You think they're behind the sabotage?"

"Weren't they initially the front-runner for the deal before you settled on Wilheimer's business instead? Maybe they want to sabotage the deal with Wilheimer, so you return to them as an alternate. Their stocks rose sharply initially when it was anticipated we'd buy them out, only to plummet when news hit it was Wilheimer's business you'd instead decided upon."

"How is it you know so much about our company, and the stock fluctuations of our competitors, when your uncle said your only interest was fossils?" he asked, placing his hand on her elbow and guiding her across the street as the traffic eased.

His touch sent an avalanche of wanting through her body, and she had to remind herself to walk and not melt into a puddle of mush by his feet.

"Well?" he asked, dropping his hand once they'd crossed to the other side of the road.

Oh, that's right, fossils, Evie's passion. Honestly, Aimee couldn't think of anything more boring than looking at old, dusty rocks. "Yes, well, as much as old rocks fascinate me," she replied, doing her best to sound genuine about a topic that didn't interest her at all, "now that I'm doing this traineeship, I felt it best to immerse myself in the world of business."

He was silent for a moment as they continued walking down the busy street. "So, you like fossils?"

"They're a, um…passion of mine, you could say." A passionate dislike of hers, though Evie did adore them.

"Interesting," he murmured, turning down another street, his footsteps barely making a noise on the cobblestones beneath. "Given you haven't mentioned anything about fossils since you arrived. Not one thing."

"I didn't know I had to." She didn't like where

this was going. He sounded highly suspicious and if he kept asking her questions about fossils, she'd flounder as she hadn't really paid much attention to Evie whenever she went on and on about them. Who cared about ancient rocks anyhow, when there were far more interesting things to discuss, such as stocks, mergers, and sabotage? "Is that the translation office just down there?" She pointed down the street to the left, to where a sign was hanging.

"It is," he said, glancing to the sign, too. "And when we get there, it could prove advantageous if they don't know you speak another language."

"Five other languages," she replied, glad his attention was now diverted back to their purpose rather than on her lack of mentioning fossils.

"So you said earlier," he murmured. "When, though, did you find the time to learn that many languages as a companion?"

"I attended all of my cousin's language lessons with her." Which was true, Evie had attended all of Aimee's lessons, though she'd always brought one of her fossil or history books with her to read instead of participating in the lesson as she was welcome to. "Who'd have thought the lessons would come in handy for some corporate espionage?"

Three minutes later her hopes of being a spy were dashed by the CLOSED sign on the door.

Harrison still knocked and rattled the knob, while Aimee peered through the glass window looking between some gaps in the lace curtains. There wasn't much to see. The front of the office had a desk in the corner with its drawers pulled out and empty, almost like someone had been in a rush to get what was inside and then get out of there.

"It looks like he's already been and gone."

Harrison stopped banging on the door and walked over to stand next to her, glancing through the gaps, too. "You're right. The place looks like it's been emptied out."

"That's because it has been," a woman's voice said from behind them.

Aimee and Harrison both spun around to find a woman in her fifties, staring at them over her spectacles as she stood in the doorway of the flower shop across from them.

"You know the people that work here?" Harrison asked.

"The one person," the lady corrected. "There was only ever Mr. Masterton in his office, though he did have a secretary who occasionally came and did some work for him, but I haven't seen her around much lately."

"Was Mr. Masterton an interpreter?" Aimee asked.

"Aye. And boy did he come through here earlier today in a rush." The woman shook her head. "Looked like the devil was after him, madly dashing about his office, shoving things in his satchel, before fleeing like he was on fire."

"Do you happen to know where he went?" Harrison asked.

The woman pursed her lips. "What do you two want with him?"

"We were in a meeting with him today and he

accidentally left behind several important documents." Aimee patted her satchel. "Which we're hoping to return to him."

"You're not the first trying to find him today," the woman replied. "Not even the second."

"Who else has been here?" Harrison asked.

The woman shrugged. "A lady was looking for him this morning, and then a couple of burly-looking blokes this afternoon. I imagine he probably stiffed them for some money like he did me. He got me to send his wife some flowers the other day, and he promised he'd pay me back given he had a big payday coming," she started to explain, "but lo and behold he hasn't, and the way he left looked like he wasn't coming back anytime soon, so I'm assuming he's gone home and left me out of pocket."

"Do you know where he lives?" Aimee asked her again.

"Just south of Waterloo Station," the woman began. "Unit twelve of sixty, Tower Street. And if he's there, you tell him to come and pay me back for his flowers, or I'll pay him a visit myself."

Aimee reached into her reticule and pulled out a shilling. "Here, that should cover it, plus a bit extra for your assistance, which we're grateful for."

The woman glanced down at the coin Aimee placed into her hand. "Aye, that will cover it and then some. But I can't pay you back."

She went to hand the coin back, but Aimee shook her head. "Keep it. Perhaps one day you might be able to return the favor and help someone else, pay a good deed forward."

"Thank you." The woman nodded, before she

spun around and returned to her store.

Aimee glanced over at Harrison who was staring at her oddly, though she wasn't sure why. "To Tower Street I'm guessing?"

He nodded. "Yes."

They walked to the main road and Harrison hailed a hansom carriage, giving the driver the address of the mysterious Mr. Masterton. Aimee preceded him into the vehicle and wiggled over to the far side, while he settled himself on the seat next to her. The heat radiating from his thigh sent a warm shiver through her and she clenched her fingers tightly in her palms to distract herself from his nearness.

"How long until we get there?" She didn't know if she'd be able to stand sitting this close to him for a lengthy ride.

"Fifteen minutes, depending on traffic." He glanced over to her. "Are you usually so generous with your money?"

"It was only a shilling."

"A generous amount for someone in your position."

"Someone in *my* position?" She was getting angry with his assumptions that Evie had nothing just because of the circumstances surrounding her birth. "What does that even mean? Are you implying my family don't give me anything simply because I was born on the wrong side of the sheets?"

"I'm implying that Thomas told me you'd refused to accept the trust fund he wanted to set up for you, stating you didn't want any charity and would work for your wages," he replied. "For someone who was adamant about that, it seems odd you would so freely give your hard-earned money to others."

"I've been lucky in my life, and if I can help someone, even a little, then I will."

"Those words you spoke to the woman, about paying a good deed forward."

"What about them?"

"Your father says that all the time, doesn't he?"

"He does." Too late she realized she'd fallen into his trap. "My uncle, that is," she hastily tried to correct herself.

"Goddamn it! I knew it!" His expression darkened and she didn't like the look that came into his eyes. "You're not Thomas's niece at all, are you?" he said, staring at her like she was Judas. "You're his bloody daughter, Aimee Thornton-Jones."

CHAPTER TWENTY

"I don't know what you're talking about," Aimee said, her heart pounding.

"Don't lie to me anymore," he ground out, his eyes pinning her with a directness she couldn't escape. "Tell me the truth."

She felt like a fox staring down the barrel of a gun. There was an accusation in his gaze along with a certainty, and she knew her masquerade really was up. At least with him. "Fine. If you must know the truth," she began, dropping her English accent and speaking normally again as a huge sense of relief ran through her with finally being able to be honest with him. "You're right. I am Aimee Thornton-Jones."

"Of course you are. I should have damn well realized that earlier!" he swore, dragging a hand through his hair and then shaking his head. "I knew something was off about you. All the signs were there, and I was a damn fool not to have picked up on them. Your interest in the business. Your confidence and boldness. Your argumentative nature. All at complete odds with the description Thomas gave of you being a reserved and accommodating young woman. Ha! I should have known the instant you walked into my office with the stride of someone who knew her place in the world. How could I have been so stupid to believe your lies?"

"I'm sorry! Truly, I am, but I only lied to you

about my identity. And I didn't want to lie to you in the first place, but I had to."

"Had to?" He scoffed. "Lady, you didn't have to do anything. What you've chosen to do is deliberately lie to me since we met. Though I must commend you on your English accent. It certainly fooled me."

"Well, I'm good with accents, probably on account of all the languages I speak…" Her voice trailed off, as she saw the full fury in the man's eyes. She wasn't scared, but she was worried he'd do something stupid like send her home.

"And what about your cousin? Let me guess, she's pretending to be you, isn't she?"

Aimee could only nod.

Harrison laughed, but there was little humor in the sound. "You sent her into the vulture's nest of English high Society without any concern, all so that you could, what? Have fun slumming it with the rest of us? Fooling us into believing you were someone else? What a great laugh you must be having at our expense."

"It's not like that," she replied, starting to get annoyed at his outrage. "I only did this because I wanted a chance to prove myself to my father. Evie is doing well pretending to be me and is enjoying herself for once." And Evie was, even if she was having to put up with her own version of Harrison, with that duke of hers.

"This has all been one big game to you, hasn't it? Not caring who you step on, or lie to, or hurt in the process. Was kissing me just for laughs, too? Something to entertain yourself with?"

"Harrison, it wasn't like that—"

"How could I have been so stupid to not realize who you were?" he interrupted her, speaking more to himself than her. "The clues were so glaringly obvious, and if I hadn't been so obsessed with you and thinking with my damn cock, I'd have realized it that very first day."

"You've been obsessed with me?" The idea was intriguing as was the second part of his statement, but she didn't have the nerve to repeat those particular words back to him.

"Damn it, Ev—*Aimee*, I should say, shouldn't I? You've lied to me! Continually since we met…"

"I know. I'm sorry, I didn't mean to."

"Didn't mean to?" he exclaimed. "All your actions have been deliberate, not accidental."

"I didn't mean to hurt you."

"You haven't hurt me. You've pissed me off by lying to me, and there's nothing more I loathe than a liar."

"I didn't want to lie. I only switched places for a specific purpose. I've been trying to convince my father to mentor me in his business since I was a little girl, and he's refused to, time and time again."

"And you thought switching places with your cousin would convince him to do so?"

"No. But I hoped by learning all I could of his business, I'd prove to him how serious I am about wanting to be a part of it all."

"You should have gone along with living the life of a pampered heiress. Wanting for nothing, having your every whim catered for."

"And would you have gotten to where you are

in life by going along with the path set out for you?"

"Lady, I was orphaned at eight. The path set out for me was fending for myself on the streets. I'd have given everything I had to have my parents alive and be living on Fifth Avenue with them. I wouldn't want to pretend to be anyone else if I had that."

There was such pain in his eyes that Aimee didn't know what to say. He'd been through so much she'd never had to, and she knew how blessed she was, but being blessed and being happy didn't always align.

"I appreciate my childhood and that my situation in life is not to be taken for granted," she replied. "And that my parents love me and only want the best for me. However, their idea of what my life should be is nothing like what I want for myself. If you hadn't decided a life on the streets wasn't for you, and you wanted to be more and have more, you wouldn't have taken the step to approach my father when you were shining his shoes, would you?"

"He told you about that?"

"Yes. You're the son he's never had and he's proud of all you've accomplished." It had always been a hard pill to swallow when she'd wanted to accomplish so much in her father's company, too.

She paused for a minute, thinking of all the times she'd pleaded, begged, and argued with her father to teach her about his business, only to be told no, every single time. "I might have had the benefit of never having had to want for anything material in my life, but I'd happily give up my inheritance to chase my dreams. That's why I did what I did. This is my one and only chance to prove to them both that this is what I want in life, not what they have mapped out for me."

"Do you think they'll care about that after they find out what you've done?" He shook his head. "They'll be enraged you've lied to them."

"What would you have done in my position?"

"I don't know, but I can confidently say I've never thought about switching identities with anyone."

"That's because you haven't had to! You're a man and your opportunities haven't been limited by your gender." It was so easy for men to succeed in the business arena, but for women it was practically impossible. "My dream in life is not to marry and be some Society wife, but to work with my father. To use the brain and gift for numbers God gave me, instead of pretending to care about who's wearing what, or what the latest scandal is. Can't you understand that?"

"I can," he conceded. "But lying is still lying, Ev—Aimee."

"The world is not so black and white, Harrison. There are many shades of gray, if only you and my father would open your eyes to them." She stared at him, trying to make him see the truth of why she'd done what she had, but his face remained impassive, and she got the feeling he'd already made up his mind and wouldn't be swayed. But she had to try. Otherwise, she was about to lose her only chance to do something with her life, apart from the path already chosen for her.

"I can't stand the future that's been laid out for me. My mother wants me to be the next Dollar Princess, which is why she sent me here. And my father is quite content to go along with her plans, despite my protests to the contrary that it's the last thing I want."

"Oh please," he scoffed. "Are you really telling me you wouldn't want to be a duchess, or perhaps a countess even, if someone asked you?" His stare was intense. "Any woman would."

"If I'd wanted that, you obtuse man, I wouldn't have swapped places with my cousin in the first place!" The man was utterly infuriating. "I couldn't think of anything worse than living in England as a duchess or countess. The weather is atrocious, and everyone is so proper and dour as they swan around from ball to ball. Such a life would be torturous."

"You'd be the only American heiress *not* to want that."

"Do I strike you as a normal sort of heiress?"

"Not even close," he agreed and then sighed. "But, damn it, you know I'm going to have to tell your parents."

"Harrison, you can't!" She reached over, and grabbed his hand with her own. "You mustn't! If you do, they'll insist I return to New York immediately, and then this whole endeavor would've been for nothing. Switching places with my cousin is my one chance to prove to my father that I should be his successor, not you!"

"Me?"

"Oh, don't pretend you don't know that's what he's been grooming you for."

"He's been grooming me to run a company, that's true," Harrison replied. "But to run my own company, not his. Now stop trying to distract me away from the topic of you lying to everyone."

"I'm not trying to distract you," she said. "What I'm trying to do is convince you that I can't let this opportunity slip away."

"And you thought lying would prove to your father you're a worthy successor?"

"I know it's not an ideal way to go about it."

"You don't say?"

"And I haven't worked out the finer details yet of how I broach that subject with my father." She dropped her hand from his, glaring at him in displeasure. "But I want to do so on my timeline, not yours."

He shook his head and exhaled harshly. "I have to tell them, Aimee. I don't have a choice. I respect your father too much to take part in deceiving him."

"You have a choice." She felt like grabbing his jacket and shaking some sense into him. Not that she'd be successful, given he was as movable as a mountain. "You're just choosing the easy way out."

"The easy way out?" He scoffed. "Nothing about you or this situation is easy! The whole thing is as messy as a dog's breakfast, but I'm choosing to be honest with your father as I've always been."

"Oh really? And once you tell him and he insists I return to New York, what will you do about the Wilheimer deal and his house party?" she asked. "Wilheimer specifically requested my attendance, and I assure you he will take offense if you attend with a different interpreter."

"He'll adapt."

"He's a stubborn old German, just like my grandmother was, so no, he won't. Instead he'll be offended, I guarantee it." When her grandmother had decreed something, that was how it had to be, no questions or changes allowed. "You'll kill this deal if you tell my father, but it mustn't be that important to you if you're willing to."

"Not important?" His voice was tinged with mockery. "It's the most important deal I've ever undertaken, and one I've been working on day and night for the past month."

"Why is it so important to you?" It wasn't the first time the Thornton-Jones Conglomerate was trying to buy out another company, and it certainly wouldn't be the last.

He stared at her for a full minute, and she could tell he was weighing up how to answer her. "About seven years ago I approached your father with a plan. If I could start up a London arm of the company and increase our shipping routes to become the largest this side of the Atlantic, then your father would agree to sell me the majority share of stocks in the London company."

"He agreed to that?" Her father always insisted that maintaining control of his companies was imperative to his overall success and wealth. "So, you don't want to take over the American side of the business."

"I want to run my own company, one I've

created from the ground up, which is what this London venture is. And your father knew I'd move heaven and earth to achieve my vision."

"But Father hates giving up control of anything."

"True, but he's pragmatic enough to know he can't be in two places at once. With this deal, though he'd be giving up his majority shares for the London company, he'd still be the second largest shareholder this side of the Atlantic, which only bolsters his share value for the American arm of the company which he retains full control over. It's a win-win for us both."

"Then why would you dare jeopardize that by telling my father what I've done?"

He pressed his lips together and stared at her. "I wouldn't be jeopardizing anything. I told you, I'll simply hire another interpreter."

"Yes, because that worked out well for Wilheimer and you last time."

"That interpreter was obviously paid off."

"And what makes you think another won't be?" she asked. "Clearly, someone wants to sabotage this deal, and I'm the only one you can truly trust to correctly interpret for you."

"Yes, my trust for you is at an all-time high, given your honesty thus far."

She narrowed her eyes at his sarcasm. "Fair enough. However, surely you'd agree that my loyalty to the company isn't in question."

"Perhaps."

"If you want this deal to succeed, you can't tell my father the truth, at least not until your goal has been achieved." He wasn't looking convinced by her argument, and she realized she was going to have to up the ante. "Plus, I don't think my father would appreciate finding out you've been kissing his daughter. He might even think you were trying to seduce me for my inheritance and fire you on the spot."

Harrison's eyes went stormy. "And how could I damn well do that when I thought you were your impoverished cousin this whole time?"

Aimee shrugged, knowing it wasn't the case at all, but desperate times called for desperate measures. "For all my father and I know, you knew who I was all along and just pretended to go along with it so you could get close to me and seduce me."

"You have one hell of a nerve to suggest that. I don't need your money. I've made quite enough of my own and will make even more once this deal goes through."

"Are you telling me you'd turn down a one-million-dollar dowry?" She had to admit to taking a little bit of pleasure using his own reasoning back at him. "No man would."

He narrowed his eyes. "Just like you couldn't stand being a countess, I couldn't stand being a kept man! And, damn it, why the devil would you even tell your father about us kissing? He doesn't need to know that."

"True, I could simply say nothing, couldn't I? It wouldn't be lying to him, simply omitting some of the details of my trip." She tapped her finger to her chin. "Much like you also don't have to say anything to him either about my identity swap with

Evie…you wouldn't be lying to him, you'd be omitting some of the details, just as I would."

"I don't take well to blackmail."

"It's not blackmail." She crossed her arms over her chest. "It's pointing out your double standards in expecting me to stay silent about our kisses yet at the same time suggesting you have to satisfy your conscience by telling my father about my swap, when all you have to do is stay silent, too! Is that not the height of double standards?"

"Damn it," he swore, raking his fingers through his hair. "It is."

Finally, some logic was prevailing with the stubborn man. "At the end of the day, if you tell him of my ruse, then you're not only risking the Wilheimer deal, but you're also potentially ruining the relationship you have with my father, because I will tell him we kissed."

"You'd be too mortified to do that."

She raised her brow and stared him straight in the eyes. "Try me."

"You really would, wouldn't you?"

"Like you keep saying how this deal is so important to you, that's how I feel about this opportunity of switching places with my cousin," she replied. "So, the question you have to ask yourself is are you willing to risk both of those things, when it would be much simpler for everyone if you stayed silent."

"If Thomas ever finds out I knew about your deception and didn't tell him, he'd never forgive me."

"Of course he'd forgive you," Aimee declared,

throwing her hands up in the air, finding the man's stubbornness beyond frustrating. "He thinks of you like a son. However, he won't find out, provided you don't say anything. It will be a win-win for us both."

"Don't throw my words back at me, Aimee Thornton-Jones." He turned in his seat toward her, leaning down until he was mere inches away and his shoulder was lightly brushing against hers. "So that's it then? I don't say anything, and you continue pretending to be your cousin."

"Is that really so hard, given you're essentially asking me to do the same thing by not saying anything about you kissing me?"

"If I remember correctly, it was you who kissed me first on the last occasion."

"Semantics." She waved a hand in the air, trying not to blush thinking about their last kiss earlier in the day. A kiss her body was begging to be repeated.

"Is it? Tell me, was kissing me all part of the ruse?" he drawled, his mouth getting dangerously close to her own. "A bit of fun at my expense while you pretended to be your cousin. Or perhaps you meant to distract me from discovering the truth about you?"

Aimee gulped, her pulse skittering out of control at his nearness. "I distract you?" She was glad to hear it, given he'd been distracting her the entire time since she'd met him.

"Every goddamn moment," he growled. "Even in my dreams."

Then, before Aimee could blink, his lips were

claiming hers, branding her with heat and fire, as a delicious flame of desire flickered to life deep inside her from his touch. She moaned, caring little that she'd told herself she wouldn't kiss him again, when all she could think about right then at that moment was Harrison.

As his lips coaxed hers open, she didn't hesitate to respond. This time, he was kissing her knowing exactly who she was, and it made it so much more enticing. She wrapped her arms around his shoulders and pulled him even closer against her, reveling at the feel and taste of him as his tongue stroked against her own.

Kissing him was so wrong, but felt so right, and no matter how she tried to tell herself she shouldn't, her body didn't care. This whole trip was the one time when she wasn't chaperoned or supervised or restricted by the tight constraints her life in New York held. The one time she could embrace passion with a man she'd hated for so long but craved with an intensity bordering on desperation.

The one time she could truly be free.

CHAPTER TWENTY-ONE

He'd intended to reprimand her for her deception, not kiss her until they were both breathless with desire. But when it came to this woman, he was beginning to realize how little control he had over his more base needs whenever she was within reach.

The idea to kiss her again hadn't been his best to date, but sitting there so close to her on the carriage seat, his thigh brushing her skirts, he hadn't been able to resist, even though he'd been annoyed out of his mind at the deception she'd pulled on him and was asking him to continue. And she was right, as much as he was loath to admit it. If he told Thomas, he would insist she return to New York immediately, and for some reason Harrison didn't want her to go.

So give in to the delight and sensations that this woman aroused in him, he did, despite the fact he knew nothing good could come from it. She was Thomas's only child and no matter how Harrison might want to pretend it wouldn't matter, as soon as Thomas found out Harrison had compromised his daughter, he'd want to kill him, pseudo-son or not. And his dreams of owning his own company would be dead in the water.

But even that wasn't enough to stop his mouth slanting over hers, all rational thought fleeing as he tasted and savored the exquisite delight that was her. He'd never wanted anyone more than he wanted this woman, who was kissing him in defiance of everything. She tasted sweet and luscious, and he knew he could taste her for a lifetime and never stop wanting her, such was the spell she'd woven over him.

The thought stopped him cold, and he dragged his lips away from hers. "Damn it, we can't keep doing this."

"Why not? Don't you want to kiss me?"

Of course he did. It was all he'd been able to think about, but the fact he was suddenly considering doing it for a lifetime scared the hell out of him. After his parents died, he'd promised himself he wouldn't love someone that much again, and he had no intention of going back on his own word to himself. "It has nothing to do with wanting to kiss you or not, and everything to do with this being a bad idea given nothing can come of it. I don't ever intend to marry or fall in love."

"Who said anything about those things?" She looked horrified at the thought. "I have no intention of marrying or falling in love, either, so whatever this is between us"—she gestured with her hand between them—"is perfect. We can enjoy kissing each other without any repercussions, and then I'll return to New York, and we can go on with our lives."

"It's not that simple," he insisted, trying to convince not only her but himself, too.

"Why not?"

"I don't know…" And for the life of him, right then he couldn't think of an argument to dissuade her, or himself for that matter.

"Well, I do." She grabbed his lapels and drew him back to her, her mouth finding his with a vigor that made him willing to do anything she wanted, consequences be damned. His mouth pressed against hers, their lips teasing and tasting each other's until they were both breathless again.

He pulled slightly back from her, staring down at her red, slightly swollen lips. "You taste so damn good. No wonder I can't stop wanting more."

With a huge grin, she wound her hands up around his neck. "That's one more thing we can agree on."

He smiled before pulling her onto his lap. She laughed and wiggled her derriere against him as she settled against him. Harrison groaned at the sensation. The woman did things to him that made him want to throw caution to the wind. "You smell delicious."

"So do you," she sighed, pressing her nose against his neck, before she started to lightly trail her lips over his skin, softly kissing down the column of his neck.

He closed his eyes in bliss as warmth rushed down his spine from her touch, but then the carriage clattered to a halt, and he cursed. Quickly, he shifted her from his lap onto the seat beside him as the driver banged on the ceiling of the carriage.

"Looks like we're here," he said, having to restrain himself from reaching out and pulling her back onto his lap, such was his urge to continue kissing her. The driver banged again on the ceiling.

"I suppose we better go," she said, sounding as

disappointed as Harrison felt while she turned the door handle and exited the vehicle.

Harrison had to adjust himself, cursing at how the woman could make him as stiff as a poker simply from a kiss. Thankfully, his black coat would hide most of his arousal while he worked on returning his attention back to the task at hand.

Stepping out after her, he paid the driver, then glanced up at the building Aimee was already staring at. It was a three-story apartment block that had seen better days. The bricks were cracking and caked in grime, the white paint of the door and windowsills had mostly flecked off, with the little remaining a dull gray from dirt accumulated on it, and the front door was wide open, the lock on it having been broken at some point.

"This isn't the best area of London, so stay behind me until I'm confident it's safe," Harrison said, motioning with his hand to his rear, glad for once when instead of arguing, she nodded and fell in behind him. "If I'd known you'd be so compliant simply from kissing you in a carriage, I'd have done so much sooner."

"Very funny," she replied, following behind him as he walked into the building. "Interpreting mustn't be a lucrative profession."

"Doesn't seem so, does it." The entry hallway was as dilapidated as the outside, with fading and cracked wallpaper throughout, and a layer of dust covering every inch of floor the residents hadn't walked a path through. A sign on the wall indicated units eight through sixteen were on the second floor.

"Do you think he's home?" Aimee asked as they began climbing the stairs up to the second level where Harrison assumed unit twelve was.

"I hope so. I have some questions I want answered." And if he was here, Harrison had no intention of leaving until he found out who'd paid him to try to sabotage the negotiations.

Cresting the stairs to the second floor, Harrison glanced at the door numbers of the apartments. "This way." He turned to the right and led the way down the corridor toward number twelve, but stopped several feet from the unit when he caught sight of the open door. He held out his hand behind him to stop Aimee from advancing, and she paused, too, her eyes following his to the door.

"Stay here," he whispered. "Until I make sure it's safe."

She rolled her eyes but nodded.

"I mean it," he said before starting to approach the door.

The first thing he noticed was the lock hanging from the door, almost like someone had taken to it with a hammer. He stopped and listened for a few seconds, but there was no sound coming from inside. Pulling out his revolver, he gently cocked the hammer, then slowly pushed open the door. He glanced around the unit but couldn't see any movement, so he slowly pushed the door fully open and walked inside.

It looked like a bomb had exploded. Furniture was toppled over, stuffing pulled out of the lounge and cushions, papers tossed all over the floor, the whole room obviously given a thorough search by someone.

Walking farther into the room, he noted an ajar door over to his left, presumably the bedroom, and then there was a small kitchen to his right, with all the cupboards open wide and the contents dumped onto the floor. Someone had been searching for something.

"What do you think they were looking for?" Aimee asked from behind him, and Harrison cursed.

"I told you to wait."

"Which I did," she replied, with a shrug. "After you entered and I didn't hear any noise to suggest fighting, I assumed it was safe. It seems my assumption was correct, doesn't it?"

Harrison holstered his pistol and shook his head. The woman was impossible. "No wonder your father always laments you getting into mischief."

"If only he really knew."

Harrison groaned. "God, I can only imagine."

She dared to grin. "Perhaps one day I'll even tell you. Anyhow, what do you think happened here? It's too coincidental to simply be a break-in."

"I agree."

"We're getting rather good at agreeing, aren't we?" She winked at him as she wandered over to the kitchen and began glancing through the open cupboards. "You'll have to be careful, or you might just start to agree with me on most things."

Harrison had to smile at that. "I doubt it." He glanced around the room and noticed some spots of red fluid on the floor near the bedroom. Walking over, he crouched down. "Looks like there's some blood here."

"Masterton's?" Aimee came over and crouched beside him.

"I'm not sure," he replied, trying not to notice how her very nearness made it near impossible to concentrate on anything else but her. "Could be, though the florist mentioned he was married, so it could be his wife's, too."

"There are too many questions and not enough answers," she said, standing and placing her fists on her hips as she stared around the room. "Why would someone want to ransack his unit?"

Harrison stood also, then shrugged. "Perhaps he had some incriminating evidence? If someone is trying to manipulate share prices, that's an offense punishable by prison, so whoever's behind it might be trying to ensure they're not discovered."

"That makes sense."

"We do seem to be agreeing with each other… far too much."

"I *agree*." She winked at him, and all Harrison wanted to do right then was sweep her up in his arms and feast upon that delectable mouth of hers. What was wrong with him?

"I don't think there's much we'll find here," he gruffly said, looking around the room, anywhere but at her. "But, still, it's worth taking a look."

Ten minutes later, after they'd gone through the unit, Harrison concluded that Masterton must have tried to flee, given he'd stuffed all his clothes and personal items from his wardrobe into some trunks in his room, but then must have been interrupted, because his trunks were still in the room but there was no sign of Masterton apart from some more blood splattered on the floor. Not enough to suggest a mortal wound, but enough to suppose the man had suffered a rather decent whack to the head.

"Well, one thing's obvious," Aimee said, standing up after having gone through the man's trunks. "It's doubtful he had a wife."

"I'd noticed that, too," he replied. There were no women's clothes in the trunks, or any feminine finishes in the unit to suggest a woman had been living there.

"So why would he send flowers to a nonexistent wife?" Aimee tapped at her chin. "Or alternatively, why would the florist lie to us?"

"Who knows," a man's rough voice spoke from the doorway. "And who cares."

Harrison glanced up to see a burly man standing in the doorway to the bedroom, holding a pistol. "And you are?"

"No one to concern ya self about. Don't go thinking about pulling out ya pistol, either." The man nodded down to Harrison's jacket. "I'll shoot ya before you can draw it." He cocked the hammer of his gun to emphasize his point. "Now slowly, with two fingers, pull out ya weapon and toss it to the floor. And no funny business, or I'll shoot this lady here." He turned his gun upon Aimee, and Harrison felt a fury burn deep in his stomach.

With a terse nod, Harrison did as instructed, slowly pulling his revolver from his holster and tossing it onto the floor, in the opposite direction of the man.

"Oy, I didn't say throw it that way." The man sounded annoyed. "I meant for ya to toss it to me."

Harrison gave a half shrug. "You didn't say that."

The man narrowed his eyes and motioned with his gun to the far wall. "You go over and wait there, while I fetch it. And you, just stay put." He said the last to Aimee.

Wandering casually over to the far wall as instructed, Harrison's eyes were anything but casual as they watched the man like a hawk, assessing the best way to gain the upper hand. Though the man had the solid build of a boxer, he'd clearly not been training regularly if the girth around his stomach was any indication. Harrison also had a good four or five inches on him, and if he could get him in close, he could wrestle the gun from him.

But he realized he'd forgotten who he was in the room with. The man strode past Aimee heading to Harrison's gun, obviously having dismissed her as no threat. A mistake, to be sure, when it came to this woman, and when the man passed her, she immediately pulled out her derringer and rushed in behind him, pressing her weapon into his back and cocking the hammer.

"Move a muscle and I will shoot you in the back," she said, with such a calm confidence that the man stopped in his tracks. Harrison covered the distance over to them and wrenched the gun from the man's hand before quickly retrieving his own pistol and returning to face the man.

"I was told you were the only one with a gun,"

the man said to Harrison, sweat breaking out on his forehead as Aimee walked over next to Harrison, her gun staying steadily aimed at the thug.

"Life is so unfair sometimes, isn't it?" Aimee answered with such composure, despite the danger of the situation, that Harrison couldn't help but be impressed. She turned to Harrison and grinned, and right at that moment, he was bowled over by just how magnificent she was. "How about that?" she said to him. "I saved *you* this time."

He was silent for a moment staring at her, wondering rather desperately if perhaps she could save him from himself...from a future of loneliness, with only his work to keep him company...

Hastily, he cleared his throat. They had no future together, not after the next few weeks, and that was that. There could never be more between them. She'd said it herself, she didn't want to be a countess and live in England, and that's where his path lay, as much as he didn't want it. Not that he wanted to marry her, even if the idea of waking up with her naked in his bed each morning was becoming an irresistible fantasy.

"Not bad at all," he eventually answered, before very deliberately turning his attention back to the man. "Who sent you and told you I was armed?"

"The man who hired me," the man replied with a shrug.

Harrison pressed his lips together. The thug certainly wasn't the brightest spark. "And who is that man?"

"Don't know," the man answered, but there was

no hint of belligerence in his tone. "I'm a contractor, ya see. I get sent instructions from my booking manager, and I follow those. The message said to come to this address and be careful 'cause you have a gun, but to get the accounts books she'd have on her." He glanced over at Aimee and then down to the satchel strapped over her shoulder. "I wasn't gonna hurt ya, neither of ya."

"You're after the ledgers?" she asked. "You're not looking for Mr. Masterton?"

"I don't know no Mr. Masterton. Just needed the books in ya bag is all."

"And where were you meant to take the ledgers?" Harrison asked him.

"There's someone waiting downstairs in a hackney for them. I was meant to give 'em to 'em."

"They're probably still there waiting!" Aimee exclaimed, glancing over to Harrison. "And if they are, we could find out who's behind all of this."

He could already see the intention in her eyes. "No. Damn it, Aimee, it could be a trap, or the man is lying to get us to rush off…" She ignored him and turned on her heel.

"You stay here and guard him!" she yelled over her shoulder, making a beeline for the door. "I'll go and see if I can find the carriage."

"Fuck me!" Harrison swore.

"She seems like a handful," the man said, staring after Aimee as she disappeared through the front door of the unit.

"The understatement of the century," Harrison growled. "You, stay there." He grabbed the bedroom key from the lock, then spun around and slammed the bedroom door shut behind him, quickly locking it in his wake. He hoped it might keep the man contained, but he didn't like his chances. However, he couldn't let Aimee confront someone who potentially was behind this whole mess on her own.

He raced after her, vowing that when he caught up with her, he was going to spank her on her damn impulsive ass.

CHAPTER TWENTY-TWO

As soon as Aimee bolted out of the unit block, she noticed two things. One, it had started to rain, and two, there was indeed a hackney cab waiting across the road. Disregarding the downpour, she checked the road for oncoming traffic, then dashed over to the carriage.

She caught a glimpse of someone behind the curtain in the back seat, but a moment later, in a flurry of motion, the carriage took off down the road, mud splattering up from the wheels, covering her in a grimy mess.

Standing there, with rain pouring down on her, and her hair and clothes now drenched, Aimee could only watch as their best lead disappeared down the street. She sighed and trudged back over to the unit block, noting that Harrison was there, standing under the entrance portico of the building, his arms folded over his chest, a scowl on his face, with his clothes and hair completely dry.

She glanced down at the mud all over her dress and felt like a drowned rat. Not the image she wanted to portray in front of him, but not much she could do about it now.

"Are you always so damn impulsive?" he said without hesitation, glaring at her like she was some errant child.

She stomped over to him, mostly because her skirt was sloshing with water and weighed about a ton. "I told you to stay with the man."

He shook his head. "Unbelievable! I couldn't leave you rushing off after whoever might be behind all this. What if you'd been hurt or kidnapped?"

"Oh, for goodness' sake. You're obsessed with me being kidnapped when it's never happened before."

"Of course it hasn't happened before, because your father has always made certain you've been well protected." His eyes traveled down her soaked outfit.

"I couldn't pretend to be Evie if I took a chaperone everywhere, now, could I?" she replied, wringing out some wet strands of hair that had escaped her bun. "Besides, I'm enjoying my freedom, and I intend to make the most of it on this trip."

"You're an impossible woman." He dragged a hand through his hair. "You're a bloody heiress who's worth a fortune. If someone found that out, you could be in danger."

"No one is going to find out." She stormed past him and began to climb the stairs, hearing him follow behind her. "Besides, of late, I always seem to be in your *fun* company. So I'm completely safe."

They got to the second floor and as soon as they were in the hallway, she felt Harrison's hand on her upper arm as he pulled her to a stop.

"Who says you're safe when you're with me?" he said, turning her around to face him, before his lips pressed hungrily down upon her own.

She all but melted under the onslaught as his full lips pressed against her own, kissing her with a thoroughness that left her breathless and wanting more. But then he wrenched his mouth from hers and strode past her down the corridor, as if their brief kiss had meant nothing to him. "Come on," he said without even looking back. "Let's see if that man is still locked in the room, which I doubt."

Fuming at his attitude, Aimee trudged behind him into the unit, only to find out Harrison was right, the man had fled. He'd first broken through the bedroom door, presumably barging through it with his shoulder, given the door had been ripped from its frame and was now hanging from only one hinge.

"Damn it!" he swore. "I knew he'd be gone." He turned to stare at her, his glare accusatory. "You shouldn't have run off like that."

"Don't blame me for this. I told you to stay here."

"I'm not one of your servants or lackeys to be told what to do, *princess*." His glare got even more ferocious.

Now it was Aimee's turn to return his glare in full. "I don't have *lackeys*, and I'm not a *princess*," she ground out between clenched teeth. "And it's a bit rich you're berating me for giving orders when you dish them out like candy yourself. *Do this, do that.* You can't seem to help yourself. Do you think you're the only one who can tell people what to do?"

"Generally, given I'm their boss, yes. What's your qualification to do so, apart from being a pampered heiress with servants galore to boss about to your heart's content?"

"I don't boss about my servants." She crossed

her hands over her chest. The nerve of the man to suggest so.

"Oh please, you've grown up watching your parents tell people what to do your entire life. Giving orders is practically in your blood." He shook his head and strode through the unit toward the front door. "Now, come on, there's no point hanging around here, seeing as we've damn well lost our only lead."

"You say *damn* quite a lot." Aimee hurried to follow him. "Did you know that?" He spun around and glared at her, but Aimee merely shrugged. "It's true."

"I don't normally curse so much," he ground out through clenched teeth, before turning around and heading along the corridor then down the stairs. "Want to take a guess as to why I have over the past week?"

"Are you implying I'm the cause?" She lifted her wet skirt as she navigated down the stairs, her boots squelching with each step on the wooden boards.

"I'm not *implying* anything. I'm stating a fact." He got to the bottom and strode out through the entrance hall to the street outside, which now only had a slight drizzle of rain softly sprinkling on the footpath.

Just her luck. Here she was looking like a wet rag doll, while Harrison looked like the golden-haired Adonis he always did. "You're annoying." Honestly, she felt like throttling him sometimes. His arrogance and highhandedness were so frustrating.

"Right back at you, princess."

"Argh, stop calling me that!" she said as he hailed a hackney over to them.

The hackney pulled up beside them and Harrison started to give the driver Mrs. Holbrook's address.

"No," Aimee quickly interrupted him. "Take me to the Mayfair Grand."

He blinked several times, and it was the first time she'd seen him appear at a loss for words.

"I'm not taking you to my hotel." His voice was low and strangled.

"It's my father's hotel," she replied. "And don't give yourself unwarranted praise. I have no intention of staying with you."

"Then why do you want to go there?"

"I've rented myself a suite for my stay, and given I'm soaked with rain and mud I want to have a bath and clean up before I return to Mrs. Holbrook's." She stepped into the carriage and took a seat as Harrison gave the hotel name to the Hackney driver and stepped in behind her, closing the door with a thud.

"You've rented yourself a suite?" His eyes narrowed on her as he sat down on the opposite seat across from her. "Why am I not surprised."

"I had to," she replied, wondering why he hadn't sat next to her like on their last trip. "I don't intend to stay there, just make use of the bath when I get some free time to myself."

They sat there in silence for several minutes while the carriage navigated through the afternoon traffic.

"Do you always do whatever you want?" Harrison's deep voice broke the silence. "Obstacles be damned?"

"I don't often get the chance to in New York, but when I do get an opportunity, I try to make the most of it. After all, if you don't go after what you want in life, you'll never get it, so you might as well chase what you want. That's what my father says, and I've taken it to heart."

"Clearly." He shook his head. "Who else would think to rent a suite for her entire stay, simply to make use of the bath on occasion, instead of slumming it like the rest of us have had to?"

"Haven't you been living there in a suite since you moved over here? All on my father's largesse?"

He pressed his lips together. "I've worked damn hard to get to where I am, and, yes, I've stayed there in a suite because it makes little sense to buy anything when I'll eventually…"

His voice trailed off and Aimee angled her head toward him. "When you'll eventually what?"

"It doesn't matter," he replied. "And staying there was your father's idea. But I still wouldn't waste money on a suite to have an occasional bath."

"You would if you had to share the bathwater with several other people."

"Share the bathwater?" He appeared dumbfounded at the idea.

"Yes. Mrs. Holbrook only allows one bath to be run per week, and that's not one bath per person, that's one bath in total, for the entire household.

Which means all of us ladies have to use the same bathwater, and I would be the last, being the new-comer. Can you imagine how dirty that water would be when it got to my turn?"

A shiver ran through her at the thought. "As much as I wish to embrace the experience of being my cousin, having to share my bathwater is a line I'm unwilling to cross, especially when I have the means to make alternate arrangements. If that makes me a pampered princess in your eyes, then so be it."

She wished that were true, because for some odd reason his opinion of her mattered. It mattered a lot. Which made no sense given she disliked him so much…well, she didn't dislike him, not really. He just made her so frustrated sometimes that she felt like screaming or launching herself into his lap and recommencing what they'd been doing earlier.

How could kissing anyone feel so good as it felt when she kissed him? The man who'd irritated her for as long as she could remember. But try as she might to understand her feelings for him, thinking about it only confused her more. So rather than focus on that, she decided to change the subject to something she was as equally confused about but would be far easier to find answers to. "Why do you think someone sent that man to retrieve the ledgers I've borrowed?"

"I'll need to have a closer look at them to try to ascertain that," he replied, accepting the change in topic without question. "Are they at Mrs. Holbrook's?"

"No, I left them in my hotel room, so I could go

through them in more detail after work today, before I eventually went back to Mrs. Holbrook's."

"Won't she get suspicious if you're always sneaking off after work?"

"I just tell her I'm visiting my cousin." Aimee shrugged.

"Lying seems to come naturally to you."

"It's simply being creative about the situation. How else would I achieve my goals?"

"And what are your goals? To work with your father in a business environment?" he asked, sounding doubtful. "Most girls your age want to go to balls and dance the night away, not read ledgers in their spare time."

"I'm one-and-twenty, Harrison Stone. I'm a woman, not a girl."

He grinned. "Yes, you're ancient."

She rolled her eyes blatantly in front of him. "Not as ancient as you."

His grin was quickly replaced by a frown. "I'm only thirty."

"Why haven't you married yet?" she asked, suddenly curious. "You're well past the age most men do."

"I've been busy creating my fortune."

"Most men marry to do that. So why not you?"

"That's none of your business." He glanced out the window, an expression on his face saying the topic was closed, but Aimee was never one to blithely accept defeat, especially not when she wanted an answer.

"I rather think it is, given you've kissed me, several times in fact. You'll probably even kiss me several more times before I leave, too."

"Excuse me?"

"Oh, let's stop pretending with each other. We might not particularly like each other, but we're certainly attracted to each other, and there's no denying that."

He cleared his throat. "I liked it better when you were pretending to be your cousin and weren't so forthright."

"Yes, I imagine you did. But, in any event, why haven't you married? Most men trying to climb the corporate ladder like to take a wife to do so. And you know my father always likes his employees to have a stable family life."

"Why haven't you taken a husband?" he replied. "According to your father, you've had ample opportunity to."

"I have. However, the simple fact is, I don't want to marry."

"Most women do."

"Neither of us are like most other people, are we?" She took in a deep breath. "I want to conquer the world, and a husband would never let me do that."

"You're very like your father."

"I am, though, unlike my father, every hurdle has been thrown my way and I've had to find ways to jump them all. A husband, however, wouldn't just be a hurdle, he'd be a mountain I wouldn't be able to shift."

"That's probably true here in England," he replied. "But in America, you know the gentlemen are much more accommodating of their wives being outspoken and daring."

"Being outspoken and daring is one thing. Wanting to run my father's empire? That's another thing entirely."

"Why do you want to?" There was no sarcasm or mockery in his question, only curiosity. "Most women are more than content to be the queens of their domestic domains, not want to run a multimillion-dollar company."

"When I was seven…" she began, thinking back to that moment when she'd been reading a journal on the floor in the library, hidden behind a desk, and her father and grandfather had come into the room discussing the succession plan of the company. "I overheard my father and grandfather talking about what they'd do in the future with the company, given my mother could never have more children after the complicated birth she'd had with me."

Ever since Aimee had realized it was essentially her fault her parents hadn't been able to have more children, part of her had always felt guilty, even though rationally she knew her parents didn't blame her. So she'd always felt the need to prove to them that she was enough, not that they'd ever made her feel she wasn't, even if that's how she felt.

"If I'd been a boy," she continued, "they wouldn't have needed to have that conversation, because it would've just been assumed I'd take over the company. It was in that moment that I decided I'd do whatever it took to prove to them that I could continue on the family legacy and be a worthy successor to my father, despite the fact I'm a girl."

"Have you told your parents this?"

She smiled, but it was filled with the ache of sadness. "Oh, we've had many heated conversations about it, with neither of them able to understand why I'd want to work when I could marry and have children, living a life of continued luxury."

"Isn't that what most people want, though? Marriage and children."

"Then why aren't you married and a father already?"

"Not all of us are destined for that path," was his gruff reply as he adjusted his legs in the confined space.

"That's certainly true."

"I'm surprised you're so jaded about marriage when your parents have an ideal marriage."

"Yes, they're still very much in love with each other even after twenty-three years." An unusual fact in their world.

"Don't you want the same?"

"I haven't yet met a man I could imagine spending a future with." And she hadn't, at least not until recently. The thought sent a chill down to her toes. No. This man wasn't even close to being someone she could spend her life with. "Even if I met someone I could fall in love with, I doubt he'd accept me wanting to run a company. Not even my father allows my mother to work."

"Knowing your mother, I imagine if she did want to work, your father wouldn't be able to stop her."

"That's true." Aimee smiled. "She's formidable. Mrs. Astor better watch out."

"Mrs. Astor?"

"The reason my mother sent me over here in the first place. She wants me to marry into the aristocracy so she can lord it over Mrs. Astor and never again not be invited to the woman's annual ball."

"Ah, yes, Mrs. Astor's famed annual ball."

"Anyhow, now that you know why I have no intention of marrying, tell me, why don't you want to marry?"

He was silent for so long Aimee didn't think he was going to answer her.

"I made a deal with myself when my parents died that I wouldn't suffer through that pain of losing someone I love again. Hence why I've never married and never will."

The raw pain in his eyes made her own heart ache for him. Leaning forward, she reached over and took his hand in her own, her fingers intertwining with his and squeezing them. "I can't pretend to imagine it." Which she couldn't. The thought of losing her parents or Evie was enough to make her want to start bawling. "All I can say is I'm so very sorry."

He didn't say anything in reply, but his thumb brushed over her palm, and Aimee felt the heat of it curl all the way down to her toes.

"I suppose that's another thing we agree on," she said, trying to lighten the mood. "Marriage is definitely overrated, and not for either of us."

His lips twitched at the corners. "At the rate we're starting to agree on things, by the time we get to Wilheimer's house party, we might not disagree on anything."

"I never took you for a dreamer, Harrison Stone." She grinned back at him. "But I think you might just be one."

The carriage came to a halt in front of the hotel, and Aimee realized she was still holding his hand. Reluctantly, she let go, missing his warmth almost immediately.

"While you tidy up, I'll study those ledgers," he said, as the door to the carriage opened and one of the hotel doormen held out his hand for Aimee and helped her down to the footpath.

Harrison followed her out, before taking her elbow and leading her through the lobby to the lifts. They stood waiting as the lights on the wall blinked with each level the elevator descended.

"I shouldn't be too long," Aimee said. "I'll have a quick bath and change into the spare outfit I've kept in the room in case of an emergency."

"Why do I get the feeling you have a lot of those?"

"You are quite the comedian, aren't you?"

"Well, enjoy your bath. Not everyone has the luxury of having them. I certainly didn't when I was young."

"Yes, I know, I've grown up with every conceivable privilege," she said as the lift came to a stop at the lobby level. "But when you get used to certain standards and ways of living, it's hard to give them up."

"That's true," Harrison said. "I suppose it would be difficult to expect a million-dollar heiress to share her bath with anyone."

"I'd share it with you." The words were out of her mouth before she could stop them, and if she weren't so embarrassed at having said them, she would have laughed at the look of pure shock that came over his face.

For a man who was always in control, right at that moment it looked like he'd been bowled over by a freight train, but there was also another expression in his eyes, something deep and primal, something she couldn't quite identify, but which sent a thrill down her spine.

"What did you just say?" His voice was husky as he tugged at his collar like it was choking him.

Aimee shrugged, feeling suddenly bold. "I think you heard me." After all, shouldn't she make the most of this trip? She'd never been as attracted to anyone as she was to this man, even as frustrating as he was, and she had no plans of marrying anyone. Why shouldn't she be like the other women at the office and enjoy having a liaison with a man she was attracted to, without any strings attached? Provided they weren't discovered, and she didn't get pregnant, which, hopefully, Harrison would know how to prevent, why shouldn't she experience all she could on this adventure?

The lift doors opened, and she stepped inside. "Level six, please," she said to the operator, turning to face the entrance and noticing Harrison wasn't getting inside. "You're not coming up?"

"I never use the lifts," he said, looking oddly uncomfortable. "I'll meet you up there."

The doors closed and she could only watch

through the glass panels as he turned and strode toward the stairs. Was it because of what she'd said that he didn't want to go up with her?

"He doesn't use the lift?" she asked the lift operator as they began to ascend.

"Not the boss, miss. He always uses the stairs," the man replied. "Always has, ever since he got here years ago."

How odd. Another mystery about the man, and Aimee loved solving a mystery. And what a mystery Harrison Stone was proving to be. One she wanted to undress and discover everything about.

Goodness, she'd turned into a wanton woman on this trip, but the thought didn't worry her in the least. Instead, she was excited, because it meant this was going to be a once-in-a-lifetime trip.

CHAPTER TWENTY-THREE

Every step he took up the stairs felt like a mountain. A mountain he wanted to climb but also dreaded, because on the other side she'd be waiting for him. Aimee Thornton-Jones, not Evie. But Aimee, his boss and mentor's daughter.

A willful heiress who liked to barge headfirst into situations, without much care or thought. The opposite to the way he normally approached matters.

And she seemed to want to barge headfirst into an affair with him… God help him. What was he to do?

His head was telling him to stay well away, but his body couldn't get him up those stairs fast enough. Damn it, but he couldn't disrespect Thomas's daughter by having a liaison with her, could he? No, of course he couldn't, even as much as his cock was semi-hard just thinking of it.

He'd never had a problem with controlling his emotions or desires before, so why was he having so much difficulty doing so with the only woman whom having a liaison with was out of the question?

Cresting the final step to the fourth level, he turned to his right and saw Aimee waiting for him in front of the lifts. One of her perfectly shaped eyebrows was raised as she watched him stride over to her.

"Why don't you use the lifts?"

Of course she'd be curious to know. When wasn't she curious about everything? She was just like her father in temperament. It was no wonder Thomas butted heads with her so much. And an even bigger wonder how Harrison hadn't picked up on her being Thomas's daughter sooner. "I don't like being stuck in a box that could potentially plummet to the ground."

"Has that happened to you before?" There was concern in her eyes.

"The plummeting part, no. The stuck part, yes. When I was six, I was trapped in one for over four hours. Since then, I've always chosen the stairs." He was brusque in his reply. "Now where's your room? I want to see those ledgers."

"And here I thought you meant you were going to have a bath with me." She sighed as she pulled out her room key from her satchel but then laughed, and he knew the vixen was having fun teasing him. "How disappointing, but understandable given I'm keen to look through the ledgers again, too. After my bath, though, seeing as I look like a drowned rat."

Harrison couldn't help but glance down at her figure, noting how the blue skirt of her outfit was still damp, and plastered rather indecently against her slim thighs. Thighs he suddenly imagined wrapping around his waist while he slid inside her and began to thrust against her until they were both panting with need.

He gulped heartily as his cock started to stir. *Focus, man, focus. Get her into her room and get the hell away from her.* "What suite number?"

"Six zero five," she replied, leading the way down the corridor.

Her suite was only a few doors down from his own. Wonderful. How the hell would he be able to concentrate on anything, let alone any discrepancies in the ledgers, knowing she was naked in a bath so close to him?

Fifteen minutes later after seeing her to her suite, then grabbing the ledgers and fleeing to his own suite, Harrison tossed the second ledger to the side and swore. He couldn't bloody concentrate on anything except the thought of her in her damned bath, and that he'd been an idiot not to take her up on her offer.

But, surely, that wasn't what she'd really been suggesting? After all, she had to be a virgin, and mustn't have known what she'd been asking of him. Unless she wasn't a virgin? The thought brought with it a scowl. She was bold and confident, and curious about everything. Perhaps she'd also been curious about men? The thought sent a simmering anger down deep in his belly.

Damn it, maybe he should've agreed to having a bath with her. He'd have peeled off her wet clothes, revealing inch after delectable inch of her soft skin. Then he'd have scooped her up and carried her to the bath, where he would have caressed every part of her supple body.

Just the thought was making him as hard as a rock.

A knock at his door jolted him from his ridiculous fantasy and he cursed once again. "One minute," he growled, shifting uncomfortably in his seat before he stood up and strode over to the door. He paused there for a good thirty seconds, while he let the wayward member of his anatomy calm down, trying to think of anything and anyone but Aimee Thornton-Jones.

He peered through the peep hole in the door and cursed again as his cock leaped to attention. It was hard not to think of the darn woman when she was standing right outside his door.

"I thought you'd be longer," he said, ripping open the door and glaring at her. She had a slight flush of pink on her cheeks from the warmth of the bath, and she'd swept up her damp hair into a bun, a few strands curling down the nape of her neck. Harrison's fingers were itching to deftly push them away and replace them with his mouth.

"I'm too excited to discuss what you thought about the ledgers." She strode past him, heading into the suite's living room. She spun around back to him as he closed the door and trudged in after her. "So? What did you think?"

For a moment, he considered telling her of how distracted he'd been thinking about her, but he got the sense that would only encourage her conversation from earlier, and he really didn't have the willpower at that moment to resist her. Even just having her here in this room was dangerous.

He'd never even entertained Jane here, preferring instead to keep his own world very separate from her and anyone else. Yet, here Aimee was. Looking so clean and fresh, and so excited to talk about ledgers of all things that he had to clench his jaw hard to stop himself from swinging her up into his arms and carrying her to his bed.

He nearly groaned with the image of it. *Resist, Harrison, bloody resist.*

"You look troubled," she said, blithely unaware of his inner turmoil. "Were they that bad?"

Taking in a breath, he shook his head. "I haven't properly gone through them yet."

"Why not?"

"Because I haven't been able to bloody well stop thinking about you in a bath is why not." He hadn't meant to tell her that, but the words came out nonetheless.

"Really?"

"Yes, really. And you need to leave now before I do something we'll both regret."

Instead of fleeing, she stayed there, staring at him. "What if I want to stay?" Her voice was a breathless whisper as she took several steps over to him, until she was mere inches away.

Harrison groaned. "Oh God, don't say that."

"I want to be with you, Harrison Stone," she said. "I want you to show me what passion truly is."

"You don't know what you're asking of me…" His voice was a choked whisper, his body tense as he resisted reaching out and pulling her to him.

"I do." She reached her hand out and trailed her fingers across the front of his shirt, then leaned up on tiptoes and whispered in his ear, "Take me to your bed, Harrison. Make me yours and yours alone."

• • •

The words were out of her mouth before she could stop herself, and rather than embarrassed, she felt emboldened. She wanted Harrison Stone with a longing she knew only he could satisfy.

"Are you sure, Aimee?"

She pulled back to look him in the eyes and smiled. "I couldn't be any more certain."

Her words seemed to be all the encouragement he needed, and with a low growl, his lips found hers, and he kissed her with a thoroughness bordering on desperation.

Aimee wrapped her arms around his neck and closed her eyes in bliss. In that moment, there was nothing else in the world but her and him, and the building heat between them.

"You drive me insane with desire, do you know that?" he whispered, trailing kisses down her neck as his fingers deftly began to unbutton her blouse, slowly exposing her undergarments beneath.

He peeled back her chemise and the pads of his fingers brushed against her bare skin. Aimee moaned; his touch was so wickedly delicious that she felt like melting. Slowly, his fingers pushed away the material, until her breasts were exposed to his view, her nipples hardening with the undisguised desire in his gaze. He lowered his head to her breast, and she whimpered in pleasure as his mouth nuzzled her nipple.

"So soft," he murmured in between kissing her breast, while his hands worked on the buttons of her skirt and petticoat, until the garments fell to the ground at her feet.

She gasped when he knelt in front of her, his

mouth kissing down her stomach, while his fingers tenderly rolled down her stockings over one thigh and then the other, until she was naked in front of him.

"God, you're gorgeous," he said in reverence, before he scooped her into his arms and carried her across the room to his bedchamber. His mouth found hers again as he laid her on the bed, his body coming down gently beside her.

Every inch of her body felt on fire, and suddenly she wanted to feel his bare skin against her own. She yanked on the buttons of his shirt, tearing it open and exposing the smooth planes of his chest beneath. He was all steel and muscle, and so very masculine, she felt the thrill of it deep inside her, the area between her thighs tingling with a need that was begging to be satisfied.

She traced her fingers down his chest toward the waistband of his trousers to where his manhood was straining against the material, demanding her attention. She began to flick open the buttons of his pants and then his drawers, and he moaned as his cock sprang free.

"Oh my," she gasped, having never seen such a sight before. She'd never thought that a man's appendage could be so beautiful, but Harrison's was. It was thick and long, proudly jutting to attention, and she couldn't stop herself from touching it, marveling at how silky smooth it was.

She wrapped her fingers around his shaft, and he groaned loudly. Quickly, she let go. "Did I hurt you?"

"No," he replied with a half laugh, half groan.

"It just feels so damn good that if you keep doing it, I might embarrass myself before I can pleasure you."

"Oh." Aimee gulped, not quite certain what he meant.

"Come here," he said, before pulling her up next to him and rolling on top of her.

Now it was Aimee who groaned as his mouth found hers and he kissed her until she was wet with need. She ran her hands across the broad expanse of his back, while his thigh nestled in between the junction of her core.

"Rub yourself against me," he murmured into her ear.

She did as instructed, and instantly a heady sense of euphoria filled her. "That feels so good."

He smiled. "How does this feel?"

His fingers replaced his thigh and began to caress her nub, and Aimee nearly bolted upright, her fingers digging into his shoulders as she arched her back in pleasure. She'd never imagined he could do that, and how ridiculously amazing it would feel. Then, he gently inserted one finger into her passage and instinctively, she began to rock her hips against his hand. He inserted another finger into her wetness, his thumb still rubbing against her as his fingers pushed in and out, bringing her to the brink of pleasure.

"Are you sure about this, Aimee?" he grunted, pausing in his machinations, and looking down at her with concern. "We can stop if you want to."

"Don't you dare stop." That was the very last thing she wanted, so she grabbed his neck and pulled him down until her lips were ravishing his own, their moans of bliss mirroring each other's.

He pulled back from her. "This might hurt a little," he murmured, sweat beading on his forehead, as he positioned himself above her. "Are you sure, Aimee?"

"I'm sure," she assured him, knowing she wanted to experience this with him.

With a nod, he slowly pressed his manhood against the opening of her passage, and he felt so large against her that for a moment she wondered if he would actually fit? But then his lips found her own, and he was kissing her with such abandon that she forgot to worry, and her hips urged themselves against him.

With a groan, his cock swiftly pushed inside her wetness, and she gasped at the pain and the fullness of him.

He stilled above her, while beads of sweat grew on his brow. "I'm sorry, my darling. The pain should settle soon," he murmured, before returning his hand to the junction of her thighs and gently rubbing against the nub of her womanhood.

Thrills of pleasure began to radiate through her core with each stroke of his fingers, and, gradually, the pain lessened, but then he started to withdraw his manhood from her.

She grabbed his shoulders and held him to her. "No, don't leave."

He grinned. "I'm not going anywhere." He slid back inside her, pushing himself in and out of her passage, in a rhythm that sent ripples of desire through every part of her body once again.

With each of his thrusts it felt like she was building to a precipice, her heart beating frantically as she was consumed by passion. And she wanted more, so much more. Her hips joined his, thrust for thrust, and Aimee felt like she was about to burst.

"That's it, my darling," he murmured against her ear as she moaned, writhing under him. Then everything froze for a split second, as wave upon wave of ecstasy flooded through her as her whole body burst in pleasure.

Harrison groaned loudly as he spilled his seed inside her, then collapsed down on top of her, his ragged breathing and racing heart mirroring her own.

They lay together there for a moment, until Harrison twisted to his side slightly so as not to crush her with his weight, then gathered her in his arms, and she nestled against him. She'd never felt so content or blissful before, and as she drifted off, she rather thought this would be the best part of her holiday, and how lucky it was she'd switched with Evie after all.

CHAPTER TWENTY-FOUR

A few hours later, after Harrison had pleasured her several times more, Aimee opened her eyes, realizing Harrison was no longer in bed with her. She glanced around the softly lit room and saw he was standing by the window, staring down into the street below.

He was naked still, but didn't seem to care, and she felt herself blushing from staring at him, but she couldn't help herself, he was that fine of a specimen of a man. She pulled up the sheet to cover her breasts and sat up in the bed.

Hearing her movements, he turned around and stared at her, but rather than the smile she expected to see, instead there was a frown on his face.

"What's wrong?" she asked, knowing it couldn't be because he didn't enjoy being with her, given he'd taken them both to the realm of ecstasy three times already.

"I'm considering the ramifications of everything," he answered. "And how to break the news to your father that we're to marry."

"Marry?" Aimee nearly screamed. "I never said anything about marrying you."

"You didn't have to," he replied. "I intend to do the right thing and make you my wife."

"You can't be serious."

"I'm dead serious," he said, his teeth clenched together. "I took your virginity, so we will be getting married. Your father would never forgive me if I didn't."

"And there it is, the true reason you want to marry me," she exclaimed, a sense of bitterness filling her. "You want to marry me because of my father." The same reason behind every marriage proposal she'd received.

"That's not it at all." He dragged a hand through his hair.

"Oh please," she scoffed, grabbing the sheet from the bed as she scooted off the mattress and began to pick up her clothes. "You probably orchestrated this whole thing so you'd be in a position to insist on marriage. And it's not just my million-dollar dowry you want, it's my father's entire company, which he'd happily give you if you were his son-in-law!"

"That has nothing to do with it," he roared, grabbing his clothes scattered across the floor. "I've already told you, once the Wilheimer deal goes through, I'll be the majority shareholder of the London portion of the company. I don't need the entire thing."

"What a load of nonsense!" She dragged on her skirt, and then turned around and shoved her hands through the sleeves of her shirt. "You're the most ambitious man I know, so why would you be content to run the London arm of the company when you could have the whole thing. I'm not stupid, though I clearly fell for your lies!"

"I never lied to you," he replied, thrusting his legs through his trousers, and then jamming his arms through the sleeves of his shirt. "Though you're being stupid to think I want to marry you for any other reason than because it's what my honor demands. I respect Thomas too much to take his daughter's virginity and not do the right thing after the fact."

"You should have thought of that before you took my virginity, shouldn't you!" she yelled, stomping over to collect her boots and ramming her feet into them.

"How was I to know for certain you were a virgin?"

"Excuse me?" Aimee didn't think her level of fury could get worse, but his words pushed her temper to boiling point. "Why wouldn't you think I was a virgin?"

"You were talking about taking a bath together. What virgin does that?"

"A curious one, you idiot!" She couldn't help it: she threw one of her boots at him, which he managed to dodge. "How dare you think I'd done this with another man. You're such a bastard!" And for good measure, she grabbed the other boot off her foot and lobbed it at him, too. When he once again dodged that, she grabbed the empty water glass from the side table and threw that at him, too. When it hit him, she felt a sense of satisfaction.

"Will you stop throwing things at me!" he yelled, rubbing his shoulder.

"I've never felt more disrespected than right now!" She glared at him, her eyes glancing around to see if there was anything else she could lob at the blockhead.

"You were the one begging me to take you to

my bed."

"Only because I wanted to see what all the fuss was about, and, let me tell you, it was overrated."

"Overrated?" he roared, stomping over to her, his eyes a burning green furnace. "You climaxed several bloody times, I made certain of it."

And they'd been some of the most extraordinary moments of her life, but she wasn't going to tell him that, not after his derogatory assumption about her. Damn it, even now, with him standing inches away, her body was begging her to grab him and get him to taste and touch her all over again.

"It doesn't matter," she said, raising her chin and meeting his stare head on. "Because it won't be happening again, end of story."

"We're getting married, end of story."

"No. We're not."

"Yes, we bloody well are, and once I tell your parents, they'll insist upon it."

"You wouldn't dare tell them!" She gasped. He wouldn't, would he? "My father would never forgive you."

He took in a deep breath and stepped back from her. "He'd never forgive me if I compromised you and didn't do the right thing to fix it."

"The right thing?" Her voice sounded rather desperate. "How is marrying each other the right thing? We argue all the time! If we married, we'd end up killing each other within the week."

"You do like to be dramatic, don't you?"

"Ooh!" She fisted her hands and shook her arms. The man infuriated her as no one else could. Not even her parents. "You're forgetting a very large thing, Harrison Stone. My mother will never agree. She wants me to marry a lord, not some self-made American. She'll have you thrown in the Thames before she agrees to us marrying."

He started laughing, though there was little humor in the sound.

"What's so funny about that?"

"It's funny because she'll have you thrown in the Thames if you refuse me."

"What are you talking about?" Was he losing his mind?

"You know how I told you my parents were English?"

"Yes. What of it?" She grabbed her jacket and put it on, determined to not stay in his room a moment longer than necessary.

"My father was Lord Edward Stone. The younger son of the Earl of Carlisle."

"Your father was a lord?" Aimee had a bad feeling about where this was heading.

"He was. Now my uncle is the current earl."

"My mother wants me to marry an earl, not be the niece of one."

"My uncle has five adult daughters and no sons," he replied.

It took her a moment for the ramifications to hit. "You're his heir?"

He nodded, then gave her a mock bow. "The future Earl of Carlisle, at your service, my lady."

For a good minute, Aimee was speechless. "Does my mother know that?"

Harrison shrugged. "I'd say so. I mentioned it a while back to your father in confidence after arriving in London and finding out. Obviously, I knew he'd tell your mother, given your parents don't have secrets between them."

"No, they just like to keep secrets from me, it seems."

"The apple doesn't fall far from the tree, does it?"

"Well, clearly you like to keep secrets, too." She pinned him with an accusatory stare. "Why didn't you say anything earlier? And why didn't anyone else mention it?"

"I choose to not tell people, especially not at work." He shrugged.

"So no one knows?"

"People in English Society know I'm Carlisle's heir," he replied. "But I didn't bother telling anyone in New York, apart from your father. The last thing I wanted was to be bothered by debutantes and their marriage-minded mothers given I don't want to get married. *Didn't* want to," he quickly corrected.

"Oh please, you don't want to marry me just as much as I don't want to marry you." For some reason, those words made her stomach feel hollow, which made no sense given she didn't want to marry him. "Let's at least be honest about that."

"Fine. Do I want to get married? No. However, I knew I'd have to eventually, so given I've compromised you and need to rectify that to satisfy my honor, then marry you I will, even if I don't really want to."

"Your honor can go and drown itself in the Thames!" Aimee roared at him, striding over and grabbing her satchel from the floor. "I wasn't going to marry you before, but I'm most definitely *not* going to marry you now!"

"I'm being honest."

"Do you think we'll be happily married when neither of us wants to be married to each other?"

"Most marriages are like that."

"My parents' isn't!" she yelled, suddenly realizing that that's what she wanted, if she ever was to marry. A man that adored his wife and would move the earth for her if he had to, not a marriage of convenience so some man could satisfy his honor.

"Their marriage is a rarity, and you know it."

"I suppose it is. But I'd rather never marry than settle for less."

"You're so damn difficult sometimes." He banged his hand on the wall nearest him. "Any other woman would beg me to marry them, knowing they'd eventually become a countess."

She felt his eyes following her as she stormed over to the bedroom door. "Then go ask your friend Lady Whitley to marry you, as I'm sure she'd jump at the chance!"

"I don't want to marry Lady Whitley."

"But you don't want to marry me, either, now do you?" She paused with her hand on the door handle, as she turned back to look at him.

His mouth opened, then closed, then opened again. "It's my duty to marry you."

"What a way to sweep a girl off her feet, *my lord*."

He narrowed his eyes. "I'm not a lord yet. Hell, I don't even want to be one. And I didn't know I was trying to sweep you off your feet."

"You couldn't sweep me off my feet even if you tried," she replied, with a tight smile. "There's not one romantic bone in your entire body, and as big as you are, that's saying something!" She wrenched the bedroom door open and stormed through his living area to the entrance door of his suite.

"Damn it, this has nothing to do with romance, and you know it!" He stalked after her. "I'm trying to be practical. What if you're pregnant?"

She froze mid-step and swung back around to face him. "We can cross that bridge if it eventuates, which I'm praying it doesn't, because I have no intention of being your Dollar Princess, ever! Now, if you'll excuse me, I need to get back to Mrs. Holbrook's."

"Damn it, wait," he yelled, as she pulled open the door and left the room. "I'll accompany you."

Ignoring him, she strode down the hallway and took the lift down to the lobby, then hurried through to the entrance, before asking the doorman to hail her a hackney.

As she got into the carriage and the vehicle began pulling away from the curb, Harrison rushed through the front doors of the hotel and caught sight of her.

"This isn't over, Aimee!" he yelled aloud, caring little of the other hotel guests who were entering and exiting the building.

"It most certainly is," she yelled through the window as the carriage pulled into traffic and he disappeared from view. She took in a deep breath and released a sigh.

If Harrison Stone thought she'd ever agree to marry him, he was delusional. No man, no matter how good a lover he was, nor how much she was starting to crave him, was going to distract her from her career path and convince her to give up her dreams, simply to become a wife. Especially not a future earl, who would demand his wife be a good little countess and look after his households.

Aimee couldn't think of a worse future.

And no man was worth giving up her dreams for, even if a tiny portion of her heart was trying to convince her otherwise.

CHAPTER TWENTY-FIVE

The rest of the week felt as if the days had turned into months, and glacial months at that, given she and Harrison had barely spoken to each other since the scene at the hotel, both actively doing their best to avoid each other.

Which was a good thing, even if it didn't feel good at all. Though how they were going to stay out of each other's way when they had Wilheimer's house party to attend tomorrow, Aimee didn't know. The idea of being with him after how things had ended was unsettling, even if Mrs. Holbrook would be there, too.

She still couldn't believe he'd conveniently managed not to tell her he was heir to an earldom. Who did that? Most men would be boasting of that fact, not actively trying to conceal it. If he'd told her that sooner, she would have stayed well away, for there was no way she was living in this country, with its weather and rigid rules that would ensure her place was in the bedroom and ballroom and nowhere else. It was not the life she'd ever envisaged for herself, even if her mother had.

Thinking about her mother, Aimee wondered if perhaps her mother had orchestrated the trip, with the knowledge Aimee would convince Evie to swap places with her, to put her in Harrison's vicinity? But that was ridiculous; her mother wouldn't do that, not with the potential scandal it could cause if it became known.

She imagined her parents must have thought Harrison would be the perfect catch given he was not only a future earl but he'd all but been groomed to take over her father's business. Well, not on Aimee's watch he wouldn't. She would make her father see she could run his companies, and she'd do it, without being married to her father's golden boy.

"Is everything all right?" Molly asked, walking over with a stack of papers and putting them on Aimee's desk, concern in her gaze.

"Yes, sort of."

"Sort of?"

"It's fine. Really, it is." Aimee smiled at her, determined not to let Harrison Stone affect her mood.

Molly returned her smile. "Yes, you sound sort of fine."

Aimee laughed lightly at that and then sighed. "I'm a bit out of sorts is all. There's a lot going on."

"Ah yes, the big meeting at Wilheimer's house party," Molly replied. "You'll be fine. I'm sure you've gotten used to attending such fancy things, being Mr. Thornton-Jones's niece."

"That I have." Truer words couldn't be said, well, except the part about being his niece. "The number of house parties I've attended over the years makes another one seem very boring." At least she was looking forward to translating for the men in their meetings over the weekend. That at least should keep her thoughts from straying to Harrison, even if the man would be right there beside her.

"It must have been fascinating," Molly said, her eyes radiating interest. "To have gone from thinking you were a regular somebody, to knowing you're the niece of one of the richest men in the world. It's a bit of a fairy tale, isn't it?"

"I suppose so." Evie had seemed shocked and amazed by it all.

"Was your cousin upset by your arrival?" Molly asked. "I imagine she wouldn't have been thrilled to share her father's affections, being an only child."

"Actually, she was thrilled to find out she had a cousin." It was true, too; when her parents had first told her they'd discovered Evie's existence, she'd immediately decided that Evie would be like a sister to her. "Aimee always wanted siblings. She was lonely as an only child."

It felt odd to talk about herself in the third person.

"How terrible for the lonely little rich girl." Deidre spoke up from behind them, obviously eavesdropping again. "I imagine she told you that nonsense but really hated knowing you existed and were going to live with them. After all, what heiress would want to share her things?"

Aimee raised her brow. "My family is so wealthy, Deidre, that nothing needs to be shared and they can buy whatever they want, for whomever they want, whenever they want."

Not that they ever did that, even though they had the means to, but Deidre didn't need to know that. Aimee's parents hadn't gotten to where they were by frivolously spending their hard-earned money, and when Aimee was a child, they'd always made sure she'd shared her toys with the servants' children, along with gifting the toys she no longer played with to the children on their estates.

"Yes, how lucky for you, going from being a poor little orphan girl to some heiress's companion." Deidre sounded bored. "I imagine it got quite tedious doing her bidding, which is why you've obviously come here and set your sights on the boss in there." She glanced over to Harrison's office and Aimee felt her cheeks go red with mortification. Was it that obvious that something had happened between Harrison and her?

"Deidre, stop being so rude," Molly said.

"What?" Deidre scowled over at Molly. "Anyone can see she's always glancing over to his doorway. Clearly, something happened between them."

"You're jealous of Evie and her life," Molly said defensively. "And the fact she's attracted Mr. Stone's attention, which you've been trying to do for months with no success."

"Oh please," Deidre scoffed. "I'm not jealous of her." She narrowed her eyes over to Aimee. "I have my future already mapped out, with certain plans in place to ensure I will be a wealthy woman who doesn't want for anything, you wait and see."

"Having a liaison with an accountant from downstairs isn't going to make you wealthy," Molly said.

Deidre smiled smugly. "At least I have a man whom I'm about to have lunch with. So I'll leave you two to your *pathetic* girl talk." She pursed her lips at them, before turning on her heel and leaving the room.

"Does she do any work apart from eavesdrop and be mean?" Aimee asked.

Molly laughed. "Not really, but she gets away with it because she's Mrs. Holbrook's niece."

"She is?" That was the first Aimee had heard about it. "Well, that explains a lot."

"Yes, but promise you won't say anything to either of them," Molly replied. "I probably shouldn't have mentioned it, given neither of them talk about it, and I don't normally gossip."

"I promise." Aimee nodded, finally understanding why Deidre felt like she could come and go as she pleased.

"Thank you. I think you and I are kindred spirits, and as we both have to put up with her, I thought you deserved to know why she gets away with so much."

Aimee grinned. "Yes, though, thankfully, I only have to put up with her temporarily, whereas you'll have to deal with her after I'm gone, permanently."

"Want to swap places?" Molly smiled back.

"No." She'd already done quite enough swapping places to last her a lifetime. "Why doesn't Mrs. Holbrook mention that Deidre's her niece?"

"Well, that's a rather interesting story." Molly glanced around the room, making sure they were still alone. "You see, I think she's a bit embarrassed by the circumstances surrounding Deidre's birth."

"Why would she be embarrassed?"

Molly pressed her lips together. "I overheard them arguing once, and apparently Deidre is the love child of Thomas Thornton-Jones."

Aimee's whole body froze. "No, that's not possible. My f—uncle would never have had an affair. He wouldn't do that to my aunt. He loves her more than life itself." There was no way her father would cheat on her mother. There was even less of a chance her mother would allow it or put up with it.

Molly cringed. "I'm sorry, I didn't mean to speak badly of your uncle. But Deidre is four-and-twenty just like me, so perhaps the affair occurred before your aunt and uncle were even together?"

The math worked out given her parents had been married for twenty-three years.

"In any event, I think Deidre dislikes you so, and more particularly your cousin, Aimee, because apparently when her mother confronted your uncle about it when Deidre was just a little girl, he refused to acknowledge their affair, claiming Deidre's mother was a liar and had fabricated the whole thing, and that Deidre wasn't his child."

"Then she's not his daughter," Aimee emphatically replied.

"She believes she is."

"My uncle would never deny a child of his, regardless of that child's birth status. He just wouldn't."

"I didn't mean to upset you, and I probably shouldn't have said anything." There was an expression of regret in Molly's eyes. "But I thought you should know why Deidre was treating you so poorly. In her mind, you've succeeded where she never will; you've integrated with the Thornton-Joneses, and are living the life she believes she should have had. Although she probably thinks it's more your cousin's life she should have, given she believes Thomas is her father. The way she speaks of your cousin Aimee, it's with venom." Molly rubbed her hands over her arms.

"There's simply no way my uncle fathered Deidre," Aimee replied, still trying to wrap her head around the information. "If he had, he would have done the honorable thing and ensured she was looked after financially, and he would have acknowledged her as his. The fact that he didn't means that Deidre's mother is lying."

"Was lying. She died shortly after she confronted your uncle," Molly said. "I heard Mrs. Holbrook say she jumped in front of a train in her sadness, or perhaps she said madness? I can't quite remember."

"Why would Mrs. Holbrook work for my uncle then, given the situation with her sister?"

Molly sighed. "I heard her tell Deidre that Deidre's mother was mad and living in a fantasy world, and that she'd most likely made it all up."

"I told you my uncle isn't Deidre's father." The very idea of it was unfathomable. Her father was one of the most honorable, trustworthy men she knew. He'd always instilled in her that taking responsibility for one's own actions was imperative to living a successful life.

"That's not what Deidre believes." Molly shrugged. "In any event, I merely told you, so you don't take anything she says to heart given she truly loathes your uncle."

"Then why is she even working here?"

"Money of course. And it's a rather easy job given her aunt doesn't bother overly with supervising her." Molly's brown eyes seemed uncertain. "I don't know, perhaps she even wants to be as close as she can to the Thornton-Joneses given her history, and this is about as close as she can get?"

"Perhaps," Aimee agreed, wondering if Deidre could be behind the alterations in the ledgers, to punish the company, and in doing so Aimee's father, who certainly wasn't Deirdre's. That required planning and calculation, and an astute head for figures, which Deidre didn't seem to possess. Though she'd been seeing someone in accounting; perhaps they could have done her dirty work for her?

"Excuse me, Miss Jenkins?" Fred said from the doorway.

For a moment, Aimee glanced around for Evie, and then remembered she was Miss Jenkins to Fred.

"This came for you." He walked over and handed her a note.

"Thank you, Fred." She smiled at him and took the paper.

Fred nodded his head before he turned and left.

Glancing down at the note, her smile faded. "Oh my God."

"What's wrong?" Molly asked.

"And here I was thinking I was the one royally screwing up the plan."

"I don't understand…" Molly said.

"My cousin has gotten herself engaged to a duke."

"She has?" Molly's eyes went wide in wonder.

"Why, that's amazing. She'll be a duchess...how lucky for her. Goodness, don't tell Deidre, though. She'll be as jealous as sin thinking it should be her in your cousin's place."

"She did the one thing I warned her not to," Aimee said, caring little about if Deidre was jealous or not, when all she could think about was Evie and the mess she'd not only gotten herself into, but Aimee, too. Because how on earth could they keep their swap a secret if Evie was engaged to a duke while pretending to be Aimee?

Aimee's parents were bound to hear about it and there would be no stopping her mother sending her father over to investigate. And if that happened, they could kiss their masquerade goodbye. "I can't believe she went and got herself accidentally engaged when I explicitly told her that was the one thing not to do. I mean, how does someone even get accidentally engaged?"

"You tell your cousin what to do?" Molly asked. "I thought you were her companion?"

"It's a companion's job to guide the person she's a companion to," Aimee improvised, thinking that did sound like what Evie did, even if Aimee didn't listen to any of her guidance, at least not most of the time. "Clearly, though, my cousin didn't listen to me as she should have."

How could her normally sensible cousin have been caught kissing a duke and, because of that, now found herself accidentally engaged to him? Then Evie had had the audacity to send a note to Aimee telling her not to worry because she had a plan.

Evie with a plan? When did Evie ever have a plan? Never was when. So it was bound to be a plan that was going to get them both caught if Aimee didn't fix things.

"Can you cover for me, Molly?" she turned and asked. "I have to go and sort out whatever this mess is that my cousin's gotten herself into."

"Yes, of course. I'll tell them there's been a family emergency you've had to attend to."

"Well, that's certainly the truth." Aimee reached over and squeezed Molly's hand. "Thank you." She quickly grabbed her satchel, flung it over her shoulder, and bolted out the door.

Who would have thought that sensible Evie would be the one to unravel their masquerade? And now Aimee was going to have to do whatever she could to rectify the problem, because rectify it she had to. She couldn't go back to New York just yet, not when she was so close to helping with the Wilheimer deal.

Yes, that was the only reason she didn't want to leave London yet, not because of some six-foot-three, stubborn bull of a man, who'd ignored her for the past week. The darn man. He wasn't the reason she wasn't ready to go just yet. And maybe, just maybe, if she kept telling herself that, she might believe it.

CHAPTER TWENTY-SIX

Harrison knew the minute Aimee left the office. The tingle of awareness just behind his neck, which had been ever present whenever she was around, had suddenly dissipated, and he'd known in that instant she wasn't in the outer room anymore.

How or why he'd gotten so attuned to her being there, to the point he knew when she left, he didn't want to examine too closely, even if he'd only ever been afflicted by such a condition with her and no one else. And despite the fact that he'd been trying to ignore her all week, he'd never actually ignored her at all.

How could he when he was so acutely aware of her in the very next room? Her laugh, her chatter, even her sighs when she was frustrated with something were all sounds he'd gotten ridiculously used to over the past week, to the point of near madness.

Wanting someone so much, but not being able to have them, was starting to mess with his head. He'd had the best goddamn sex of his life, and she'd carried on like it had meant nothing, and he was acting like a fool for insisting they marry after he'd taken her virginity.

Most women would have been begging him to marry them in such a situation. But, no, not Aimee Elizabeth Thornton-Jones, who seemed to think it was more than acceptable to have a liaison with him, and nothing more. Would she have thought that if she'd known beforehand that he was the reluctant heir to an earldom? Actually, that probably would have scared her away.

"Miss Mitchell," he yelled out suddenly, startling Mrs. Holbrook, who'd been running through the notes she'd taken in the meeting with Wilheimer last week, with both him and Ben.

"Yes, sir," Miss Mitchell replied, sticking her head around the doorframe.

"Where has Miss Th-Jenkins gone?" How did Aimee pretend so easily? It was bloody hard to remember to call her by her false identity now that he knew who she was.

"She had a family emergency and had to rush off," Miss Mitchell said nervously. "I'm sure she'll be back once she's sorted things out."

"Where did she go, Miss Mitchell?" God knew what sort of shenanigans she was up to, if she'd managed to recruit the normally by-the-book Miss Mitchell into her scheme.

"Her cousin did something she shouldn't have so Miss Jenkins went to talk to her," Miss Mitchell said, biting her bottom lip.

"Berate her, don't you mean?" He could only imagine how her cousin doing anything she wasn't meant to could throw a wrench into Princess Aimee's grand plans.

"Yes, probably," Miss Mitchell admitted with a little nod of her head, her spectacles bobbing precariously on the bridge of her nose, her hazel eyes looking remorseful.

"And I'm guessing she went alone?" The woman had no sense of the potential peril she faced, even pretending to be her cousin.

Miss Mitchell nodded her head. "She did."

"Of course she did." Harrison sighed and stood up. "Continue going through the notes without me," he told Ben and Mrs. Holbrook. "Then come up with some strategies I can employ against Wilheimer over the weekend. We'll discuss them after I'm back."

He had one reluctant fiancée to go find, then haul back to the office, because if she thought he'd allow her to traipse about London on her own, at least not without him behind the scenes to ensure she was safe, she needed reminding that that wasn't happening on his watch.

• • •

Aimee came out of her visit with Evie feeling more confused than when she'd gone into the Countess of Brexton's residence. Because contrary to her initial belief that Evie had gotten herself into a mess she wouldn't be able to get out of, Evie had managed to sort it out rather effectively, convincing the duke to go along with merely pretending to be engaged for the remainder of her trip, rather than actually being engaged.

One fewer thing she needed to worry about, she supposed. Cutting down a walkway through a park, Aimee glanced over at some of the people she was walking past, and nearly did a double take when she recognized the Earl of Brexton.

"Miss Jenkins?" he exclaimed, coming to a stop in front of her, while he waved at his other companions to go ahead. "What a pleasure it is to see you again!" He bowed, taking her hand and placing a deft kiss across her knuckles. "What are you doing in this part of town?"

"I was visiting my cousin and am now heading back to work."

He smiled. "Ah, so you've heard about their accidental engagement. I hope you don't intend to shoot my cousin."

"Not at this stage." Aimee smiled back at him. "But let's see what unfolds in the next few weeks, my lord."

"That's a relief." He grinned. "But, please, call me Sam, given we're to be related, even if you don't sound too enthusiastic about their engagement."

His green eyes were curious, and Aimee couldn't help but compare them to the green of Harrison's, which were a deeper, more vivid shade, and were usually filled with annoyance. Unlike the friendly and comforting green of Sam's.

Aimee sighed. "It's not that I'm not happy, it just complicates things."

"I suppose it would. You'll be returning to America eventually while your cousin will be staying here."

"Yes, that's it." She couldn't very well tell him the true reason for her concern. "You're not worried about how quickly they've gotten engaged?"

He grinned at her. "Not in the least. I think our cousins are perfectly suited to each other. Not many people like to talk about rocks, let alone study them in detail and go digging for them, as they both do. Personally, I find the topic rather boring."

Aimee couldn't help but laugh. "That's exactly how I feel, too. Though E—Aimee still tries to spark my interest in them, which never works."

He laughed, too. "Alex does the same with me. Honestly, he's an encyclopedia when it comes to fossils, and doesn't quite understand when others don't share his enthusiasm."

"They do sound perfect for each other, don't they?" The fact made Aimee both angry and sad for her cousin, because if the truth of Evie's identity was ever revealed, a duke, no matter how scholarly or seemingly perfect he might be for her cousin, simply wouldn't marry someone who was illegitimate. It was so unfair.

"Which is why I'm thrilled with their engagement," Sam said, blissfully unaware of the truth of the matter. "For too long, Alex has closed himself off to love, and I believe your cousin might just help him heal."

"I didn't realize you were such a romantic, Sam."

"I'm a big believer in love."

"Then why haven't you fallen in love and married yet?"

"I've fallen in love many times, and out of it just as quickly," he said, laughing, "so I'm not in any rush to find a wife."

"You're a Lothario, then," she replied, raising a brow, thoroughly enjoying their banter. Sam was so good-natured and happy compared to Harrison that it was nice to flirt a bit without repercussion, especially with an attractive man whom she wasn't attracted to.

He laughed again and shook his head. "I respect women too much to be a true Lothario; however, I do admit to adoring and appreciating them greatly."

"Yes, I imagine you do." The man was a flirt through and through, but a fun one.

"Speaking of which, can I escort you back to your work?" he asked, an eager glint of interest in his eyes.

"That won't be necessary, Brexton," Harrison's deep voice drawled from behind Aimee, and instantly she stiffened, her whole body vibrantly aware of him.

"What are you doing here?" Aimee turned around to face him.

"Going for a walk."

She didn't believe him for a second.

Sam glanced over to Harrison. "Stone? Do you know Miss Jenkins?"

Harrison flicked his gaze to Sam. "She's my fiancée."

Sam looked taken aback. "She is?"

"I'm not his fiancée," she told Sam before turning to Harrison and glaring at him.

"You will be." He crossed his hands over his chest, his expression implacable.

"No, I won't." Aimee smiled through gritted teeth, before turning back to Samuel. "I'm sorry for such a display, Sam—"

"You're on first-name terms with Brexton, too? Is there not a man in London you don't call by their first name?"

"Sam and I are to be cousins given Aimee is

engaged to the Duke of Hargrave." At least temporarily.

"Your cousin is engaged to Hargrave?" Harrison's anger was replaced with bafflement as he glanced over to Sam. "But he's always been against marrying."

"Thought you were, too, old chap," Sam said, clapping him on the back. "Seems a lovely lady can change anyone's mind, doesn't it?"

"You two know each other?" Aimee glanced between them both.

"We attend many of the same Society events," Harrison replied.

"Of course you do, given you're a *secret earl in waiting*." She still didn't quite know how to feel about that revelation. Surprisingly, she found herself more disappointed with that bit of information than she should have been. At least before when he was just Harrison Stone there was maybe a hint of the possible. As an earl, everything was impossible.

"It's not a secret, I just don't advertise it, and I'm called an heir," Harrison grumbled. "Only the Queen has ladies-in-waiting."

Sam laughed. "I think earl in waiting has a certain ring to it. In any event, I was going to go and wish Miss Thornton-Jones well on her engagement, so I'd best head off and do that." He turned to face Aimee. "Unless you wish me to accompany you?"

"I'm accompanying her," Harrison answered, with a scowl. "So bugger off, Brexton."

"Answering for me is not the way to go about getting me to change my mind about marrying you." Aimee crossed her hands over her chest and shook her head at him. "Honestly, Harrison Stone, you might know the ins and outs of business, but you have a great deal to learn about women." She turned to Sam. "But thank you, Sam, I'll be fine with the jackapanny here."

"Jackapanny?" Harrison raised a brow.

"I heard it from one of the girls the other day, and thought it more than appropriate for you," she replied. "It's a way to describe someone as being an annoying idiot."

Sam began to laugh but when Harrison turned and scowled, he had the good sense to cover his mouth and feign a cough instead. "In that event, I shall wish you both a good day, and I'll look forward to seeing how whatever this is between you two resolves itself." Sam grinned at them both, before turning on his heel and walking toward his mother's house.

"You'll have to deal with a damn difficult female one day, Sam," Harrison called out after him. "And, trust me, you won't be grinning then."

"I can't believe you followed me again," she said as soon as Sam was out of earshot. "Shouldn't you be focused on the Wilheimer deal instead of me?" She turned and began to walk through the park toward the office.

"I promised your father I'd look after you," he replied, following alongside her.

"I don't think taking me to your bed was the looking after my father had in mind."

"No, it wasn't," he ground out. "But, regardless, you're now my responsibility, and I will ensure your safety."

"How lovely to be a *responsibility* to you." She shook her head. He'd taken her father's request to keep an eye on her to ridiculous proportions. "I can see why you're worried. Cleary, the nannies pushing the babies in their prams could be a danger to me. Or perhaps it's the old ladies taking a walk you're suspicious of?" She pointed over to several elderly women, who were happily strolling along the footpaths.

"Be sarcastic all you want, London is not the safest of places, even in Mayfair," he mumbled, as they left the park and turned right onto the main thoroughfare. "You just have to accept that I'm protective of certain things."

"I don't have to accept anything. And I'm not a thing. I'm a woman, in case you hadn't noticed."

"Oh, I've noticed." He glanced down at her and there was heat in his eyes. "I can't help but notice every damn time I see you."

Suddenly, Aimee forgot she was upset with him and wanted to kiss him until they were breathless. She nearly groaned at how badly she wanted that. Shaking her head, she dragged her eyes forward and well away from him; she couldn't encourage that sort of behavior until he'd dropped the issue of marriage completely.

"Is your cousin really engaged to the Duke of Hargrave?" Harrison asked, abruptly changing the subject.

"Yes and no," Aimee replied, not sure exactly how much to tell him, but given he knew her secret, and she was tired of lying to him, she told him the truth.

"You two ladies have woven a tangled web, haven't you? Hargrave will be furious if he finds out he's been lied to."

"Do you think my cousin is in danger from him?" She stopped on the footpath, prepared to turn around and march back to the countess's.

"He won't hurt her," Harrison said. "He'll just be damned furious. Far more than I was, given he's previously been betrayed by an American heiress."

Aimee nodded as they resumed their brisk walk, turning onto Fleet Street. "I was only young when that happened, but even I heard about it."

"Do you think your swap isn't going to be found out?" he asked after several minutes.

"I hope not." It had been so simple at the start but had quickly turned very complicated. "If it does, it could prove to be a bit messy."

"A *bit* messy?"

"Fine, very messy, but it will all work out. I'm certain of it."

He shook his head, looking thoroughly unconvinced. "It will when you agree to marry me."

"Oh, for goodness' sake, not this again." She was getting thoroughly sick of him mentioning it.

"I'm not going to stop mentioning it just because you say no."

"That's exactly what you should do," she replied, glad that the office was close. "I've never had this much trouble from the men I've rejected in the past. Once I said no, that was the end of the matter."

"How many proposals have you had?"

"Five, if you count your half-baked one."

"Half-baked?" He looked as if he was about to choke on her description.

Aimee shrugged. "What else would you call it? My other proposals have at least been a lot more creative than a blunt demand that we get married. I would have to say the other proposals were all done rather decently, some more formal and businesslike than others, but all had much more deference in their requests to ask for my hand in marriage than you continually blustering on about the subject like a caveman."

"A caveman?"

"How else would you describe your badgering?" She felt like rolling her eyes at the man. "Just find someone else to marry. I'm sure some women would overlook your bossy tendencies given you're heir to an earldom."

He stopped in the street, and Aimee paused to look back at him.

"Why don't you want to marry me?" he asked, genuine confusion on his face. "A marriage between us would make good sense from a business and social perspective."

Aimee knew it made sense. Except for the part about her having to give up all her dreams to be a countess, something she didn't even want in the first place.

"Do you love me, Harrison?" She found herself bracing for his answer. Not that she wanted him to answer yes...at least she didn't think she did. But she'd always imagined that if she did ever marry, it would be to a man who loved her, the same way her father loved her mother. Adored her was more like it.

"Who said anything about love?" He seemed uncomfortable even mentioning the word.

Aimee shrugged. "That would be the only reason I'd ever consider getting married. And given you don't love me, then it's pointless for you to ever mention marriage again."

"I have no intention of loving anyone," he grumbled. "Besides, most marriages are arranged and have nothing to do with love, your parents being the only exception I know."

"Which is why if I ever marry I want that, too."

"Your parents' marriage is a rarity."

"It is. Which is why I never thought I'd marry." And she hadn't, until she'd met Harrison. But he refused to love, and she could never marry without that. Not that she was in love with the man, goodness no, far from it. Yet at the back of her mind was the small thought that he was the only man she could envisage a future with. The only man she could possibly give her heart to.

The thought left her terrified. No. she couldn't fall in love with Harrison Stone. He was her nemesis. Or at least he had been. Not to mention his life was completely entwined here in England. She could never leave New York or her family. The very idea of being an idle countess, hosting balls and soirées, with no possibility of ever running her father's company, was enough to send a cold shiver through her entire body.

Such a life was what she'd rallied so hard against. To go back on her convictions and settle for a life like that would be torture. She couldn't do it, not even for a man who might just possibly have stolen a little piece of her heart without her even knowing he had, until right then.

"We're nearly back," Harrison said, glancing over to the office building taking up the entire next block. "We can discuss this later."

"There's nothing more to discuss. You don't love me, and I'll never marry a man who doesn't love me, so do stop mentioning the topic. Oh, and one more thing." She narrowed her eyes upon him. "Don't tell people we're engaged when we're not."

His jaw clenched. "I told Brexton that because he was flirting with you."

"Why would you care if he was flirting?" she replied, feeling weirdly glad that he'd noticed.

"I care."

"You do?" A small seed of hope blossomed in her heart with his words.

"Yes, I bloody well do," he continued. "You're mine, and he damn well needed to know it."

"Yours?" Aimee roared, the seed burning as her anger flared back to life. "I'm not yours! I'm no man's, and the sooner you accept that, the less chance you have of me shooting you in the nether regions!"

He stepped closer to her and lowered his head until it was only inches from hers. "The moment you gave yourself to me, you became mine, just as I became yours," he said, his voice a deep rumble that reverberated through to her very core.

She briefly closed her eyes, part of her thrilling at his possessiveness, her body wanting him to possess her again. To touch her. To thrill her to the point of bliss.

"We belong to each other, Aimee Thornton-Jones," he murmured, his breath a soft whisper against her earlobe. "And the sooner you accept that, the sooner I can make your body writhe in ecstasy once again as I slowly slide inside you, filling you with my cock and thrusting against your hips, over and over again, until you orgasm harder and longer than you ever have before."

Aimee couldn't help a low moan from escaping her lips. The man was causing chaos in her body, a deep burning need that was growing to the point of no return and wouldn't be content until he satisfied her again. "You will?"

He took a step back from her, his eyes burning bright with desire. "I will. As soon as you agree to marry me and not a second before. Now come on, let's get back to work."

His words broke the spell in an instant. Was he trying to seduce her into agreeing to marry him? How dare he! Especially as part of her was worried it just might work.

Strength, Aimee. Strength.

Just because he could do wicked things to her body, and make her want him with an insatiable appetite, was no reason to allow him to seduce her. She couldn't let him.

A weekend away wouldn't help that, but thankfully with Mrs. Holbrook there, things should stay respectable. At least she hoped so, because she got a feeling that if she let Harrison touch her again, she wouldn't say no.

CHAPTER TWENTY-SEVEN

The carriage ride to Wilheimer's Dorset estate had been excruciating. Harrison had spent the four-hour trip doing his best to keep his knees and thighs from touching Aimee, who was sitting directly across from him, while Mrs. Holbrook sat next to her.

Being so close to Aimee had been torture, when all he kept thinking about was pulling her onto his lap and kissing her senseless, despite his ultimatum to her yesterday that he wouldn't unless she agreed to marry him. His lack of self-control when it came to her was confounding, but having Mrs. Holbrook there meant he had to control himself. He just hoped he could do so for the entire weekend.

Thankfully, they were nearly at Wilheimer's estate, and he'd have a cold shower when he got to his room—which he desperately needed, given all he could think about was how damn good it had felt touching and pleasuring her, and how much he wanted to be inside her again. Damn it, why couldn't she just say yes and then he could happily continue where they'd left off?

But she was far too stubborn for that. What he needed was to convince her that marriage to him was worth giving up on her dreams for. But was it? His own dreams had been what saved him as a boy when despair nearly took over. Could he ask her to give up her dreams to marry him? He didn't think he could. But how else could he rectify the situation of dishonoring her?

In the distance, he saw Wilheimer's estate come into view, an enormous Tudor-style mansion, fully restored to its former glory and looking like something out of a gothic novel. A backdrop that would play a pivotal role in determining Harrison's future, which should be what he was focusing on instead of Aimee.

He glanced over at Mrs. Holbrook, who was snoring lightly with her head propped against the side padding of the carriage, before he turned to stare at Aimee, who was peering out the window up at the carriages slowly winding their way up the drive.

"What was your take on Wilheimer and his grasp of English?" He broke the silence that they'd managed for the entire trip, speaking softly to not wake Mrs. Holbrook. "Do you think he can speak and understand it better than he lets on?"

"Oh, he definitely has a basic grasp of English," she whispered back, turning her attention to him, her big blue eyes piercingly gorgeous in the early afternoon sunlight. "But no, I don't think he understands it enough to discuss business principles or the legalities and intricacies of a company buyout. He was genuinely surprised and furious to find out he'd been lied to by the translator."

"Are you sure?" he asked, rubbing his chin in thought. "What if he was behind the interpreter misinterpreting everything?"

"Anything is possible," she replied with a light shrug. "But why would he have insisted I come along and interpret this weekend if that were the case?"

"Aside from the obvious fact that you're stunning, and the man probably wants to add you to his harem of mistresses?"

"His *harem* of mistresses?"

"He has a wife and at least three mistresses on the side."

"That is practically a harem. But the man must be in his mid-sixties; what's he doing with three mistresses and a wife?"

"Staying physically active, I'd say." Harrison winked at her. "I can only wish for that sort of stamina when I'm his age."

She crossed her arms over her chest, an expression of acute distaste on her face. "Do you intend to have a harem of mistresses, too?"

He laughed at that. "I can't even keep the one lady I intend to marry happy. How on earth would I manage even one more?"

Aimee pressed her lips together before quickly glancing over to Mrs. Holbrook, who was starting to stir. "Perhaps you can't keep her happy because you keep mentioning the *M* word, which she doesn't want anything to do with."

"That's only because she's somewhat naive about the inevitable." He managed to keep a straight face, even when her eyes narrowed and he could tell she was biting her tongue to keep from berating him and waking Mrs. Holbrook.

"An interesting way of describing her behavior," she whispered. "When one might call you delusional for even thinking she'd agree to marry you in the first place, when you know she's more likely to shoot you."

He couldn't help but laugh, thoroughly enjoying bantering with this woman more than he had with anyone else in a long time. The realization stopped him short. He did truly enjoy spending time with her, even when they butted heads. The woman was quick-witted, bold, and didn't step on eggshells around him. She fascinated him without even trying to.

And when all his other paramours had tried to corral him into marriage, here she was running for the hills. Who'd have thought a Dollar Princess would ever say no to marriage with a future earl?

Would that change if he loved her? Not that he did, even if he'd never felt this way about anyone before. But liking her a lot, probably more than he'd ever liked another woman before, wasn't love, was it? Certainly, he enjoyed her company, and if he was being honest, he even looked forward to spending time with her. But that wasn't love, either. He couldn't feel love for anyone. That emotion was far too dangerous to fall into. Even if for some reason, the idea of it suddenly wasn't so foreign or terrifying as he'd once believed it to be.

Mrs. Holbrook stirred and then blinked at them both, a sheepish expression in her eyes as she slowly woke from her nap. "Oh dear, did I fall asleep?"

"Yes, but you waking was good timing as we're practically here." Aimee pointed out the window to her right, to the estate ahead.

A few minutes later, the carriage crested the

drive and began to slowly wind its way to the front entrance where Wilheimer and a woman were greeting the new arrivals from the carriage ahead of them.

"His wife or one of his harem?" Aimee asked Harrison, with a raise of her brow.

"The man has a harem?" Mrs. Holbrook gasped.

"He has a wife and three mistresses," Aimee replied.

"Good gracious!" Mrs. Holbrook exclaimed, and both he and Aimee grinned at the woman's expression of outrage. "How shocking."

"It is, isn't it," Aimee replied. "One wonders why women even get married when their husbands carry on like that."

She directed her last words straight at Harrison, and he frowned. He'd never cheated on any of the women he'd had liaisons with, and he had no intention of doing so when he did marry. "There are many benefits to marriage, Miss Jenkins."

"For a man, Mr. Stone," she pertly replied. "Not a woman. In any event, I'm sure the lady with Wilheimer is his wife."

"Given his mistresses are half his age, you're probably right." He looked over to the woman next to Wilheimer, noting she was probably in her early fifties, with a trim figure. "Though he'll probably have one of his mistresses here, too, tucked away for the weekend."

"You say that without blinking an eye," Aimee said with a frown.

"It's just how it is," he replied, to which her frown turned into a furious scowl. He grinned and held his hands up in mock surrender. "It's not what I would do, but it's generally how gentlemen in Society behave."

"That's because most of Society don't marry for love," she said. "So they go looking for it elsewhere."

"One doesn't have to marry for love to be faithful, especially not if there's an attraction and desire for each other present." For a moment, he couldn't disguise the hunger for her in his eyes. And if Mrs. Holbrook hadn't been there, he would have hauled Aimee onto his lap and kissed her until she was moaning his name aloud.

Thankfully, the carriage came to a halt and the door opened, bringing Harrison back to his senses. The two ladies exited, while Harrison followed behind, stepping out onto the path as Wilheimer and the lady stepped forward to greet them, their butler beside them.

Wilheimer extended his hand and Harrison took it in his own, shaking it thoroughly while staring intently into the man's eyes. Wilheimer returned his stare before Harrison released his grip, and the man turned to both Aimee and Mrs. Holbrook and said welcome in a heavily accented English. He then bent down and kissed both ladies on their gloved knuckles, while Harrison did likewise with the woman next to Wilheimer.

"Mrs. Wilheimer, I'm presuming?" Harrison asked the lady as he straightened, frowning when from the corner of his eyes he noticed Wilheimer's hand lingered a bit longer on Aimee's hand than it had on Mrs. Holbrook's.

The lady's eyes followed his, an expression of resignation crossing her features before she masked it and turned back to regard Harrison. "Yes, I am Maria Wilheimer, and my husband and I welcome you to our country estate," she replied in a heavy accent.

"You speak English well," Harrison commented, wondering again how much English Wilheimer did or didn't speak.

Maria shrugged. "Enough to be understood. Seeing Franz still refuses to learn." She glanced over at her husband, who was now watching Harrison like a hawk.

"Deutsche Männer können sehr stur sein," Aimee said.

The woman's gaze swung with great interest over to her. "Du sprichst Deutsch?"

"I do speak German," Aimee replied in English. "It's the reason Mr. Wilheimer requested I attend this weekend so I could translate."

"Yes, I'm sure *that's* the reason he wanted you to attend," Maria replied, with a small sigh.

Wilheimer said something in German, and his wife frowned before replying back to him in rapid German, too.

"He wants to discuss business with you," Aimee said to Harrison. "But his wife is saying later."

"I'd rather discuss it now, too," Harrison replied, subjecting himself to a frown from Maria.

"Business later," Maria said with a definite shake of her head, her gaze pinning first Harrison and then Wilheimer with a no-nonsense glare, until both men reluctantly nodded. "Good," she said with a bob of her chin. "Now, you follow my butler, who'll show you to your rooms where you can freshen up. Everyone will meet for tea and cake in two hours out in the greenhouse in the far gardens." The woman gestured over to the entrance behind her, while the butler ushered them to follow.

With a reluctant nod to their hosts, Harrison followed Mrs. Holbrook and Aimee as the butler led them through the foyer and up the marble staircase to the first floor.

"That was interesting," Aimee said over her shoulder to him as they followed the butler down the hallway.

"How?" Harrison asked, somewhat distracted by the alluring sway of her hips in the deep sapphire-blue skirt that molded her figure to perfection. His hands itched to draw her to him and press himself against her softness.

How the hell was he going to get through a weekend without touching her? At least Mrs. Holbrook was there to play chaperone, which he imagined she'd do well, given she'd been suspicious of them both all week.

"Well, Maria Wilheimer clearly speaks English. Not enough for the intricacies of a business transaction, but enough that Wilheimer could have made use of her skills to discuss the basics with you," Aimee replied, pausing in response to the butler stopping and showing Mrs. Holbrook to her room.

"If you both don't mind," Mrs. Holbrook said as she paused at the door and glanced back at them both. "I might have a small lie-down as I'm feeling a tad unsettled in the stomach."

"Can I get you anything?" Aimee asked, her face crinkling in concern.

"No, I'll be fine. I'll call for a pot of tea but otherwise, rest is what I need," Mrs. Holbrook said. "I'll meet you both down in the greenhouse in two hours."

Mrs. Holbrook entered her room then closed the door, while the butler continued ushering them down the corridor to their rooms.

"This way, please," he said to them, striding down to the end of the hall and turning right.

Aimee and Harrison quickened their pace to follow as the butler walked down to the end of the hall and turned right. A few moments later, he showed them both to their rooms, adjoining rooms, which made no sense given Harrison was certain Wilheimer had asked Aimee here with a view to try to charm her himself.

"If you need anything, there is a bell pull in each of your rooms," the butler said. "The greenhouse is in the far back gardens, about a five-minute stroll from the back of the residence, through the gardens and forest. There will be some footmen along the way to guide you." He then nodded to them both and turned on his heel, striding back the way they'd just come.

"Adjoining rooms, how convenient," Aimee said, walking over to the adjoining door and opening it. "And it's not locked, either. How handy." She glanced back at him and grinned.

Harrison blinked. "Excuse me?"

The minx had the audacity to wink at him. "We'll make good use of these doors into each other's room this weekend, won't we?"

"We will?" Was she really talking about what he thought she was? Suddenly, his necktie felt suffocatingly tight.

"Yes, to discuss the Wilheimer deal, of course." She was staring at him with eyes as wide as saucers. "Did you think I meant something different?"

He caught the little twitch at the corner of her lips and knew the woman was teasing him. Tormenting him, too, given the images that had arisen over just what they could get up to without interruption…images he was having a hard time shaking.

"Are you purposefully trying to provoke me?"

"Perhaps." She grinned at him. "Is it working?"

He couldn't help himself. He stepped into the room, kicked the door shut with the heel of his boot, then strode over to stand in front of her. Glancing down into her bright blue eyes, eyes that he could have sworn were sparkling brighter than the stars, he realized she really was quite the most gorgeous woman he'd ever known, and it wasn't just her looks that made her that way.

There was a vibrancy about her, a zest for life and adventure that he was drawn to, despite all his reservations to the contrary. She was the light to his darkness, and he needed to feel her again, to be surrounded by her warmth and her essence. His marriage ultimatum be damned.

Almost tentatively, he reached out and cupped her cheek with his hand, a fission of heat scoring his palm and shooting down his spine. "It's working."

"Good, because I've been wanting to do this for days."

And before he could gather his wits, she launched herself into his arms, winding her hands around his neck and bringing his head down to her, until their lips met in a clash of pent-up heat and frustration. All thoughts of why he shouldn't be doing this with her fled in an instant, as an all-consuming desire filled him to the point where nothing else mattered but her.

They tore at each other's clothing, pulling at the material in a frenzy as they stumbled over to the bed, their hands and mouths all over each other.

They fell onto the mattress, Aimee on top of him. She unbuttoned his trousers, her fingers flying over the material, and Harrison lifted his hips to help her, his cock springing free of the confines a moment later.

He shuddered in pleasure when her fingers began to stroke his cock, but then when her mouth replaced her hand, he nearly came on the spot. He dug his fingers into the sheet, desperately trying to control himself, but her tongue flicked across his shaft, teasing and tasting him until he didn't think he'd be able to stand it.

He flipped her over onto her back and pulled her skirts up and pushed down her drawers. Then he buried his head in her curls at the junction of her thighs.

"Oh my," she moaned, her wet passage tasting like the sweetest nectar he'd ever sampled. He sucked on her nub and gently pushed his fingers inside her, her hips thrusting against his hand, as she began panting and grabbing at the sheets, too. He flicked his tongue against her and feasted on her mound, until she began bucking under him, screaming in pleasure.

He replaced his mouth and fingers with his cock, pumping inside her over and over until she began writhing under him again, and her wet passage squeezed tightly around his cock. As she orgasmed again, he began to pump his seed inside of her, waves of ecstasy gripping him, before he collapsed on the bed beside her, completely spent, but feeling so goddamned satisfied that he never wanted to let her go.

But rather than the thought scaring him, he wrapped his arms around her and breathed her in as she snuggled against him. And as exhaustion began to overtake him, he realized he felt something he hadn't ever before.

He felt at peace.

CHAPTER TWENTY-EIGHT

Cocooned in Harrison's arms, Aimee felt more content than she ever had, her whole body having experienced an ecstasy she hadn't understood was possible until she'd met him. No wonder so many couples partook in such delights with each other, though she suspected Harrison's skills in the bed-chamber were more impressive than other men's, given he excelled in anything he put his mind to.

And he'd certainly put his mind to pleasuring her; she could still feel the aftermaths of his exquisite touch upon nearly every inch of her body. Even the thought of how she'd orgasmed around him as he thrust inside her was enough to simultaneously make her blush and send a delicious thrill of excitement down to her toes.

"I suppose we'd better dress and head downstairs for afternoon tea," he murmured against her ear before beginning to trail kisses down the back of her neck.

Aimee sighed, not quite ready to leave this bubble of bliss just yet. "Must we?"

Harrison laughed. "Unfortunately, we must. However, I'll be more than happy to satisfy your every desire later tonight, and every night once you're my wife."

"That would be wonderful," she replied, but then his words registered, and panic started to claw at her chest. Very real, very raw panic, and not because he was talking of marriage, but because it had sounded so natural that she hadn't even flinched...almost as if she was starting to consider it.

"Are you agreeing to marry me?" he asked, his body tensing behind her.

"No," she was quick to assure him, and herself, as she pushed away from him and sat up, pulling the bedsheet to her chest. "I was referring to the first part of your statement, not the latter part, which you know I won't agree to." She couldn't seriously consider being his wife...not unless she wanted to throw away all her dreams. Which she wouldn't do. She couldn't. Not even for Harrison... could she?

"Why do you have to be so stubborn about it?" He sighed, a long, drawn-out sound tinged with frustration.

She twisted around to face him. "And why do you always have to ruin these moments by talking about it? Can't you leave well enough alone and accept we're simply having an affair?"

A frown was his answer. "You're Thomas Thornton-Jones's only child and heir. You can't simply *have an affair*. Marriage is an inevitability for you, and you know it."

She was worried he was right, especially because the more he mentioned it, the more a small part of her was getting used to the idea. "It's not inevitable at all." At least she sounded convincing, given she felt anything but.

"You know it is, and the sooner you accept that, the better." He raked his fingers through his hair and sat up in the bed, staring at her. "The two of us marrying makes perfect sense, and if you think about it with logic instead of emotion, you'd realize it, too."

"Perfect for you, not perfect for me. You're the only one who benefits from us marrying. You'd get my million-dollar dowry, inherit my father's company, and have a wife to bear your heirs and run your households. What would I get, except having to give up all of my dreams?"

"Why do you assume you'd have to do that?"

"You'd allow me to play an active role in running the company if I was your wife?" She stared at him with undisguised skepticism.

"Honestly, I don't know. It's not something I've had to consider before I met you. Though I'd never want you to give up your dreams."

"You wouldn't?" Her heart skipped a beat at the thought.

"No, I wouldn't," he replied. "But you know women in our circles don't work, let alone run companies. It's not done."

She gave a mirthless laugh. "I've been trying to convince my father to let me be part of his business since I was a little girl and I've been so unsuccessful that I've had to resort to swapping place with my cousin simply to learn what I can of the company. So, yes, Harrison, I'm aware it's not done. But it can be. Someone has to do it first and lead the way. Now, if that's something you could accept me doing, then I'm willing to consider marrying you."

And, in the moment, she realized she was...if

he'd agree to abandon the traditional notions of what a wife's role should be, and if any man liked to push the boundaries of what could be done, it was Harrison Stone. Not to mention he was the only man she could ever see herself marrying. The only man, aside from her father, she cared about… The only man she'd started to fall in love with…

The dawning awareness of her feelings was as terrifying as it was liberating.

Was she really falling for Harrison Stone? Or was she caught up in their whirlwind ride of passion? It had to be the latter, but with a sinking heart she suspected it was the former, especially given she was considering marrying him when she'd never thought she'd marry at all.

"If you want a wife who's happy to run your households and be a perfect little countess," she continued, "you need to look elsewhere because I intend to play an active part in my father's company, marriage or not."

"Do you think you'll convince him to let you?"

She pressed her lips together and nodded. "I'm determined to. He's stubborn but I'm even more stubborn."

He was silent for several seconds. "Before I met you, I'd never have thought a woman would want to have anything to do with business, and I certainly never envisaged my future wife working."

No man ever did. "Which is why I refused you, and unless you're willing to reconsider, then I'll continue to refuse you."

"So let me see if I understand you correctly. If I do agree to let you help run the company, you'll agree to marry me?"

"Are you agreeing to?"

"I'll agree to consider it."

It wasn't the answer she'd wanted. Not even close. "My father taught me the devil is in the details, and I know he taught you the same. Agreeing to *consider* it is not agreeing to it at all."

"You're right, it's not," he said without a hint of expression on his face.

"It doesn't matter anyhow, because, in the end, who are we fooling?" Aimee shook her head. "You're the heir to an earldom, and Society will never condone your wife being involved in running a company alongside you."

"You're right. They wouldn't."

His words sent an unexpected pang of hurt right through her heart. "I'm glad you've finally accepted the futility of us marrying." She was lying through her teeth, because how could she be glad when she felt so heartbroken? And why she felt heartbroken when she should be relieved was something she'd consider another time. A time when she could look back on the whole situation and laugh instead of wanting to cry.

"I wouldn't say that," he murmured. "I'd say it's more a case that I've finally accepted how determined you are to pursue your dreams, and who am I stop you, even as your husband."

She tried to make sense of his words. "Are you saying you'd agree to let me work if I was your wife?"

"I am," he replied with a definite nod of his head. "I intend to be an unconventional earl, so why shouldn't my countess be unconventional, too?"

Part of her desperately wanted to believe him, but the other part wasn't quite ready to. "You're not just saying that to get me to agree to marry you, and then you'll change your mind after."

"I promise you, if that's really what you want to do, I'll support you, and I'll even speak with your father about how much of an asset you'll be to the company."

She couldn't believe what she was hearing. It was as if her dreams, which had seemed so far out of reach only moments ago, were now so close she could touch them.

He leaned over and took her hand in his. "Now, will you agree to marry me?"

She stared into his eyes, trying to see if there was any hint of artifice in the green depths, but all she could see was honesty. She nodded her head. "Yes."

"You will?" Now he was the one who seemed hesitant to believe her.

"I will." She couldn't believe she was agreeing to marry him, but she was, and rather than fear she felt excited.

A grin spread over his face. "Good."

"Good?" She grabbed one of the pillows from behind her and swatted his chest with it. "I finally agree to marry you, and all you can say is *good*?"

"How about very good?" He winked at her, before his lips swooped down and captured her own, silencing any of her further protests.

She wrapped her arms around his neck and

kissed him back with ardor, a part of her still reeling. Her parents would be thrilled of course, and news of their engagement would definitely lessen the scolding she'd get for swapping places with Evie.

Hmm, already she could see the benefits of being engaged. That and Harrison's kisses. God, he was a wonderful kisser. She imagined she could kiss him forever and never tire of his touch.

He gently pulled away from her. "As much as I want to again explore every inch of your delectable body, we probably should get dressed and go downstairs before Mrs. Holbrook sends out a search party."

Aimee laughed. "You're right."

"I usually am." He winked at her again before swinging his legs over the edge of the bed and striding completely naked to where his drawers and trousers had been tossed to the floor.

"Very funny." She lay there happily watching him as he pulled on his drawers over his muscled legs, followed by his trousers. Her fiancé had a very fine figure indeed. Her fiancé…it sounded so odd yet felt so right. "How will we get any work done after we're married, when your kisses are so distracting?"

He laughed before grabbing his rumpled-up shirt from the floor and putting it on. "It could prove difficult. But who knows? You may end up changing your mind about wanting to work."

She went from happy to furious in the blink of an eye. "Is that why you agreed to let me work as your wife, because you think I'll change my mind?"

"No." He shrugged. "But your priorities might change, especially after having children."

"They won't." She narrowed her eyes at him before scooping up the bedsheet and storming out of the bed toward where her clothes were in a bundle on the floor. "And if that's what you're hoping will happen, you're going to be sorely disappointed."

"I'm not hoping for anything. I'm being realistic about the fact that people can, and do, change their mind about things," he replied, tying up his shoelaces with more force than needed.

"Like agreeing to marry someone?" She raised her brow at him before bending down and picking up her clothes.

His hands paused over his shoes. "I walked right into that one, didn't I?"

"You did."

He nodded and finished tying his laces before glancing up at her. "Are you reconsidering marrying me then?"

"I said I'll marry you, so I will." She stalked over behind the dressing screen and yanked on her pantaloons, then her petticoats, nearly ripping the stitching in the process. "But don't be under any illusion that my priorities will change after we marry, because they won't."

Aimee grabbed her blouse and began to put it on, and then a question began to burn at the back of her mind, and she stopped buttoning up her blouse midway. "Why do you even want to marry me, Harrison? I'm not so naive to think my dowry isn't a part of it—"

"I've already told you I don't want your bloody dowry. I never want to feel beholden to you, or to anyone, ever again."

"Again?"

He blew out a breath. "Did you know that after my parents died, my grandfather came to New York?"

"No, I didn't know that."

"He came to retrieve my father's body and take him back to England to be buried in the family plot on his estate."

"What about your mother? Surely, they should have been buried together."

"Oh, she was only a maid according to my grandfather, and she'd done the unforgivable by marrying well above her station, hence she wasn't worthy of being buried alongside my father." A muscle in his jaw twitched, while his hands clenched by his sides. "And why I as her son also wasn't worthy of returning to England with him."

Aimee's heart broke for the little boy he had been, and she had to anchor her legs in place to stop herself from running over and hugging him, knowing he wouldn't appreciate her sympathy, even if it was warranted. "Your grandfather was a monster."

"He was," Harrison agreed. "He wouldn't give me a dime to bury her properly, so she was buried in an unmarked grave in the paupers' cemetery on Hammond's Hill."

Aimee gasped. "You're the anonymous buyer who bought the cemetery and had that beautiful monument built." The land was prime New York real estate and all of Society had been abuzz when the new anonymous buyer hadn't developed it into small lots, but instead ordered an elaborate monument be built and placed in the center of the cemetery as a tribute to all the nameless souls resting there.

"It was the least I could do for my mother and all the others buried there without even a name holder to mark their graves."

"Your mother would have been proud of you." The more she found out about Harrison, the more she realized how wrong she'd been to judge him.

He unclenched his fists. "Perhaps. In any event, after I'd begged my grandfather for some money to bury her with and he refused, I promised myself I'd never ask for money from anyone again, nor would I accept it. So the only way forward was to make a fortune and prove my grandfather wrong."

"You've certainly done that." Her heart broke for the eight-year-old boy he'd been. How scared he must have been to be on his own, with absolutely no support from his family. "Your grandfather was a bastard."

"He was," he replied. "But, in the end, his rejection and cruelty made me into the man I am today. Which is why I don't want a cent of your dowry. You can put it into trust for our children."

Aimee gulped. He said the word "children" so casually and with such certainty that it scared her, especially as she'd never really thought she'd have children given her life goals. "What if I don't want children?"

"Don't you?"

"I don't know," she answered truthfully, tugging

on her earlobe. "I never thought I was going to marry, so I never thought I'd have children. Not to mention my mother had such complications giving birth to me that she could never have children again… I don't know if I want to go through that. Perhaps you should marry someone else, someone who wants to be a wife and have children, instead of running a company."

"I don't want another woman. I want you."

"But why?" she beseeched him, still trying to comprehend his motivation. If it wasn't for her dowry, could she dare to hope that he was starting to care for her, as she was him? That perhaps he was even falling a little in love with her, too?

"I've dishonored you," he replied. "I need to do the right thing and rectify that."

A bitter sense of disappointment rose in her throat. Had she really expected him to profess any love, when he'd made no secret that he had no intention of loving her? She was a fool to have hoped, even for a moment, he might. "Of course that's the reason why."

"It's not the only one." He rubbed his temple, looking oddly uncertain. "And it's not because of your father or the company, either." He paused and took in a deep breath before exhaling. "I suppose, aside from being insanely attracted to you, I actually like you, Aimee Thornton-Jones."

"You sound surprised by that."

"Aren't you? We've been at loggerheads since meeting, yet I think you might even like me, too."

Like him? She'd come to do more than just like him.

"Which is why I'm not going to keep dishonoring you, or your father, by having an affair with you. I respect you too much for that."

She took in a big breath, not sure how she felt about his answer. Was him liking her going to be enough? Somehow, she doubted it, especially after growing up seeing how much her parents loved each other.

Suddenly, almost desperately, she wanted that sort of marriage for herself, but not with simply anyone. She wanted it with Harrison. She wanted him to love her as she was starting to love him.

"Do you think you might ever do more than just like me?" Gathering her courage, she raised her chin until her eyes were staring directly into his. "That perhaps one day you could possibly even... love me?"

Silence followed her question, Harrison's whole body going rigid and his eyes turning completely impenetrable.

"I've told you I can't do that." There was a finality to his voice that suggested he wouldn't say a thing more on the topic, but Aimee wasn't one to give up.

"Can't or won't?"

"Both, and you know the reason why," he said, his brows knitting together.

"I don't think your parents would want you to forgo love for the rest of your life because they died."

"You say that so flippantly! But you have no idea what it was like... Life took away the two people I loved most in the world. Hell, they *were* my world. Then they were gone in the blink of an eye, and I was all alone." He took in a deep breath and then exhaled it slowly. "The only thing that's given me comfort since is succeeding in business, which is the only thing I'll ever love. I'll never subject myself to the pain of loving someone then losing them, ever again. Not even for you."

He spun away from her and stalked over to the closed door.

"So that's it?" Aimee called out after him. "End of discussion?" She felt like raging at him, or bawling. But she wouldn't give him the satisfaction of showing him how his refusal to love or even consider it was devastating her.

"I've said all I need to on the topic," he replied, pausing at the door as his hand reached out for the handle. "And we need to get to Wilheimer's afternoon tea."

She bit her bottom lip to stop herself from crying, unwilling to let him know how upset she was with his refusal to even consider loving her. Which, clearly, he didn't. The realization opened a hole in her heart she didn't think would heal. So instead of saying anything further, she simply followed him out the doorway and down the hall.

Had she really expected him to say anything else when he'd never been anything but blunt about never wanting to love again? Perhaps her heart had hoped he might have changed his mind, but her head knew otherwise. And at least he was being honest with her, unlike the men who'd previously asked for her hand, professing their supposed undying love and admiration in the process, when they'd barely spent two minutes alone together.

Her marriage to Harrison wouldn't be the same as her parents' marriage, not by a long shot, but most people married for a lot less, and if she couldn't have his love, then at least she could put all her energy and passion into her dream of being an active part of her father's company, couldn't she?

At least she hoped so, because, in the end, business was what had made her happy in the past and it would make her happy in the future. It had to, because if it didn't, she didn't know what she'd do.

CHAPTER TWENTY-NINE

Harrison's boots clipped loudly on the footpath as he walked through the back gardens of Wilheimer's estate, heading toward the greenhouse where the afternoon tea was being held. Aimee was walking silently by his side, still not having said a word since they'd left his room.

Why had she spoken of love when he'd already told her it wasn't something he could give her? But she had, and now they were at odds because of it. He didn't like it at all.

Already this engagement business was proving complicated, but, hopefully, she'd realize they could have a perfectly amicable marriage filled with mutual respect and attraction, rather than anything so fickle as love added to the mix. Love led to heartbreak and loss, and it was something he never wanted to experience again. Part of him knew if he let himself fall for her, he'd never want to let her go, and with life having a bad habit of taking away those Harrison loved, the odds were it would take Aimee away from him, too.

He glanced over to her as the greenhouse came into view. Her eyes were affixed firmly ahead and she had a determined tilt to her chin that suggested she wasn't going to budge an inch. "Are you going to speak to me at all this afternoon?"

She pressed her lips briefly together, her eyes remaining forward as they arrived at the greenhouse entrance and a footman opened the door for them. "That depends entirely on how much you further annoy me."

He felt like sighing in exasperation. Women could be so confusing and frustrating at times. His fiancée most especially of all.

They headed to the adjacent garden terrace just off the greenhouse, where Wilheimer's guests were mingling, and where the man himself was holding court at the far end of the terrace.

Aimee came to an abrupt halt. "Why didn't you tell me Lady Whitley would be here?"

Harrison followed her gaze and caught sight of Jane, who had begun weaving her way over to where they stood. "I didn't know she would be."

"Harrison," Jane said a moment later, looking the picture of elegance dressed in a light green day dress and matching bonnet. "How lovely to see you again."

"What are you doing here, Jane?" he replied bluntly, taking her gloved hand in his and giving her knuckles a perfunctory kiss.

"Always straight to the point, aren't you?" She laughed lightly, her hand coming up to tap him on the arm, resting there briefly. "Franz and my late husband used to do business together, and I still get invited to his weekend house parties, though I rarely attend them given most of the guests only speak German." The lady shrugged. "However, I decided to attend this weekend."

"After you found out Harrison was attending, I imagine," Aimee said, her face a picture of inno-cence and her English accent firmly back in place.

The woman was good at accents and languages, he'd give her that.

Jane's smile slipped as she turned to face Aimee. "Ah, Miss Jenkins, how *wonderful* to see you here, too," she replied, sounding anything but happy about it. "And being so bold and direct, as I thought only Americans could be."

"You're forgetting I am half American," Aimee replied with a smile of her own. "Clearly, such traits are in my blood."

Lady Whitley returned her smile, though there was nothing friendly in the tight twisting of her lips. "That and many other things I imagine, seeing as you're so liberal with your favors…"

"Jane, that's enough," Harrison warned, knowing she was referring to when she caught Aimee and him in an embrace.

"No, Harrison, let her say whatever she wants," Aimee said. "I'm capable of defending myself."

"No, he's quite right," Jane said. "That was rude of me and I do apologize."

She seemed sincere, which was so at odds to her demeanor from a moment ago that Harrison began to question just how good of an actress the lady was.

"Excuse me, Mr. Stone?" the butler said, interrupting them as he came to a halt next to Harrison. holding a silver tray with a folded-up note lying upon it. "Your secretary has asked me to deliver this to you."

Harrison took the note from the butler, then unfolded it, recognizing Mrs. Holbrook's penmanship on the parchment. "It's from Mrs. Holbrook, who sends her apologies but says she's come down with a stomach ailment and will rest in her room for the remainder of the day. And she's asked for you to attend her room, Aim—Evie," Harrison said, correcting himself before slipping up.

"She's asked for me?" Aimee asked, doubt filling her eyes. "She must be unwell then."

Harrison shrugged. "She says she wants to give you some instructions about dealing with Wilheimer, seeing as you're here in a work capacity."

"Now that makes sense," Aimee said. "Well, I better go and see her." Her head swiveled between Harrison and Jane, her brows knotting together as she did so. "If you'll both excuse me."

"I can go with you if you'd like."

"There's no need, I'll be fine."

"Of course she'll be fine, Harrison," Jane said, her arm lightly looping through his elbow. "It's only a short walk through the gardens to the house, and besides, I've spoken to several of Wilheimer's friends about your plans for the future of the London company, and they're all eager to meet you and possibly invest, too."

He gently but firmly extracted Jane's arm from his. "As much as I appreciate your efforts, Jane, I will go with—"

"I said I'll be fine," Aimee interrupted him, a determined glint in her eyes. "So go with Lady Whitley, Harrison, and cultivate business for the company, which is your one true love after all."

She gave him a nod and then turned on her heel and marched back to the inside of the greenhouse and out of his sight.

Part of him wanted to chase after her, but that was foolish. She'd start to think he cared more for her than he'd told her he ever could...which a small part of him was terrified was the case. But that couldn't be. Even the thought of loving her sent him into a cold sweat.

"Are you quite all right, Harrison?" Jane asked, her eyes filled with concern, but Harrison could also see a calculation in their depths he'd not noticed before.

"I'm fine," he said, parroting Aimee's words, and rather than follow his instincts and follow Aimee, he followed Jane, who began regaling him of everyone she was going to introduce him to that would further his empire in London.

Which was exactly what he wanted, he reminded himself.

At least it had been before he'd met Aimee. Now he wasn't so sure. Because as much as he denied it, he was worried the ice he'd encased his heart with was starting to crack, and if he let it get any bigger, it just might shatter.

So he pushed down the voice in his head telling him he was being a fool, and focused on what was most important in his life—business and growing his fortune. Which he reminded himself was the reason he was marrying her in the first place, to ensure this deal went ahead and there would be no future business repercussions from her father. Because if Thomas ever found out Harrison had dishonored his daughter and not married her, the man would do all in his power to destroy him. It was a fight even Harrison was reluctant to take on, especially when it would jeopardize his dream of owning his own company. A dream that had got him through the dark times as a child when he was so desperately alone. A dream he'd pursued more passionately than anything in his life, until recently.

A dream he couldn't abandon for anything so debilitating as love.

CHAPTER THIRTY

Aimee marched down the footpath back to Wilheimer's residence, her annoyance with Harrison growing with each step she took. The man was even more stubborn than her father, unable to accept that love didn't have to equate to loss. And even if it did, surely it was worth it?

She knew to the bottom of her soul her parents wouldn't trade their love to soften the heartbreak that would occur if anything happened to either one of them, preferring to have loved each other than never loved at all. But then perhaps that wasn't being entirely fair to Harrison. To have lost both of his parents as a child, and then been discarded by his grandfather when he needed the man most, would probably steel anyone's heart against loving someone.

It was as frustrating as it was heartbreaking, because Aimee knew he had a lot of love to give, if only he'd let himself do so, but given his constant protestations otherwise, it was unlikely he ever would. The thought was depressing, because as much as she was starting to love him, she didn't think she'd be able to go along with having a marriage that was mutually agreeable but lacked love.

"Aimee?" a man said from behind her.

"Yes," she said, only realizing too late she'd responded to her real name, which no one should know. "It's Evie actually," she quickly corrected, spinning around to the voice. It took her a second to recognize the clerk from the telegram office, and another second to see the pistol he was pointing at her.

"Don't lie," the man spat out with a smirk as he waved the pistol about. "I know who you really are. And don't you dare scream or run, Miss Dollar Princess, or I'll shoot you."

She nodded, not wanting to startle him, given the hand he was holding the pistol with was shaking lightly. "I won't." How had he found out who she was? Surely, he wouldn't have assumed that from the telegram she sent. "William, isn't it?"

His eyes narrowed. "It is."

"So, William, why are you pointing a weapon at me?"

There was a glint of resolution in his eyes. "Isn't it obvious? We're kidnapping you."

"Of course you are." Did Harrison always have to be right? He'd never let her forget it, she was sure. But then William's use of the term *we* registered in her thoughts. "We?"

Leaves crunching underfoot sounded to her right and Aimee swiveled her head in that direction.

"Yes, we," Deirdre said, emerging from some trees just off the footpath, dressed all in black and holding a pistol in her hand. "And you're going to make us a pretty little penny, too."

"Is this your kidnapping attire?" Aimee couldn't help but ask, hoping that if she could rattle her, it would give Aimee a chance to pull out her own pistol.

Deidre pinched her lips together before twisting them into a tight smile. "So overly confident as I'm sure only a million-dollar heiress could be, but you won't be so confident shortly with what's planned for you. And if you don't shut up and do as you're told, you'll be a dead heiress."

A sliver of fear ran down Aimee's spine at the absolute certainty in Deirdre's eyes. If she was as obsessed with her and her father as Molly warned, then Deidre could be very dangerous. "Look, Deidre, I know you think we're sisters—"

Deidre laughed. "You're really not right in the head like I was told, aren't you?"

"Who said that?"

"Never you mind," Deidre replied, before she glanced behind Aimee. "Now, William."

Before Aimee could even react, William's hand darted around from behind her, pressing a wet cloth against her mouth. She reached up and grabbed his arm, trying to wrench it away from her, but the sickly sweet smell of the rag was making her head spin, and she found her arms losing all their strength.

"Have a nice little sleep, princess," Deidre cooed, before a blackness started to engulf Aimee's vision. "And don't you worry, we'll look after you. You're our golden ticket, after all."

• • •

Harrison pulled out his pocket watch for the fifth time since Aimee had gone to see Mrs. Holbrook. How long could it take to give her some instructions? Yes, Mrs. Holbrook was thorough, but it had been over an hour, which seemed far too long.

"Looking at your watch again, Harrison?" Jane purred, sidling up to him after retrieving a glass of champagne from a passing waiter. "Anyone might think you're bored with my company, which is the last thing I'd want." Her free hand traced up along his right bicep through the material of his jacket. "I'd much prefer to entertain you this weekend… especially in the evenings while we're both naked in your bed."

She was batting her eyelashes up at him in a manner he used to find attractive but now found oddly false, and there was a calculation in her eyes again that suggested she was trying to manipulate him. Had she always been like this? Or was he only just now seeing it?

He gently removed her hand from his arm and took a step back. "Jane, I've agreed for us to be friends, but that's all."

"You know friends can still occasionally enjoy each other's company," she said with a decided pout. "Most especially at a house party."

"That won't be happening."

Her eyes narrowed. "This is because of Miss Jenkins, isn't? You're sleeping with her."

"That's not your business, Jane." He was getting frustrated with this conversation and the building sense of urgency that Aimee was taking too long.

"I thought you had a rule to never become involved with your employees?" Jane's voice was getting louder with each word. "Yet here you are fornicating with your secretary."

"She's not my secretary, Jane—"

"A trainee secretary then—"

"She's my fiancée."

Jane's face blanched, her fingers squeezing the stem of the champagne glass until they went white. "You're jesting, surely?"

"No, I'm not. She agreed to marry me this afternoon. At least I think we're still engaged."

"But you told me you weren't interested in marriage only a few months ago." Her voice had turned deceptively soft. "And yet here you are now engaged to someone completely unsuitable to be a future countess, given she's an illegitimate bastard whose mother was a maid!"

"You're forgetting my mother was a maid, too," Harrison said, his voice clearly showing his displeasure.

"At least she was clever enough to marry your father, unlike that harlot's mother!"

"That is enough, Jane. I will not have you disrespecting my fiancée."

"Yet you've obviously disrespected her enough to have become engaged to her," Jane hissed back. "But the joke is on you, Harrison, because Society will shun you for your choice, at least they will after I'm done ensuring they do."

"If I hear that you've even looked unkindly at my fiancée, let alone spoken a single word about her to anyone, I will make certain your bank forecloses on your loans and no other bank will lend you a penny more. You will be the one Society shuns given you won't even be able to afford rags to dress in."

She blinked repeatedly, gulping in a breath. "I don't know what you mean."

"There's no need to lie to me, Jane," he replied. "I know your late husband gambled away most of your dowry within the first month of your marriage, and that you've been living on what little is left and the largesse of your paramours since."

"How did you know…" Her voice trailed off, as fear replaced the anger in her eyes.

Harrison shrugged. "I always check the financials of whomever I'm getting into bed with, be that in business or in the bedroom."

"You knew all along?"

"Information is power, Jane. I didn't have a problem with it before, and I don't now, provided you do everything you can to ensure my fiancée is happily embraced by Society."

A panic-stricken look crossed her face. "How can I do that given her illegitimacy?"

"That won't be an issue in a few weeks' time." Once he'd settled everything with Aimee's father, and their engagement became public knowledge, everyone would know of Aimee and Evie's masquerade. Initially, it was bound to create a scandal, but with Harrison's clout in Society, and Aimee being Thomas Thornton-Jones's sole heir, they'd have enough influence between them to ensure Society viewed the charade as a harmless bit of fun. And if they didn't, he'd make them.

"How will a few weeks' time change that?"

"Trust me, it will," he said, unwilling to outline any details to her. "Now if that's all, I have a fiancée to find." He bowed briefly to her, then turned on his heel and strode through the guests mingling on the terrace.

Just as he entered the greenhouse a woman barreled into his chest. Steadying her, he realized it was Mrs. Holbrook, and there was an expression on her face he'd never seen before—worry.

"Where's Aimee? And, yes, before you ask, I know she's Thomas's daughter, not Peter's. Now where is she?"

"She's meant to be with you," Harrison replied. "You sent me a note requesting her to attend your room."

Her gaze swung back to Harrison and the worry turned to alarm. "I didn't send you a note."

"It was in your handwriting." He pulled out the note from his jacket pocket and handed it to her, desperately pushing aside the fear that was starting to clutch at his heart.

Her eyes scanned over the paper before returning to his. "It does look exactly like my handwriting, but it's not...it's my niece's."

"Your niece?"

She inhaled shakily. "Yes, and I think Aimee might be in terrible danger from her."

CHAPTER THIRTY-ONE

The muffled sound of voices gradually penetrated Aimee's sleep-shrouded mind as she began to wake up, her eyelids feeling like lead as she slowly glanced around and blinked in confusion.

She was lying in the middle of the floor in a room she didn't recognize, and her arms were tied together in front of her, while another piece of rope was binding her ankles to each other. And most disturbingly there was a large camera on a tripod in the corner of the room. What was going on, and where was she? Panic gripped her as she pushed up on her elbow and then swung her lower legs underneath her as she sat up on her haunches.

Apart from a desk under a window with a few papers scattered across it and a glass lamp burning brightly on top, there was nothing to give any hint of her location. There was barely any light coming in from the edges of the curtains on the window, suggesting it was getting dark, too. *Focus, Aimee, focus,* she told herself over and over, trying to relax her breathing, knowing she'd need a clear head to get through whatever this was. And then she started to remember… Deidre had kidnapped her after her sidekick, William, had knocked her out with chloroform or ether.

Frantically, she patted the pockets of her skirt in search of her pistol, but it was gone.

"Looking for this?" Deidre's voice purred from

behind her, her feet not making a sound as she walked around to stand in front of Aimee, reverently holding her derringer. "I found it in your pocket while you were sleeping. It's so pretty and petite," she continued, "though it would still occasion a fair bit of damage if I shot you with it, wouldn't it?"

"It would," Aimee replied, wondering just how she was going to get out of the situation. Thankfully, they'd made the mistake of tying her hands in front of her, which meant that if she could get Deidre close enough, she might be able to wrench the gun out of her hand.

"Good. If you don't want me to test that out, I'd suggest you don't try to stand up and give me a reason to."

"What do you want, Deidre? Money? Is that what you're risking the gallows for?"

"Trust an heiress to be so disdainful about the topic," Deidre replied, walking over to the desk, while placing the gun in her skirt pocket as she did so. She perched her backside on the edge of the desk and faced Aimee, assessing her for a moment before she spoke. "You have no idea what it's like for the rest of us not to have money."

"You're right, I don't. But I do know kidnapping isn't the way to go about getting it."

"It's the perfect way," Deidre replied. "I've barely had to do anything apart from helping kidnap you and assisting in taking some pictures to soon reap a large reward."

"Pictures?" Aimee asked, her eyes swiveling over to the tripod in the corner of the room.

Deidre smiled. "Yes. William took some photos of you tied up on the floor in case we need to prove we have you for the ransom."

"He did?" She felt like scratching at her skin at the thought of being unconscious while a man she didn't know took photos of her.

"Yes, but don't worry, I was here the whole time, and it was all above board." Deidre laughed, obviously sensing her discomfort. "In any event, why don't you relax and enjoy your surroundings while I organize things. Night is soon approaching and there's much to be arranged."

"You do realize Harrison will be looking for me."

"*Harrison*? My, you've gotten rather chummy with him to be calling him that, haven't you?" Deidre winked at her. "Does he even know who you really are?"

"He does. How do you know?"

"A little birdie told me," Deidre replied. "Goodness, though, it's no wonder Mr. Stone's so interested in you then, is it? You being a million-dollar heiress and all. In any event, he has no idea you're missing yet, and when he does find out, you'd best pray he'd doesn't come looking for you, or he'll be shot for his efforts."

Her chest clenched at the thought of him hurt and bleeding. She had to get out of here before he even came close to finding them, because contrary to Deidre's belief, Aimee knew Harrison would realize she was missing. And when he did, he'd probably leap to his usual conclusion that she'd been kidnapped...something she'd never hear the end of if she got out of this situation. "Where's your sidekick?" She couldn't hear or see him, and she'd have a better chance of escaping Deidre if he wasn't close by.

"Don't worry, he should be back very shortly after having sent off a telegram in the little town just over the hill." Deidre grinned as she stood up and walked over to Aimee.

Her heart sunk. "A telegram to my father?"

"Of course," Deidre purred. "How else will we get our ransom?"

"Kidnapping is a felony, Deidre," Aimee replied, imagining how terrified her parents would be once they got the news. "If you let me go, I promise I won't say anything, and you won't get in trouble." She had to convince her, given Deidre and William had made no effort to conceal their identities, which didn't bode well for what they had planned for Aimee after receiving a ransom.

Deidre laughed. "Do you think I'm stupid? If I let you go, you'd have me arrested and tried. So, no, I won't be doing that. Oh, and by the way, we call them crimes here in England, not felonies."

"You do realize there's only one way out of this for you."

"Yes, I'll get the ransom money and flee to Europe." She raised her chin at Aimee in defiance.

"After killing me, correct?" Aimee didn't blink as she stared up into Deidre's eyes.

Deidre turned her head away, unable to meet Aimee's stare. "That is not my job to do."

"Do you think my father will care who pulled the trigger?"

"What do you mean?" Deidre asked, the fingers of her free hand reaching up to tug nervously at the edge of her collar.

"I mean that if anything happens to me, my father will not rest until he finds you and destroys you. And that is not overexaggerating what he'd do, trust me on that."

"You're just trying to scare me."

"Am I? Tell me, what do you think one of the wealthiest, most powerful men in the world will do to someone who harms his only child? Do you think he'll be lenient and simply accept that fact? Or do you think he'll want to exact vengeance upon those responsible? Chasing them to any corner of the globe to do so."

"Stop it." Deidre shook her head fiercely, standing and beginning to pace across the short span of the room, backward and forward, a bundle of restless and fearful energy. "I was warned you'd try to do this and to not listen to a word you said if you did."

"Who warned you of that?" Deidre had referred to someone else earlier, too, and Aimee didn't think she meant William.

"That's not your concern."

"Was it your aunt, Mrs. Holbrook?" It had to be. Deidre didn't strike her as the one pulling the strings.

"What are you talking about?" Deidre stopped in her tracks and spun around to face Aimee. "Mrs. Holbrook isn't my aunt."

"She's not?" That made no sense. "But Molly told me she was."

"Well, Molly's mistaken, because Mrs. Holbrook is most definitely not my aunt." Deidre shook her head vehemently.

"No. She's mine, in fact," Molly said calmly from behind them.

"What are you doing here?" Deirdre said, sounding cross. "You're meant to stay away until we receive the ransom."

"The plans have changed," Molly replied, wandering into the room.

"Molly? You're part of this?" Aimee exclaimed, belatedly noticing the pistol Molly was holding.

"Part of it? I'm the mastermind behind it," Molly said with such a genuine smile that it seemed like she was talking about having planned a picnic rather than Aimee's kidnapping.

"But why? I thought we were becoming friends."

"Friends don't lie to each other, *Aimee*, which is what you've been doing ever since you got here," Molly replied with a smile, a second before she raised her pistol and pulled the trigger.

CHAPTER THIRTY-TWO

"What do you mean Aimee could be in terrible danger?" Harrison demanded, his sense of urgency building. "Where is she?"

"I don't know." Mrs. Holbrook twisted her hands together. "And I could be wrong, which I hope I am, but I do think Molly means her harm."

"Molly? As in my undersecretary, Miss Mitchell?"

"Yes." Mrs. Holbrook nodded. "She's my niece, which I know I should have told you earlier, but I didn't think it would be an issue…at least I hoped it wouldn't. However, given I saw her about twenty minutes ago from my window striding through the grounds of the estate heading east to the forest, when she's meant to be in London, I fear I was wrong. Especially now that Aimee appears to be missing, too."

"Why the hell would Molly mean Aimee harm?"

The woman straightened her shoulders like she was steeling herself for whatever she was about to say. "Because she thinks her father is Thomas Thornton-Jones."

"Is he?" he asked bluntly, thinking such a thing was doubtful. The Thomas he knew would most certainly have looked after a child of his, even if conceived out of wedlock.

"No, of course not," Mrs. Holbrook was quick to

answer. "But she believes so, contrary to my vigorous assertions otherwise."

"Why would she think she is then?"

Mrs. Holbrook sighed. "Her mother, my younger sister, Flora, became infatuated with Thomas when he first visited London, and she and I were assisting him and his brother as their temporary secretaries. Thomas never returned Flora's interest of course, never even looked twice at her, but she thought they were destined to be together. Convinced herself of it even. So, to get closer to him, she seduced his valet, but got pregnant as a result."

"And Molly was that child?"

"Yes," Mrs. Holbrook replied. "Though Flora insisted Molly was Thomas's child, even though they'd never been together. It was mad, of course, but well, my sister lived in a deluded state after she had Molly, and nothing I said would get through to her. Instead, she preferred to live in a world of fantasy. When Thomas next returned to England three years later, Flora confronted him, presenting Molly as his child, which he denied, of course. Then later that day Flora jumped in front of a train, leaving a journal with her outlandish accusations written about him inside it, on the platform beside her purse.

"I should have thrown her journal out that day, but instead I kept it with her belongings in my attic, and unfortunately Molly discovered it about five years ago. She confronted me and I explained the truth to her, but she wanted to believe her mother's lies, preferring to think her father was a wealthy millionaire instead of a valet."

"She wishes to take revenge on Thomas through Aimee?" Harrison surmised.

"Yes, I believe she wishes to punish him for never recognizing her, by hurting his actual daughter."

A montage of images cascaded through his head of what could be happening to Aimee right then, but he refused to let them overwhelm him. "We need to find them. You said Molly was heading east on foot. Was she alone?"

"She was. By the time I got downstairs to try to follow her, she'd already disappeared. Where exactly, I don't know. I asked several servants if they'd seen her, but no one had, which is when I came to seek you out," Mrs. Holbrook said. "I didn't see Aimee with Molly, though, so I could be completely wrong about all this, and perhaps Aimee is in my room waiting for me? Though I rather think she would have come back here."

"She would have, and seeing she hasn't, I'll assume the worst." And if she had been kidnapped, then it was doubtful Miss Mitchell was working alone. She would have needed help, and a secluded place to take Aimee, but somewhere close as they wouldn't have been able to get horses or a carriage inside Wilheimer's estate without being questioned.

Harrison glanced around the room until he spotted Wilheimer and his wife beside him, talking to another couple. Without a word, he strode over to them. "I need your help," he said, interrupting their conversation before quickly explaining the situation.

Mrs. Wilheimer translated in German and Wilheimer nodded emphatically. "Of course, we help," he said in broken English, before calling over his butler and quickly speaking in German to him.

"My husband is getting our butler to gather our servants to begin searching for her," Mrs. Wilheimer said.

"Thank you. Are there any abandoned buildings or cottages or barns around the estate? Particularly to the east," Harrison asked, clamping down on the debilitating thought that he might be too late to save her. He couldn't let that overwhelm him or he wouldn't focus. "Somewhere she could be taken and kept without being discovered?"

Wilheimer and Mrs. Wilheimer spoke back and forth in German for a moment, before Mrs. Wilheimer answered, "There is an old hunting lodge to the west that is vacant, but the only thing to the east is our gamekeeper's cottage and I doubt they'd go there with Mr. Sanders in residence. Though the village of Marston is only a short walk beyond the hill at the back of the cottage, where there'd be any number of possibilities they could hide."

"Direct your servants to start searching the house and the grounds of the estate in all directions, and have some head to your hunting lodge and others head toward the cottage."

Mrs. Wilheimer translated, and Wilheimer himself nodded and then said, "Da, da."

"And tell them to arm themselves, just in case." Harrison didn't know if Mrs. Holbrook's assessment of her niece was accurate, but the woman was never prone to exaggeration, so he wanted them all to be prepared. "I'll go ahead toward the cottage first." Molly had been heading that way, so that was his best bet, even if someone was occupying it.

"Wait," Wilheimer said, before hurriedly speaking in German to his wife, who then translated.

"Franz says he will go and get his gun and come with you," she rushed out. "He wishes to help."

"Thank you, and he's welcome to follow as I'm certain to need all the help I can get." Harrison pushed back his jacket to reveal his gun. "But I'm already armed, and night is fast approaching. I need to go now and not waste another moment."

"Of course," Mrs. Wilheimer said. "When you leave the greenhouse, turn right and follow the path through the grassed lawns to the edge of the grounds, where there's a smaller gravel path that leads through the woods to Mr. Sanders' cottage. It's about a twenty-minute walk to get there."

"Thank you." He nodded to them both and hurried through the terrace and out of the greenhouse, Mrs. Holbrook following beside him. "You should wait here," he said over his shoulder to her before he grabbed a lantern from the wall and turned to the right as Mrs. Wilheimer had instructed. "It's getting dark out and I'll be hurrying as much as I can through the woods."

"I'm not waiting anywhere," Mrs. Holbrook replied, taking another lantern for herself, before following him down the footpath through the grassed area. "As misguided as Molly has become, she's my niece and I feel responsible for what's happening, so I need to do what I can to help. And I'll try to keep up with you, but go ahead if I don't."

"Don't worry, I will," Harrison replied, his boots crunching along the stone footpath until they continued along the grassed area toward the woods just as Mrs. Wilheimer had told them to. "Are you involved in any of this?"

"Excuse me?"

"Molly couldn't kidnap Aimee alone," Harrison said, glancing to his side. "Are you helping her?"

"Of course not!" Mrs. Holbrook exclaimed, shock and outrage flashing on her face, before an expression of dismay followed. "Though I can't really blame you for questioning me given I haven't been fully truthful with you about Molly."

He didn't know why, but he believed her. "Why didn't you tell me Molly was your niece?" he asked, starting along the dirt path, holding his lantern aloft trying to stave off the ever-approaching darkness as he hurried to the cottage, his pace hindered by the branches scattered on the path, which were getting harder and harder to see in the twilight as the sun began its descent.

"Molly asked me not to," she replied, her breathing getting slightly labored as she struggled to keep up with his quick pace. "She said she didn't want anyone treating her differently at the office, so I agreed not to say anything, which in hindsight was a mistake, but I didn't think she'd do anything. At least not until Aimee arrived. Though given Molly didn't know it was actually Aimee, I didn't think there'd be a problem."

"I will hold you responsible if anything has happened to her."

She nodded. "I would expect you to, given I'd blame myself if anything did."

"How did you know who Aimee really was?" Harrison asked, leaping across a large log that had fallen across the path.

"When you sent me to New York about four years ago, I saw her visiting her father at the office," Mrs. Holbrook began, taking the hand he was offering as she, too, jumped over the log. "She was the spitting image of her mother, with her father's eyes. She never saw me, but while I was waiting in his outer office to deliver some papers, I overheard her begging him to let her learn his business."

"That much hasn't changed." He stopped when he noticed fresh footsteps in the dirt. There were several. "Why didn't you say anything about who she was?"

"Women don't get a lot of opportunities to fulfill our ambitions, and given she'd gone to such trouble switching places, even putting on a very convincing English accent to do so, I decided not to interfere," Mrs. Holbrook replied, pausing beside him and taking in a deep breath. "I should have said something to you then, but a part of me understood why she was swapping places, so I didn't."

He grunted, half listening to the story, half focused on the path ahead and how best he could quickly get to the cottage, where hopefully Aimee was. But with the approaching darkness and the branches strewn across the path, it was too dangerous to do anything apart from walk as quickly as he could with the lantern lighting the way.

His boots crunched on the gravel underfoot while his eyes scanned through the trees, but apart from their branches swaying in the wind, he saw nothing out of the ordinary. Perhaps Mrs. Holbrook was right and Aimee was safely back at the house. Though, that seemed doubtful, and the longer it took him to check the cottage to see if she was there, he feared it was going to be too late.

"We'll get to her in time, Harrison," Mrs. Holbrook said, almost like she, too, could feel Harrison's sense of impending doom.

"We must, Ann," he replied, using her name for the first time.

It felt like life was about to take away another person he'd started to care for. Another person he'd even started to love. The thought was enough to turn the small fissure of ice surrounding his heart into a giant crevice that he was terrified would destroy him.

CHAPTER THIRTY-THREE

The gunshot reverberated like a cannon, echoing through the darkening room.

Aimee watched as Deidre jolted backward, the bullet slamming into her chest with a sickening thud, propelling her to the floor. Blood poured from her wound onto the wooden planks beneath, a crimson pool spreading rapidly around her body.

There was so much blood.

"Molly, we have to help her! She's bleeding to death!" Aimee yelled, frantically struggling to stand, the ropes at her ankles hindering her greatly.

"Don't move another inch!" Molly yelled, turning to point the pistol at Aimee, an expression of loathing on her face. "Now sit back down on the floor."

Aimee stopped in her tracks and slowly nodded, doing as she was told. "All right, but Deidre needs our help."

"Oh, she's already dead," Molly replied, walking over to Deidre, then nudging the girl's unmoving body with her boot. "I made certain of that when I aimed for her heart."

Aimee's whole body froze. "Why would you kill her?"

"I need someone to take the blame for all this," Molly said matter-of-factly as she pocketed her own pistol, before turning back to face Aimee. "Otherwise, how else will I get away with kidnapping and then killing you?"

"You intend to kill me, too?" There was a calmness to Molly's demeanor that sent a shiver of dread down Aimee's spine.

"Yes. You see, if I let you live, you'd tell everyone of my involvement. So the sooner you die the better. Then once you're all dead, and I've received the ransom, everyone will believe Deidre and William were responsible, with no idea of my involvement. It's the perfect plan."

Again, Molly was so matter-of-fact about it all that for a second Aimee questioned whether this was real or a dream. "I can't believe you're behind all this."

"You didn't really think Deidre had the brains to plan this, did you?"

"Actually, I haven't had time to give it much thought," Aimee replied, suddenly feeling furious that this woman in front of her had the audacity to discuss the matter like they were speaking of the weather. "Being drugged as I was and now tied up." She raised her hands, bound together at her wrists, to emphasize her point.

Molly laughed lightly. "I do so admire your forthrightness and spirit. In fact, when we first met and I thought you were Evie, it felt like we were kindred spirits: two smart ladies, struggling in a world we didn't fit into, destined to be the best of friends. But then I found out you were lying to me, just like our father has lied to me for my entire life." Her smile slipped into a tight line. "That you weren't Evie at all, but instead my half sister, a pampered heiress who was playing at being her poor cousin and taking us all for fools in the process."

"It wasn't like that," Aimee replied, realizing that what Molly had told her about Deidre thinking she was Thomas Thornton-Jones's daughter was what Molly thought to be true about herself.

"Of course it was," Molly snapped back. "And you didn't think anyone would find out, did you? But I did."

"William told you about the telegram I sent that day at the telegram office, didn't he?" It was the only way she could have put it together.

"Yes, and I was subsequently able to recruit him to help me, given he does love money. And Deidre barely had to be convinced at all after I told her you were worth one million American dollars and that William would help us."

"I should never have used my full name to send that telegram with," Aimee replied, annoyed she'd done so in the first place.

"It wouldn't have mattered. I already knew something wasn't right about you when you started speaking back to Mr. Stone. No illegitimate child born into poverty, as I thought you and I both were, would dare to do that. And as soon as I spoke to William, I started to put it all together. It wasn't too hard to figure it out in the end, though I am rather clever."

"I wouldn't have thought kidnapping and murder were all that clever, to be honest." She probably shouldn't antagonize her, but Aimee was starting to get furious. The woman, who so callously and without emotion murdered Deidre and intended to kill her, too, had the nerve to stand there talking about how clever she was?

"I'm not surprised you'd think that. Your world has been sheltered." She gave a half shrug. "Whereas mine has not, since I grew up without a father to protect me after my mother killed herself, following a confrontation with him when I was only three. Did you know he called her a liar and refused to acknowledge me? He said she was mentally unbalanced and needed help. That he'd never even kissed her let alone slept with her. And everyone believed him and not her! It was no wonder she jumped."

"And you remember all this from when you were three?" Aimee replied, unable to disguise the doubt in her voice.

"Of course not," Molly scoffed. "My mother wrote it down in her journal, which she left on the platform beside her purse before she jumped in front of a train. A train owned by your father, too. I think she was trying to make a point, don't you? In any event, as much as I blame our father for denying me all that should have been mine, I really should thank him, for it did give me a purpose in life."

"Yes, kidnapping is a noble purpose, isn't it?"

Molly's whole body tightened for a minute and she took in a long and sustained breath through her nose. "Perhaps before you comment, you should remember I'm the one with the gun." She emphasized her point by pulling out her pistol and thrusting it toward Aimee.

"You're right, I'm sorry," Aimee said, putting

her hands up in front of her, tied up together as they were. She knew she shouldn't provoke her but was finding it difficult not to.

Molly nodded, somewhat placated. "As I was saying, it gave me purpose. Five years ago, when I discovered my mother's journal in the attic and finally learned the truth about who my father was, which my Aunt Ann had kept secret from me for my entire life and still denies to this day, I knew then I had to take away what he loved most, just like he took away my mother from me."

"My father wasn't responsible for your mother taking her own life."

"*Our* father most certainly was!" Molly stomped her foot on the ground. "And once I knew it was his fault, I made a vow I would make him pay, which, at first, I could only do trying to sabotage his business—"

"So you're the one responsible for altering the ledgers." It was starting to make an odd sort of sense.

"Yes. What better way to hurt him when he was half a world away then by trying to ruin the share price of the company that he loved. At least until you arrived."

"And the translator not correctly translating in the Wilheimer deal... Were you responsible for that, too?"

Molly shook her head. "No, I can't take credit for Lady Whitley's work."

"Lady Whitley? Why would she care about the Wilheimer deal?" There weren't many ladies Aimee knew who took an interest in business, let alone actively trying to sabotage a deal.

"When she overheard Mr. Stone talking about his new deal, she purchased a great deal of shares in the company he was originally going to take over. But then he broke things off with her, and she had no idea he'd changed directions and had set his sights onto Wilheimer's company instead."

"Rendering her new shares worthless."

"Exactly. She then bribed the translator to do all he could to sabotage the deal with Wilheimer, so Mr. Stone would be forced to go back to the original company, which you got in the way of."

"How do you know all this?"

"I caught her rifling around Mr. Stone's desk a few weeks back and blackmailed her to tell me."

"I'm sure you would have been supportive of any plan to make my father's shares lose value."

"*Our* father's shares," Molly corrected her once again. "And, yes, I was supportive, though by that stage I'd already moved on to making him pay for his sins through you. A far more effective punishment that will wound him to the point of madness, just as he did to my mother by refusing to acknowledge me."

"*My* father would have acknowledged you if you were his daughter."

Molly's grip tightened on Aimee's derringer. "He *is* my father! And you're just like him and my stupid aunt saying I'm not, continuing to deny the facts while lying through your teeth. Well, I'll show you all. After he pays the ridiculous ransom I've set, he'll find out you're already dead, his precious little princess. Then he will feel my pain...and I'll finally have my revenge and be free to live a life of luxury that has been denied to me for too long. A life that was meant to be mine!"

The woman was dangerously unhinged. "Perhaps we can talk to him together, and he'll take care of you, just like he did with Evie, when he found out about her being his niece."

"Stop lying! He knew about me when I was three and refused to accept me! He's not changing his mind twenty-one years later, now is he?" Molly yelled, the early evening shadows from the lamp on the desk distorting her face, making her seem slightly demonic. But then she pulled back her shoulders and a smile replaced the fury from a second ago as she cocked the hammer on her gun. "In any event, let's get back to business, shall we? I hope you're ready to meet your maker, for I'm done explaining things and it's time to move on to the second part of my plan."

"You can't kill me! At least not yet," Aimee rushed out, unable to help the cold shiver that ran up her spine seeing the intent in Molly's gaze.

"I certainly can."

"What if my father demands proof I'm alive before he pays your ransom?"

Molly smirked, her eyes looking down on Aimee with pity. "That's why I had Deidre and William take some photos of you."

"But what if he wants date proof?" Aimee replied. "Like a picture of me with a newspaper for the day? If you kill me now, you won't be able to give him that, and as much as my father loves me, he's a businessman at heart and will not part with a cent if he thinks I'm already dead." Aimee rushed the words out, her tone beseeching Molly to listen.

"Yes, he will. For *you* he'd do anything." There was a note of bitterness in her voice she wasn't trying to disguise.

"And what if you're wrong?" Aimee replied. "You might have your revenge, but you won't have any money and you'll still have to work for a living."

Molly inhaled sharply, her pistol dropping slowly to her side as she tapped it restlessly against her thigh, appearing agitated with the thought. "Damn it. You might be right." She pulled out a pocket watch and glanced down at its face.

Just then a loud *bang* came from beyond the room, followed by footsteps rushing down the hallway toward them.

"Stay put," Molly said to Aimee as she raised her pistol to face the door.

"I heard a gunshot," William said, bursting through the doorway and skittering to a halt as he caught sight of Molly, then glanced down and saw Deidre's body. "What happened to her?"

"She was going to kill us both so she could take the ransom for herself," Molly replied, lying without hesitation. "I had to kill her to protect us."

"You're lying," Aimee cried out. "You killed her in cold blood—"

"Shut up!" Molly swung the gun to Aimee. "Or I will kill you, proof of your life be damned." Her eyes then turned back to William. "What are you doing back here anyhow? You were meant to send the telegram to my father."

"I've sent it," William replied. "And as I was returning, I saw some lanterns in the distance heading this way, so I ran the rest of the way here. Tripped over a few times, too."

"No one should be looking for her yet!" Molly glanced around the room, panic flaring in her eyes.

"It's Harrison," Aimee said, feeling equal parts relief and terror. "I knew he'd know I was missing."

"This isn't how I planned things," Molly screeched. "And how did he even know to come this way? He'll ruin everything!"

"We've only got about ten minutes or so until they come upon the cottage. We need to get out of here now, unless you want me to use the shotgun out the front on them…" He sounded ill at the thought.

"No, if it is Stone, we can't kill him," Molly replied. "He has access to the office safe, which is where the ransom will come from." She paused and glanced over to Aimee, her eyes narrowing. "Damn it, we'll have to leave now and take her with us. Cut the ropes at her feet but not her hands," she directed William, raising her gun again back to Aimee. "And if you give him any trouble, I'll shoot you."

There was such a steely resolve in her eyes that Aimee knew she meant it. But Aimee also knew if she didn't do something and soon, she'd be dead shortly anyhow. So she nodded as William approached her, his eyes not meeting hers as he bent down to where she was sitting and began to untie the ropes around her ankles.

A tingling sensation ran through her feet as the

ropes loosened and Aimee sighed, having not realized how tight the bindings had been against her legs.

"Up you get," William said, grabbing her elbows and hauling her to her feet.

Aimee stumbled into him, her legs wobbling slightly. William tried to steady her, but she used the momentum to push against him with all her might, knocking him backward and into Molly.

Chaos erupted as William and Molly fell onto the desk and then tumbled to the floor, sending the lamp crashing to its side. The flames from its wick hungrily lapped at the papers on the desk before a whooshing sound filled the room as bright orange flames flared to life, hungrily crawling up the curtains as smoke began to spread through the room.

"You bitch! I'm going to kill you," Molly yelled from underneath William, as she pushed against him. "Get off me, you idiot!"

Aimee didn't waste another second and sprinted through the doorway, her gait slightly unbalanced with her hands still tied in front of her as she searched desperately for an exit. She ran to the end of the short hall and followed it to the right, where she saw what looked like the front door ahead. With a burst of speed, she ran toward it, her hands reaching for the handle, desperately clutching it and praying it was unlocked. It twisted in her hands and she wrenched it open, racing outside across the clearing toward the thick trees, heedless of the darkness around her. She had to get away and quickly; there was no other choice.

Just as she reached the tree line, a gunshot rang

out to her right and the branch of a tree splintered not more than ten feet away from her. She ducked to her left and took cover behind a tree trunk, before quickly glancing around it to the cottage, where she saw Molly reloading a smoking shotgun while William unstrapped a lantern from the outside wall. Then, they both ran across the clearing heading toward where she disappeared into the woods.

Aimee pushed off from the tree, darting through the woods, using the foliage for cover. Her heart was pounding so hard, she could only just hear the distant sound of footsteps behind her as they gave chase.

"Get back here!" Molly screamed, her voice echoing somewhere behind her, but Aimee didn't look back and instead kept running deeper into the woods, veering to her left, doing her best to use the moonlight to see in front of her, but tripping lightly on a few of the tree roots. After a few minutes, she began to circle back around to the cottage to where Harrison would soon be, a path that hopefully Molly wouldn't think she'd take.

As she weaved through several trees, the smell of smoke hit her, and she paused, worrying that they'd set the woods on fire to flush her out. But then she noticed an orange glow in the direction of the cottage and realized it was the cottage on fire. Her heart plummeted. What if Harrison was there now? What if he'd gone inside to rescue her, thinking she was inside?

With a burst of speed, Aimee pushed herself to run harder. She had to get to him, but then a rumble of thunder clapped overhead as the skies opened up and a torrent of rain began pouring down, drenching her in a matter of seconds. The ground became muddy far too quickly but she knew with a sense of urgency she had to get out of the woods and get to Harrison, before it was too late.

CHAPTER THIRTY-FOUR

A loud crack echoed in the distance, and Harrison came to an abrupt stop, his eyes scanning the woods ahead of him, listening intently for any threat, but the only thing he could hear was the birds fleeing their canopy of trees in response to the sound.

"What was that?" Mrs. Holbrook panted, coming to a halt beside him, her hands dropping to her knees as she dragged in several haggard breaths, resting her lantern on the ground.

"A gunshot," Harrison replied, handing Mrs. Holbrook his lantern before he shrugged off his jacket and gave her that, too. He pulled out his pistol then took back the lantern with his other hand. "Go and get help, now." Without looking back, he took off up the path, his lantern held in front of him as he raced up the uneven surface, sprinting as fast as his legs would carry him, heedless of the dangers of the night.

His heart was pounding like a freight train, not from the physical exertion, but from the terror of what he might confront ahead.

Please don't let it be Aimee, he kept repeating over and over in his head as he urged himself to run faster up the path toward the cottage, jumping over the branches and rocks he caught sight of, while stumbling over some he didn't see. He was probably still five minutes from the cottage, but even that could be too long. *Faster*. He had to move faster. He had to get there and save her if he wasn't already too late…

No. He couldn't think that way. He couldn't. She was going to be fine. She was. She had to be.

But a few minutes later the smell of smoke hit him and his faith plummeted.

Ahead in the distance, where there should only be darkness, was an orange glow lighting up the night. A bright, incandescent sheen that could only be one thing… *Fire*. And it was coming from the direction the path was taking to the cottage.

It felt like the longest few minutes of his life as he ran toward the light, his legs pumping as hard as they could, while sweat dripped down his brow and the sky overhead cracked with thunder and then opened up, unleashing a deluge.

Heedless of the rain, he kept running until he crested a rise, only to be confronted by the sight of a cottage in the middle of a clearing, completely ablaze. The flames were bursting through the door and windows, fighting desperately against the sudden downpour, but lighting up the area as if it were day. It was then he noticed an old man on the grass, watching the fire burn while sobbing loudly, his clothes soaked to the bone.

Harrison ran up to him, holstering his pistol and putting his lantern on the ground. "Is anyone in there?" he yelled loudly, trying to be heard over the rain starting to fall in earnest.

Slowly, the man glanced up at Harrison and nodded, uncaring as the raindrops slammed onto his face. "Aye. I couldn't save her, though…"

Without thought, Harrison raced for the cottage, but the wall of flames were viciously fighting to stay alive, the heat from them blistering in their intensity, despite slowly starting to be tamed by the rain. He ran around the house, trying to find some way in, but each opening was blanketed by flames, and there was no way through. He could only stare in frozen horror at the cottage and the inferno inside.

"She was already dead," the man said beside him, having followed him.

Harrison spun around and grabbed the man's shoulders, his words echoing like a dagger in his heart. "What do you mean she was already dead?"

The man sobbed lightly. "When I woke up after being clonked on me head, I could smell the smoke, so I rushed through the place seeing if anyone was still in there, and then I spotted her lying on the floor in the back room. Looked like she was asleep, but I saw all the blood pooling around her, and the horrible gunshot wound in her chest." The man's breath hitched. "I ain't never seen such a horrible sight before. Her glassy eyes will haunt me forever…"

"You just left her there?" Harrison roared.

The man dipped his head and nodded. "There was no saving her, and by then the fire was licking at my feet, so I had to get out."

"But what if she was still alive?" Harrison shook the man's shoulders, much like he was a rag doll. "You could've tried to pull her out. You should have tried to save her!"

The man shook his head, deep remorse on his

face. "There weren't no saving her. God had already taken her." He made the sign of a cross over his chest. "There was no mistaking that."

"No. That can't be!" Harrison glanced back to the cottage, the flames battling a hopeless fight against the rain, but having already been effective in their destruction...and Aimee was in there, dead? With an anguished cry, he dropped to his knees, unable to drag his eyes away from the blaze. He was too late to save her. And the pain of losing her was unbearable, like someone had ripped his heart from his chest and torn it in two.

He felt numb all over.

What a fool he'd been to let himself feel again, especially knowing the pain of losing his parents. And now he was going to have to live with the agony of losing her for the rest of his life.

"Harrison!" Aimee's voice screamed from the tree line to his right, jolting him out of his stupor and making him question his sanity.

He whipped his head around as she raced across the clearing toward him, stumbling slightly with her hands tied in front of him, and her clothes and hair a wet mess, but she was alive... He staggered to his feet, a part of him disbelieving what he was seeing. "Aimee? You're alive? But who's dead in the cottage?"

"Deidre," she replied as she rushed up to him. "Molly killed her. She's behind everything and she's got a shotgun."

"Where is she?" Harrison asked, his voice thick as he resisted reaching for her and pulling her into his arms. But before Aimee could even answer,

Molly and another man burst through the tree line about forty yards away. There was shock and anger on Molly's face as she caught sight of him and raised her shotgun toward them.

He dragged Aimee behind him and drew out his revolver, then without hesitation he pulled the trigger, knowing there was no room for error. His bullet found its mark, hitting Molly in the chest. She jerked backward and collapsed to the ground, unmoving.

The man next to her stopped in his tracks and raised his hands up high in front of him as Harrison ran toward them, his pistol pointed at the man.

"Don't shoot!" the man yelled, his voice a nasal plea. "I ain't got no weapon."

"Put your hands on your head and sit down," he yelled to the man, scooping up Molly's shotgun with his free hand, while Aimee bent down over Molly and checked her pulse.

"She's dead," Aimee said, glancing up at him.

Harrison nodded. He'd known she would be. He hadn't had another choice.

"Molly?" Mrs. Holbrook's voice echoed from the woods behind them and Harrison turned and saw her with Wilheimer and a contingent of his servants.

Mrs. Holbrook's eyes darted down to Molly's body on the ground. "Oh no, Molly," she cried, rushing to them, her lantern bobbing up and down as she stopped just short of Molly, catching sight of the bullet wound in her chest. "Is she…dead?"

Harrison nodded. "She is. I'm sorry, Ann, I had no choice. She would have killed us if she'd gotten a shot off."

"But why couldn't you have just shot her in the a—arm?" Ann said, her voice catching. "Then she'd still be alive…"

"I might have missed," he tried to explain. "She was running toward us."

"She might have missed, too," Ann replied. "She might have—"

"She had buckshot in her shotgun, Mrs. Holbrook," Aimee interrupted. "So even if she'd missed hitting us directly, from this distance, the spray from her bullet would have been fatal." She glanced up at Harrison, her eyes staring steadily into his. "He had no other choice but to aim for her chest to stop her, and he saved my life by doing so."

Ann nodded. "I see… It's just hard to believe she's gone." She glanced down at Molly and gulped, before averting her eyes back up to Aimee. "I know she wasn't well, and had obviously become far more fixated on harming you than I'd realized, but can you tell me what happened this afternoon?"

Aimee nodded and recounted what had occurred after she'd left Harrison. Tears streamed down Ann's face the entire time, while Harrison felt a gut-wrenching sickness to his stomach realizing how much peril she'd been in. She'd been so close to being taken from him forever…which had nearly undone him. It would only be all the worse in the future if he did succumb and give his heart to her, more than he already had.

He didn't think he was strong enough to risk such devastation again. Not after his parents. Not ever again.

CHAPTER THIRTY-FIVE

After finishing telling Harrison and Mrs. Holbrook of all that had happened, the reality of the situation slowly started to penetrate and Aimee's whole body began to shake. She'd been so focused on surviving that she hadn't had time to give in to her fear, but now that she was safe it was all she could think of…

That and the fact that two people were dead, and she was the catalyst for their deaths. "I'm so sorry, Mrs. Holbrook. It's my fault. I never should have switched places with my cousin."

Mrs. Holbrook swiped away her own tears and a stalwart expression grew on her face. "It's not your fault, Aimee. It's mine, and mine alone. I shouldn't have kept my sister's journal, and then Molly never would have embarked on any of this."

"Neither of you are to blame," Harrison said, his voice gruff. "Now let's get you back to the house." He glanced over to Aimee, his expression distant and cold. "You're soaked to the bone and freezing."

"S-so are y-you both," Aimee said, her teeth suddenly chattering against each other as the cold of the night began to hit her and she felt so tired that she didn't know how she'd have the energy to walk back.

"We're not the ones shaking like a leaf," Harrison replied, before bending down and scooping her up into his arms.

Aimee didn't have the energy to object, nor did she want to. Instead, she looped her hands around his neck and snuggled into the warmth of his chest as he cradled her to him. He was so vibrantly warm and strong, and she felt so safe in his arms, that she never wanted to let go.

Everything became a blur after that, and she was only just aware of him talking to Wilheimer through a servant, and arranging things, before the gradual movement of him walking through the woods began to lull her to sleep. As much as she tried to resist the pull, her eyelids grew heavy until she'd couldn't keep them open and sleep took her.

When she next opened her eyes, confusion gripped her, and then panic. She was alone in a bed, in a mostly dark room, lit only by a lamp on a bedside table.

"It's all right," Harrison's voice whispered from the shadows. "You're safe."

Aimee sat up and swung her gaze over to him. He was sitting in a chair beside her bed, his eyes crinkled in fatigue and what looked like regret. "Where are we?"

"In your room at Wilheimer's," he replied. "You fell asleep as soon as I picked you up and didn't even wake when I put you to bed."

She glanced down at her nightgown and blushed. "You changed my clothes?"

"Yes. They were soaking wet and I didn't think you'd mind, given I've seen you naked before."

She cleared her throat. "Yes, I suppose that's true." She still felt slightly mortified she hadn't even woken up to change herself. "Um, thank you, then."

A brief smile twisted at the corner of his lips before he replaced it with a frown. "There's no need to thank me given you'll shortly be cursing me, I'm sure."

She narrowed her eyes at him. "Why? What have you done?"

"It's not what I've done, it's what I'm about to." His voice sounded ominous. "I intend to change the scope of our marriage agreement."

"How?" she asked, swinging her legs out of bed to sit and face him.

"I wish for our marriage to be in name only, going forward," he began. "Which means I have no intention of sharing your bed again or having children with you."

"I know what it means," she replied, trying to process his words. "But I don't understand why."

"You don't need to understand," he said, standing and buttoning up his jacket.

"Of course I need to." She swung her legs to the side of the bed and stood to meet his gaze. "What's suddenly changed, Harrison? Don't you need an heir or want a proper wife?"

"No. I don't want or need either." His voice was cold and clipped, with a finality that Aimee found devastating.

"But why not?"

"You nearly died, Aimee," he said, like he was discussing the weather.

"How does that change anything?"

"It changes everything! I can't fall in love with

you any more than I've started to, or I'll be ruined when you're taken from me."

"You're starting to love me?" Her breath caught. "But that changes everything."

"It does. It means this marriage will only go ahead if it's a business arrangement. Nothing more and nothing less."

"If you love me, then we can have a proper marriage like my parents."

"We will never have that."

"Why not?" What was wrong with him?

"Because nearly losing you tonight was devastating, and I will not go through that again! I'd be utterly destroyed if I had to. And if we had children, it would be a thousand times worse…" His voice trailed off and he took in a deep breath. "I'd rather be alone now than face that inevitable heartache in the future."

"But isn't a life without love a half life?" Perhaps she could make him understand.

"I don't wish to discuss it further with you."

"Well, too bad, because we're going to."

"No, we're not," he replied curtly, getting his jacket from the back of the chair and putting it on. "I've explained the situation to you and we will leave it at that. You can go back to your sleep. There's a few hours left till dawn."

He began to walk around the bed but she rushed in front of him and put her hands out against his chest. "You're not going anywhere."

He glanced down at her hands and raised an eyebrow. "Do you really think you can stop me?"

She dropped her hands and took a step back

from him, knowing full well it was pointless to pretend she could. "You can't tell me you've fallen in love with me, but then decree we're going to have a marriage in name only. That's not how it works."

"If I hadn't dishonored you, I wouldn't be marrying you."

The blunt honesty in his words sliced through her heart.

"But since I have," he continued, "I will do the honorable thing and marry you. So long as you understand it will be in name only."

"Oh, you've made that perfectly clear." An unholy rage filled her. "But there's something *you* need to understand, Harrison." She pressed her lips together for a moment, praying she had the strength not to cry in front of him. "Death is an inevitability for all of us, and if you don't have the courage to love me, even with the possibility you might one day lose me, you don't deserve my love or my hand in marriage."

"It's the only honorable—"

"Stop saying that!" Aimee cut him off. "I don't care about your honor. I care about your heart, and if you can't give me that, then I won't be marrying you!" She marched over to the door and yanked it wide, never having been so angry and devastated all at the same time. "Please leave."

"I'm under an obligation to marry you—"

"Don't you dare keep saying that!" she yelled, caring little if she woke the entire household. "Now leave. I intend to go back to New York and I don't want to see you ever again. Not unless you stop being a coward and have the courage to love me as

I deserve to be loved."

His whole body braced as if she'd slapped him. "I'm being realistic, not a coward."

"Call it whatever you will. Now, please leave. I don't want to see you again."

"We can't *not* see each other again," he muttered, walking over to where she stood by the door. "I have to get you back to London."

"I'm perfectly capable of returning to London with Mrs. Holbrook, while you can arrange transport with one of the other guests. I'm sure Lady Whitley would oblige." She crossed her arms over her chest and stared pointedly out the door.

"I don't want to end things like this," he replied as he walked out into the hallway and turned back to face her.

Neither did she, but she was too proud to beg when he'd made his feelings clear. "There's no other way they can end." And with that, she closed the door in his face and collapsed against it.

When she heard his footsteps finally recede, she let go of the tears she'd been desperately holding at bay, wondering if they'd ever stop.

CHAPTER THIRTY-SIX

The trip from Wilheimer's estate back to Mrs. Holbrook's townhouse had been a solemn affair, with Mrs. Holbrook mourning her niece while Aimee mourned the end of whatever she'd had with Harrison, who'd thankfully done as she'd asked and arranged to return to London himself, separately.

Small talk had been kept to a minimum, with both ladies preferring the company of their own thoughts rather than further discussing what had occurred.

Initially, Aimee had considered going to the Mayfair Grand and staying in her suite until her passage back to New York had been arranged, but given there was a much higher chance of bumping into Harrison there, she'd decided to stay with Mrs. Holbrook instead, and all her clothes were there, too, or rather Evie's.

Another situation she was going to have to face the ramifications of…her switch with Evie. The thought was exhausting, but she took in a steadying breath, and then another, and gradually the feeling subsided.

As the carriage began to slow, she glanced out the window and saw Mrs. Holbrook's townhouse ahead. She gasped seeing Evie and her father at the top of the entrance steps.

Her father was here in London? The most

profound sense of relief overwhelmed her, and tears began to course down her cheeks. Barely waiting for the carriage to come to a halt, Aimee yanked open the door and jumped out as her father bounded down the steps toward her and she ran into his arms.

"Oh, thank God, you're all right," he said, hugging her fiercely.

Aimee returned his embrace, wrapping her hands tightly around his neck, never wanting to let go.

"I've never been so terrified in all my life hearing you'd been kidnapped!" he said, pulling back from her slightly and staring into her eyes. "Are you all right?"

"I'm fine," she replied with a nod, wiping away at her tears, trying to convince him of something that was most definitely not the case. "But how are you even in London, let alone know what's been happening?"

"That is a story best left for when we're all settled back at my hotel. But tell me this, were you hurt?" he asked with such concern that Aimee felt like bawling even harder.

Instead, she shook her head. "No, I wasn't. I managed to escape and then Ha-Harrison saved me." Even just saying his name was excruciating.

"And where is he?" There was anger in his voice. "I would have expected him to accompany you back here given the situation."

"I didn't want him to," Aimee replied, before she buried her face in his chest and soaked his shirt with her tears.

He gently began to pat her on the back just as he'd done when she was a child. "There, there, my darling," he murmured. "You're safe now. Everything's going to be all right, Papa's here to protect you," he continued to reassure her, his strong arms like a band of steel around her, keeping the world at bay and protecting her as little else could. "Now let's go inside and you can tell me what happened."

Ten minutes later, seated in the sitting room, Aimee finished recounting all that had occurred, except the part involving her and Harrison. That she'd take to the grave before she'd tell anyone about. Silence echoed in the room for several moments after she was done, her father appearing as equally concerned as he was furious, while Evie nervously wrung her hands together and Mrs. Holbrook sat stoically on the armchair across from them.

"I'm sorry for your loss, Ann," her father said, glancing over to the lady with compassion in his eyes.

She nodded. "Thank you, Thomas. And I'm so sorry for all your daughter had to suffer because of Molly. I should have known something was wrong. I should have sought help for her a lot sooner..."

"It's not your fault," he replied. "You weren't to know what she was up to." He glanced pointedly over to Aimee and she knew he was talking of her masquerade.

"But I can't help but feel responsible—" Mrs. Holbrook's voice broke off and she suddenly stood, tears beginning to cascade down her face. "I'm sorry, I think I need to be alone now. If you'll all excuse me." And with that she hurried from the room, the sound of her crying gradually getting more distant as her feet pounded up the staircase.

"I never should have agreed to swap places with you in the first place," Evie said, breaking the silence following Mrs. Holbrook's departure. "Then you never would have been kidnapped."

Aimee reached over and hugged her cousin. "None of this is your fault, Evie. It was all my idea, and you know I wasn't going to take no for an answer."

"And it's something we shall all be discussing at length later," her father added sternly, before he let out a sigh. "However, we must get back to the hotel as I need to let your mother know you're safe, Aimee, and then I shall have to sort out the messes you've both gotten yourselves into with this swapping places business." He stood and walked to the door. "I shall go and have my carriage brought around and organize with Mrs. Holbrook's housekeeper to have your things sent on to the hotel."

"I don't want to go back to the Mayfair Grand," Aimee blurted out.

Her father paused in his stride and turned back to look at her, his brow raised. "*Back* to the hotel? Pray tell, daughter, when have you been there at all on this trip?"

Why did her father have to pick up on everything? Now it was Aimee who sighed. She might as well tell him; he'd find out soon enough anyhow. "I rented a suite there so I could have an occasional bath given Mrs. Holbrook only has one bathroom to be shared by several women."

"Why am I not surprised." He took in a deep breath. "I shall have to have a talk with the hotel manager about why he didn't inform me of that."

"He didn't tell you because he didn't know it was me renting a suite. I used an alias."

"Of course you did." He shook his head in resignation. "Tell me, is there anything else I need to know about this trip of yours?"

"Not that I can think of." He certainly didn't need to know about her and Harrison.

"That doesn't particularly fill me with confidence." His eyes narrowed but her expression remained impassive under his scrutiny. "In any event," he continued, "I'll get things sorted and be back in a moment." Turning on his heel, he left the room.

"Are you sure you're all right?" Evie asked as soon as they were alone. She reached over and squeezed Aimee's hand.

"Not really." Aimee returned the squeeze and managed a small smile. "But I will be. Eventually."

"Does it have anything to do with Harrison Stone?"

"Why would you think that?"

Evie shrugged lightly. "I know you've been through a terrible ordeal, and of course that would terrify anyone, but it was only when you mentioned his name that you truly started to seem upset."

Sometimes, she wished her family weren't all so observant. "I appreciate your concern, Evie, but I really don't want to talk about it. I don't think I ever will."

"Yes, I can understand that."

It was then Aimee noticed the sadness in Evie's eyes, a sadness that hadn't been there the last time she'd seen her. "Evie, what's wrong? And, come to think of it, my father never explained why he was even here in London in the first place."

"He came to England to surprise us both but was instead the one surprised when he found out of your supposed engagement to Alex," Evie replied, trying for what Aimee thought was a stoic expression, but failing miserably. "He followed me to the duke's country estate, though he thought it was you he was chasing, and it was there our swap was revealed to everyone."

"Oh, Evie, what happened with your duke?"

"He was never my duke. Not really." Evie swiped away several errant tears, doing her best to smile. "But when he found out I'd been lying to him, he called off the wedding. Not that I can blame him…"

"But I thought it was a pretend betrothal?"

"It was meant to be in the beginning, but it turned quite real in the end." She gave a self-deprecating laugh. "I was a fool to have thought anything could have come from it, given he's a duke and I'm who I am—"

"You are perfect just as you are!" Aimee interrupted fiercely. "You are the kindest, loveliest, most genuine person I know. He should be grateful to have you as his wife and is a fool for not recognizing that!"

Evie smiled through her tears. "He's a *duke*, Aimee, and I'm illegitimate. He could never have married me in the end, even if a tiny part of me was perhaps hoping for a fairy tale, as impossible as I knew it to be."

The pain in her cousin's eyes was heartbreaking. "I'm so sorry, Evie," Aimee said, her own eyes misting over. She leaned over and hugged her tightly once again, the two of them crying silently together. "If he couldn't love you for the amazing woman you are, then he doesn't deserve you. Not even for one minute."

"I'm trying to tell myself that, but part of me still wishes he could have loved me. That I was enough for him, despite everything."

"Oh, my darling cousin," Aimee cried, hugging Evie even harder, as her words echoed Aimee's own desperate longing. She pulled back and stared at Evie. "Men can be the biggest bastards sometimes, can't they."

"Not all men, I hope?" her father's deep voice spoke solemnly from the entrance to the sitting room.

Aimee pulled farther back from Evie and glanced up at him. There was such concern in his eyes that she quickly wiped away her tears and managed a brilliant smile. She couldn't allow her father to suspect something had happened between her and Harrison, or he'd mostly likely try to kill him, or ruin him… And as much as Harrison had hurt her, she didn't want anything to happen to him. She still loved him, as much as she wished she didn't. So, stay strong and pretend she was fine was what she would have to do. "No, not all men are bad, Father. Except for dukes."

He stared intently at her for several moments. "If you say so."

She kept her face perfectly neutral as his eyes searched her own, almost like he knew she wasn't telling him everything.

But then he nodded. "In any event, I've organized the carriage for us, so come along, ladies."

Aimee and Evie both stood and followed him through to the entrance. They walked down the stairs and then her father gestured for Evie to get into the carriage, but as Aimee began to follow her, he stepped in front of her and blocked her path.

"Did he hurt you?" His voice was a low grumble as his gaze intently searched her own.

"I've already told you I'm perfectly fine, Father."

"I'm not talking about the kidnapping. I'm talking about Harrison," he replied.

"I don't know what you're implying—"

"I saw you flinch earlier when I mentioned his name."

Of course he had. He never missed a thing. "I flinched because I can't stand him," she said. "Nothing more and nothing less."

"Did he hurt you, Aimee?"

"Not for one moment," she said with honesty, because the pain of her heartache would stay a constant companion to her for the rest of her life, not merely for one moment. "Now if you don't mind, Father, I would like to get to the hotel and have a bath. The sooner I can wash away the weekend's events, the sooner I can get on with my life."

Slowly, he nodded. "Which clearly I'm going to

have to readjust my position on."

Aimee cocked her head to the side. "What do you mean by that?"

"I mean that I'm finally realizing how serious you are about wanting to be part of my company."

"You are?" Her pulse quickened in excitement as hope blossomed in her heart.

"Yes," he replied gruffly. "You've obviously gone to a lot of trouble to concoct this elaborate masquerade, which means you're a lot more determined to follow in my footsteps than I ever believed you to truly be. And rather than continue to fight with you about it, instead I'm going to support you."

"Are you serious, Father?" She couldn't believe what he was saying. "You will?"

"Yes. I nearly lost you." His voice cracked on the last word and he pressed his lips together for a moment and cleared his throat. "You have no idea how terrified I was after I arrived at the hotel this morning and there was a telegram waiting from your mother telling me of your kidnapping. I thought I might never see you again, my darling girl…" His voice broke and the tears he'd been holding onto spilled over. He pulled her roughly into his arms again and held on to her tightly. "It nearly broke me, and I will never let anything happen to you again. And if learning my business and helping me run the company is what will make you happy, then that is what you will do."

"But what about Mother and her plans I marry a title?"

He pulled back from her and smiled. "Let me

handle your mother. But I must ask, are you truly certain you don't want to marry and have children? That this is the path you want to take?"

It had been all she'd wanted only a month ago... until she'd thought she could have it all, but in the end, a marriage without love was no marriage at all. "Yes, I'm sure, Father."

"All right then." He nodded his head. "Though I must warn you, it won't be easy, especially with the biases many men have about doing business with women. However, I do know several women running successful businesses both here and back home, and I'm sure they will be more than happy to mentor you."

"But I want you to mentor me, Father."

"Oh, don't worry. I will. But if you are serious on this path, then first you will learn from these women how to successfully navigate the world of business and effectively deal with men who are less than willing to conduct business with a woman. The experience you gain will be invaluable, but alas is not something I can teach you. However, once you've learned all you can from those ladies, then I will mentor you. It's time your mother and I gave up on you leading a conventional life according to Society's standards and embrace what it is you want for your life."

"Oh, Father, thank you so much!" She leaned over, hugging him again as happiness filled her. Her dreams were finally coming true and she couldn't wait to tell Harrison.

The thought stopped her cold.

There would be no telling him. In fact, once he

sorted out the Wilheimer deal, which she knew he would, her father would sell him the majority stake in the English side of the company and she'd probably never see him again. Which was a good thing, though, wasn't it? After all, her heart had just been shattered and she didn't think it could take any further heartache, which seeing him would surely do.

She had to focus on her dreams for her future. Dreams that no longer held as much excitement as they once had, all because of Harrison suggesting she could have the world, with him by her side. He'd promised her everything, except for his heart, which in the end was what she'd wanted above everything but was something he could never give her as much as she wished he could.

She took in a deep breath. It was better this way. It had to be, and eventually she might start to believe that.

CHAPTER THIRTY-SEVEN

Four months later, London, November 1890

The sound of his pen scratching across the parchment as Harrison signed the contract symbolized the culmination of all of his dreams in one swift stroke, but rather than the satisfaction he'd been expecting, instead he felt empty inside. And it was a feeling he hadn't been able to shake since Aimee had left him and returned to New York, no matter how hard he tried.

At first, he'd immersed himself with work, staying at the office until late and sometimes even sleeping there, desperately trying to stay as busy as possible to forget her, but to no avail; everywhere he looked he was reminded of her. So then, he'd thrown himself into attending all the various balls Society had to offer, hoping against hope that perhaps one of the young ladies he danced with might interest him enough to finally forget her.

Instead, all he'd done was compare them to Aimee and find them wanting. None had her stunning blue eyes or contagious smile. None had her wit or keen intelligence. None challenged him or made him feel so alive as she had. And, in the end, he'd realized, none could compare to her because they weren't her. But, then again, none would leave him broken and shattered if he loved and lost them…not like she would.

"Congratulations, Harrison, you now own fifty-one percent of the London company." Thomas paused as he handed him a copy of the contract. "You've finally achieved what you set out to, which I hope will bring you some measure of happiness."

He'd hoped so, too, but happiness had always been an elusive emotion that he didn't think he was destined to achieve. "Thank you, Thomas." He took the man's outstretched hand and shook it. "Ultimately, none of this would have been possible if you hadn't taken a chance on me when I was a boy."

"How could I not? A twelve-year-old wanting to invest all his savings in my company, after paying keen attention to all of the conversation between the gentlemen he shined shoes for? I was more than impressed, and I could see your potential. I've never met a young boy more determined to succeed than you were back then, and look at you now," Thomas replied, the first hint of a smile creasing the corners of his mouth since he'd arrived. "It's been a privilege to mentor you over the years, and I am proud of you, despite recent events."

Thomas was obviously alluding to what Harrison had told him had occurred between him and Aimee, or at least a heavily edited version of it. After all, no father needed to know the true extent of what Harrison and Aimee had gotten up to, simply that he had proposed and she had declined. Thomas was canny enough to have worked out things had been a bit more complicated than that, but he hadn't pressed Harrison for a more detailed explanation, instead simply commenting on the fact that whatever had happened between them, his daughter's heart was broken, and Harrison was to stay away from her.

Which had been easy enough to do given Aimee was either in New York, or when visiting here seemed to avoid every social event he attended, including not attending her own cousin, the new Duchess of Hargrave's balls. Probably just as well. It was much easier to forget her if he didn't see her. Knowing that still didn't stop him from constantly looking around a ballroom hoping to get a glimpse of her and feeling disappointed when he never did.

"I am grateful to you, Thomas, more than you know. And I want you to know I'm sorry for all that occurred with Aimee. You placed your faith in me and I let you down, greatly."

"I still have faith in you, Harrison," Thomas said. "But now we must focus on the future instead of lamenting the past. And the future of the company is bright with the Wilheimer deal you've secured, and the new deal with the Rousseau Group in France that Aimee's working on."

"Aimee's working on a deal?"

"Yes, she's in Paris now charming the Countess of Rousseau, who took over running the company after her husband recently died."

"You've certainly changed your tune about Aimee working for you...embraced it even." Harrison knew Thomas had finally agreed to mentor his daughter; he just hadn't realized she'd progressed to helping her father win over a new market, a position Harrison had previously filled.

"It was either embrace her or continue to fight with her over it." Thomas shrugged. "And given the elaborate masquerade she concocted for her trip here, her mother and I agreed that the only way forward was to help her rather than hinder her. And though her mother isn't entirely happy about it, I myself couldn't be happier. Indeed, it was her idea to approach the countess about a possible merger."

"It's a clever idea." The Rousseau group controlled the largest shipping ports in not only Paris, but in Egypt, too, and if Thomas could acquire the company, it would see the Thornton-Jones Conglomerate as the world's largest trading and shipping company.

Thomas's smile returned. "Honestly, Harrison, you should see Aimee in action. She's charming and personable, and so clever that I feel like such a fool for not embracing her in my business long ago. She had the countess wrapped around her finger in minutes with her ideas, not to mention her flawless French. Her son, too, was entranced by her."

"Her son?" Harrison felt his jaw lock tight.

"Yes, he's the new count and sole heir to the Rousseau fortune," Thomas confirmed. "Actually, I have hopes that this business deal might not just be solely a business deal after all. You see, he's taking her on a tour of the Eiffel Tower this weekend, and well, who knows what will happen there. I hear it's quite the place to propose to someone nowadays…"

Harrison whole body jolted, almost as if someone had sucker punched him in the stomach as a bitter sense of betrayal rose up in his throat. "She said she would never marry." At least not without love, and she couldn't have fallen in love again so soon after professing her love for him. Unless she'd never really been in love with him in the first place and had instead mistaken lust for love, which she probably had.

"People do odd things after they've had their heart broken, don't they? Some even accept the next man to ask them to marry them. But how thoughtless of me to mention such things given your own proposal was rejected." He didn't look contrite in the slightest. "In any event, though she does seem to adore the count, they've only known each other a few weeks, so I doubt it's anything serious." He paused, then glanced to Harrison, his stare intense. "You also only knew her a few weeks before charming her to the point of her believing herself in love with you, so I suppose anything is possible, isn't it?"

"I never charmed her," Harrison said, a horrible sense of anger and fear jostling inside him. "I annoyed and frustrated her more than anything, as she did to me, too."

"Yes, I'm sure that's true. Though, in the end, you were the one who broke her heart."

"I'm surprised she's confessed such a thing to you." The Aimee he knew was far too proud to have confessed that to her father.

"Of course she didn't," Thomas said, waving his arms around. "But she didn't have to. I know my daughter and can see her heart's been broken."

"I never meant for that to happen. I even

warned her I could never love anyone." Harrison pressed his lips together, the memory of her telling him she loved him so bittersweet he could taste it. "The last thing I wanted to do was hurt her."

"And yet you did."

"For which I am sorry," Harrison replied, dragging a hand through his hair. "But, as you mentioned, she was the one who ended our engagement, not me."

"You didn't give her much of a choice. My daughter would never settle for a marriage of convenience, not when her heart is involved."

"It can't have been that involved if she's already considering marrying another man," he said, unable to disguise the bitterness in his voice.

"Like I said, people do odd things when their heart's been broken." Thomas was staring steadily at him, and Harrison got the impression he wasn't talking about Aimee. "In any event, it doesn't really matter now. Her interest in a wealthy count is better than her interest in a man looking to marry a Dollar Princess to save his future estate after his uncle has nearly destroyed it with his poor investments and debts."

"I never proposed to her for her money!" Harrison roared, crossing his arms over his chest. "I proposed because I wanted to make things right, and because..." His words trailed off as the truth hit him in the face. "Well, because she's the only person I've ever wanted to marry."

Thomas scoffed. "Then why did you let her get away?"

"Because I couldn't stand the thought of losing

her." Harrison stalked over to the side table and poured himself a stiff brandy.

"But you did lose her, Harrison."

"Better to have lost her now before falling even more in love with her, and then losing her later, which would destroy me." He swallowed the liquid in one mouthful, part of him relishing the burning sensation down his throat, which very briefly took away the ache around his heart.

"True." Thomas walked over next to him and poured himself a brandy. "Why would you want to love someone and create wonderful memories with them when something might eventually happen to them, leaving you all alone? It's far more sensible, and safer, to simply be done with it and be alone right now, for the rest of your life."

"You mock me, but you don't know what it's like to lose your world in the blink of an eye." Harrison slammed down his glass. "I went from being loved and happy, with a family, to being alone and terrified, with no food, no place to live, and no one who cared whether I lived or died. I never want to experience that again."

Thomas took a sip of his drink and was silent for a moment. "I can't pretend to know what you went through when you were a young boy and lost your parents. But I do know that no parent would want their child to be alone, ever. Not as a child and certainly not as an adult. If they were alive, I'm certain they'd tell you to embrace love with both hands, because yes, life can be fragile, but it's the memories we make with those we love that keep us company in times of sadness. Tell me this, Harrison.

When you think of your parents, what is it you think of?"

Taking in a deep breath, Harrison let the memories of his parents float into his thoughts. Him and his mother laughing as his father told one of his outlandishly funny bedtime stories. His mother's arms wrapping tightly around him as she gave him a hug good night, before his father ruffled his hair and tucked him in. "I think of the good memories with them. But I still feel the pain of their deaths down to my soul."

"I know you do. But would you trade those good memories of your parents to get rid of the pain?"

Harrison sighed. "No. I wouldn't." As much as it had nearly killed him to lose his parents, he held those memories of them close to his heart.

"I didn't think so." Thomas nodded sagely. "And as difficult as the thought of losing someone you love is, I know from my experience I wouldn't trade the memories of the ones I love for anything in the world, not even to save myself any future potential pain. So now, my boy, you must ask yourself, do you really want to be alone for the rest of your life, letting your fears win? Or do you want to create future memories with the woman you love, and let courage triumph? It's as simple as that."

Was it? Could he live with the risk of loving and then possibly losing Aimee? He was silent for several minutes as he wrestled with the demons inside, until he finally looked back up at Thomas. "I need to get to Paris immediately."

CHAPTER THIRTY-EIGHT

The lift to the top of the Eiffel Tower took just over eight minutes to make its climb, an ascent of nearly one thousand feet in an iron box nestled inside the pillars of the tower itself. She'd never been in a lift that went so high, and when it reached the summit, the doors opened and Aimee stepped out onto the landing of the wrought-iron lattice tower.

She gasped at the sight of Paris spread before her. It was a concrete jungle that stretched as far as the eye could see in all directions. It was a breathtaking sight, and she finally understood why it had attracted close to two million visitors in the year since it had opened.

"Isn't it marvelous?" Henri Valois, the Count of Rousseau, enthused in perfect English beside her, his green eyes shining with excitement as he eagerly glanced around the monument.

Aimee could only nod as she slowly spun around, trying to see everything. "It's amazing, my cousin Evie said there's even a post office here in the tower. Is that true?"

"It is, it's down on the first level. I shall take you there on our way down and you can send your cousin a postcard direct from the Eiffel Tower!"

"That would be wonderful, thank you."

"My pleasure," he said with a grin. "It's a shame, though, that the spiral staircases leading up and down from the first floor are closed for cleaning today. Otherwise, they're great fun to walk up and down. A little scary given the incline of the stairs and their narrowness, but you have such a good uninterrupted view of everything that it's well worth it."

Aimee glanced over at one of the narrow spiral staircases that had a locked gate at the top of it, with a sign in French warning visitors that they were temporarily closed. She'd read in a brochure that morning that there were three hundred and eighty steps from the first floor to the second, and the stairs spiraled around a pillar of the tower, leaving only enough width for one person at a time, with what looked to be a narrow iron banister to hold onto. She was glad they were closed. "Yes, what a shame."

Henri grinned, obviously picking up on her sarcasm. "I suppose they're not for everyone, though when the tower first opened, everyone had to walk up and down them from the ground, as the lifts still weren't open. Anyhow, come on then." He gestured toward one of the viewing platforms overlooking the Champs-Élysées. "Let's take a closer look at Paris. *That* you'll want to see, and there are some observation telescopes we can use, too!"

"That sounds like much more fun." She laughed, eager to see all she could from the world's tallest structure from the safety of the landing.

Henri ran ahead of her and Aimee delighted in his excitement. It was so contagious and such a nice change from the disheartened mood she'd found herself in more often than not of late. A mood that not even working for her father could lift, though spending time with Henri had certainly helped. His enthusiasm for life and his playfulness were catching, and just what she needed to try to forget Harrison.

Even his name brought with it a sharp fission of pain, but she pushed it away, determined not to let her day with Henri be marred by thoughts of her past. Shaking off the gloom, she rushed after him, coming to a halt at the edge of the viewing platform. "Oh my, it's breathtaking…"

"It's the most marvelous spot in the whole world," he replied, his eyes shining brightly with pride as he gazed over the vista of Paris in the distance.

"It certainly is," Aimee agreed, marveling at how high up they were. "Your mother says you've already been up here over twenty times, though. Aren't you bored of it yet?"

"I could never be bored up here. The design and the engineering fascinate me every time I visit. So much so that I know I want to be an engineer and build such structures all around the world, too."

"What about your family's company? Don't you eventually want to run that?"

"Now that's what I would find boring. Besides, I've heard you and my mother talking about a merger, and if that happens, there won't be a company for me to take over."

"That doesn't bother you?"

"Not at all. If she sells it then I won't have to learn how to run it." He grinned again at her, before his eyes swiveled over to a kiosk selling candied chestnuts. "Oh sweets, that's just what I feel like! Shall I fetch us each a bag?"

"All right," she said with a smile, and before she could say another word, he raced over to the kiosk and lined up in the queue. Aimee smiled; his enthusiasm was a breath of fresh air and had the ability to divert her attention from things she'd rather not dwell on. Things like a certain six-foot three-inch man, the memory of whose touch was still able to send a shiver through her body and caused such longing that it felt like a physical ache.

When would she forget him and stop thinking about how much she missed him? Forget how angry she still was at him for not having the courage to take a risk on love... Probably never was when.

She sighed and strolled over to one of the large observation telescopes. Perhaps Paris itself could distract her from her thoughts. Pulling out a franc, she inserted it into the machine and peered through the lens, bringing the streets of Paris into sharp relief. It was amazing; she could see the carriages and the people walking on the sidewalks along the Champs-Élysées from all the way up here.

A niggling at the nape of her neck sent a sharp pang of awareness through her body, and she abruptly pulled away from the telescope and spun around, only to be confronted by the very person she hadn't been able to get out of her thoughts, no matter how hard she tried. Was she daydreaming and he was an illusion before her? But he looked real enough, though slightly ill at ease, but still solid and real. "Harrison? What are you doing here?"

"Your father said you'd be here," he said, his

voice a rough whisper.

She straightened her spine, determined not to let him see how much she'd missed him. "And here I am. You still haven't answered why you're here, and come to think of it, how did you get up to this level? The stairs are closed."

"I…um…used the lift."

"But you never use the lifts."

"I know, but I had to speak to you, and, well, it was the only way to get up to you in time."

"In time for what?" She wondered if the lift ride had seriously addled his senses, given she had no idea what he was after. "If it's to do with the Rousseau deal, you shouldn't have bothered, because I have everything well in hand, and I don't need your assistance."

"Your father mentioned the count was bringing you here, but I don't see anyone with you," he said, his eyes swiveling around in search of Henri.

"He's buying some sweets for us at the kiosk. But what does Henri have to do with anything?"

His gaze swung sharply back to her, a frown now marring his forehead. "You're on a first-name basis with him?"

"Yes, of course I am. But surely you didn't come here to talk about the count. What was so urgent that you braved the lifts to speak with me?"

"Has the count proposed to you yet?"

"Are you out of your mind?" Aimee's jaw dropped open. "No, he hasn't proposed to me."

"Would you accept him if he did?"

There was such an intensity in his eyes that Aimee didn't know whether to play along with what was surely a joke or knock some sense into the man. Perhaps some sense was needed. "No, I would not accept him, because I have no wish to become engaged to a ten-year-old boy."

"Ten?" Now it was Harrison's jaw that had dropped. "He's only ten?"

Aimee nodded. "Yes, and as much as I have fun spending time with him, I certainly have no intention of marrying a child. The fact you could even suggest so is ludicrous."

"But your father implied he was going to propose…"

"I highly doubt that," Aimee said, now certain the lift ride had affected Harrison's senses, and not in a good way.

"He did…or at least he mentioned this being a place where people propose…" He shook his head and muttered under his breath. "I think your father was trying to play matchmaker."

"Matchmaker?" Aimee exclaimed. "For me to marry Henri?"

"No, not you and Henri. Matchmaker for you and me."

Her heart skipped a beat, but she carefully schooled her features into a neutral position as her mother had taught her when dealing with a situation she wasn't certain of. "I thought I made myself perfectly clear that I wouldn't marry you unless you were prepared to give me your heart, and you were adamant you'd never do that."

His eyes were locked upon hers, his stare intense. "I was a fool."

The four simple words rendered her speechless.

"On that we can agree." She paused for a moment, gathering up her courage, not wanting to read too much into the situation. "If that's all you came to say, I can see Henri's nearly done, so I'll bid you good day."

She went to sweep past him in what she hoped would be a dignified exit, but her heel caught on a cross section of the iron floor and she went tumbling toward the ground.

Harrison reached out and caught her before she fell, pulling her up against him and steadying her in his arms. Her fingers clutched at his shirt and she gulped at his nearness. For a brief moment she closed her eyes and inhaled his scent, the sandalwood and soap so familiar that all she wanted to do was sink into his embrace and never let go. Instead, she hastily straightened up and pulled her hands away from his chest.

"Thank you," she mumbled, trying to smooth out her skirts, her eyes unwilling to meet his as she took a step back from him. "Now, if you'll excuse me—"

"Aimee, wait," he murmured, closing the distance between them, then reaching his fingers out under her chin and tilting up her face until her eyes met his. "I'm so sorry for being a fool, and for not having the courage to stop you from leaving in the first place. But I won't make that mistake again." He paused and took a deep breath. "The truth is, I love you, and I'm hoping you'll forgive me."

Her heart desperately wanted to, but her head was far too stubborn to risk such pain again. "I'm sorry, Harrison, I can't. You broke my heart and

I'm not sure you won't do the same again in the future." Quickly, she pushed past him, rushing to the lifts, not wanting him to see the tears about to spill down her cheeks.

"Aimee Elizabeth Thornton-Jones," he said from behind her, his voice booming across the entire level and causing everyone to stop in their tracks, herself included. "Who's being the coward now?"

Her whole body straightened in fury as she turned around to face him. "Excuse me?" she yelled back at him. "You dare throw my words back at me?"

"Damn right I do! Especially because you were right. I was being a coward."

He looked thunderous as he stalked over to her, but there was also such vulnerability in his eyes that she didn't know quite what to say to his blunt honestly.

"And I'm not done telling you what I came to," he continued, stopping in front of her, "and given I had to brave getting into a lift for you, and not just any lift, but a lift for the highest bloody structure in the world that took eight minutes to get up here in, you damn well will listen to me. Then if you don't want another thing to do with me after, I'll never bother you again."

"Fine then!" she fired back at him, staring defiantly up at him and trying her best to stop herself from throwing herself into his arms. "Say what you need to, but your words won't change my mind." Even if his *I love you* was still swirling around in her head on repeat.

"You're so damn stubborn!" He dragged a hand

through his hair, in a gesture she'd missed so much.

"Really? *That's* what you came to tell me?" She crossed her hands over her chest.

He exhaled harshly. "You're not going to make this easy for me, are you?"

"Not in the slightest."

His lips twitched at the corners. "I suppose I deserve it given I was an idiot to let you go in the first place."

"Another thing we can agree on." Aimee crossed her hands over her chest and raised a brow. "So is that all then?"

"No." He shook his head. "The truth is, I want to marry you, Aimee Elizabeth Thornton-Jones. And not because of my honor, or your father, or your dowry. I want to marry you because of you. I love you so damn much that the thought of never seeing you again, or hearing your voice, or seeing that cranky frown on your face, doesn't just break my heart but shatters it. To the point where I'll be lost without you, my life a half life without you in it."

"You broke my heart, Harrison." She had to fight against the tears still threatening to spill over. "How do I know you won't do the same in the future? That you won't suddenly get terrified again of losing me, and that you'd rather leave me than go through the pain of that again?"

"I'm already terrified I've lost you," he replied, the pulse at his neck thrumming heavily as he gulped. "And of course part of me will be terrified of loving you and losing you every single day, but I'm even more terrified of not loving you every single day. Of not waking up with you next to me each morning and working alongside you through the day…of not making the memories with you that I long to. I'm terrified that you're my only chance for happiness, and through my fear and cowardice, I've let you slip away…"

He took a deep breath and exhaled it loudly. "Aimee, I've not only fallen in love with you, but I love you with my whole heart and soul, and I promise I will never leave you or push you away ever again. I will give my life for you, and I will do all in my power to make you happy for the rest of our lives together, no matter how long or how short that may be, if you'll agree to marry me and be my wife."

There was such naked vulnerability in his eyes that Aimee wanted to hold him and reassure him it would all be all right. But would it? Could she risk believing him and giving him her heart completely?

"I want to share my life with you, Aimee, and start a family with you," he continued. "And if you don't love me anymore, as hard as it will be, I'll accept that, and you won't hear from me again. But I need you to know I was wrong to ever push you away and not embrace your love when I had the chance, and that I'm willing to be courageous for you. If you still love me and will have me as your husband?"

"Love you?" Her voice cracked slightly. "I've never stopped loving you." And it was the truth. There wasn't a moment she hadn't loved him, since first meeting him if she were being honest. The man challenged her, thrilled her, frustrated her, but most of all he loved her, and she loved him, more than she'd known was possible. And if he was

willing to risk loving her, despite having lost his whole family and vowing to never love another again, then she was willing to embrace that and love him back with her whole heart.

"You do?" he whispered.

Slowly she nodded. "I do. I love you, Harrison. That hasn't changed and it never will, even when you act like an idiot."

"So you will marry me?" he asked, almost in disbelief.

Aimee grinned. "Yes, I will. Just don't go breaking my heart ever again, or I will shoot you like I've threatened to in the past."

He laughed, and then with a holler he scooped her up into his arms and swirled her around, caring little for the audience that had gathered around them and were now cheering and clapping.

She clung onto Harrison's neck and laughed, too, her heart filled with so much joy, she didn't think she'd ever felt happier or more excited than right then.

Placing her gently back onto her feet, he grinned down at her. "I love you so damn much, Aimee. You have my heart and my soul, and I will love you with every fiber of my being and cherish you, for the rest of my life. I promise you that, my love. Always."

"I love you, too, Harrison, more than words could ever say," she whispered an instant before his lips came down tenderly on hers. It was a kiss filled with the promise of a love to last a lifetime, and Aimee knew in that moment her heart would be forever safe in his hands.

EPILOGUE

SIX MONTHS LATER, LONDON, JUNE 1891

"*The Titled American*?" Aimee wandered into the breakfast room, noting the magazine her husband had his head buried in. "That's a bit different to your usual morning read, isn't it?"

The *London* or *New York Times* were what normally held Harrison's attention, not a magazine dedicated to listing the marriages between wealthy American heiresses and foreigners of rank, along with a register of the titled bachelors still left on the marriage market and advertisements from some of them basically hinting at looking for a wealthy bride.

He grinned up at her, placing the magazine on the table next to where he was sitting as he came to his feet and strode over to pull out her chair, beating the footman to the job as usual. "Good morning, my love." He kissed her gently on the lips. "And, yes, I usually prefer reading the news rather than gossip. However, Hargrave said it was a must read." A chuckle accompanied his pronouncement. "And it certainly is."

"Alex reads *The Titled American*?" She couldn't imagine any man, most especially Evie's husband, a duke, reading the magazine let alone recommending it to anyone.

"Not normally," Harrison replied, picking up the

magazine and sliding it over to Aimee. "But he did for this addition. Page thirty-five might be of interest."

Her curiosity piqued, Aimee reached over and flipped open the magazine to the page he mentioned. "The Earl of Brexton is the eighth earl of a long and proud lineage in the Peerage of Great Britain. His entailed estates amount to fifteen thousand eight hundred acres, yielding an income of over ninety thousand pounds, and his family seat is the great estate of Tottenbury House, in Cambridge. The earl is thirty-one years of age, passable in appearance and manners, and is an excellent prospect." Her mouth dropped open and she glanced over at Harrison. "Sam has listed himself as an available bachelor?"

Harrison laughed again but shook his head. "I don't think Sam knows anything about the advertisement. Though he soon will."

"But who would..." It was then the penny dropped. "Alex paid for the advertisement, didn't he?"

The duke was one of the most scholarly, serious-minded people Aimee knew. Perfect for her cousin Evie, but not someone she ever would have suspected to play a practical joke on his cousin Sam.

"Sam's been happily teasing the duke about being the one to play matchmaker between Alex and Evie, so I think this is Alex's way of getting a bit of revenge and having some fun with his cousin at the same time."

"Some fun?" Aimee exclaimed. "Every Dollar Princess and their single-minded mothers will be booking passage on the first steamer across the Atlantic to try to entrap him. Sam will be bombarded, hounded even. He's not going to know what hit him, and for a man that doesn't need to marry a Dollar Princess, or even want to marry just yet, he's going to be beyond vexed."

"A tame way to describe having to fend off a multitude of determined American women all with their eyes firmly fixated on being a countess." Harrison laughed again. "What a way to even the score on one's cousin, a self-confessed ladies' man, then by sending a fleet of women after him. It's ingenious, and I'll have to applaud Alex on his cunning when I see him next."

"Poor Sam," Aimee replied, taking a sip of her coffee. "I feel sorry for him already."

"Don't feel sorry for him," Harrison said, reaching over and taking Aimee's free hand in his own, kissing her knuckles; his very touch still sent a tingle right the way down to her toes. "He might find the love of his life and marry his very own Dollar Princess. After all, it worked extremely well for me."

"For both of us, my love," Aimee replied, leaning over and meeting his lips halfway as he gave her a thorough kiss. She sighed in bliss before reluctantly pulling away. "I suppose we best hurry with breakfast. I have a lot to do today in preparation for our own voyage."

"I imagine your mother will be thrilled to see you when we return to New York for our visit."

"She will, though what she's truly thrilled about is for us all to finally be attending Mrs. Astor's ball next week." Her mother had gotten the coveted invitation to the exclusive event and had been in a frenzy of organizing ballgowns since. Regular trips to Paris had ensued for both Aimee and Evie, with her mother sparing no expense to ensure the House of Worth created the most dazzling gowns for them all. "I, on the other hand, would much prefer to stay here and work."

The Rousseau merger had been her baby from its inception and now that they'd taken over the French company, Aimee was even more determined to increase their shipping routes and global dominance.

"We could always delay our trip. Your mother would still be happy having Evie and Alex attend with her and your father."

"Yes, but she doesn't want to just be happy, she wants to lord it over Mrs. Astor that not only is her niece a duchess, but her daughter will be a countess, too." It was her mother's dream, not her own, but having experienced her own dreams coming true recently, Aimee was more than happy to see someone else's also come to fruition. "I still wonder if she knew I'd swap places with Evie, bringing me into your vicinity."

"You are impulsive and determined." Harrison shrugged. "It's not beyond the realm of possibilities she suspected you might."

"True, though she couldn't have predicted you might jeopardize it all by trying to rescue me that first day we met."

"*Try* to?" He raised a brow.

"You know I could have rescued myself."

"I do. My wife is a capable and clever lady."

The praise brought a flush to her cheeks. "Oh, Harrison, you say the most wonderful things sometimes."

"What? You are clever." He took a bite of his toast. "You married me, didn't you?"

She threw a bit of her toast at him, and he dodged it with ease, then grinned.

"Yes, I did marry you, my earl-in-waiting," she said, unabashedly teasing her husband with the moniker.

His grin turned into a grimace. "You're always going to call me that, aren't you?"

"Always." She winked at him and laughed. "Do you think you can handle it for the rest of our lives together?"

"Oh, I can handle it." Then before she knew what he was about, he stood and scooped her up from her chair into his arms. "Because you're the best thing that's ever happened to me."

Aimee wound her hands around his neck and breathed in the delicious sandalwood scent of him. "I feel the same way about you."

"Leave us," he directed the footmen, who were both trying not to grin at the regular display of affection while they did as instructed, closing the door behind them and leaving Aimee and Harrison alone.

"I thought we agreed we'd get to the office on time today?" It was becoming a deliciously bad habit of theirs to get there a tad later than usual.

"We're newlyweds, my darling," Harrison's voice rumbled softly in her ear as his mouth began to trail soft kisses down her neck and his fingers began to work on the buttons at the back of her gown. "Everyone at the office expects us to be late on occasion."

She grinned. "On occasion? This will be the third time this week, and it's only Wednesday."

"Excellent, then we still have three more days we can be on time, don't we?"

"Yes, I suppose we do," Aimee said, needing no further convincing when his lips found hers and drew her into his exquisite touch. His touch that always bought her so much joy and contentment, and filled her with such a sense of belonging, knowing they would always be together.

He pulled away from her and stared into her eyes. "You have my heart, my beautiful wife, and I love you with every fiber of my being. And I will *always* love you until my very last breath. I promise you that."

Aimee didn't think she could love him any more than she did right now, but with every moment that passed, her love only grew. "I will always love you, too, Harrison," she whispered. "You've captured my heart and it will be forever yours."

"I will treasure it my love, just as I treasure you."

ACKNOWLEDGEMENTS

First and foremost, I want to thank my family. Their unending support, encouragement and love, is a true blessing that I'm so very grateful for. I love you all so much!

Next, I want to thank the amazing team at Entangled—the behind-the-scenes work you all do is nothing short of brilliant, and very much appreciated. I'd also like to thank my editor, Alethea Spiridon, whose suggestions have helped polish up Aimee and Harrison's story, beautifully. Thanks Alethea, you rock!

And finally, a huge thanks to all of the readers out there who've picked up my books and left a review—it means the world to me when I hear how much you've enjoyed my stories.

*Don't miss the exciting new books
Entangled has to offer.*

Follow us!

 @EntangledPublishing

 @Entangled_Publishing

 @EntangledPub